The Cliff's Edge

Also by Charles Todd

The Cliff's Edge

A Bess Crawford Mystery

CHARLES TODD

WILLIAM MORROW
An Imprint of HarperCollins*Publishers*

THE CLIFF'S EDGE. Copyright © 2023 by Charles Todd. All rights reserved. Printed in the United States of America. No part of this book may be used or reproduced in any manner whatsoever without written permission except in the case of brief quotations embodied in critical articles and reviews. For information, address HarperCollins Publishers, 195 Broadway, New York, NY 10007.

HarperCollins books may be purchased for educational, business, or sales promotional use. For information, please email the Special Markets Department at SPsales@harpercollins.com.

FIRST EDITION

Designed by Kyle O'Brien

Library of Congress Cataloging-in-Publication Data has been applied for.

ISBN 978-0-06-303994-0

23 24 25 26 27 LBC 5 4 3 2 1

This book is especially for Martha Teachey, a sister, aunt, and a very special person in both our lives. Through it all a survivor today and always.

For Fran and Don, dear friends and family to us. Family born of caring rather than mere blood. Their kindness and dedication are beyond comprehension.

For sweet little Button, who brought joy to the lives of her family. Always friendly, always happy, she had a tail wag and smile for everyone. Button was a member of the family for fifteen years, and they miss her every day.

The Cliff's Edge

CHAPTER ONE

Somerset, July 1919

SIMON BROUGHT IN the post, set it on the salver in the hall, and went on through the house and out across the back garden to his cottage just beyond the wood. I'd watched him go from my window.

Since we'd returned from Ireland, he'd spent most of his time there.

Iris, our maid, claimed he was writing his war memoires, like all the generals were doing just now. I reminded her that he wasn't a General. But, of course, Iris just shook her head and said, "There's no rule says a Sergeant-Major can't do the same, is there?"

"Well, no," I'd told her then. Iris always has her own interpretation about any situation. Still, I didn't believe her, because most of Simon's war, like the Colonel Sahib's, was still officially secret.

I was just coming down the stairs as she collected the post from the salver.

"Mostly for the Colonel Sahib," she said, looking up at me as she sorted the letters. "I'll set it on his desk, shall I?" Then she stopped. "Oh, look, Miss, something for you."

She acted as if I never received any letters at all and this was a treat. Which warned me that it wasn't the usual post. Now she was holding up the last envelope. "And for your mother, Miss. Shall I take it back or will you?"

"I'll take it. I wanted to ask her about making new curtains for my bedroom."

"Oh, Miss, what about spring green? I've always fancied spring green," she said. She was still holding on to my letter, as if reluctant to go on about her duties until she's seen me read it.

"I haven't decided yet," I said diplomatically, and held out my hand.

Mine wasn't a letter after all. It was a postal card. From Australia.

No wonder she was curious!

My second thought was, *Had Simon seen it?*

Iris was pretending not to watch me as I looked at the front of the card—a drawing of a kookaburra bird—and then slowly turned it over.

I knew who it was from, and why. Sergeant Lassiter . . . It read simply, *Changed your mind yet?*

There was no signature. I didn't need one. He'd proposed to me near the end of the war, and I'd said *no,* and I hadn't seen him since then. I'd assumed—rightly, it seemed—that he'd returned with his regiment to Australia.

Clearly disappointed that I hadn't satisfied her curiosity about the sender, Iris handed me the letter for my mother.

I was still standing there when she went on about her duties.

The Sergeant and I had had a history. I hadn't been in love with him—besides that, I was still a nursing Sister, and the rules set out for us by the Queen Alexandra's was no romantic attachment while serving, on pain of dismissal. But the Sergeant had saved my life and I'd saved his, during the war, and somehow he'd always found out if I was in any difficulty. I'd hear that strange laugh—the call of that bird—and there he would be. I'd wondered sometimes how he managed it, with a war going on all around us.

Sighing, I tucked the card in my pocket and turned to walk back to the morning room, where my mother was working.

As I did, to stop the direction my thoughts were running—back to the war, where oddly enough, everything seemed so much clearer—I idly turned over the other letter. The postmark was Kent, and that usually meant Cousin Melinda.

My mother was just finishing writing a letter. She was no longer officially serving with the regiment as the Colonel's lady, but the wives of many officers and even men in the ranks from our old regiment treated her as if she were still, asking advice, sharing news, or just staying in touch.

"Here's another," I said lightly, setting it on her desk.

"Melinda?" she asked, smiling. "I expect she wants us to come and visit. Your father isn't back from London, and he may not wish to leave again so soon. But it would make a nice change, wouldn't it?"

She picked up the brass letter opener—there was a carved elephant in place of a handle, one of our purchases in a bazaar in Calcutta—and opened the envelope. "That's odd. Two letters . . ."

My mother began to read the first one. "She's well—Ian is out of the clinic and she has been worried about him returning to the Yard so soon. I expect he was ready to put the war behind him as quickly as possible. But you know how much she cares for him. Ah—this is about the other letter.

"'Clarice, this is from an acquaintance of many years. Lillian Taylor was Nanny to an officer I knew, and we've kept in touch. At present she's companion to a woman who is about to have her gallbladder removed, and the doctor insists that Lady Beatrice must have a nurse to attend her when she comes home from hospital. Lady Beatrice is refusing outright. And so I've been asked to come at once and persuade her to heed her *doctor. I can't leave at the moment, and I wonder if Bess might go in my place? It's lovely there this time of year, and I'm sure you'd like Lillian as much as I have done. But whether you go or stay, please do me another favor and don't—' "*

My mother stopped, glanced at me, and then said, "I expect it's about Richard's birthday. Let's keep this between us, shall we?"

Now when my mother asks me to keep something from my father, I'm doubly suspicious.

"What does the other letter have to say?"

She picked it up and unfolded it. "Hmmm. Not very much. Well, of course you ought to read it. Melinda is recommending you. Still, I know how much you have to do just now—"

"Mother—" I knew what was on her mind—that I'd only just got home, we'd had a number of people staying with us for nearly a fortnight, and she would very much like to have me to herself, at least for a bit.

"Darling, I thought you were looking at samples of curtain fabric? Have you made a decision?"

I really wasn't interested in curtain fabric. The problem was, I was restless. For the first time in over four years, I had time on my hands. I'd helped my mother design and plant a new rose border, I had helped her make jam, I had even helped with the rigorous spring cleaning she and Iris had given every room in this house.

Yet I had been accustomed to wounded being brought in to the surgical tent at all hours, one after the other, as fast as we could work with them. I'd taken a line of ambulances back from the Front to a base hospital, trying all the while to keep men alive until we could give them more care than we were able to provide so close to the fighting. I'd worked in a forward aid station when German aircraft strafed the site, and I'd been overrun by the German Army, dealing with wounds no matter which uniform a man was wearing.

I loved working with my mother, watching her happily planning where to put the yellow climbing rose. But I wondered sometimes if *she* missed India or South Africa or Kenya, the excitement of the regiment, a foreign country, dealing with a Maharani today and a tribal chieftain tomorrow. She would have followed my father anywhere, made the best of anything. With cheerfulness and enthusiasm. And here she was, finally planning a new garden.

I'd been standing next to her desk. I sat down now in the chair beside her.

"Mother . . . I don't really need new curtains. What I do need is something new to think about."

She frowned. "Are you unhappy here, darling? It's very different from France."

And she had worried for me there every day of the war. I felt a surge of guilt.

Taking a deep breath, I said, "Do you miss India?"

She looked away. "I'm delighted to be in my own home again. We traveled most of our marriage. Most of all, it's nice not to have to worry about your father—or for that matter, Simon—when I heard a troop coming in late from an action."

"I understand that. I worried too. But you enjoy going into London with me. Let's do ourselves a favor, and one for Cousin Melinda as well, and run up to Yorkshire together. Florence Dunstan lives in York, we could spend a few days with her, as well. Father wouldn't mind, and Simon can fend for himself for a week. I'm sure Lillian, whoever she is, wouldn't mind having both of us stop in first, to deal with a gallbladder."

She turned and looked at me thoughtfully. "What went wrong in Ireland, Bess? You've been restless ever since you got home. And don't tell me it's the war, and coping with the wounded." She hesitated, and then added, "It isn't the young Irishman you left behind? You were worried about him."

Oh, dear.

How to answer that?

I smiled and told the truth. "Terrence is in love with someone else. And while I came to like him in the end, I didn't fall in love with him."

"Well, that's a relief." She smiled. "I don't know what the neighbors would have thought if you had brought him home with you."

A man with a price on his head . . .

I said wryly, "I remember telling Simon just that. Still, I think the Colonel Sahib would have come to like him too."

We laughed together, as I'd intended for us to do.

"If this woman needs a nurse until she's fully recovered, why don't you go and persuade her it's necessary? I know, she sounds a terror, but you've dealt with worse."

But I didn't want to be someone's nurse, I'd resigned from the Queen Alexandra's when I came home from Galway. And the last thing I wanted was to be the nurse of a woman like this one promised to be. At her beck and call, treated like a servant and threatened with dismissal five times a day. I'd met women like her during my training, and I heartily disliked them. Besides, she probably had a lapdog that bites.

My mother must have read my mind. "I don't think Melinda would have asked you to do this favor for her if she thought it would be anything but a short visit."

I held back a sigh. "Read the rest of the letter."

She picked up Lillian's letter, rose from her chair, and moved to the cold hearth to read it. I saw her eyebrows go up.

"What is it?"

"See for yourself." She handed the letter to me.

Dear Mrs. Melinda Crawford,

I write to you because you've always taken an interest in my welfare. You know how grateful I am for that! And I've been grateful as well for this lovely position. But I'm worried about Lady Beatrice. Her doctor has told her she must have her gallbladder removed, and that a nurse must be at hand when she comes home. She refuses, in spite of the fact she has a tricky heart. Neither I nor her doctor can convince her to change her mind. You knew her in Kenya, she has the highest regard for you, and your encouragement could make her reconsider. I have come to care for her myself, and I am truly worried about her. Nor can I think of any other way to persuade her. I wouldn't ask if I could find any other solution. It's such a long way to Yorkshire, I know. But please think about it. At present her surgery is scheduled for Friday next.

"Who is Lady Beatrice?" I asked, passing the letter back to my mother. "Do you know anything about her?"

"I've heard Melinda speak of her. She was a cousin of the Governor of Kenya, and went out there in 1905, after her husband's death. She was so distraught, the family decided she needed a change of scene. She stayed a year or two, and then came home again. I think Melinda met her out there."

"Surely she has family who can step in now?"

"I have no idea, darling. But I expect Lillian has no authority with her—or perhaps she fears losing her position if she pushes too hard."

"Worse and worse."

"Well, if Melinda liked her, she can't be all that bad."

I leaned back in the chair beside my mother's to contemplate this situation and my other issue. What my mother wasn't aware of was that the estrangement between Simon and me was something I didn't know how to repair. It had begun in Ireland, and it was gnawing at me. When my parents were there, Simon appeared to be his usual self, but he avoided me, and I had begun to avoid him as well, which probably only served to make matters worse, I'm sure. But it lessened the pain I was feeling.

And so to my own surprise, as well as hers, I changed my mind and said, "If we can visit Florence in York on our way home, I'll go."

"I'll write to Melinda this very minute. I'll leave it to you to ask Florence if a visit is convenient just now."

But two days later, when we were to travel up to London to take the train north, Cook accidentally scalded her hand and couldn't use it for the next week. And my mother had to stay behind to prepare meals.

That's how it happened. I traveled to Yorkshire alone, to meet the dreaded Lady Beatrice.

There was a stop in Peterborough, and the family sharing my compartment got down. I was glad to have it to myself, because it had been rather crowded with two restless children in such a small space. I was hoping, when no one came, that I might have it to myself for the rest of the journey. And then just before the guard gave the signal to pull out, the door to my compartment was opened by a nursing Sister. She peered in, smiled at me, then turned back to speak to someone I couldn't see. A man stepped forward, and she assisted him into the compartment, said a cheery farewell, and shut the door again.

I couldn't see his eyes, for bandages covered them, only the lower part of his face, high cheekbones and a strong jaw, and he had a walking stick by his side to help him find his way.

Shrapnel in the eyes? I'd seen it often. Some cases cleared up without treatment, while others resulted in partial or permanent blindness.

I said, "Good morning," so that the man would know someone was sitting across from him.

His gaze swung toward the sound of my voice, out of habit, but of course he couldn't see me. "Good morning."

He was cold, indicating that I shouldn't ask questions about the bandages.

"Are you traveling to York?"

"I am." Again, curt enough to indicate a lack of desire for conversation.

And so I returned to looking out the window.

But when we got there, no one was waiting to meet him.

I offered my help, but he said, "I can manage."

"Don't be silly. I was a nursing Sister during the war. I'm accustomed to being useful."

So he did accept my assistance descending from the carriage, and I was starting toward the stationmaster when a nurse came hurrying through the passengers milling about as some got down and others were eager to get aboard.

She came up to him and looked shocked at the bandages, then recovered quickly to say, "How lovely to have you home at last! Oh, my dear!" But he pulled away as she attempted to take his arm.

"I can manage," he said again in the same harsh tone, and she dropped her hand as quickly as if he'd struck it away.

I watched them walk on, his cane tapping, and sometimes losing his direction.

He—whoever he was—was home. But it was not going to be a happy homecoming.

I was still watching the pair when someone coming toward me said, "Pardon, Miss. Could you be Sister Crawford?"

I turned to see a middle-aged man in dark green livery heading my way in the thinning crowd. The train was beginning to move out, and he was looking rather disturbed, as if he thought he had missed me.

"Yes, I'm Sister Crawford." I could understand his confusion, for I no longer wore my uniform.

"I'm Wilson, Miss. Lady Beatrice sent me to collect you. Do you have luggage?"

"How kind of her." I looked around, then pointed to the cases that the guard had set down for me. "Yes, just those."

"I'll see to them, then. If you'll follow me, please?"

I did.

I'd been told I'd be met, but not by whom. We went out to where a matching dark green Rolls was waiting. He dealt with my two valises—it still felt strange not to travel with my kit—then settled me comfortably in the long Rolls. He took his place in the chauffeur's seat, and we set out toward the north.

As it turned out, the little village that was associated with Lady Beatrice's estate was thirty miles to the northwest of York, and it was a long drive. Even with the blanket over my knees, I could feel the difference in the temperature from Somerset.

Wilson assured me that today was chillier than usual, and that the wind would drop by nightfall.

The countryside was striking. Outside the city, we were soon in rolling dales that were as beautiful in their own way as Somerset. We passed through a number of villages, where the dark stone houses crowded the street, and one small town even had a market in progress. The people seemed to be less friendly than those at home, staring at us without smiling. Or perhaps, I told myself, it was Lady Beatrice's motorcar they recognized.

I was already regretting coming.

But I was here, and I would make the most of it, for Melinda's sake.

When we finally reached the village where Lady Beatrice lived, it was close to dusk, the streets were empty, and the day's chill had become *cold* evening.

The manor house sat just outside the village, close to a mile away, and a man stepped quickly out of the gatehouse to open the gates for us to pass through, waiting to close them behind us.

The "manor house" I was expecting to find at the end of the long drive through parkland was in fact a stately home. Not palatial in appearance, but still large enough to lose the Colonel Sahib's old regiment in it, and have rooms left over.

Built of mellow stone, it had a parapet running around the roof and several wings, one a tower that looked possibly fifteenth century, maybe the oldest part of the house. The grand entrance was framed by a pillared portico, and the crest above the door was rather impressive.

And so when I walked up to the grand doors and they swung open to allow me to enter, I wasn't prepared to meet my hostess straightaway. I had been expecting her to see me at her convenience—especially as she would not be pleased with my arrival. *She* hadn't sent for me—Lillian Taylor had.

But to my surprise, as I walked through the heavy inner doors, she was waiting for me in the great hall. She swept forward to welcome me as if I were the daughter of a friend, and greeted me warmly.

"Welcome, my dear. You must be exhausted by your journey."

Lady Beatrice was a tall, attractive woman in her seventies, her gray hair beautifully set, and her gray dress simple in design but expensive. Her only piece of jewelry was a lovely thistle pin, silver and amethyst. And her smile reached her eyes as she spoke to me. Behind her stood a quiet, slim woman of perhaps sixty, who must, I thought, be Lillian Taylor. Her hair was still fair, and her eyes were blue. She also smiled—in relief, I thought—as we were introduced.

After inquiring about my journey, Lady Beatrice turned me over to a housekeeper by the name of Mrs. Bennett, and I was whisked upstairs to my room. I was politely informed that I had thirty minutes to change for dinner, but that it would be informal tonight. And then I was left alone.

My room was enormous, with long windows overlooking a garden in full bloom, and furniture that appeared to be Georgian. A tray with a silver tea service stood on a table in the middle of the room, and I saw the coat of arms on each piece. The pot was hot, the tea ready to pour, if I felt like refreshing myself after my journey.

I quickly bathed, then changed my traveling dress for something suitable for dinner in a house this size. My mother had wisely suggested

I pack a pretty shawl, and I was grateful for it across my shoulders as a maid appeared to escort me down the stairs. It was quite chilly outside in the passages.

I tried not to gawk like a schoolgirl, but there were such lovely things everywhere I looked, that I couldn't stop myself from enjoying them. The hall where the stairs ended was a pale blue trimmed in white and filled with Roman statues and busts that would have done justice to a small museum. Another door led to the salon, where I was seated to have a sherry with Lady Beatrice before the meal. This room was decorated in golds and reds, and one could imagine standing here conversing with one's fellow guests while awaiting the King's pleasure.

Only, I was the sole guest. Lady Beatrice asked after Melinda, and then my mother, with a kindness that quickly won me over.

"Have you been to Yorkshire before, my dear?"

I told her that I knew York and had visited Fountains Abbey. She nodded. "We're a long way from both, but it's amazingly beautiful here. Although, when I first came to this place as a young bride, I was certain that this must be the most desolate place in England." There was a sudden sadness in her eyes as she added, "But ours was a love match, and I'd have lived in a cottage with Hugh. His mother was still alive, and happy to teach me how to run this house. Now it's home, and I love it dearly."

We chatted for a while. Lillian spoke when she was addressed but mostly sat quietly and listened. I thought she might be shy, but I soon realized that she was worried. She'd hoped for Melinda, and instead had gotten me. And she wasn't quite sure whether I could cope.

We were called in to dinner, and the meal was excellent. After we finished, we were joined for tea by Dr. Halliday, Lady Beatrice's physician, who would see to her care after the gallbladder surgery. He appraised me, as if uncertain whether I was fish or fowl. Too young to be a competent nurse, surely . . .

But when we began to talk about the war, he seemed to change his mind. In fact, he knew several of the doctors I'd worked under at the Front. That too must be reassuring, I thought. At first glance, he must have believed me to be just out of training, with little or no experience to speak of.

We called it an early night, I think out of courtesy for me, tired as I was. We went up to bed as soon as the doctor departed. The fire had been replenished, and there was a hot water bottle between my sheets.

I was just about to fall asleep when there was a tapping at my door. I found my robe and went to open it.

Lillian Taylor stood there.

"I'm so sorry to disturb you at this hour," she said quietly, "but Lady Beatrice found it hard to sleep tonight. She's nervous, as the surgery is only three days away. I have found that reading to her is soothing."

"Come in," I said, and led the way to the chairs by the hearth.

"You said you were in the war? I should have known that Mrs. Crawford had found someone who could manage. Thank you for coming!"

She began to tell me a little more about the surgery. "It will be performed in York. At least for the first two or three days, Lady Beatrice will stay in hospital to be sure all is well. And then a private ambulance will be ordered, to bring her home. We've persuaded her to have a bed made up in one of the smaller sitting rooms, so that she won't have to climb the stairs. Dr. Halliday and I have tried to think of everything. It isn't that she's being difficult, but she is used to being independent, and it's hard to face being immobilized for two weeks or more."

"What is the problem with her heart?"

"I'm not quite sure. With the need for an anesthetic during the surgery, there is some concern. But the gallbladder is making her wretched, and so she has come to the conclusion that the only hope for less pain is to be rid of it."

"Yes, I understand. At least arranging that procedure hasn't been a problem."

Lilian sighed. "She wanted the surgery done here, but Dr. Halliday told her in no uncertain terms that he would not allow it. She likes him, and so she didn't argue very much."

"Does she have any family?"

"She has a son. He sits in Parliament when it's in session. The rest of the year he prefers his house in London because it's more comfortable."

"Will he come up for the surgery?"

"Oh no, we have been forbidden to mention it to anyone. Least of all to Jonathan." She smiled. "Lady Beatrice dotes on him, but you'd never know it. She tries not to show how much she misses him. The doctor refuses to allow her to travel to London just now, or she would have had her surgery there. She told Dr. Halliday that she'd ask the Queen to lend her the Royal Train. And she would have done, you know. Very likely they'd have agreed!"

I told Lillian that I planned to visit a friend while Lady Beatrice was in surgery. Her eyebrows rose. "Oh—I'd thought you would be available for the surgery. I heard her tell Dr. Halliday that she was pleased with you and would agree to having you with her for the whole two weeks."

"Tell me about her?"

"Her father was an Earl, and she married another one. But you'd never guess. She's kind and thoughtful and cares about the people around her. Nothing pompous about her. I've come to love her." She smiled a little. "How could I not? It's a lovely place to call home, and after years of being a governess to impossible children, and companion to demanding women—and one man—I'm grateful."

Indeed, that had been my impression as well. But I didn't say what was on my mind, that Lady Beatrice also seemed to have a marvelously developed skill at getting her own way.

The next morning, I broached the subject of my staying here to Lady Beatrice herself. She said bracingly, "Not a problem, my dear! Why don't

I ask Wilson to drive you to York directly, and you can visit your friend there over the weekend, while I am having my operation. He'll return for you on Monday morning, and you'll be here to care for me when I return from hospital."

"Lady Beatrice—"

She waved her hand in dismissal. "No, my dear, I'm delighted to arrange this for you. And while you're in York, perhaps you can do one small errand for me. I've ordered new dressing gowns for my convalescence. They are ready to be collected—I can even have them delivered by hand to your friend's house. You have only to bring them back with you."

"Lady Beatrice—" I began for the second time, but she said, "Evensong at the Minster is lovely. I'll have Wilson arrange for both of you to attend. I believe you would enjoy that. The sound soars. It's truly beautiful. I could almost wish I were going with you."

When I found Lillian afterward looking for a book in the handsome library, I said, "She's impossible. How on earth do you manage?"

Lillian shut the glass door that protected that set of shelves and turned to me. "What's wrong, Bess?"

I realized she had no idea what I was about to say.

Sighing, I tried to explain. "I only came to Yorkshire to persuade her that it was wise to have a nurse in the house while she recovered. Isolated as this estate is, it would take hours to reach a doctor in an emergency. Not that it's likely, of course, but at her age, with her heart, it's for the best. I hadn't intended to stay here myself. I was going to visit a friend in York on my way back to London. I don't have two weeks to spare."

A little voice of conscience reminded me that the only major decision on my calendar was to choose the color of my curtains. I ignored it. Something else was making me restless, and the thought of staying here for a fortnight, playing nurse, felt unbearable.

"I couldn't get a word in," I continued. "She just kept arranging my visit to York, and my return here. What am I to do? Short of wandering on foot across the moors, like Jane Eyre?"

She smiled. "Lady Beatrice does have a habit of taking over. I don't mind. I've been safe and comfortable here. She's kindness itself, and I really am grateful for this position. Couldn't you stay? Would that be so truly impossible?"

What to do, then?

I tried, "I had packed for only a few days—"

Lillian Taylor smiled. "If that's the only problem, Lady Beatrice has a seamstress in the village who does lovely work. She can make up whatever you need. Lady Beatrice will insist on providing anything you might require." She made a deprecating gesture. "She likes you, Bess. I've been amazed by her taking to you so quickly. She's had a difficult life, losing her husband so young, and a daughter too. She withdrew from Society for a number of years. The doctor called it depression, but I think the truth was, she wasn't sure she could go on. Jonathan took his father's seat in the House of Lords, and his wife doesn't care for Yorkshire at all, which means he seldom visits. That is why as soon as Lady Beatrice returned from Kenya, Mrs. Crawford asked me to come and live here. And I think I've helped, a little."

I said, "I need to write to my mother—" And Melinda as well, but I didn't mention this.

"Yes, of course. Wilson will see that it's posted in the village." Rising, she said, "Write your letter, and give it to me tomorrow."

I went to the small desk between the windows and found stationery in the drawer with the family arms at the top, beautifully embossed.

I drew out a sheet, sat down, and began to write.

CHAPTER TWO

Mother,

Lady Beatrice insists that I stay for her surgery, even though I have tried my best to explain to her that I hadn't come for that. Meanwhile, she has even arranged for me to keep my visit to Florence. I truly don't know what I'm to do, without being terribly rude and upsetting. It's a quandary.

I ADDED A few more lines about my journey north and I sent my love to the Colonel Sahib. I remembered to ask after Cook's poor hand, and to tell Iris that I missed her.

I wrote much the same letter to Cousin Melinda, asking that she use her good offices in persuading Lady Beatrice that a perfectly fine nurse was surely available in York, if not here, to take my place.

Still not completely satisfied, I went ahead and folded the letters, put their proper direction on each, and set them aside for the morning post.

The next day, I discovered that a Mrs. Foster, the village seamstress, was waiting for me after breakfast to take my measurements.

Now what to do? I could hardly let her begin uniforms for me, if I was going to leave shortly.

In the end, as we were alone in my room, I explained that it was uncertain whether I was to stay or not, and that it was best to wait before starting any actual sewing.

Mrs. Foster, a motherly woman with a great eye for color, as it turned out, merely smiled, asked me to hold out my left arm again, if I would be so kind, and added that there would be no uniforms, that Lady Beatrice had asked her to make dresses instead.

"She says she will be much more comfortable, not being reminded every day of the hospital."

Oh, *dear.*

It also appeared that Lady Beatrice kept quite a stock of colors and fabrics in Mrs. Foster's shop, so that any clothing she might require could be made up without traveling all the way to York for a fitting. Indeed, Mrs. Foster told me she had made the dress that Lady Beatrice was wearing when I arrived—the gray one.

At that point, I asked Mrs. Foster to excuse me for a moment, and went in search of Lady Beatrice, or failing her, Miss Taylor. I got lost only twice.

With some help, I found her finally in the Dresden Room, supervising the dusting of some exquisite porcelain figurines.

She turned to me with a frown. "I hope you like the samples Mrs. Foster brought. If not, please tell me, and I'll have Wilson take her back for others more to your taste."

Drawing a breath, I said, "Lady Beatrice. Truly, I appreciate your thoughtfulness—"

The frown became a smile. "Not at all. You've helped me enormously, you know. It's the least I could do. You didn't bring everything you might need, and I know how uncomfortable it is to have to make do."

Gathering my courage, I said, "Lady Beatrice, you aren't listening. I can't possibly stay two weeks!"

"I agree with you, Bess, it's ridiculous to think of keeping me in bed or lying on a couch for two weeks. I'll summon Dr. Halliday, and we can tell him to his face that it's nonsense." And then she added, with a conspirator's smile, "I'd much rather go to Cornwall—we have friends there. Or even Scotland. I do love it there in midsummer, and the hunting lodge was one of Hugh's favorite places. You must come too! I think you'd enjoy it as well. Think about it, my dear."

She went blithely on—as if we might actually be planning the summer.

"Have you visited Cornwall, my dear? It's a long journey, of course, but we could break it in London, spend a few days with Jonathan, then travel on."

Before I could find a suitable argument to present, to indicate that I would have to miss the joys of all this travel because I was involved in projects of my own, Lady Beatrice was distracted by the housekeeper, Mrs. Bennett, who had just come into the room to ask whether or not a tapestry on the inner wall might need attention.

Later that day, Lillian came to speak with me. "You must understand, Bess. She is extremely anxious about this operation."

I felt ashamed. I hadn't cared for the way Lady Beatrice was ordering my life, but it hadn't occurred to me that her behavior might have been rooted in fear. That all this talk of making plans together was really a way to persuade herself that all was well. Would be well. That she would live to go to Cornwall, and her invitation for me to join her was ensuring that it would happen. That the future was there, waiting for her.

I realized something else as well. I truly had no reason to hurry away. I was only seeking more distance from my own heartache—from Simon, and his coldness, which had so shocked me in Ireland. I had never seen him so hurt with my making light of his seemingly jealous remark about Terrence. And yet, I knew as well that it was like picking at a wound, to be there and see him almost daily. I had no idea how to bridge the gap between us.

Perhaps a fortnight with Lady Beatrice would give me the time I needed to come up with a solution to this problem. And I wanted to do that, not because I had fallen in love with him, but because I missed his friendship that had been so precious to me since I was five. If there was never anything else between us, I needed to keep my oldest friend.

Miss Taylor noted the anxious expression on my face. "What is it, Bess? What's wrong?"

I couldn't tell her, could I? I barely understood it myself. But I knew that my restlessness had worried my mother, and I realized now that it was the gnawing uncertainty in my personal life that had caused it.

I swallowed the sadness I could feel bubbling up in me before it could reveal itself in sudden tears.

"I'm sorry for dismissing Lady Beatrice," I managed to say in a nearly normal voice. "I'm so sorry. I didn't know—I didn't see—"

She put out her hand. "Call me Lillian." She smiled. "I understand. And I couldn't think of a way to help you see. Until I told you the truth. But please, don't tell Lady Beatrice that I've persuaded you. Let her believe you stay for her. And I do hope you will."

Lady Beatrice was quite cheerful as we sat down at the table in the small dining room, which was still large enough to seat twenty guests with ease. And then Mrs. Bennett came to tell her that Jonathan was on the telephone, and she hurried out to speak to her son.

I hadn't been aware that Linton Hall was on the telephone. Lillian Taylor, seeing my look of surprise, said to me, "We had that put in when the Earl decided to stay in the London house. He calls regularly, when he isn't sitting in the House of Lords."

And it was clearly a pleasant conversation, because when she came back to the dining room, Lady Beatrice was beaming.

"How is his lordship?" Lillian asked.

"Well. Quite well. Last night they dined in The Ivy, one of Hugh's favorite restaurants. My son was telling me that the waiter remembered us from the grand opening, and asked after us." She chatted on. "I had to tell him about the surgery—Dr. Halliday insisted. He was happy to hear I'd found a nurse I liked. I told him we were planning on inviting her to stay on and come down to London with us, and he was pleased. He asked if he should come up, but I told him we would manage nicely now. And not to worry."

Lillian glanced briefly my way, and I guessed she was telling me how much my presence had already done to make the surgery seem less terrifying.

I could see it for myself.

After the meal, Dr. Halliday came to see his patient to ensure she was well enough for the surgery at the end of the week. While he was examining Lady Beatrice, there was another telephone call, this time for me. I went to the small room—hardly larger than a closet—where the telephone had been put in.

It was Cousin Melinda on the other end of the line.

It was too soon for her to have received my letter. And so when she asked how I was faring, I confessed, "We got off to a rocky start, but all is well. I'm staying for the surgery myself."

"I'm glad to hear it. Lady Beatrice was going to make herself ill before the doctors had a chance to do their work."

And she went on, asking how I liked Lady Beatrice and Lillian, and the dales—as if my being in Yorkshire was no surprise, my staying on was no surprise, and the fact that Dr. Halliday approved of me as well was not one either.

"Melinda. Did you know from the start that I would be persuaded to stay on?"

"No, of course not. But I do know Lady Beatrice, and I was hoping you would like her as much as I have done through the years. Do let me know how she does, after her surgery." And then she added, "I hope you'll like Lillian Taylor as well. She's had quite an adventurous life."

"She's been very helpful," I answered.

We talked for a few minutes longer, and then she said goodbye.

I had the oddest feeling as I put up the receiver that something was wrong, and that Cousin Melinda had called to keep me from worrying while it—whatever it might be—was sorted out. The thought niggled at me all through the evening, and finally I asked if I might use the telephone to let my mother know the change of plans.

"Of course, my dear," Lady Beatrice replied. "I should have thought of that myself. By all means, put a call through."

It was almost my mother's bedtime—just after eleven—but I thanked Lady Beatrice and hurried back to the telephone closet.

My father had had a telephone put in as soon as the lines had reached us in Somerset, and I'd been glad of that a number of times. I told the operator the number I wished to reach, then stood there, biting my lip as I waited for the call to be put through.

When my mother said, "Hello?" there was anxiety in her voice, I could sense it.

"I'm just calling to let you know there's been a change in plans," I said quickly.

"Oh—hello, there, love. I was going to telephone you in the morning."

"Lady Beatrice has asked me to stay on with her, during her convalescence. She has suggested I visit Florence in York—as planned—while she is having her surgery, and then I'll come back to the Hall with her until Dr. Halliday decides she is fully recovered."

"I see," she replied, distractedly. "Well, that should work out, I should think. I know Florence is looking forward to seeing you. And as to that, love, I shan't be meeting you in York after all. Cook's hand has not healed as well as it should have done, and I was waiting to hear from Dr. Johnston when you called. I'm worried about infection setting in."

"I'm so sorry—is she in great pain?"

"Yes, and the swelling has got worse, I think. We've taken care of it, from the start, as you know."

Mother continued. "We haven't starved. All my culinary skills have returned—I've only burnt the bread once."

"I'm reassured," I told her. "But please keep me informed. And give Cook my love." I wanted to ask about Simon, and if he was still at the cottage. But I contented myself by asking about the Colonel Sahib.

"I'm sorry to not be there," I said. "I never intended to be away this long."

"Look on the bright side, love," she said with what I recognized as false cheer. "We won't have to choose your bedroom curtains for another fortnight."

On Friday we left for York.

It was an entourage. The motorcar with Lady Beatrice, ensconced among half the pillows in the Hall to lessen the jarring of the road, led the way. Behind that, Miss Taylor—Lillian—and I rode together in the smaller motorcar. And behind us came the shooting brake, filled with all the luggage.

When we arrived, Lady Beatrice was taken directly to hospital, where Dr. Halliday's assistant was waiting to greet her and settle her. Lillian stayed with her, and I was driven to Florence's house just outside the city's border.

I watched the city pass by through the window. During the war, when most able men were away fighting for their country, we had grown accustomed to seeing only young boys and old men in the villages. Sadly that hadn't changed much. So many soldiers hadn't come home. The ones who did return were wounded, and most would never recover. Legs and arms missing, blindness, and terrible scars were everywhere. Even sadder were the thin beggars in uniforms that had seen better days. People hurried by them, heads averted, unwilling to aid the men that had kept them safe for four years.

I turned away, wanting to weep.

My friend was happy to see me, running out to greet me as the unfamiliar motorcar pulled up in front of her house.

"Bess! How lovely to see you! I thought it must be you, although I was expecting you to come by train. Only you could manage to arrive in a motor with a coat of arms on the door! Come in, come in, and tell me all about it! And did you know, there's a box waiting for you, with the name of a very nice shop on the lid."

Florence and I had been to school together, and our mothers had been fast friends. She was married now to a barrister and—I could see behind the scarves and shawls that concealed it—she was expecting her first child.

"Congratulations," I said when we were in her pretty sitting room and the maid had gone to bring us tea.

Florence blushed. "I should have written—told you. But I was rather superstitious, I didn't want anyone to know until I was sure—" She smiled. "And the truth is, the larger I grow, the less I seem to accomplish. Still, it's wonderful, and I can't wait. Bruce is over the moon."

"He should be. Tell me all about it, do!"

And for the next two days we talked of nothing but setting up the nursery, her lying-in, baby clothes and blankets and what I thought of the crib. I found myself thinking that this could have been me, if there hadn't been a war, if I hadn't chosen to train as a nursing Sister.

I wasn't sure I'd have traded places with Florence. Despite the horrors

I'd seen and the tragedies and the deaths, despite the long hours and heartbreak and danger, I was glad I'd made my choice.

The time flew by, and then it was Sunday and Bruce escorted the two of us to Evensong at the Minster. This time, as we drove through the city toward the church, I kept my eyes on Florence, to avoid seeing the wounded. I only partly succeeded.

CHAPTER THREE

THE NEXT MORNING, the motorcar collected me and I was taken to meet Dr. Halliday. The familiar smells and sounds of a hospital raised my spirits.

"It was a good clean surgery," he said as we walked together down the passage toward Lady Beatrice's room. "You shouldn't have any trouble. If you do, call me at once. Don't try to deal with it yourself."

"No, Doctor," I answered obediently. But he would be hours away. "You've arranged for her to be comfortable on the journey? And what about medicines as we return to the Hall?"

"The ward Sister has all that for you. Try your best to keep the patient quiet, and don't let her get out of bed too soon. I know she'll test your authority."

I shouldn't be at all surprised if she did, I thought to myself, but replied only, "Yes, Doctor, I understand."

The ward Sister did indeed have everything in hand, giving me copies of instructions, a report on the actual surgery, and a list of the medicines she had packed in a kit for me.

When we reached Lady Beatrice's bedside, she was restless and eager to leave.

I thought she looked rather pale still, and her voice was merely a thread, but she made it clear what she wanted and when.

A quarter of an hour later all the formalities had been dealt with, Lillian had seen to the collecting and packing of all their belongings, and the proper care for the flowers that Lady Beatrice's son had ordered to fill her private room. Wilson was waiting with the motorcar, and this time I rode with him, to keep an eye on the patient, while Lillian sat among all the flowers we were taking back to the Hall.

Dr. Halliday told Lady Beatrice in no uncertain terms to behave herself and mind every instruction I gave her, if she wanted to see a full recovery.

We stopped four times on the journey north, so that I could check on our patient and see to giving her the food that the hospital had prepared for her. She made a face at the thin soups but drank them obediently. But by the last stop, she was tired and hurting from the bouncing on the roads, and her temper was fraying.

I was glad to have her back at the Hall and safely tucked into the bedchamber that had been a sitting room. Mrs. Bennett and the staff had made it as comfortable as possible, and as little like a sickroom as they could manage, collecting some of her favorite things from her usual bedroom, to make her happy. Included among them was a gilt-framed portrait of her husband in Highland dress that had been hung across from her bed. She had pointed out several likenesses of the late Earl, but this was the one she preferred. And I could see why—he was tall, darkly handsome, and he wore the kilt with a flair that was clear even in the painting. He had been in one of the Scots regiments before their marriage.

Lillian and I had a late supper in the small dining room, and then she went upstairs while I slept in a cot at the foot of Lady Beatrice's bed.

I was glad she was tired enough to sleep the night through. I slept as well, but with an ear ready to hear any change in her breathing or signs of restlessness or fever.

She was a trying patient for the next few days, in pain and impatient with everything from the plumping of her pillows to the nasty (her words) medicines she was asked to swallow.

But as postsurgical pain began to subside, her spirits improved, and she was back to the woman I'd met on my arrival. We'd arranged a chaise longue by the window, and as soon as it was safe to move her to it during the day, she could lie there and look out at the gardens. I was very watchful, but there were no signs of infection, and the incision was healing quite nicely. Dr. Halliday came to call several times and nodded with satisfaction as he noted her progress.

"You must be feeling much better as well," he informed her. "I told you it was one of the benefits of having the surgery done."

She glared at him, but it was more playful than serious. "Yes, you always tell me that. And then gloat when I admit you were right."

"By Saturday, let her walk a little bit more each day," he told me, "but don't let her climb stairs or tire herself. I don't intend this as permission to overdo."

"Yes, Doctor," I replied.

But it was easier said than done, keeping her quiet. She insisted on engaging with her staff but then she would be tired and rather querulous afterward. Still, it was good for her mind and her spirits to feel she still held the reins of her life here.

It was Wednesday, a week past the surgery, when everything changed.

We were just sitting down to breakfast when Mrs. Bennett came in with a silver tray with a telegram on it.

Lady Beatrice frowned as she took it, then sat there staring at it rather than opening it.

Lillian said quietly, "If it was Jonathan, Sylvia would have called. Or Bartlett . . ."

Lady Beatrice gave her a grateful smile, saying, "Yes, of course." Using the knife by her plate, she slit open the little envelope and drew out the sheet inside.

The smile changed abruptly as she opened it and read the message. Drawing in a harsh breath, she crumpled the sheet in her hand.

"Oh my God. Lillian—"

Lillian was already out of her chair. Reaching out she took the sheet from Lady Beatrice's clenched fingers, spread out the sheet, and began to read.

Chapter Four

LADY BEATRICE HAD closed her eyes in pain.

Lillian said softly, "Oh my dear!" She passed the telegram to me.

Gordon had accident. Come at once.

It was signed simply, *Arthur.*

I had no idea who Arthur was, nor Gordon either for that matter. I couldn't remember Lady Beatrice ever mentioning them.

I must have looked as puzzled as I felt, for Mrs. Bennett, just behind me, said softly, "Her godson."

I still didn't know which man, or perhaps a child, she meant.

Lady Beatrice was still sitting there as if turned to stone, her eyes closed, her breathing ragged. I rose and took her right hand, reaching for the pulse. It was fast, irregular—

"Let's move her—" I began, worried, but Lady Beatrice opened her eyes. I could see the unshed tears.

"No! I'm all right." Clearly she wasn't, the shock had been severe. I was about to say so when she went on, her voice husky, but clear. "I must go to him."

"Where is he?" I asked. A telegram—some distance, surely—

My words crossed those of Mrs. Bennett and Lillian.

Mrs. Bennett said, "You can't."

And Lillian was saying, "You mustn't think—"

"No," Lady Beatrice interjected. "He's hurt, I want to be there."

I tried again. "Let me telephone Dr. Halliday—"

"He's in York. He won't be here in time," Mrs. Bennett reminded us.

Lady Beatrice attempted to rise from her chair, but we all leaned toward her to stop her. She sighed. "If I cannot go, then you must, Bess, please. Lillian, go with her. Wilson will drive. Bess, if he's had an accident, I'd feel much happier if you were there. I trust you to do what's best."

She was herself again, back in command and barking orders.

I stayed where I was, standing just beside her, and said, "You must do your best to stay calm. Your heart—"

"Will improve quickly when I know you are with him. Go on, Bess, hurry!"

I had already realized that the best thing I could do was obey. I nodded, hurried from the room, and went to find Mrs. Bennett.

She was in the linen cupboard on the second floor, pulling out sheets and blankets for use in the car.

I said, "Tell Dr. Halliday to hurry. I'm worried for her."

"Yes, Miss, I will." She was already gathering up the armload of pillows and linens. A maid came hurrying to help her.

"I sent for Mr. Wilson," she said as she took the extras. I had turned and was already on my way to my room.

Accustomed to having to leave quickly during the war, I gathered what I needed, and then hurried to Lady Beatrice's room to collect what I thought could be spared for an improvised kit. I hadn't brought my own, I hadn't expected to need medical supplies.

I met Lillian coming down the stairs to the main hall, and someone came rushing up with a hamper of food. "You'll be needing this, ma'am," she said to Lillian, and we added it to the pile of things waiting for the motorcar to be brought around.

Mrs. Bennett was already opening the heavy doors, and I saw Wilson rounding the last bend in the drive. When he arrived, we began to load everything into the vehicle. There was barely room for the two of us to fit beside everything.

I was just closing my door, thanking Mrs. Bennett for her help, when I saw Lady Beatrice walking toward us.

"I can't get through on the telephone. It must be a madhouse there. Call me. Please." She placed a hand on my forearm. "And, Bess, please do whatever you can to help Gordon. Even as a child he would always underplay the truth about the amount of pain he was in, thinking he could spare us the worry. Both those boys are very dear to me, but Gordon, my godson, in particular . . . promise me you'll do whatever you can to help him."

"I promise," I told her. And Wilson was letting in the clutch, and we began to move away from the house, around the circle, and down the drive.

Clearly Wilson knew where he was going. I had no idea. Beside me, Lillian was leaning her head back against a pillow, drawing a deep breath.

"I don't know anything about Gordon," I said. "Or where we're going."

She turned to look at me. "I'm so sorry. Of course. We were in such a rush to be on our way. But the sooner we were gone, the sooner Lady Beatrice would be able to rest."

"It will depend on what's happened. What's wrong. The question at the moment is, who is he?"

"Oh—her grandnephew, Lady Beatrice's husband Hugh's sister's grandson is Gordon Neville. Gordon inherited the farm from his father. Arthur is his brother. He is a solicitor now, in Richmond with his wife. Gordon and his mother live deeper into the Dales near the town of Scarfdale."

"If this was an emergency, why didn't someone telephone Lady Beatrice, so that she could learn more than the telegram could tell her?"

"I don't believe they're on the telephone." She coughed. "Hugh's sister married for love," she explained coyly.

"Was Gordon old enough to be in the war?"

Lillian half-smiled. "He's thirty-five. Arthur is thirty-three. They served in a Yorkshire regiment. And survived, somehow."

Somehow, I'd thought of "Gordon" and "Arthur" as being younger, barely out of their teens. I was beginning to follow the family tree, now. "Are either of them married?"

"Arthur is married, his wife's name is Margaret. Gordon never married. There *was* a girl, but she chose someone else. Gordon was very bitter over that."

"Are they close to Lady Beatrice?"

"Yes, of course. Jonathan never cared for them. He's a little bit of a snob, having inherited the title so young." She smiled, but it wasn't more than an attempt to make light of what she was saying. Lady Beatrice clearly had a blind spot where Jonathan was concerned.

Lillian leaned her head back against the seat and closed her eyes.

It was the end of confidences.

Wilson drove as fast as he dared, on the winding roads. I stared out at the passing scenery. Yorkshire was so empty compared to my part of England where one had only to go a few miles in any direction to find a crossroads or a village, even a small town. We passed a few lanes that went off to isolated farms, but for each one of those, we went miles without seeing anything but sheep. Around us the valley began to shrink inward, narrowing rather than opening out. And the landscape was more rugged.

After we turned off the winding main road, we found ourselves on an even more narrow lane that followed a rocky stream—a beck, according to Wilson—and in a few more miles turned again, leaving it behind. I could see the land ahead of us rising into the blue sky, cutting off the sun and leaving us in shadow as we drew closer. The hills were crisscrossed with lines of gray stone walls, and dotted with sheep. Gray stone outcroppings, some of them rather high, broke the monotony, as if the earth beneath them had washed away over the millennia until the face was bare. In some of the folds and crevices, water ran in little trickles. I could imagine them in spate after a storm. There were sheep here too, and sometimes grazing cattle lower down.

I'd seen no one for miles, and I was beginning to think that there were more sheep than people in Scarfdale, when the motorcar began to slow.

Ahead I could see stone pillars, the gates between them standing open. Each pillar was topped with what appeared to be a boar's head, staring at us from blank stone eyes. Wilson turned in through the gates and drove up a winding, looping drive. I could see the house, now because there were only a handful of ornamental trees, rather than the parkland that surrounded Lady Beatrice's home. This wasn't the usual grim stone found in many parts of the dale—not the dark, bleak sort that formed those snaking dry stone walls that marked the landscape, just as hedgerows did at home. This was lighter, and offered a quiet contrast to the handsome style of the house. A narrow side lane cut away to the left before the drive reached the manicured lawns and flower beds. For service vehicles and farm carts, I thought, for I could see, as the lane disappeared behind a stand of tall bushes, that it was less well tended than the main drive.

I touched Lillian's arm, and she opened her eyes. I didn't think she'd slept at all either, because her breathing hadn't changed.

"Ah—we've arrived," she said, making sure her hat was still properly settled.

The house came into view—unlike the villages, which tended to be in protected valleys, it was set on a slight hill, which must offer grand views all around. A large manor house, not the seat of an Earl, but attractive, with ivy running up the facade and over the sheltered porch.

Someone must have been on the lookout—the door was opened just as we reached the circle in front of it, and a man in the dark clothes of a butler stepped out to greet us and help us step down.

He tried to conceal his surprise at seeing only Lillian and me in the rear of the motorcar—he was clearly expecting Lady Beatrice to come.

Lillian said, "Hello, Davies. I'm sorry we have to meet again in these circumstances."

"Miss Taylor," he said in acknowledgment, and then she presented me.

"Lady Beatrice is indisposed at the moment. But she has sent Sister Crawford in her place, to see what can be done for dear Gordon until the doctor arrives."

"Sister," he replied with a nod, adding, "the local man, Dr. Menzies, has been in. But a second opinion will be welcome."

He led us into the house as a younger man, a footman, came out to help Wilson with the baggage. Davies was saying, "The house is rather full at the moment. Mr. Arthur and his wife are here along with Lieutenant Frederick Caldwell and his wife, for Lady Neville's birthday. Would you mind sharing a room?"

"Not at all," Lillian told him, looking at me for confirmation, and I smiled in response. "Perhaps we should look in on Mr. Gordon before we go up?"

"He's in the gun room at the moment," Davies said.

An unusual place for an accident victim, I thought, but said nothing as I followed Lillian and Davies down a passage toward the back of the house. A door stood open near the end of it, and I could see lights and hear voices.

Davies stepped aside to allow us to enter, saying, "Miss Taylor and Sister Crawford, sir."

We walked in.

Two men, presumably the Neville brothers, looked up. They looked very much alike, dark like the portrait of Hugh, with blue eyes and strong faces. The one by the hearth was slimmer and not quite as tanned. Perhaps Arthur Neville, the solicitor? He stepped forward. "Welcome to the Hall." He greeted us politely enough, although his gaze had moved behind us. "Has Lady Beatrice gone up?" he asked Davies.

I was looking at the other brother, who was sitting uncomfortably in the large leather chair on the other side of the hearth. Gordon Neville, I thought, because he was heavily bandaged around the arm and shoulder, and his face seemed more weathered from managing the estate.

"Hello, Arthur," Lillian said, before Davies could answer. "This is Sister Crawford. Lady Beatrice has just had surgery and isn't allowed to travel. She sent us in her place."

"With all due respect," he said, frowning, "it's my aunt we need, not a nurse. Lady Beatrice knows what needs to be done for this grave matter."

"The telegram said only that Gordon was hurt. How are you, my dear?" Lillian stepped into the room, speaking to the second man, and I followed her. Behind us, Davies closed the door.

"In pain," Gordon Neville answered from the chair. "Dislocated shoulder, broken arm, and a lump on the head. Dr. Menzies wouldn't give me anything for it."

Lillian crossed to the chair. "And rightly so, with a head injury." She saw the glass in his hand. "Whiskey isn't much help, either."

"For the shock," he replied.

I kept out of it. Dr. Menzies had already dealt with the patient, and I was clearly not needed.

But Gordon was looking at me, now, saying, "Sorry you've had the journey for nothing, Sister."

I smiled. "We were worried. I'm glad to see you in better circumstances than we'd expected."

"We couldn't put anything more into the telegram," Arthur was saying. "I didn't know my aunt had had surgery." She was actually his great-aunt, but it was clear he was fond of her.

"She didn't want anyone to worry," I answered. "She'll be fit to travel in a few more days."

Arthur Neville shook his head, clearly in shock. "We were counting on her. The police will be here soon. Lady Beatrice knows the chief constable and her guidance is vital."

"Police?" Lillian said, turning to Arthur. "What on earth for?"

Gordon said, his voice strained, "There's a dead man upstairs in one of the bedrooms. I killed him."

CHAPTER FIVE

WE STOOD THERE, Lillian and I, staring at Gordon Neville.

"I'm to blame for his death," he amended. "The local Constable saw fit to send for someone with more authority."

"What in God's name has happened?" Lillian demanded, looking from one to the other.

Arthur shook his head.

It was Gordon who said, "I was out on The Knob with Frederick. There's a stretch of moorland just below it. Where the sheep like to scratch themselves on the heather. We were looking for some that had got themselves lost in that storm last week and hadn't come down. At any rate, we'd had no luck, and when we came to that outcrop of rock, I went up it for a better view, and then Frederick came after me. I turned to tell him no luck, and there was some loose scree at the edge. I slipped, started to fall, and he tried to stop me." He stopped; his mouth tightened as if a wave of pain had caught him unprepared. "Both of us went over the edge. I landed—he cushioned my fall. We must have been unconscious for a bit. When I came to my senses, I saw that he was in bad shape. There was no one to help—I walked down to the house, and Arthur and I went back for Frederick. We had a hurdle, we had no choice but to bring him home on that; it was freezing out there."

"He was alive, when we got there, although he told us he couldn't feel his legs or arms," Arthur put in. "We got him into bed just as Davies came back with Dr. Menzies. He died in the small hours of the morning."

They should never have moved him. It most certainly had made matters worse. But it was too late to say that, and wouldn't serve any purpose now. Was that why the police had been summoned? Was it the doctor who'd had questions and sent for them?

"Who is Frederick?" I asked. "What did Dr. Menzies say about his injuries?"

"Frederick Caldwell," Arthur Neville interjected. "He is a childhood friend of ours. He and his wife, Grace, came for my mother's—Mrs. Neville's—birthday party."

"His back and neck—" Gordon shook his head. "There was no blood, except where his head struck a rock. Falling on him did the rest."

"Dr. Menzies told you this?"

"He didn't have to. I was in the war. I could see that it was bad. But we had to get him off the moor. There was no other choice." He drank more of the whiskey. His coloring was not good. Setting his shoulder must have been agony, and the broken arm, already taped to a board, must hurt nearly as badly.

I said, "I'm sorry. But you, Mr. Neville, ought to be in your own bed."

Gordon Neville wasn't having it.

"I'm all right."

"Mr. Neville, you are still in a state of shock." I turned to Arthur, his brother. "He shouldn't be sitting here, drinking whiskey. The sooner he lies down, even if he can't sleep, the better." And I added for good measure, "If the police are coming, he will need a clear head."

Arthur said to his brother, "She's right, you know. Let's have you up the stairs, old son, and out of those clothes. I'll help you."

It took some persuasion to get him on his feet, and I quickly saw why. His own back was complaining loudly, and he found it difficult to walk properly, forcing himself to manage it. I saw the tightening of his mouth and the color draining out of his face.

"He will need a hot water bottle—several of them—around him, to keep that back warm. Otherwise he'll be as stiff as a board."

Arthur cast me a glance, and said, "Aunt Beatrice knew what she was about when she sent you."

We got Gordon up the stairs with the help of Arthur and the young footman, down the passage, and into what I assumed was his room. We took off his boots and his trousers, got him into the bed, while the footman lit a fire in the room. Gordon clenched his teeth with a cry of pain as he tried to lie back, and I thought for a moment that he was going to lose consciousness. I moved some of the pillows under his bad shoulder and arm, to make them more comfortable, and he nodded his thanks.

Lillian had stayed in the passage until he was in bed, and she came in now to take his hand and say, "That was rather brave of you. It couldn't have been easy."

Davies came back with the hot water bottles, and we arranged them around the patient. He was no longer protesting—I think the sheer relief was overwhelming. For all I knew he'd sat in that chair since Frederick had been brought home. How Gordon himself had got to the house, then gone again to the scene of the accident and helped carry the hurdle back was surely a matter of will alone. Or a guilty conscience? Still, every step he took must have been almost unbearably painful. He was my patient now, and I could feel that sense of responsibility for his well-being returning to me. Habits of a nursing Sister.

Arthur was pulling the curtains while Davies lit a lamp on a desk across the room from the bed, then saw to the fire, which was just catching well. The house was chilly, and it sounded as if a wind had come up, for I heard the windowpanes rattle once or twice.

When all was well, Arthur and Lillian left, taking the staff with them, and I heard Lillian say, "What shall I tell Wilson? Lady Beatrice will ask him a hundred questions—and if he tells her what's happened . . ." Her voice faded down the passage.

I took a seat by the fire, wishing for a cup of tea and a chance to freshen up. I had given my coat to Davies when we arrived, but that was an hour ago.

Gordon spoke from the bed. His voice was low, drowsy. "I didn't intend for any of this to happen." I wasn't sure he was aware that he'd spoken aloud. "God knows I didn't."

I didn't respond. And soon afterward I could hear his breathing change as he slept. I wondered if he'd slept at all the previous night.

After a while, Lillian came back with a middle-aged woman carrying a tray, followed by a younger maid bearing a pitcher and fresh towels.

They moved quietly into the room, and Lillian whispered, "Hot water for you, Bess, tea, sandwiches, and slices of strawberries from the walled garden."

They arranged everything, then left.

I washed my face and hands, took off my hat and set it aside, did what I could about my hair, then poured myself a cup of tea, before touching the food.

I stayed there another hour, to be sure Gordon was resting quietly. When I looked at him, I could see that this was indeed a deep sleep. I wasn't sure what it was, his helplessness or his saying "I didn't intend for any of this to happen" that brought forth this surge of protectiveness. I assured myself it was my training during the war. Then I set my tray in the passage outside the door, and went to the stairs.

There were voices coming from a room to the right of the staircase, and I hesitated, and then tapped at the door before walking in.

Arthur and Lillian broke off what they were saying. "How is he?" she asked.

"Deeply asleep at the moment," I assured her, and then turned to

Arthur. "It might be a good idea for me to have a look at Frederick's body."

He was appalled at the very idea, but before he could object, I said, "I was with the Queen Alexandra's in France. A surgical nurse. If the police are coming, it might be helpful if someone other than Dr. Menzies examine the body."

Both Arthur and Lillian stared. And then Arthur rose. "A very good idea. Come with me."

We went back up the stairs to another bedroom.

The sun was still bright outside, but it was late afternoon, and this room was rather gloomy. Nor was there a fire on the hearth or a lamp lit.

The figure on the bed was covered with a sheet. We walked over to it, and Arthur asked, "Are you certain of this, Sister Crawford?"

"Yes."

We lifted the sheet back. Rigor hadn't passed, but I could see the stark bruising against the man's pale skin.

There was dried blood in the man's fair hair, and when I lifted the body a little to look at its back, I could see dark bruising along the spine and at the nape of his neck. He must have hit the rocks below the outcropping hard enough to do damage to the spine, but it was the back of the neck that worried me. It looked as if there had been a blow there, just at the base of the skull. Of course, it could have been that his neck landed on another rock, higher perhaps and more pointed than the flatter ones that had bruised his spine.

Arthur was watching me. Noticing what I was noticing. I remembered that he too had served in France—and that he was a solicitor.

I gently lowered the body back in place. The sheets hadn't been changed, nor the pillows, and the head wound had bled into the pillows' cases.

"Did the Constable walk out to the scene of the accident?" I asked.

"No, he didn't. He simply looked at the body. Not as closely as you have done, but enough to see something that worried him." He cleared his throat. "Constable Woods should have retired during the war, but there was no replacement for him. There hasn't been anyone sent up since then, either. Besides, he doesn't much care for us."

"Why?" I asked, surprised.

"This is my parents' house. We grew up here, Gordon and I, and we were rather a handful," he said wryly. "We gave poor Constable Woods more trouble than he could ever have deserved. He hasn't forgot."

We pulled the sheet over the dead man again.

"Why are you all here, just now?"

"It's my mother's birthday—or will be in a few days. We have only just come back from France, and she wanted us here. My wife came with me. They're in York along with Mrs. Grace Caldwell, Frederick's wife, at the moment."

"And the—Frederick? Is he a member of the family?"

"He's a childhood friend." There was something in the way he said it that was a warning not to pursue the matter. "That's why he and his wife are here as well."

Small wonder, with so many guests for the birthday, that Lillian and I were sharing a room.

We left, closing the door behind us.

"You don't seriously believe that the police will blame Gordon, your brother, for what occurred on the moor?" I hoped as a solicitor, that Arthur would have some insight.

"I don't know." But I thought he did.

The housekeeper, a Mrs. Roper, was waiting at the foot of the staircase to show me to my—our—room. Lillian had already gone up, and she waited until the door had closed behind the housekeeper to say, "I shall have to tell Wilson something. And I still don't know what to do."

"If he was in the kitchens, sitting with the staff, he already knows more than it's best to tell Lady Beatrice."

She looked tired, drained. "Then it's a question of how much he's allowed to pass on."

"For the moment, why not say that Gordon was injured in a fall, and I'm needed at present, until Dr. Halliday—"

"Oh, I'd forgot that Dr. Halliday was to follow us." She shook her head. "Is he needed, Bess? Is there any way to put him off? From what you say, Gordon will recover on his own."

I'd have liked someone else to have a look at the dead man, but I took her point. Dr. Halliday would report to Lady Beatrice. And might be—if things didn't go well with Gordon—called to testify at the inquest.

"They were able to send a telegram before. You must send one now telling Lady Beatrice that Dr. Halliday isn't needed, that Gordon appears to be recovering on his own."

"Yes. Of course." She reached for her coat and hat. "I'll have Wilson take me to send it, and that will give me a chance to speak to him privately."

I thought back to Arthur Neville's comments about Constable Woods. Why did the Constable feel it was necessary to summon someone higher in authority to look into this business? It seemed to be an accidental death.

Still, there was that injury on Frederick's neck. It *did* look as if someone had struck him from behind, and that the fall might have occurred because he took Gordon over the edge with him as he went down. But that wasn't enough evidence for everyone to assume the worst. Or that Gordon was lying about what had happened.

Was there some part of this accident that I didn't understand?

CHAPTER SIX

WITH LILLIAN GONE to find Wilson, I set about settling in. That took me all of ten minutes. Then I decided I should check on Gordon one more time, so I found my way back to his room. I had to pass the door to Frederick Caldwell's room as I went, and I thought about the dead man. He couldn't have been more than thirty-five, with a strong, attractive face, broad shoulders, and a scar across his back that I recognized as a shrapnel wound. He had been in the war then.

Gordon was still deeply asleep when I entered his room. I felt his forehead and took his pulse, and he didn't stir. Tiptoeing back into the hall, I was on my way back to my room when I heard a bustle as I passed the staircase.

Thinking it was Lillian, already back from the village, I paused to wait for her.

The footman was bringing in luggage—

Not Lillian, then. Surely not Lady Beatrice, worried enough to set out on her own!

I could hear voices now, women's voices. Lillian had encountered Lady Beatrice on the drive!

But I didn't recognize either of the two women as they reached the door and stepped inside.

I heard Arthur, coming quickly down the passage beyond the stairs, saying, "Margaret—" in a tone of voice that was more shock than welcome.

A woman, laughing, said, "Surprised? Well, we tired of the shops and the crowds and the *noise* of a city, and decided to cut our visit short."

The second woman added lightly, "As it was, we left nothing in the shops. Although sad to say, there was so little to buy. Nothing has changed, the shelves are depleted still. Not even something for your mother's birthday. I'd counted on finding the perfect gift."

There was a third voice, older. "Never mind that. I thought the cobblestones in the streets would be the death of me!"

Arthur had reached them, and Margaret said to her husband uncertainly, "I thought you'd be happy to see us."

He was ushering them into a room just out of my line of sight. I could just see his back, and beyond him, the skirts of the women.

The door was closed, but I stayed where I was, knowing what was to come.

And it was barely a minute later when I heard a woman's cry of despair. And then footsteps rushing to the closed door, and Arthur's voice saying, "No, Grace, you mustn't—"

She pleaded with him, but he was speaking forcefully, telling her to wait until Frederick was presentable.

Then the tears came. Shuddering tears, as if her heart was breaking. Another woman, comforting her, and they moved away, as if the sobbing woman had been persuaded to sit down.

I could hear someone else coming down the passage now. Mrs. Roper the housekeeper, I thought, and I was right. It was likely that Arthur Neville had rung for her.

Hurrying away so that I wouldn't be caught eavesdropping on a family's grief, I had just sat down by the hearth in my room when there was a knock at my door.

"Come in," I called, and Mrs. Roper opened the door, stepping just inside. "It's Mr. Arthur Neville, Miss. He asks that you come down. Mrs. Caldwell is in a state, and she needs your assistance."

"I'll come at once," I said, and thought to pick up the satchel with the medicines we had brought from Lady Beatrice. And then the name struck me. Caldwell.

"Is Mrs. Caldwell Fredrick Caldwell's wife?"

"Yes, she is indeed," Mrs. Roper replied. "Grace Caldwell."

No wonder, then, she had taken the news so hard.

I followed the housekeeper down the stairs, and taking a deep breath, I opened the door to what turned out to be a lovely drawing room, done up in rich blues and creams. Arthur was there, his face set, and two women, one of them older, were comforting a third, whose face was buried in a handkerchief. The older woman rose and then held out her hand. "I'm Mrs. Neville. Arthur and Gordon's mother. And this is Margaret, Arthur's wife."

"Elizabeth Crawford. I was staying with Lady Beatrice when the telegram came. Thinking that your son might need medical care, she sent me with Miss Taylor in her place. I was a nursing Sister in the war." I added, "This is hardly the homecoming you were expecting."

Arthur Neville said, "Mrs. Caldwell has had a shock. Is there anything you can give her?"

"Brandy would be best. Laudanum would put her to sleep for several hours."

"Laudanum," the older woman said quietly, glancing toward Arthur.

Mrs. Roper spoke from behind me. "I've put her things in the blue bedroom, sir. Away—"

"Yes, thank you, Mrs. Roper," he said, cutting her off.

The older woman turned to me as I set my satchel down and looked inside. I'd brought a little laudanum, not knowing what I'd find here in the way of injuries. "Thank you, my dear. What do you need?"

"A glass of water, please."

She went to a cabinet against the wall, and found a jug of water. It was for the drinks in that cupboard, but it would do, as would the wineglass she brought as well. I mixed a very little laudanum in the water, stirred it, and handed it to her.

She went to the distraught woman in the chair. "Here, Grace, this will help. Drink it all, my dear."

Grace obediently took the glass and drank it. I think she would willingly have swallowed poison just then, she was in such straits. A very pretty woman with fair hair and a sweet face.

The two women went on comforting her, giving the drug time to take effect. Arthur came to stand beside me. "Frederick's wife," he said softly. "They're—they were very close."

I could see that, for she seemed completely lost, as if the mainstay of her world had been taken away. For clearly it had.

"The other two women?" I asked, keeping my own voice low.

"Ah. Yes, sorry. My wife Margaret, and my mother. Tomorrow is her birthday."

As the sobs began to subside, changing to hiccoughs, I stepped toward the women.

"You'll be more comfortable upstairs," I said to Grace Caldwell in the voice I'd used for four years to comfort and manage patients. "Let us help you with your hat and coat, Mrs. Caldwell."

She rose unsteadily, and we helped her out of her traveling coat and Mrs. Neville gently removed her hat.

"That's much better, isn't it?"

She barely nodded.

With the help of Margaret Neville and Mrs. Neville, we got her to the door and up the stairs, but at the top of the staircase, she seemed to collect her thoughts. "I want to see him . . ."

"In a little while," I said, taking her arm. "You will want to wash your face first, and arrange your hair."

"Yes—yes, of course. I am so tired, I can't think properly. It was a long journey after the train."

"The last hour or so of a journey is always the most tiring, I find."

"Yes."

Mrs. Neville was opening the door to a room. It was cool, the fire had only just been lit, but there were lamps burning, and the wallpaper, a Chinese print, was very pretty.

"This isn't our room," Grace Caldwell said, pulling away.

"There's no fire in there," I told her. "It's warmer in here. Can you tell?"

We got her to sit on the edge of the bed, Margaret and Mrs. Neville were talking to her while I unlaced her boots and pulled them off. The covers had already been pulled aside, and Mrs. Neville said, "Why don't you lie here for just a few minutes while I change? Margaret and I will be back in only a minute or two."

"Yes, all right," she said frowning but too drowsy now to think what she had been on the point of doing. We tucked her in, the other two women left, and I said, "I'm going to turn down the lamps. They must be in your eyes."

I turned them down, leaving mostly the fire to light the room. Arthur's wife had drawn the drapes across the windows, shutting out the late afternoon sunlight. By the time I'd finished, Mrs. Caldwell was asleep. I pulled the covers up over her, then went to the door, hoping to find Mrs. Roper and ask if one of the maids could sit with her until Mrs. Caldwell woke up.

I met Margaret and Mrs. Neville in the passage.

"She's asleep," I said quietly. "I was just going to ask Mrs. Roper if someone could be spared to sit with her, so she doesn't wake up alone."

"I'll see to it," Mrs. Neville said. "Such a horrid thing. Sadly, there was no way to reach us and give us a little warning. Where is Gordon, do you know? Out on the farm somewhere, I expect."

Oh, dear. There had been no opportunity to explain all the circumstances in the drawing room. Taking a deep breath, I said, "Your son would want to tell you—"

Color drained from her face. "No—it isn't—Gordon isn't dead as well—"

I said quickly, "He was injured in the same fall, and he's resting in his room. If he's asleep, please don't wake him. He was very tired and in some pain."

"Oh, dear God." She turned to her son's wife. "Go and ask Arthur to come up to my room, would you, love? And, Sister Crawford, would you come with me—and tell me what is wrong with my son?"

We walked down the passage together. "I haven't had an opportunity to examine him fully," I said, "but his right arm is broken, the right shoulder was dislocated, and he struck his head. Dr. Menzies saw to his injuries, and Mr. Neville and I have managed to convince him to go to his bed. He was sitting in the gun room when I arrived. I don't think he'd moved from there since the doctor left. He's going to be in some pain for a time—he walked back to the house alone, then went back with his brother and the footman to bring Mr. Caldwell down on a hurdle. This didn't help his own injuries, and he was still in a state of shock when I arrived with Miss Taylor."

"Yes, yes, I just want to see him, reassure myself that he's all right. Where is Beatrice? I thought Arthur mentioned that he'd sent for her. But then I hardly had time to think about anything but Grace."

"Lady Beatrice just had surgery in York, and she's now recuperating at home. The doctor hasn't cleared her to travel yet. That's why she sent me."

"I don't understand why Arthur sent for her. I sent him a telegram relaying that we'd be home a day early." She opened the door into Gordon's room.

I said softly, "Perhaps she was closer."

"I'm sure that must be it." She walked across to the bed and looked down at her sleeping son. "Are you sure," she whispered, "that he'll be all right?"

"Unless there are internal injuries I don't know about, he should recover."

He stirred a little in his sleep, as she put out a hand and gently smoothed his hair.

"Poor darling!" she said, and leaned forward to kiss him, then thought better of it and straightened up. "No matter how old they are, they are still one's children." With a last look, she turned, and I followed her from the room.

We met Arthur in the passage, just coming toward us.

"How is Grace?"

"Asleep," I said,

"Good."

His mother took his arm. "Come with me, I need to know what's happened."

I left them to it.

Lillian had come back by the time I'd reached our room again. She was sitting in a chair by the fire, looking quite sad.

"Did you manage to send the telegram?"

"We had to go to the next village. But yes, it's sent. I see that Mrs. Neville has come back from York. It must have been difficult to break the news to Mrs. Grace Caldwell." She rose, held out her hands to the blaze in the grate. "Who was it who told her?"

"Arthur."

"I should have guessed. I couldn't envy him that. Where is she?"

"She's in the blue bedroom. I had to give her a little laudanum to calm her down. It was such a terrible shock. I believe Margaret Neville—Arthur's wife—is sitting with her."

"They are close—were close, Frederick and Grace. I don't know how she'll manage." It was almost word for word what Arthur Neville had said to me.

"Do they have children?"

"No. She had a miscarriage before the war. There haven't been any others."

"Poor Mrs. Neville. It's not going to be a memorable birthday."

"No." She sighed. "I wish we'd never come. That Arthur hadn't sent that telegram. It would be easier, at a distance."

I understood. She knew these people well. But a man had died . . .

I said, curious, "There's an Inspector coming from somewhere, to take over the inquiry. I should have thought that Frederick Caldwell's death was just what it appears to have been. A terrible accident. Not a matter for the police."

Lillian looked across at me. "I expect it's because they were alone when it happened. A formality, surely. An inquest."

But it appeared to me that she didn't really feel certain that it was.

She'd been wandering about the room, putting everything in order, as if in doing so, she could also order her own thoughts.

I said, "I must look in on Gordon. I don't know why Dr. Menzies hasn't come back. I think he could help Mrs. Caldwell."

"He probably has other patients and he is the only doctor for miles around. Didn't someone mention a lying-in, just before he was sent for?"

I left and went down the passage. Margaret Neville was just stepping out of the blue bedroom as I passed.

"Sister Crawford?"

I stopped. "Is she still asleep?"

"Yes, thank goodness. She wants to see Frederick. Is—should she be allowed to do that?"

I knew what she was asking. "He isn't . . . marred."

"Thank you."

I said, concerned, "You should rest as well, Mrs. Neville. She will need you and your mother." They must have set out at first light, to make it here as soon as they had.

She took a deep breath. "I know. Arthur told me what happened. I can't imagine how horrid that must have been. How is Gordon?"

"I was on my way to look in on him. Why don't you come with me?"

Together we walked on down the passage, past the staircase and past the room where Frederick lay. As we did, she asked, "Has anyone sent for the undertakers?"

"I don't know. There is an Inspector coming. The local man sent for him. That could be what your husband is waiting for."

I opened the door quietly to Gordon's room, and she followed me inside. He was asleep, but restless, as if his arm and shoulder were hurting. I watched as Mrs. Neville went up to the bed and looked down at the patient. "When Arthur was wounded in the war," she said in a low voice, "it was Gordon who got me through the fright of waiting for news. He wrote nearly a dozen letters, whatever he could learn about Arthur's injuries and how he was healing. Until he could write, himself. I was so very grateful." After a moment, she turned, and with a nod of thanks, left the room.

After a cursory examination, I turned to leave as well. And met Arthur just coming down the passage.

"Is there anything you need, Sister? You have only to ask. You've had two patients thrust upon you."

"Is Dr. Menzies coming back today to look in on your brother?"

"I don't know. He didn't say." He grimaced. "I don't know what to do. Gordon keeps telling me he's to blame."

"He feels a natural sense of guilt. After all, he survived the same fall."

But Arthur wasn't as certain. "He walked down from the place where it happened. He was as white as his shirt when I first saw him. He was in the most extraordinary pain—his arm and shoulder were in rough shape—and yet he insisted on going back with us. That was a good three miles or more."

"When something must be done, like finding help quickly for Mr. Caldwell, people can do amazing things. I saw that in the war."

He looked at me, frowning. "You served in France, you say?"

"Yes, very often in forward aid stations. I saw severely wounded men bring in a comrade whose wounds were even worse. Medically, they shouldn't have been able to do it, but they did."

"I saw it myself. How did you come to act as nurse for my great-aunt?"

I smiled. "You must know how persuasive she is. Mrs. Crawford, my cousin, had asked me to come up to Yorkshire to persuade Lady Beatrice to allow a nurse to attend her after her surgery. Instead, I found she'd decided I would do very well."

He nodded. "God knows, she's a master at it. Still, it's been our luck that you were available. Has Grace managed to sleep?"

"Yes, the laudanum did its work. But she will wake up eventually. And will want to see her husband's body."

"Oh God, I don't think I can face that." He looked away. "This was to be a happy weekend, wishing my mother a happy birthday. The first time we've all been here for it since 1914. It *will* be memorable . . ."

He turned and walked off.

The housekeeper was coming up the stairs as I passed them. "Sister? Could you tell Miss Taylor and Mrs. Neville that tea will be served in the small drawing room?"

"Yes, of course." It was nearly six o'clock, late for tea, but this hadn't been an ordinary afternoon.

I looked in on Grace, but Mrs. Neville wasn't there. Nor was Lillian in her room. I discovered that she and Mrs. Neville had already gone down and were sitting in the chill of the morning room, quietly talking. The door was half ajar as I walked by, and I passed on the message.

It was a somber gathering in the small drawing room, no one feeling at all festive as Mrs. Neville poured at the small tea table. I don't think anyone had much of an appetite for the sandwiches or the little cakes. It was the tea all of us needed more. I took my cup and stood by the windows, watching this family that had already suffered so much.

Arthur had just finished and was about to set his own cup on the tray when we could hear someone hammering on the door. His mouth tightened, and he looked at his mother. She barely nodded, and he turned and went to answer it without waiting for the staff to come up from the kitchen.

I think we all knew who was there.

The police had arrived.

CHAPTER SEVEN

INSPECTOR WADE WAS a thin man with sandy hair that was just beginning to recede. When Arthur returned to the drawing room with him, to present the rest of us, Arthur looked haggard.

Inspector Wade nodded to each of us in turn, hard gray eyes seeming to miss nothing. Then he said, "I'd like to see the dead man, if you please."

"Yes. He's upstairs . . ." Arthur turned and walked out into the passage.

But the Inspector hadn't finished with us. He said, in a voice that brooked no argument, "I'd like all of you to stay here, if you please."

We listened as the two men went up the staircase. Then Mrs. Neville said, "We mustn't give him any reason to be annoyed with us. It will only make matters worse."

"He needn't be so rude. Why did Constable Woods send for him in the first place?" Margaret asked.

"I don't know. Perhaps because he didn't wish to seem to be favoring us." She drew a breath, and said to me, "What if he wants to speak to Grace?"

"I'll explain that it was necessary to give her laudanum because of the state she was in. What's more, she wasn't here when the accident occurred. There's little she can add to his report."

"Yes, yes, that's quite true." But she still seemed wary.

No one spoke after that until we heard the two men coming back down the stairs.

As they came back into the drawing room, Arthur said, looking directly at me, "Inspector Wade would like us to wake up my brother. He wishes to hear his account of the fall."

"I'm sorry, Mr. Neville was still in a state of shock when I arrived earlier. We managed to convince him to lie down, painful as it was for him, and eventually he managed to fall asleep. I don't think anyone was able to rest last night." And all the while I was wondering how carefully he'd searched Frederick Caldwell's body. "If you could wait a little longer?"

"Then I wish to be taken to the site of the accident. While it's still light."

Arthur said, "I'll just go up for my coat."

Inspector Wade was staring at me. "And what is your medical training?"

I told him.

"Has Dr. Menzies come today to examine Gordon Neville?"

"I don't believe he has," I answered. "There was a lying-in, I'm told, last night. There may have been some difficulties with that."

Arthur came back, slightly out of breath from hurrying, sparing me from more questions. I said, "Would you mind if I went with you?"

"I don't believe that's necessary—" Wade began but Arthur cut across his words.

"Yes, I'd appreciate that."

I went for my own coat, and by the time I got back, the Inspector was asking the housekeeper, Mrs. Roper, about the state of mind of the two men as they set out to search for the sheep.

Looking flustered but determined, she replied, "They were talking about where to begin. It was Mr. Gordon who suggested going up Old Grumble. Mr. Frederick wasn't sure the sheep had got that far, but the thunder had been quite loud, and the rain had come down heavy. And it was more likely they'd look for shelter amongst the heather."

Inspector Wade seemed skeptical. "Wouldn't they have come down on their own, once it was clear? The sheep?"

"Most have lambs with them."

He nodded, as if that made perfect sense. Turning toward me, he said, "Let's be off, then."

We left the house through the kitchen passage, walking past the small gardens by the door, past the outbuildings, in the same stone as the house, and then began to climb. Above us was a high summit, and there were sheep dotting the fields most of the way up. Stone walls separated some of the flocks, others roamed free.

"Why is it called Old Grumble?" I asked Arthur, hoping to ease some of the tension I could feel rising in him.

"Storms seem to sweep down over the summit," he said. "We hear the thunder first."

I could well imagine.

We crossed several small rills, tiny streams that seemed to bisect this lower stretch. I saw sheep far to my left drinking from it, one down on her knees to reach the water. It must be quite cold, that water. I was grateful for my coat, for the wind I'd heard earlier was still with us, and as the sun moved west, the shadows on this side of Old Grumble were growing longer.

As we began to bear more to the north, I could see The Knob, a hill that appeared to have part of it broken off, leaving an outcrop of rock and a fairly long drop from there to broken rocks and heather below.

Oh, dear, I thought to myself. I could see now why one man had died and the other had been badly hurt.

Inspector Wade was saying, "Surely this is familiar land to your brother. Constable Woods told me you'd grown up here, both of you."

"Yes, of course it is. We were helping with the sheep when we were eight or ten. We thought it great fun to go out with Stevens—he manages the flocks."

The Inspector had laid his trap well. He stopped and turned to face Arthur. "Then he must have known about that loose scree. He'd have been careful not to come too near the edge."

Arthur flushed. "That's ridiculous. You haven't even reached the outcropping."

"We'll see. According to Constable Woods, you and your brother are a devious lot." He walked on, and Arthur, still angry, had to call to him. "This way, Inspector."

It was not the easiest walking. Under the thick grass were lumps of stone protruding from the ground, and I nearly stumbled twice. I heard Inspector Wade swear to himself when he tripped too. Arthur seemed to know how to avoid them.

The occasional ewe stared at us without fear, then went back to eating the grass, while this past spring's lambs gamboled about in the late afternoon's sun without a care. We made our way toward our destination in silence, and as it grew closer, I examined it.

I'd thought earlier that the dirt had washed away over the centuries, leaving the underlying stone bare. It wasn't the case. If one climbed the grassy slope on this side, one could walk out on the large boulders, which formed a sort of platform. From there, high above, one could look out and see that the drop-off was sheer, because part of the lower stones that formed the platform over time had crumbled away and rolled down the slope. The drop was approximately just over twenty feet, I judged. If someone falling was lucky, he might land on a thick carpet of heather—rough, but better than striking where smaller stones were and appeared to be unforgiving.

We struggled up the slope, the wind against us, and moved warily out onto the platform, staying well away from the edge. It was crowded with three people standing together here. I was admiring the view—I could see the house to my right, and to my left, the line of a beck leading to a small village a mile or so away. Sheep owned the rest of what I could see.

We were quite high, here, for we'd climbed even as we'd crossed the slope. The narrowness of the dale was also obvious, for I could see the opposite side, the fells dark and craggy as clouds began to move toward us. I could also see why the road had zigged and zagged as we had arrived, for at the bottom of Scarfdale, scrubby trees followed the line of the stream there, called a beck, I remembered. It zigged and zagged too, and the road had, perforce, to follow where it led.

Behind me, Arthur was saying, "You can see that there isn't a great deal of room up here. If my brother began to fall, and Mr. Caldwell started forward, he would find it difficult to brace himself as he reached out to stop it from happening."

I could also see that the opposite was true. That if Frederick Caldwell had started forward with an eye to shoving Gordon over the edge, he risked going over with him.

We stayed there for a good five minutes as Inspector Wade examined every inch of the shelf, going down on one knee to scoop up a handful of the loose scree at the edge. Rising, he nodded.

"I'll see where they landed," he said, and led the way off the shelf and down the slope.

There was a bit of space just under the outcropping above. Perhaps wide enough and deep enough for one person to shelter for rain. But beyond that there were scratchy banks of heather, green now, with buds for the late summer color, and spaces where nothing grew because a bed of stones lay scattered about. We could see where these had been disturbed by the men who had come to bring Frederick Caldwell back to the house.

It was a wonder that either man had survived the fall, much less lived to reach the Hall.

I hadn't expected much in the way of blood to mark where either man had landed. And the out-of-place stones made it difficult to see what had struck Frederick's neck so hard.

I said to Arthur, "How was Frederick lying, on his face or his back, when you found him?"

"On his back. That's why all the damage was along his spine."

"Yes, of course." But I wondered if Gordon, as badly hurt as he was, had tried to make the other man more comfortable. Or had he felt that it was best not to move him at all?

"How long was he left here?" Inspector Wade asked.

Arthur said, "Perhaps two hours. We got here as quick as we could, carrying the hurdle."

"Then another hour to take him back?" the Inspector went on.

"Yes. I expect if this had happened closer to the house, he'd have had a better chance of surviving." Then realizing what he might be conveying to the policeman standing next to him, he added, "But that's the nature of sheep. They move and graze all summer long. Often miles from the house."

"What's that stone building there? The ruin?"

Arthur and I turned to follow his pointing finger.

"That's what's left of an old laithe. Stock barn. That's a Norse name for them."

It stood perhaps three hundred yards downhill from us, just by a narrow little stream that appeared to have been dammed at one time, for it broadened just past the barn.

I was looking at the stream, noting the same dark stone, when I noticed that the branches of a heather closer to where the men had come down were broken, as if they had rolled a little. Or was it where the men with the hurdle had set it down?

The Inspector, staring suspiciously about, as if he expected answers to pop up if he kept searching for them, was making me see shadows too.

He stayed for a good fifteen minutes, going back briefly to the out-cropping and peering over the edge, as if to be sure where the men had come down. Arthur, watching him, swore quietly as Inspector Wade himself put a foot perilously close to the edge.

Finally, Arthur said, "We should be heading back. Those clouds mean rain is coming."

Inspector Wade looked up at them, as if to judge for himself what they meant. And then, reluctantly, he turned to leave, saying, "If you are satisfied, Sister Crawford."

As if it were I who had dragged us out here . . .

I could feel myself coloring.

On the way back, he was asking Arthur how many sheep the Hall ran, and how they were collected for shearing or for market, and lis-tening closely to the answers with all the air of a man about to buy a sheep run himself. When questioned about the breed, I heard Arthur an-swer, "Some generations back we crossbred with the Swaledale breed. The ewes lose very few lambs, and our wool was finer. It was a very good decision."

It began to rain as we came down toward the outbuildings, just scat-tered drops at first, and then with increasing force. We ran the last twenty yards to escape a soaking.

Once inside, we left our coats in the hall and went into the drawing room, where the fire's warmth greeted us. Inspector Wade went to stand in front of it, as if by right.

He said, "I have examined the site of the accident. I should now like to speak to Mr. Neville."

Gordon.

I said, "I'll just go up and see if he's awake."

"We will both go," he told me, and together we climbed the stairs. Arthur reluctantly followed us.

When I reached the door of Gordon Neville's room, I held up my hand and opened it quietly. Then in full view of the two men behind me, I crossed the room to the bed and leaned forward.

"Mr. Neville," I said clearly so that nothing I said could be misconstrued, "are you asleep? Inspector Wade has arrived from Richmond, and would like to speak to you about the accident."

His eyes had opened as soon as I'd said his name, still dark with pain, but alert enough. I thought perhaps he'd been awake, and trying not to move at all, for some time. I didn't think they could see that from the doorway.

"Sir? Are you awake enough to speak with the Inspector?" I repeated.

"Yes." The answer was rough. He cleared his throat and said, again, "Yes. If I don't have to move at all."

The men were already coming toward the bed. Inspector Wade was saying to me, "If you please, will you light another lamp?"

I did as I was asked, then came to stand at the foot of the bed. Arthur was at Inspector Wade's shoulder.

He identified himself to the man in the bed, then said, "I understand you left the victim of the accident in order to go for help."

"There was no one else," Gordon replied in a low voice. "I didn't move him, there was something about the way he lay that worried me. I thought it best to find help as quickly as possible."

"In spite of your own injuries."

"I could walk. I couldn't move him with one arm."

"How did you get on with the dead man?"

Gordon frowned at the unexpected shift in subject. "Well enough. He's a childhood friend, we thought of him as a cousin. His family lives in Harrogate."

"You appear to be of an age. Did you attend university together?"

For the first time there was the slightest hesitation in Gordon's voice. "Yes. Oxford. Not the same college."

"Why is he here this weekend?"

"My mother's birthday."

"Did you lure him out onto the fells in order to kill him?"

Arthur moved as if to stop the Inspector, as Gordon also moved, then swore in pain. "Why in hell's name would I do that?"

"The ladies were away. It was an opportunity."

Gordon said in a harsh voice, "If I wished to kill anyone, I shouldn't choose my mother's birthday to do it."

"Yes, that's what everyone would suppose."

Gordon tried to rise, and fell back again. "Get him out of here, Arthur."

Before Arthur could speak, I stepped forward. "You may question the patient, but you will not upset him. That shoulder has only just been reset. He must remain quiet."

"I have no more questions to ask." He scowled at me, then turned and walked out of the room without looking back. Arthur hesitated, then followed him. I stayed to put Gordon's pillows back in place.

When the door had shut, the man in the bed said, "Who the devil is that man?"

"He's from Richmond."

"I heard the collieries in his voice."

The coal mines. I rather thought he was right, that the policeman's educated accent slipped sometimes. As if it didn't come naturally to him.

"He'd have taken me into custody on the spot," he went on, "if I had been sitting in that chair in the gun room." Sighing, he added, "Why does he believe it wasn't an accident? Because clearly he suspects foul play?"

"I don't know. Earlier we went to that outcropping, so that he could see where the accident happened."

"I didn't kill Caldwell. Have the others come back? My mother and sister, and Frederick's wife?"

"They have. We were having a late tea when the Inspector arrived."

Gordon closed his eyes. "I'm so sorry." Then, as if against his will, he asked, "How is Grace?"

"I gave her a sedative. She took the news rather hard."

His mouth twisted. "I never intended it to happen this way . . ."

I said, "No one could have foreseen such a thing."

"I should never have let him come with me. Foreseen or not." His voice was grim. "Please, go. I need to rest."

"Of course."

I turned out the extra lamp and then quietly left the room, shutting the door. I had only just reached the bottom of the stairs, on my way to the drawing room, when I heard a door slam upstairs so hard that it reverberated through the house.

I could hear footsteps coming fast this way, and then I saw the wraithlike figure of Grace Caldwell pass the top of the stairs.

Dear God—she was going to see her husband—

I called sharply, "Mrs. Neville—" and started back up the stairs.

I got there just as Mrs. Caldwell was fumbling with the doorknob. Perhaps the laudanum was still clouding her mind, but was the memory of what she needed to do driving her to act?

"Mrs. Caldwell—"

"No. I *will* see him!"

She got the door open and flew across the dimly lit room to the bed. "A fire—we must build a fire. This room is too cold."

Reaching the bed, she pulled the sheet down from her husband's face, and cried out when it came into view. Pale, the lips blue, the mouth slightly open, the eyes as well.

Arthur and Mrs. Neville came hurrying into the room, but Grace Caldwell had already reached out to touch her husband's face. Rigor hadn't completely passed, and he moved like a statue under her hand.

She cried out again, this time in horror. Putting myself between her and the bed, I wrapped my arms around her and turned her away. I'd dealt with delirious patients, I knew what I was about. Then Mrs. Neville was there, to take Grace into her arms as she began to weep. I pulled the sheet back in place, and Arthur Neville was ushering the two women out of the room.

But in the passage, Grace broke away from Mrs. Neville and ran back down it, pounding on doors, shouting Gordon Neville's name, accusing him. It was Arthur who stopped her this time, and he and his mother between them got her back to the blue room.

At the top of the staircase as we passed it, Inspector Wade stood silently, watching.

The tea tray had been removed when we came back to the drawing room. Inspector Wade had gone as soon as we had come back down the stairs. Exhausted, we sat in front of the fire, listening to the wind and rain lashing the windows and sometimes gusting down the chimneys. I was glad that, unlike Inspector Wade, I didn't have to return to Richmond in this weather.

Mrs. Neville said, "I don't know whether I can swallow my dinner, I'm so weary."

"You must eat, Mama," Margaret Neville urged her. "You'll need your strength. And that awful man has said he will be coming back."

"I shan't forgive Constable Woods for bringing him here," she said, and I knew she meant it. There was an undercurrent in her voice that told me how worried she was.

I'd tried to see what the Inspector had seen, and I still couldn't find any reason to believe this was anything more than a tragic accident. But the Inspector clearly felt differently. I wondered if Gordon was right, he was from the collieries and didn't care for those who had had more advantages in life. Or perhaps it was just his nature to be difficult.

Lillian said, "I think we could all do with another cup of tea to strengthen us."

Arthur got up from his chair and rang.

Mrs. Roper, the housekeeper, came at once, and he explained that it would be best if dinner could be brought forward an hour.

She said, "He'd a Sergeant with him, that man. He badgered us with his questions until he had Cook in tears."

Most of us hadn't known that, I could see the surprise in their faces.

"Soup and sandwiches will do. Do you think that's possible?"

Mrs. Roper said, "I believe she could manage that, sir. Shall we say in half an hour?"

"Yes, please. Thank her for us."

Mrs. Roper asked, "What about Mr. Gordon and Mrs. Caldwell? Will you be wanting a tray for them?"

Mrs. Neville answered. "Yes, that will be lovely. If you could wait until we've finished, Margaret and I will see to dealing with it."

Mrs. Roper left to speak to Cook.

Mrs. Neville said, "That man, you know, don't you, will cause as much trouble as he can, before this is finished. He saw Grace shouting at Gordon, calling him a murderer."

Arthur sighed. "Yes, that was very unfortunate. I don't think he's the sort of man who would understand the strain she's under."

Lillian and I sat quietly, not adding to the conversation. We were the strangers in their midst.

As if she realized that, Mrs. Neville said to us, "I'm so sorry you had to be witnesses to this evening. None of us are at our best."

Lillian answered for us. "We're here to do whatever we can. You must know that. Lady Beatrice trusts Bess implicitly."

Arthur asked again, "Do you think Aunt Bea—Lady Beatrice—will be able to travel here?"

"If she's careful. In a few days. I do know she was quite worried about your son, and wanted very badly to be here. That's why she sent us ahead."

Mrs. Neville said, "She's close friends with the Chief Constable and his wife."

I understood what she was saying. Lady Beatrice might be able to convince him that Inspector Wade had gone too far.

There was a loud clap of thunder just overhead, seeming to shake the house, and everyone jumped at the noise. A sign of how tense all of us were.

After the meal, we had tea in one of the sitting rooms, then went up to bed. Margaret and Mrs. Neville were to take turns staying with Mrs. Caldwell. Arthur had a cot made up in Gordon's room.

Lillian and I, with no duties, retired to our own room. She sat down by the fire, holding her hands out to the blaze.

"Are you all right?" I asked after a while.

"Yes, of course. No—" She straightened, looked up at me, and shrugged. "I never dreamed we'd have the police here, upsetting everyone. It's beyond belief."

"Why is everyone so on edge? I even found myself jumping at that clap of thunder. I have the distinct feeling that there's something that's worrying everyone, and I don't know why there is so much concern over what happened out there on the fell. I mean, Frederick Caldwell died of his injuries, and it's very natural to be upset over his loss. But there's almost a—a conspiracy of silence, as if everyone is afraid something will be said that will cause a problem for Gordon Neville."

Lillian sat down at the dressing table and began to take off the bracelet and necklace she had worn for dinner. She took her time about it, and in the mirror, I could see her frown.

"I think it must be your imagination, my dear. Perhaps Arthur told the family that Gordon felt it was his fault that Frederick was so badly hurt. But he couldn't prevent falling on him. That was just how they happened to fall. Still, people do feel guilty because they survived as someone else suffered."

But wasn't it more likely in the nature of a fall that Gordon had gone down first and Frederick fell on *him*?

I didn't say it aloud. After all, the poor man's injuries indicated just the opposite.

Still, I wasn't there to see just how they came down, if they were twisting as Frederick tried to stop Gordon from going over.

I liked Gordon Neville and his brother. I really didn't want to think either one of them could be capable of harming anyone.

But I was an outsider, and I couldn't help but see . . .

Into the silence when I didn't answer, Lillian said, "That policeman. Inspector Wade. He doesn't appear to like us. I can't think why. I asked Mrs. Neville if she had met him before, and she told me he was new to Richmond and even Arthur hadn't come across him there."

New—and trying to prove himself? Or perhaps Gordon was right, the man really didn't care for people with money and position. I'd met soldiers who felt the same way, intensely disliking officers who came from a very different social background. I'd heard them talking among themselves about just that. They'd had to scrape for their living, and resented those who had been given more of life's blessings.

Surely a man like Inspector Wade wouldn't carry his personal grudges over into his professional opinions? And yet it seemed that he was doing just that.

I got myself ready for bed, and as I climbed in, Lillian said from the hearth, where she was sitting again, as if drawn to the dancing flames, "I wish this hadn't happened. Any of it. I wish we were back with Lady Beatrice, talking about Cornwall. Silly though it was, it did pass the time pleasantly."

I had to agree. Looking back, it was soothing compared to the situation here.

I thought during the night that I had heard Grace Caldwell calling out in her sleep. But the rain was back sweeping across the fells like a wet broom. I wondered what the sheep did in such weather, picturing them huddled in the lea of a stone wall, the oils in their coat keeping out the wet. I fell asleep again on that thought.

Breakfast was interrupted by the return of Inspector Wade and, I presumed, the Constable or Sergeant who had unsettled the Nevilles' cook.

Arthur asked and was given permission to summon the undertaker. I thought everyone would all be happier without Frederick's body in a room just down the passage.

Dr. Menzies arrived as well, soon afterward, to look in on Gordon and Mrs. Caldwell, and answer the questions that the Inspector put to him privately in one of the sitting rooms.

Arthur had fed his brother breakfast as well as last night's dinner, and he looked very tired when he passed me on the stairs. It was a gloomy morning. Although the worst of the storm had passed, there was a lingering drizzle that made walking in the garden impossible. I'd have liked to do that myself.

Grace Caldwell came down for lunch, already in widow's black, which made her look even paler, if that were possible. She must have borrowed the clothing from Mrs. Neville or sent someone out for the proper attire. She had very little to say, her eyes mostly on her food while the rest of us tried to make a little conversation to ease the sense of gloom that appeared to have seeped from the outside to the inside of the house.

We were just finishing the meal when Mrs. Roper came to tell the family that a visitor had arrived.

Arthur looked as if this was the last straw, a burden beyond his strength to carry. Thanking her, he rose and left the room.

Mrs. Neville quickly followed.

Margaret asked Grace if she would care for another cup of tea, but she shook her head. Her grief had truly overwhelmed her, and I felt a welling of sympathy for her.

I left the breakfast room with Lillian, who said, knowing the house from previous visits, "I think we might take refuge in the library, Bess. There will soon be a stream of visitors offering condolences."

"A very good idea."

She led the way, but as we arrived at the door, Mrs. Roper appeared and asked if Lillian would mind sitting with Grace for a bit, while Margaret and her mother-in-law were interviewed by Inspector Wade.

"Go on," she told me. "I'll be back as soon as they're free."

And so I opened the door and stepped into a beautiful library, the dark wood of the shelves arranged around an oval room, with a pair of windows breaking the line and looking out on a sheltered walk.

I didn't realize at first that there was someone else in the room, his back to me, standing at the far end, idly spinning a globe on a walnut stand. My heart leapt in my throat when I first noticed him.

Simon—

How on earth had he come to Scarfdale? Was something wrong in Somerset, and he'd been sent to bring me home?

I swallowed hard, not sure what to say.

Just then he turned to face me, and I saw that it wasn't Simon after all. And yet, with his back to me, a tall man with dark hair and the bearing of a soldier, the resemblance was startling.

"I'm so sorry," I said at once. "I didn't know anyone was here."

I turned to go, but he said, his voice tight with anger, "I've been banished here. I wanted to see my brother before the undertakers came for his body."

"You are . . . ? You are Frederick's brother?" I asked, surprised. While there was a little resemblance to the man in the darkened room upstairs, they could have been distant cousins rather than brothers.

"Mark Caldwell. Yes. Do *you* know where my brother is?"

Instead of answering his question, I said, "Everything is rather at sixes and sevens. The police are here—" I realized at once I had said the wrong thing.

He frowned—just like Simon. But his eyes were hazel, edging toward green. "The *police*?"

"Apparently, it's strictly a formal visit." That wasn't true, but I couldn't tell him how unpleasant the Inspector had been. "A serious accident, causing a death. I'm sure Arthur will be here to explain shortly."

"And you are?"

"Elizabeth Crawford. I'm a guest in the house."

"Well, Miss Crawford, guest in the house, do you or do you not know where my brother is?"

It wasn't my place to take him to the bedroom where Frederick lay. On the other hand, the Nevilles were beset on all sides just now. Surely there would be no harm in letting a family member see his brother?

"Yes, of course. If you'll follow me?"

I still didn't know the house very well, but I got us back to the main staircase. No one was close by—if they were, I couldn't hear voices. We started up, Mark Caldwell at my heels, and went down the corridor to the room where his brother lay.

"How did you hear the sad news?" I asked, curious. No mention had been made in my hearing of a brother, much less one expected to arrive momentarily.

"Arthur had the decency to send me a telegram."

We walked into the room. I felt obligated to stay there, since I'd taken the responsibility of showing Mr. Caldwell the way here. But after I'd lit one of the lamps, I went back to stand by the door, to give him some privacy.

He stood there by the bed. This had been the room where Grace and her husband were staying, and I tried to look everywhere but at the bed. I saw Frederick's hat sitting on top of the armoire, and a pair of Grace's shoes by one of the chairs. Little things were on top of the dresser and the tallboy. A folding picture frame . . .

I was aware when he bent and pulled the sheet away from the body, and aware again when he moved it to look at the injuries to the back. He had, I thought, been in the war. The dead held no terrors for him. When he had settled the body back among the bedclothes again, he took a last look, then pulled the sheet in place once more.

"Where's his killer?" he asked me as he crossed the room to leave. I busied myself turning out the lamp to hide my surprise.

"Killer? Gordon carried him down, despite his own injuries. He is still and can't be disturbed."

"He waited long enough for his revenge, didn't he?" he said harshly as we left the room and started down the passage.

"I'm sorry, I don't know what you are talking about. I don't know the family terribly well, so I can't answer that."

He looked at me, as if seeing me for the first time. "No, of course you don't. You'd have been too young to be included in discussions of the family's scandal. But there is a murderer in this house, and I will get to the bottom of this."

We walked in silence to the stairs, and as we started down Arthur was just crossing the hall and turning down the passage that ran behind the stairs. He looked up, saw us beginning to descend the steps, and stopped short.

"Hallo, Arthur," the man beside me said. "Are the police still here? I should like to have a word with them before I go. And you haven't told me when the funeral service will be."

Arthur looked at me.

"I'm sorry," I said, not really sure what I should be apologizing for.

Turning back to Mark Caldwell as we reached the bottom of the stairs, Arthur said, "The Vicar and the undertaker will be here today."

"What, you sought no comfort for a dying man?"

Holding on to his temper with a visible effort, Arthur said, "Dr. Menzies felt he would live at least until Grace returned. Sadly, he took a turn for the worse in the middle of the night. But," Arthur continued, "Inspector Wade has ordered that everyone in the house must continue to stay here until the inquest."

I didn't want to stand here and listen to any more. But I couldn't move around either man without making it obvious. And then to my relief, Lillian came down the passage. She looked at the tall man beside me and her mouth tightened.

"Hello, Lieutenant Caldwell," she said formally. "May I offer my condolences . . ."

He glanced at her, said, "Thank you," abruptly, and turned back to Arthur. "The staircase isn't the place for this."

Arthur gestured down the passage. "We can be private elsewhere. This way."

Lieutenant Caldwell, to give him his courtesy title, turned and followed him without a word.

I waited until they were out of hearing. "He was in the library. I didn't see him until I was already inside the room."

She shook her head. "Let's go to our room."

And so I found myself following *her*.

The fire was burning nicely, and the room was much warmer than the passage. We sat down, and she leaned her head back, closing her eyes for a moment.

I waited, then said, "I hadn't heard that Frederick had a brother. Is there any other family?"

"A sister. She died in the epidemic. Cousins. Most of them too far along in years to come to the service." There was distaste in her voice.

"You don't care for them." It was a statement, not a question. "I must say I wasn't terribly impressed with the Lieutenant."

"Old history," Lillian replied. "Frederick was more like his mother's side of the family. She was a Lindsay, and such a lovely person. Kind, thoughtful, just lovely," she said again.

"How did you come to know her?"

"We were invited to the wedding. Lady Beatrice was, that is, but I was included, which was a kindness. Grace was such a lovely bride, and Frederick's mother was truly fond of her. They kept it small, because the family had just come out of mourning."

"After the Lieutenant had seen his brother, he asked to see his killer. He meant Gordon. Why is everyone—including the police—so ready to believe that Gordon is a murderer?"

She didn't want to tell me. I could see that. Finally she settled on, "There has been bad blood there. Of long standing."

"Is that why Lady Beatrice's son, Jonathan, doesn't care for Gordon? He sides with the Caldwells?"

Lillian couldn't stop the flare of surprise in her face. "How did you know—oh, I expect I said something to you when we were asked to come here in Lady Beatrice's place. I shouldn't have mentioned it. It's a family matter."

Which effectively stopped any further questions into the ill will between the two families.

I said, changing the subject, "I haven't seen Grace since breakfast. Is she any stronger?"

Lillian said, "I couldn't believe that Inspector Wade demanded to speak to her! She wasn't even here, and it's her husband who died. Mrs. Neville put a stop to that, and Dr. Menzies had just arrived, which was fortunate, because he could also tell that man not to disturb Grace. And the undertaker will be here by three o'clock. She wanted to sit with Frederick for a while."

That must have been why Lieutenant Caldwell had been asked to wait before he saw his brother. I was just grateful that I hadn't inadvertently interrupted her vigil.

We were silent for a time. I stared out the window. It was still gloomy out there, although the drizzle may have stopped, I couldn't be sure. We had been very lucky, getting to the scene of the accident before the weather turned.

Lillian broke the silence. "I don't know whether we ought to go or stay."

Surprised, I said, "I hadn't considered that." We had come to help with the injured Gordon Neville; Lady Beatrice had asked me to do whatever I could to help him. He was stable, a doctor had come again. Maybe there was really no point in staying, and the house was already full enough. There would be others who might wish to stay for the funeral. Frederick's family, and of course Grace's.

"Should we say something?" Lillian asked.

"Let's wait until the Inspector has gone tonight. Just now I think the Nevilles have about as much on their minds as they can cope with." It was the best advice I could think of. We'd have to send for Wilson . . . it would be at least another day.

There was a knock at the door, and Mrs. Roper stepped in. "Miss Taylor, Mrs. Neville asks if you could sit with Mrs. Caldwell for a bit. Perhaps in the solarium? They'll be removing Mr. Frederick soon."

Lillian rose at once. "Oh. Yes, of course, I'll be happy to."

As she crossed to the door, Mrs. Roper turned to me. "And Dr. Menzies has asked if you'll step into Mr. Gordon's room, please?"

And what was that about?

I thanked Mrs. Roper, and went down the passage, tapping lightly on the door as I would in hospital, then opening it.

Gordon was still lying flat in the bed, just as he had been when I last saw him. He looked flushed, but I couldn't be sure whether it was fever or anger.

Dr. Menzies was standing by the window. He was a slight man with a receding hairline and pince-nez perched on a bony nose. As he turned, sharp gray eyes peered at me over the rims of his glasses.

"Ah. Sister Crawford." He came forward and introduced himself. "I understand you were trained by the Queen Alexandra's and served in France?"

Clearly someone had told him that. And where was this going?

I replied truthfully. "Yes, indeed."

"Then I must rely on your training and your word as an officer in His Majesty's forces to assist me in a sensitive matter."

"I promise to do my best."

He nodded. "How well do you know our patient here?"

"I only just met him yesterday."

"Good." He started toward the bed, still speaking to me. "I have been asked to inform Inspector Wade that our patient is well enough to travel as far as Richmond, to be held in custody there while the death of Frederick Caldwell is being thoroughly investigated."

Oh, dear!

"I should like you to help me determine whether Gordon Neville has recovered sufficiently from his injuries to be taken away."

His eyes were different behind the pince-nez. Larger, more difficult to read. I couldn't judge whether he wanted me to agree with the police, or to prevent them from taking Gordon Neville away.

"Why are they so certain he ought to be held in Richmond?" I asked.

"That is not the issue here, Sister, it's his state of health."

No help there, then.

"Very well, Doctor," I replied, as I had so many times during my training and the war.

We had reached the bedside. Gordon Neville stared up at us with all the emotion of a dead cod. He must feel, I thought, rather like an interesting specimen being studied under a microscope.

But behind the coldness, there was the faint glitter of fever.

That couldn't be feigned.

Without a word, I began to examine the cut on his head, which was not healing properly but couldn't be responsible for the fever. Moving to the dislocated shoulder, I watched Gordon Neville clench his jaw in pain. It had been reset but was still very uncomfortable. Turning to the broken arm we removed the bandages holding it to the board, and I could see it was swollen and bruised. Where the bone had penetrated the skin, there was an inflamed rim around the cut. And that was the source of the fever.

How in heaven's name had this man walked back to the house, then gone with the rescue party to bring Frederick back to the house? He must have been in intense pain. But I had seen soldiers with ugly wounds bring in a dying comrade to a forward aid station and demand that he be treated first.

Dr. Menzies went to the table where he had laid out his instruments and medicines, bandages, and so on. He found alcohol to clean the wound, and a salve to put on it before wrapping it again in clean bandages. "You must take every care of this wound, Sister. I will leave what you need, but the arm should be unwrapped and left to air, then cleaned again and more of that jar of salve applied before it is covered again.

"Yes, Doctor."

"I had waited to unwrap the arm until you were here as witness. I'd expected it to heal, but apparently it has not. Do you think this could be causing a fever?"

"Yes, I do. There are sheep everywhere in the field by the outcropping. I have no idea what might have entered an open wound."

"Exactly."

We had finished our work. Dr. Menzies began to sort out what I would need after he left, and put the remainder of his medicines back where they belonged.

"You're to give the patient this in a small amount of water when he appears to be restless. Two drops, no more. The aspirin as you see the need. This for cleaning and disinfecting the wound, this for the inflammation."

He set a small vial, another larger with the alcohol, and the pot of salve in a row, with sufficient bandages until his next visit.

Satisfied that I was well supplied, Dr. Menzies closed his satchel and turned back to the bed. "I'll return tomorrow, Gordon. Unless the Sister requires me to come sooner. Please listen to all her instructions and answer her questions just as if I were standing before you. Do you understand?"

His voice was husky. "Yes, Doctor. I do."

The doctor ushered me out of the room, and closed the door behind us.

I said, as we walked down the passage, "May I ask what killed Frederick Caldwell?"

He stopped, turning to me. "What do you mean, Sister?"

"If the police wish to take Mr. Neville into custody, there must be a reason."

He took off his glasses and with a handkerchief from his pocket, polished them vigorously. "I wasn't here when they came to examine the body. I haven't been told just what it is they saw. What they cannot see is that Frederick Caldwell's vertebrae were cracked in two different places. C4, in the neck and T7 in the spine. Sadly, the jostling necessary to bring him back to the house probably made matters even worse, and damaged the spinal cord beyond repair. Or it could have happened in the fall, I can't tell because I didn't examine him in situ. But a man who helped bring Mr. Caldwell back said he was sure that he saw Mr. Caldwell move his arm, which could be interpreted that he was still able to survive. But there was something about the neck wound that convinced Inspector Wade that someone had seen to it he didn't survive."

He finished polishing the glasses and returned them to his nose. "It will be difficult to prove. Either way. But Wade feels he must see that justice is done." For a moment he considered me, as if trying to decide how far to trust me.

"Mr. Caldwell," he continued, "the brother of the deceased—has a tendency toward leaping to conclusions. And he has some authority in Richmond, as he owns extensive property there. I believe the good Inspector is not above taking these circumstances into consideration."

Mr. Caldwell, who looks so much like Simon from the back. Who was angry to be put off, viewing the body of his brother.

I took the intended warning to heart.

CHAPTER EIGHT

WE WALKED ON, descending the stairs in silence.

"This way," he said, and I followed him to the small drawing room. Inspector Wade and Mark Caldwell were waiting there. I had the distinct impression that they had been pacing impatiently.

"Well?" Wade demanded as we stepped into the room.

"Mr. Neville has become feverish. The wound from the compound fracture has become infected. I expect that is the source of his fever."

"But you aren't sure." This from Frederick's brother, Mark Caldwell. "You can't trust him."

"I have asked Sister Crawford, who has had extensive experience of battlefield wounds, to examine the patient."

Inspector Wade swung his gaze from Dr. Menzies to me, glaring at me angrily.

"If you move the patient now," I said, "and in the conditions available for treatment in a cell, if the fever continues to mount, Mr. Neville could lose his arm. I have seen cases of gangrene that began with a similar injury. Mr. Neville was out on a fell where sheep and other animals range free. It is impossible to guess what he might have picked up with an open wound of that type. Of course the final responsibility must be yours, Inspector. As a nurse, I would advise you to reconsider." That was delivered in my best imitation of Matron speaking to an officer insisting that a soldier was sufficiently healed to return to the Front.

He considered me, something in his expression that made me think of a cat playing with a mouse.

"Exactly how much experience have you had with wounds, Sister?"

"Three and a half years of battlefield forward aid, base hospitals, and hospital ships returning the wounded. I was aboard *Britannic* when she went down, and in appalling conditions treated those wounded and dying, until help could reach us. If you wish to verify these credentials, I refer you to Matron in Charge at QAIMNS headquarters in London."

He hadn't expected that.

"Indeed," he replied. The mouse had unexpectedly turned on the cat. I looked down to hide any satisfaction showing in my eyes.

This must have come across as modesty to Mark Caldwell. I glanced up again and he was looking decidedly put out.

I realized that he must have expected me to try to defend myself, leaving me open to more questions. If he had been in the Army, he would know precisely what I was describing as my experience.

Inspector Wade turned to Mr. Caldwell. "However regretfully, I must accept the medical advice we've been offered."

Mr. Caldwell made a face, a mixture of frustration and anger.

Dr. Menzies said, "If there are no other questions, gentlemen, I must return to my surgery. Good day." And then, to me, "Sister, I shall have a few more instructions, if you don't mind."

And we escaped together. I was grateful and saw him out to the horse he'd ridden from the village, a lovely bay mare.

I walked back into the house, thinking to myself that the good doctor had hidden qualities, among them a strong conspiratorial ability.

No one was about when I walked back inside, and so I went quietly up the stairs and down the passage to Gordon Neville's room.

He was lying there very much as we'd left him. Staring at the ceiling.

Moving his head to see who had entered the room, he said, "What now?"

I said, "It must be difficult to lie there, no one to talk to, no one to distract you from the pain. Not even able to read to pass the time."

"I review all my sins," he said, irony in his tone. "Apparently I have more of them than even I knew."

I pulled a chair closer to the bed—apparently the one Dr. Menzies had been sitting in before I'd come in—and sat down.

His eyes still had the brightness of fever, and there were spots high on his cheekbones. But he said sharply, "I don't need to be entertained."

"I have no intention of entertaining you. Nor will I read to you or write letters for you, or listen to a confession of those sins. I have just put my own professional reputation on the line in front of witnesses. Inspector Wade, Dr. Menzies, and Frederick Caldwell's brother, Mark, whose fury toward you, I don't understand. I have earned the right to ask you, Gordon . . . Did you murder Frederick Caldwell, out there on the hillside?"

Gordon frowned, gazing at me with suspicion. Then his eyes flicked toward the closed door.

"No one is listening in the hall." I kept my voice low, so that no one could hear us even if they tried. "I agree with Dr. Menzies that you shouldn't be moved to Richmond or anywhere else. But that opinion aside, I believe his purpose in establishing that a fever existed was to protect you, not simply treat you."

"I don't know what happened out there on the outcropping," he said finally, and looked away, toward the window. "I was tired of searching for sheep, tired of listening to Frederick, and I went up on the top of the boulders, for a better look over the hillside. Hoping to God I'd see no ewes in need of being rescued. That all of them had finally been accounted for.

That much is clear enough." There was a pause. He raised his good hand to rub his eyes. "I saw something and took a step forward for a better look. I can't remember what it was. At any rate, there was movement behind me. And nothing after that." He dropped his hand from his eyes, and took a deep breath. "The next thing I knew, I was lying half on Frederick, half on the rocks. I couldn't move at first, and when I did my shoulder hurt so badly, I stopped. As my senses came back to me, I realized somehow Frederick was there as well. Under me. That we'd both fallen. I couldn't remember why. What we were doing out here, in the first place."

He was silent for so long I was about to ask him to go on, when he said, "At some point I began to realize too that Frederick hadn't stirred. Hadn't moved. I had to struggle to get to my feet without hurting him or setting my shoulder on fire again. I was wearing a jumper, I didn't notice my arm, at first, the shoulder overclouded everything else. I got to my feet and turned to look at Frederick."

That pause again. This time I said, "What did you see?"

"He was unconscious but he was breathing. I saw that straightaway. I bent down to try to wake him, and almost went out myself. It must have taken some minutes before I could see that he was not moving, not coming out of it. That he was in trouble. I was afraid to go on trying to wake him. I couldn't lift him—I couldn't help him at all. But I could walk. I set out for the house. You know the rest."

Was he telling me the truth—or a well-rehearsed account he'd had hours alone to work out?

I couldn't be sure.

And so I said, "I think you're lying to me."

Gordon tried to move and was stopped short by the pain. "I'm not a liar."

"But I don't know you, Mr. Neville. I've only just met you. How can I judge that?"

He lay back among his pillows. "Damn it, you're worse than Wade."

Even so, he didn't try to persuade me that he'd told the truth.

"I have no reason to trick you or make you do something you don't want to do. I'm just trying to protect myself, to be able to say to the police that I gave an honest opinion and I had no knowledge of your guilt or innocence that might affect my decision. But my own conscience is not at all happy with being put into that position at all. You must understand that."

He was silent again.

I was about to rise and leave him to his quiet room when he said, "All right. Which am I? An innocent man? Or a murderer?"

"Honestly? I don't know. I saw Frederick Caldwell's body. The evidence is confusing."

"Why?" Sharp as a shot.

"Because I didn't see his body lying among the rocks. I have been there, to the outcropping. But there is so little evidence to help me."

"You went to the scene?" He was startled by that.

"Yes. Inspector Wade asked your brother to take him there. I asked to accompany them."

"You're a strange one," he said, shaking his head a little.

"I have seen death close at hand for nearly four years of war. I don't fear the dead." Rising, I said, "Were you in France?"

"Yes."

"Then you know what I am saying."

He took a deep breath. "I'd thought I'd seen the end of it. God knows, I brought enough of the dead back with me in my dreams."

I didn't tell him that I too had those dreams. The patient I was struggling with all my skills to save, slowly bleeding to death, no matter what I did. The young men who held my hand night after night, calling me by the name of a sister or mother or lover as the darkness came down. And those who died screaming and we had nothing to end their pain before death did . . .

I said only, "It is finished. That's all that matters." And closed the bedroom door behind me.

I was not particularly happy about persuading Gordon Neville to confide in me. And I'd been rewarded for my efforts only with renewed uncertainty. Even so, that uncertainty was enough for me to continue to defend him until I knew more. And my promise to Lady Beatrice, given that she was an old friend of Cousin Melinda's, weighed heavily on me.

I went down the passage just as the body of Frederick Caldwell was being removed from the room where he had died. I stopped some distance from the men, and watched the still form beneath the sheet start its progress toward the stairs. Just as I was about to follow, Mark Caldwell stepped out of the room and shut the door firmly behind him. He didn't look my way, his gaze was on his brother's stretcher. They walked toward the stairs, moving slowly and carefully. They had reached the top of the steps and were turning the stretcher to begin the journey down them to the hall below.

But before they could finish their turn, I heard another door open on the far side of the passage, and Grace came out of her room. She saw the stretcher being borne away, and screamed. Racing forward, she insisted that the men lower their burden so that she could throw herself across her husband's body one last time.

It was rather wrenching to say the least. Her brother-in-law walked around the stretcher and put his hands on her shoulders, apparently intending to comfort her. Or so I thought, until he almost lifted her bodily off the stretcher.

"He's no longer there," Mark Caldwell said. "You are wasting your tears on the shell of the man he was."

She struggled against his grip. "You don't understand. He'd only been home for a few weeks. I've waited four years—I've done nothing to deserve this! I'm not ready to be a widow, not now. Not after he *survived*."

He paid no heed, holding her tightly, stroking the back of her hair and nodding to the stretcher bearers. They didn't move, uncertain what to do in the face of her reaching hands and cries. Then Grace gulped, holding Mark Caldwell's wrist, before weeping again.

Arthur's mother came hurrying down the passage. "My dear!" she exclaimed as she drew near enough. "You will make yourself ill of grief. And then you shan't be able to attend the services—"

She was there, reaching out to take the weeping woman from Mark Caldwell's hold, turning her so that she was gently pulled into Mrs. Neville's arms, her head on Mrs. Neville's shoulder.

By then, Grace Caldwell's cries had become sobs, and she allowed herself to be led away.

Mrs. Neville mouthed, *How did she know?*

But Mr. Caldwell was already directing the undertaker's men to continue taking the body down the stairs.

For an instant as they raised the stretcher in preparation for the descent, I thought they were about to drop the body on the top step. I heard Mark Caldwell break off swearing at them. The two men, anxious now, began their slow journey down the long staircase.

As soon as they were a little in advance of him, Frederick's brother started down as well.

I hadn't intervened. Grace Caldwell barely knew me, and it was her husband they were removing. While her behavior was a little dramatic, this wasn't an ordinary death, expected and prepared for emotionally. Still, if Mrs. Neville hadn't appeared, I would have done my best.

When the undertaker's men had arrived safely at the bottom of the stairs without mishap, I turned and quietly carried on down the passage to our room.

Lillian was there. As I opened the door she said, "Mrs. Neville and I were talking when we heard poor Grace's cries. Is she all right? I was asked to stay here, and let her attend to it."

"Mrs. Neville has managed to take her back to her room." I didn't add that I'd thought Lillian was sitting with Mrs. Caldwell. "It was rather upsetting."

"You can just see the front portico from her room. She must have heard the horses. She had fallen asleep—I don't think she's really closed her eyes except when she had taken the laudanum. Mrs. Roper came to spell me, or I'd have been there to deal with her."

And Mrs. Roper would have had difficulty stopping a guest in the house from doing what she'd set her mind to.

Lillian sighed. "I wish I felt free to go and speak to Gordon. Lady Beatrice wished me to. I promised to write to her. But with that Inspector slithering about the house, I'm not sure it's a good idea."

I managed to keep a straight face.

"His injuries are healing slowly," I said, not mentioning the fever, knowing it would worry her. "But a cell . . ." I knew something about cells, having spent a night in an Irish one. "And besides, he is hardly going to flee. They can do their investigating while he recovers."

"But a cell, why? Arthur told us it was an accident. Both men were badly hurt, as well. And apparently Gordon came to summon help at some cost to himself."

I took a deep breath, uncertain of what to tell her. For that matter, I myself wasn't sure of the evidence that the Inspector appeared to be so certain of. "I expect the police feel that it's better to do a careful investigation, even though the family is a prominent one. To avoid any feeling of favoritism."

"I don't know," Lillian said, getting up to poke the fire. "This is a different generation of policemen. They have no respect for anyone." As she sat down again, she added, "I've found them difficult to deal with myself."

I said, "Tell me a little more about Frederick Caldwell. What sort of man was he?"

"He was quite lovely. Quiet, well read, but when there was something that he felt strongly about, he could fight for it. He was a protector. The sort of man people naturally respect. He adored Grace. He'd have done anything to make her happy. It was hard for them to be separated all these years. But he did his duty. As did Arthur and Gordon."

It was clear that she liked all three of these men. And to my surprise, I realized why. They had been kind to her. She wasn't just Lady Beatrice's companion, a paid servant. She had become in a sense an accepted part of the family. After all the years she had so often been treated badly in her various posts, she finally felt safe. In turn she was very fond of them, the children she herself had never had.

"What do you know about Mark Caldwell?"

She was suddenly uneasy. Not wishing to speak ill of a family friend. "He's not the easiest man to get along with. I try, but he's always rather— well, Lady Beatrice says he's got a disruptive temperament."

To say the least!

"And he has always been very protective of Grace."

There was a knock at the door. I rose to answer it and found Arthur standing there.

"Could I have a word, Sister?"

"Of course." I smiled at Lillian and walked out into the passage.

"There's really no place to talk quietly except the room where Frederick died. Would it bother you to go inside there?"

"No, not at all." We walked in silence down the passage and went into the room. I noticed at once that all the personal things belonging to Grace Caldwell had been removed, to her new room. The belongings of her husband lay forlornly just as he'd left them to go out onto the fells with Gordon.

Arthur frowned, seeing them too. "I shall have to do something about these. I don't think Mark is in the mood to take care of them."

He moved to the window, flung back the long drapes, and let in the pale light of the gloomy day. Turning to me, he said, "I've had a telegram from Aunt Bea. She wants news. I don't know precisely what to tell her. I need to know, for instance, if she can travel. Frederick's death will upset her enough, but if that Inspector takes Gordon into custody for it, she will be on the road, gallbladder or not."

"I had a telegram from her doctor. She has now healed enough to travel. I thought it best for her not to, back when Miss Taylor and I came in her place. Her heart—we were afraid that her godson had died and you were not breaking the news . . ." I purposely used the relationship between Lady Beatrice and Gordon. I wondered if Arthur realized that his brother was her favorite . . .

Arthur seemed to understand. "Yes, just as I thought." He rubbed his forehead with one hand. "Mark wants to stay. He insists there will be nothing short of a miscarriage of justice if he doesn't. And he's rather reluctant to sleep in the room where his brother died. I am at a loss where to put her. I can't very well ask her to double up with Mother in the master bedroom."

It was his mother's place to worry about such matters. But I could see that Arthur was trying to take some of the burden from her, and there was the inescapable fact that it might be impossible to stop Lady Beatrice once she knew the situation here.

I said, "I expect the truth will bring her here posthaste. Is there no place in the village where he could be put up?"

"The room above the pub is hardly suitable."

"Then move Lillian and me to a lesser room, and give that one to Lady Beatrice."

"There's the maid's bedroom next to yours. It's rather plain—but it has a hearth, and a large bed . . ." He hesitated, then said flatly, "If you'll come and see?"

I followed him back down the passage to a door that I'd seen just down from our room. He opened it, and went to the windows to pull the drapes.

It was indeed rather plain by the standard of other rooms I'd seen, like Gordon's, the one where Frederick had died, and the one Grace had been moved to.

Smaller, with only a single pair of windows, a large bed, two chairs, an armoire, and a small writing desk, but the heavy early Victorian pieces made the room seem smaller than it was.

"It should do nicely," I said. Then, before I could stop myself, I said, "I didn't know Frederick of course. But everyone tells me he was quite a nice man."

"He was. A good friend since university. And we served together in France in '17. It's just a damn—terrible thing to happen, least of all here, and much less in the company of my brother."

"I don't quite understand why everyone is so afraid that there might be more to the incident than an ill fated mishap."

He had been looking around the room, as if hoping it would grow larger or finer or in some way seem less a reflection on the house that guests should have to be put here. Even a nursing Sister and Lady Beatrice's companion. Frowning, he seemed to debate with himself. "There's a history of sorts between Frederick and Gordon. Mark knows it." Having said that much, he realized he had to explain, as if to make it less violent. "They were the best of friends. Well, the three of us were more or less inseparable. Yorkshire men against the world, at Oxford. Then Gordon met Grace. He fell in love with her. Asked her to marry him, and she said yes. They put off announcing it because our father was ill, and Gordon was sent for. We'd been told he didn't have long to live. And so Gordon and I stayed here for several months. My father surprised the doctors by recovering, and I went back to Richmond and he went to York to join Grace."

The silence lengthened. Finally he said, "She told him that she believed she'd been mistaken in her affections, and rather than announce the engagement, she wished to end it." He turned away. "A month later, she announced her engagement to Frederick."

That, I thought, could be viewed as a motive for murder. Long-delayed revenge—but then both men had only just come back from France. Had that suddenly stirred up feelings Gordon had thought he'd put behind him?

"Surely Frederick must have known—as a friend, he must have had some notion of how things stood between Grace and your brother?"

"I don't know who was at fault. Grace or Frederick. Or the simple fact that she had been mistaken about where her affections lay. At any rate, it was just before the war when Gordon and Frederick made their peace. Gordon appeared to accept what had happened and come to terms with it. But it was awkward when Frederick and his wife came for the weekend. I don't know why that should be, but it was. My mother noticed it. I did as well. And then the accident, while they were out there alone, hunting those blasted *sheep*."

"It could very well be true, that the fall happened exactly as your brother described it."

"I wish I knew . . ." Turning toward the door, he said, "I'll send a telegram to Lady Beatrice. She will want to be here for the funeral service. I'll simply say nothing about the police. It's not something to put in a telegram anyway." He opened the door and waited for me to step into the passage. "There's no haste in moving. Until we know my great-aunt is coming. My mother will ask one of the maids to help you when the time comes. Thank you, Sister Crawford."

And he strode down the passage, leaving me to return to our room.

"Is there any trouble?" Lillian asked as I stepped in and shut the door.

"Arthur received a telegram from Lady Beatrice asking for news.

He believes she may decide to come as soon as he replies. But Mr. Caldwell is staying. They're short of rooms for everyone."

"There's no place for him to stay in the village," she told me, echoing what Arthur had said. "It's rather tiny and there's really no need for accommodations. Most people who come to visit this part of Yorkshire prefer Wensleydale or Swaledale."

"How did the family come to settle here?"

Lillian smiled. "The story goes that when Richard III fell at Bosworth Field in 1485, the Nevilles fled to Scarfdale, where they had a minor holding. They were his wife's family, you know. It was thought that Henry Tudor would see to it that everyone who supported Richard would be punished in one way or another. And some of them didn't intend to risk that. But the wool here is particularly good, and they quietly prospered."

That explained the boar heads on the gateposts. A small defiant gesture even in exile. It was Richard's emblem, after all. That had been a turbulent period in history.

The wool market had collapsed at the end of the Great War. I'd heard the Colonel Sahib talk about it. The demand for blankets and uniforms had ended with the war. I wondered if that had affected the Nevilles at all.

Lillian rose. "I ought to see if I can help Mrs. Neville. I'm used to staying busy . . ."

I thought she was also uncomfortable talking about our hosts.

I too felt like a sixth finger. Partly because I could no longer claim to be a nursing Sister, I'd resigned. And partly because I had no business involving myself in this family's affairs. As soon as Lady Beatrice was released by Dr. Halliday, I could quietly return to Somerset.

I just couldn't turn away when a patient was involved. That had always drawn my attention, because something disturbing my patient was disturbing his ability to recover. Yet, Gordon wasn't truly my patient . . .

The rest of the day passed uneasily. One of the maids who was sister to a tenant farmer reported to Mrs. Roper—who told Arthur and Mrs. Neville—that Inspector Wade was seen walking about the farms, asking questions. Margaret passed the news to Lillian and me.

"What is he doing there?" Margaret pondered. "I don't believe you can see that outcropping from any of the farms. I don't see the point."

Lillian said, "He's a troublemaker. I don't know what his motive is, but he seems to feel antipathy toward this family. Arthur tells me that he's from a strong union family in coal country. The mine owners were the enemy. I expect he simply transferred that aversion to anyone with land, money, and standing."

It made sense. Gordon had said much the same thing.

"I expect," I said, "he's hoping that someone among the staff or on the farms might tell him more about Gordon and Frederick than he can learn from the family—"

The expression on Margaret's face stopped me.

I suspected that Arthur did and didn't want to tell her.

"It hardly constitutes a motive for murder, all these years later. They weren't twenty years old," I said.

But the situation with Grace some years later, could be seen as a motive . . .

I liked Margaret. She was sensible and pleasant, took her role in this family seriously, and was loyal to it. More to the point, she seemed to be defending Gordon rather than suspecting him. And yet beneath the loyalty were there creeping doubts? I thought perhaps it was Inspector Wade who had sown those . . .

Unable to stand the tension in the house any longer, I put on my walking shoes and went out into the fine mist that had replaced the drizzle. The gardens were heavy with moisture, blossoms dropping, limbs lower than they ought to be. I stayed near the house, but I remembered the stream—beck—I'd seen earlier before we turned into the road that led to the gates of the house. I wondered where that went, and in which direction the village lay—how far it might be, whether I could walk to it or must borrow a horse.

I realized that I was exceedingly damp now, and turned back to the house, wondering if Arthur had sent the telegram to Lady Beatrice or was holding off until tomorrow.

Needless to say, many of us around the table that evening strove not to appear uneasy, but it was a far cry from the birthday celebration they had been anticipating. We all retired later with no loud summons at the door. The man's visit to the farms hadn't been successful, I hoped.

I had looked in on Gordon from time to time, and someone had fed him his meal. When I visited him before joining Lillian in our room, his mood was black.

"How is the pain?" I asked, resting my hand for a brief moment on his forehead. The fever was still there, and I thought it had gone up a little.

"The shoulder is better, I think. The arm throbs. And I'm going mad lying here. Arthur says he has given my orders to everyone who depends on them, but it isn't the same, relying on someone else. Even my own brother."

"You can ask him tomorrow. Meanwhile, is that a book I see on the table over there? Is it one you've been reading? Shall I read a little of it, to settle you for the night?"

One foot kicked at the coverlet. "I don't need to be read to, I'm not a child with the measles."

It was said in a man's angry baritone, but there were distinct overtones of a child's tantrum. I wanted to laugh but couldn't insult him by letting him see.

"Then shall we talk?"

"You've already heard my confession. There's nothing more to say. Just get me out of this blood—this bed before I rot here."

"Yes, of course. And as soon as you can sit in that chair over there by the window, Inspector Wade will descend and drag you off to gaol."

That was a sobering reminder. The tantrum subsided.

"Dear God." He raised his good arm, wincing at the effort and put it across his eyes. "I'm often out at the farms or on the fells dealing with some problem among the sheep. I think sometimes I live in my Wellingtons, or my riding boots. You have no idea how difficult it is to be treated as an invalid, being fed my food and a glass or cup held for me. My meat diced into small portions, easier to swallow lying down."

"Did your brother tell you that earlier this afternoon, Inspector Wade was seen moving around among the farms?"

The arm moved from across his eyes and he turned to stare at me. "No. He did not."

"He's not giving up."

"What is the family saying? They're very consoling when they come but tell me nothing that might upset me."

"I think the Inspector's persistence has put everyone on edge," I said carefully.

"Does that mean they believe him?" When I hesitated, he said, angry again, "I want the truth."

"If one repeats a story often enough, people begin to wonder if there might be some truth in it. We haven't reached that stage. Everyone knows the history between you and Frederick Caldwell. And it makes them uneasy."

He took a deep breath. "Grace. I was in love with her. Or believed I was. She was the center of my life. At the time, I blamed Frederick for taking her away from me. I should have blamed Grace for being so shallow. He had a great deal more money than me at the time, you see. And he didn't live in such an out-of-the-way dale."

"Are you saying you think she was tempted by that?"

"God knows."

Again, I couldn't be sure whether he was building a case to prove his innocence, or if he was telling the truth. Was it the fever talking?

More to the point, I could be a factor in keeping him safe from a cell. If my sympathies were involved strongly enough.

I nearly missed what he was saying.

"Have you ever been madly in love?" he asked then. "It's torment and joy and blind devotion. You no more know the truth about the other person than you could fly. You see them through the eyes of adoration, and make them more perfect than they could possibly be."

Did I see Simon that way? Was I searching for something I wanted so badly to be there, but wasn't? Or was I not seeing what had been there all along?

It was a painful thought.

CHAPTER NINE

WHEN I REACHED the room, I found Lillian in tears.

I went to her at once. "My dear—what is it?"

She hastily wiped them away. "I must have something in my eye," she said, giving me a rather rueful smile.

"What is it?" I asked again.

She sighed. "There's nothing, really. I expect I've forgot what it was like to work for uncaring people. Afterward I just reminded myself that sticks and stones . . ."

"I can't imagine that anyone here would have upset you so. Unless it was Mr. Mark Caldwell?"

From the sudden flush rising in her face, I'd guessed right.

"What did he say to you?"

"I was just starting up the stairs when he came down the passage and called to me. I stopped and asked if I could help him. And he said, 'I should think there would be no use for you or the Sister, now that the danger to Mr. Neville has passed. If you will have your belongings ready in the morning, I'll drive you to Richmond, where you can take the train to York.'"

"And what did you reply?" I asked, feeling my anger rising.

"That I believed Lady Beatrice would be arriving shortly, and she would expect to find me here. Arthur had told me he was sending her a telegram. And you know she won't listen to reason, she'll be on the road at first light. The only thing that has surprised me is that she hasn't arrived by now."

"Was that enough to put him off?" I asked.

"He told me that he ought to have a word with Jonathan, that I was hardly the person to act as companion to Lady Beatrice. A woman of a better class would be more suitable. And then he stalked off. It's the only word for it, Bess. This isn't his house, he has no right to order people about. But what if he *does* write to Jonathan?"

"I should think it's nothing but bluster."

"You don't know the Caldwells," she said, shaking her head. "Even Frederick could be rather—unpredictable at times."

"How do you mean, unpredictable?" I asked, surprised. Everyone had sung his praises.

Lillian walked away, smoothing the coverlet on the bed, even though in ten minutes or so we'd be turning it down for the night.

I waited, but she didn't answer, as if she hadn't heard me. And so I let the subject drop.

She was no longer crying, but the hurt would take longer to go away.

And then she said, still busy with the small things that allowed her to keep her face averted—the lampshade that didn't need straightening, the fallen petal from the vase of flowers on the nightstand that could have been left till morning, the pillow slip that didn't need straightening—"I have no right to say such things. Forgive me. Mr. Caldwell has had a shock, he's lost his brother. And he's always been very kind to Grace. We must make allowances for his being ill-tempered."

"No, we don't," I told her. "He was rude. He has been rude to me as well. You needn't fear what Mr. Caldwell says or does. You answer to Lady Beatrice, not to Mark Caldwell."

She gave me a wavering smile that told me she didn't believe me but was too polite to tell me so.

We went to bed, but I don't think either of us slept for some little while. I watched the play of firelight reflecting on the ceiling above my head. Beside me, Lillian lay quietly, but I knew she wasn't sleeping either. She hardly moved at all, her body rigid as she pretended.

Lillian was finally asleep when I woke up. I tried not to disturb her as I slipped quietly out of bed. It was only a little after seven, and she could sleep for another hour.

I was dressed and on my way down to the dining room when the summons we had been dreading finally came.

I stopped, and hurried back up to the head of the steps. I didn't want to be there when the door was opened. Standing in the shadows of the landing, I waited.

Davies, the butler, came through the door from the kitchens and went to answer the now-pounding blows on the wooden paneling that sounded as if an axe was being taken to them. But it was only Inspector Wade's fist.

"I am here to speak to Mr. Neville, the younger."

"I will see if he is receiving guests at this hour," Davies replied with the calmness of long experience.

"No, damn it, this won't wait for his convenience. It's a matter of police business."

"Indeed, sir. If you will wait here."

Davies turned toward the passage, intending to find Arthur. The Inspector followed him.

Davies continued down the passage, and both men were quickly out of my line of sight.

Arthur Neville must have been in the small dining room, because I could hear what went on.

The sound of a door opening, a chair being pushed back hurriedly as Davies entered with the Inspector at his heels.

"Good morning," I heard Arthur say before Davies could announce the man. And then, "Inspector." There was a sour note in the late addition of the man's title.

Inspector Wade's voice came from inside the room. "I'm afraid there is nothing good about it, sir. I have found a witness who tells me that Mr. Gordon Neville, your brother, was seen sitting on Bald Willie, sometime after the fall must have occurred. Sitting there without a care in the world, while Mr. Caldwell lay suffering at the foot of the outcropping awaiting help to arrive as quickly as possible. Time that might have been critical in preserving his life."

"*What?*" This was another voice. It sounded like Mark Caldwell's. And then savagely, "I told you that bastard was a killer."

"Watch your tongue. This is my table, and my wife is present." Arthur, angry now.

"I apologize for my language," Mark Caldwell said, "but not for what I have said."

"I don't believe any of this," Arthur snapped, clearly speaking to Inspector Wade now. "Who told you such a tale?"

"What is Bald Willie?" Mr. Caldwell asked sharply, interrupting again.

"It's a half-buried boulder, some six feet long that overlooks the house. My grandparents made it a favorite seat for viewing the gardens from higher up the fell." There was reluctance in his tone, as if he resented sharing such personal information with either man. Then he added harshly, "Well, Inspector? I'm waiting."

"I prefer not to tell you who spoke privately with me. Suffice it to say, Mr. Neville, that this puts a poor light on your brother's rescue efforts."

"Such unsubstantiated information has to be viewed skeptically," Arthur told him. "If you can't give me a name, then I refuse to take the accusation seriously. And maybe he was in shock? He's already said that he has no idea how long they were both lying there."

His voice grew louder as he spoke, as if he were stepping into the passage. "This way, gentlemen. We'll continue our discussion in my study, if you please."

They had no choice but to follow him down the passage. I heard a door close behind them.

How had I even fleetingly thought that Mark Caldwell reminded me of Simon? He wasn't as tall—his manners were appalling—he was callous of the feelings of nearly everyone around him. I sent a silent word of apology to a very different man in Somerset.

I didn't wish to be caught eavesdropping, and so I began to descend the stairs. And just as well I did, because Mrs. Neville had just left her own room. I stopped to wait for her.

"Good morning," I said.

"Good morning, Bess. Was that pounding I heard at the door the good Inspector returning?"

"I expect it was." We descended the stairs together. I didn't think it was my place to tell her what the Inspector had said. "How is Grace this morning?"

"Calmer, I think. This was so unexpected—" She broke off as we reached the hall. "I am still horrified that it should happen at my house, when they only came to honor my birthday. But I can't give over to worry, not with Gordon in danger."

Greeting Margaret as we walked into the dining room, Mrs. Neville said, "Good morning, love. What does that wretched man want this time?"

As we filled our plates from the buffet—still as lean as it must have been during the war years—and took our seats, Margaret told us what the Inspector had said. Her account was exactly what I'd overheard, she hadn't added anything to make the visit sound worse than it was.

Mrs. Neville pushed her plate away, as if she had lost any appetite she may have had. "If Rover and Betty hadn't died, I'd be tempted to put those dogs on him. Even so, I doubt they could have chased him far, at fourteen and fifteen." She sighed, then turned to me. "Bess, would you mind terribly slipping up to Gordon's room and letting him know what is being said? I think it might be best if Margaret and I can swear we have said nothing to him, if we're questioned. And as you are not part of the family, no one can accuse you of trying to protect him from the police."

She gave me a conspiratorial smile. The smile of a mother.

I wasn't quite certain Inspector Wade would see it that way, but I understood her dilemma.

"I don't recall seeing Bald Willie on our way up to the scene of the accident."

"I don't know which path you took when you went with the Inspector. There's a shorter way. More difficult, but shorter. You would have passed the stone then."

I finished my breakfast, expecting any moment to hear Inspector Wade going down the passage toward the stairs, on his way to speak to Gordon Neville. Apparently he was still closeted with Arthur.

Finally, excusing myself, I left the dining room. In the passage I could hear raised voices from behind a door farther along. Arthur, I remembered, was a solicitor. He must be arguing his brother's case with the Inspector. I didn't envy him.

I ran lightly up the stairs, met Lillian at the top, and she said, "Is something wrong, Bess?"

I hadn't meant anyone to see me.

"A little exercise," I said, smiling. "Don't tell Mrs. Neville!"

She returned the smile. "Have you finished breakfast already? You should have waked me."

"Everyone is still in the dining room. You aren't late at all. I'm on my way to look in on Gordon—"

I broke off as Grace opened her door and stepped into the passage.

I had expected swollen eyes and a husky voice, but she appeared to be much improved this morning. I put it down to the body of her husband being taken away. After all, she knew where he was, it was a constant reminder that he was dead, when he lay in the room they'd shared.

"Going down to breakfast? I'll join you," she said.

Lillian asked how she was this morning.

"I finally fell asleep shortly after five," she said. "It helped."

"I'm glad to hear it, Mrs. Caldwell," I said, and meant it. "I'll join you later. I must retrieve something from my room." I walked on and left the two women to go down together. As soon as they were gone, I turned and went down the other wing, to see my patient. I'd felt uncomfortable mentioning Gordon Neville to Frederick's widow. I wondered if Arthur had sent telegrams to Grace's family, and if they would come here to take her home with them. There was a funeral to plan . . .

Although he was awake, and cross, I found my patient's fever rising, and when I looked at the wound over his protests that it was doing well enough, I found that infection had taken hold. The flesh around the wound was swollen and a deep red, while the edges of the cut where the bone had broken through the skin were raised and there were signs that it was draining.

There was a brightness to his eyes, and his face was flushed. He'd managed to draw up a blanket against the chill he was feeling, despite the roaring fire in the room. Indeed, it felt stuffy and overly warm to me.

Gordon Neville tried to raise his head and see the lower arm for himself, but that hurt too much and he dropped back. I went across to the tall chest where I'd noticed a shaving mirror, and used that to show him just how it looked. He grimaced.

As I set about cleaning and sprinkling disinfectant in the wound, I said, "How did you ever manage to come back to the house, with a broken arm and dislocated shoulder?"

"I had no choice," he said shortly. "Frederick needed help."

"It's a long walk. I told you, I went to the scene with your brother and the Inspector."

"I took the shorter path. I had the devil of a time with the stone walls, nearly fell getting over one. But it was worth it, saved almost a quarter of an hour."

He winced as I wrapped the wound again.

I said, finishing the task, "Margaret told us at breakfast that Inspector Wade has a witness who saw you sitting on some stone or other."

"Oh, God, I remember. A wave of nausea hit me, and I thought I was going down."

Breaking a bone was a shock to the body. Nausea and light-headedness were symptoms of that. I knew from my own experience—my arm was fractured when *Britannic* went down, and the wave of pain was so intense I felt sick.

Still, he hadn't told me that he'd stopped at Bald Willie, or for how long.

I said, "How long did it take to recover?"

"I can't tell you that. It passed. I was losing blood from the exertion, but I had nothing to wrap around my arm, much less tie it in place. I kept telling myself that I had to hurry. I couldn't see anyone in the gardens or outside the house. No one to shout to. And so I kept going." He took a deep breath. "It was like the war. We did what was asked of us somehow. I saw men who had lost an arm trying to drag a wounded comrade across the wire . . ."

"The Inspector interpreted that as waiting for Frederick to die."

"Damn the man." He didn't apologize for swearing. "If I'd wanted to kill Frederick, I could have done it without falling off the overhang in the bargain."

The words were still hanging in the air between us when there was a knock at the door, and Arthur came in with Inspector Wade. I was glad to see they'd left Mark Caldwell behind.

"Good morning, gentlemen. I was just cleaning and dressing Mr. Neville's wound. It's infected and he's running a fever. I must ask you to be brief."

"Indeed," Inspector Wade replied. "I must ask you to leave. I have some questions to put to the accused."

I said to Arthur, "Please see that your brother is not unduly distressed." Then to Gordon Neville, I added, "I will bring some aspirin when they have finished. It will help the fever and the pain."

As I left the room, I heard Inspector Wade say to Arthur Neville in a low voice, "Sisters have no respect for authority."

I wanted to tell him that our duty was to the patient, and we were responsible to Matron, not the police.

I went to our room and found my coat. The sun was trying to come out this morning, but there was a wind—I could see the trees outside our windows moving.

And it was brisk, but as I walked through the kitchen gardens and moved past the outbuildings as we had done when I climbed with Arthur and the Inspector, I could see sheep moving about on the flanks of Old Grumble, but didn't at first see anything that might be called Bald Willie. My gaze followed the lines of the stone walls that formed the patchwork of dry wall sheep folds across the land. Nothing leapt out at me as a possible seat.

And then I saw it. Higher than the path we'd taken, a long low profile of gray rock half buried in the earth. Closer to, it would be larger than it appeared from here, I thought. And I noticed too that the folds just there were offset slightly, as if older. While I couldn't see it from this vantage point, a path could run from Bald Willie almost directly up to the outcropping. It might even, for all I knew, connect with the path we had taken, which had slanted upward in a more irregular pattern.

I was so absorbed in what I was seeing that I jumped when someone spoke just behind me.

"It's a fair sight."

I turned. A famer stood there. I could tell because he wore a dark coat over his flannel shirt and trousers.

"It is," I agree.

He touched his forehead, in an older generation's traditional acknowledgment of those living in the House. And he was of that generation too, his iron-gray hair and lined face, his calloused hands and muddy boots marking him as a man who worked the land.

"I've lived here, man and boy, all my life. T'ain't a fairer place in all England."

It was, to his eyes, though empty and bleak in places to mine.

I smiled.

"How's Mr. Gordon?" he asked. He must have read the surprise in my face, for he went on. "I saw Chester and Sons carry out poor Mr. Frederick."

Not sure how I ought to respond, I said, "He's in some pain still."

"Aye, I saw that bone sticking out of his forearm, and the blood dripping with every step he took. Arm was hanging odd, too. That would be the shoulder, I expect."

He was observant, I realized, and he had been there when Frederick Caldwell was brought down.

"You were with them? When they brought him down?"

"Oh, aye. He were a terrible sight, lying there. Face gray, knocked out of his senses. I thought he were dead, before I seen his chest rise and fall. Mr. Gordon told us he had to move Mr. Frederick to get himself to his own feet."

So no one could tell if his head or neck had hit a raised stone . . . Even one like Bald Willie that was partly buried in the soil, the rest, like an iceberg, hidden below out of sight. No one but Gordon Neville would ever know what had caused that blow to the back of Frederick Caldwell's neck.

For all I knew, he himself might not know—or remember.

Still, I had to remind myself, he could have lifted a stone and brought it down on the helpless man's neck, even with his own injuries. Given the fierce desire to kill at any cost.

The farmer was saying, "It were the devil's own task to get him down. I've brought ewes back easier. Mr. Arthur, he said we must be careful not to jostle him. Not to do more damage than was done. And over rough ground at that."

"Did you bring him back by the short path or the longer one?"

He seemed surprised that I knew the difference. "It had to be the longer one, with us carrying the body. T'wasn't room, ye see. No, not on the short path, there wasn't."

I said, "Did anyone try to stop the blood from Mr. Gordon's arm, when he reached the house?"

"I heard the maids, they went screaming when they saw the bone. Mrs. Roper tried to do a bandage, whilst Mr. Arthur and I and the footman went to find a hurdle. But it weren't no good, the bandage was dripping before we'd got halfway there. She did have the doctor waiting, give her that, when we got down from the fell. Sent one of the maids running into the village."

I said, "How far, exactly, is the village?"

"'Bout a mile. Quarter mile back to the turning, then follow the turning, straight on."

I heard someone shouting a name. He touched his forehead again with grimy fingers. "That'll be the missus. Good day to you, Miss."

And he was gone, strong strides taking him toward the house. A man accustomed to walking on the fells.

I stood there for a bit longer, then walked around to the front of the house in time to see Inspector Wade's horse trotting purposefully down the drive.

He was alone.

Drawing a breath of relief, I went in the door. It was standing wide, and I saw why when I stepped inside.

Arthur was there with his mother. She was as flushed with anger as he was, and I heard him say to her, "The man's a fool. But he's dangerous too. You have to respect that. And walk carefully."

He stopped when he saw me.

I said, "I'm grateful to see that he left without taking your brother."

"I'm grateful to you for protecting my brother."

"He's not likely to escape the Inspector's clutches," I said. "But for now, he can't even feed himself."

Mrs. Neville said, "The infection. Is it true? Or were you simply trying to convince the Inspector that my son was too ill to move."

I told her the truth. "I've watched the wound since the start. The infection is becoming more serious with each hour. My advice is to send for Dr. Menzies." When she frowned, skeptical, I added, "Where the bone protruded from the arm, there is no way to know what got into the wound. We have cleaned it, put antiseptic powder on it, and let it air before putting the brace back on the arm to hold the two ends of the bone together so that they can knit. If they don't, the arm will require surgery to clean and reset the ends. In breaks of this sort, the danger is that any jostling will change the position of the bones, making them rejoin crookedly."

I saw at once that she had not known the full extent of her son's injuries. I glanced quickly at Arthur Neville and caught the expression that flashed across his face. He'd tried to protect her . . .

"I didn't know," she said faintly, looking up at him. "I had no idea . . ."

I said to her son, "You were in the war, you know what I'm saying. It's best to face the truth. For your brother's sake."

He understood. Gordon Neville had come back from France with scars but with all his limbs. This break in his arm could lead to amputation if it didn't heal and gangrene set in.

Arthur said to his mother, "There was enough worry over Frederick. I didn't want to add to your burden."

"I'm stronger than you realize, my dear. I ought to *know*."

Still, I could see for myself that she was badly shaken.

"Can I see him, Bess?"

"Yes. I think he would enjoy company. It's difficult lying there all day and all night."

She reached out and touched my arm, then crossed the wide hall to the stairs and began to climb them.

Arthur watched her go.

"I'm sorry. I didn't realize—"

"No, it had to be done sometime. Best coming from you. I must go saddle a horse. The sooner I find Dr. Menzies the better." He paused. "Do what you can for him. Please."

"It's what I was trained to do," I reminded him.

He hesitated. "You must know what is being said about my brother, that he tried to kill Frederick Caldwell. Will that make a difference?"

"I treated German wounded when we were caught in a surge. They needed care, and it didn't matter what uniform they were wearing. The patient always comes first."

After a moment he nodded. "Thank you."

And then he was striding down the passage toward the kitchen door.

I knew I could continue a little while longer to treat the infection. But it had occurred to me that if Dr. Menzies could give his opinion of the situation, it might go further with Inspector Wade than my diagnosis.

Lillian was coming down the stairs, eyeing the hall warily, then saw me by the door.

"Bess," she said, glad to see me. "Where were you?" She dropped her voice to a whisper. "There was an awful row with Mark Caldwell. We could hear them shouting from where we were. I thought they would come to blows."

"What about?"

"There was a telegram from Lady Beatrice. She's coming, and she's bringing Dr. Halliday from York with her."

"When? Did she say?"

Lillian shook her head. "I'm afraid not. As soon as the Doctor arrives at the Hall, I should think."

"We'll have to move to the smaller room next to ours."

"Yes, of course. But it wasn't the bedrooms worrying Mr. Caldwell. He was furious that Lady Beatrice was coming at all."

"Why?"

"I don't know."

I said, "Dr. Menzies is coming. Arthur just went for him."

"Oh dear God." She looked stricken. "What's wrong?"

"It's the infection in Gordon Neville's arm. Before it becomes more serious, I think it's best if the doctor has a look at it." I didn't want to upset her with the worrying details.

"I'm glad to hear it. I don't think I could take much more anxiety."

"Come and walk in the gardens a bit," I said. "It will do both of us a world of good."

We got back to the house just before the doctor arrived with Arthur Neville. Mrs. Neville was sitting in Gordon's room when we opened the door, and we asked her to leave while the doctor examined the wound.

She shook her head resolutely. "No. I'll stay."

"Mother, no," Gordon told her. "It's best if you come back later." When she tried to argue, he said, "No, I'm quite serious. Let the doctor do his work."

She left, but under protest.

I removed the bandages that held the splint in place, then uncovered the wound.

Dr. Menzies bent over it and sniffed. I knew he was looking for the first hint of gangrene. Then he examined it thoroughly while I held the lamp for him to have a better view.

He finally shook his head. "We've taken the very best care of this. It shouldn't be getting worse. I'd like to send him to hospital in Richmond."

"Neither Inspector Wade nor Mark will agree to that," Arthur put in.

"Still." He cleaned and wrapped the arm.

Gordon, who had said nothing while we stood over him probing and peering, spoke testily. "It will be all right."

I had given him the promised aspirin, but his eyes were still brighter than they should be.

Dr. Menzies had seen that as well. He said, "Yes, that's a very fine attitude."

He smiled, gathered up his things, and then said to me, "Increase the aspirin, and I'll leave you a pot of a different salve. See how that works, and I'll come back tomorrow. Send for me at once if there's any change."

I walked with him as far as the door of the room, then turned back to the bed.

"I know you'd rather be looking after your sheep than lying here. But once more you've thwarted Inspector Wade. That's something to be grateful for."

"I expect in the end he'll have his way." Then he said, "He asked me about Bald Willie. Thank you for the warning."

"It wasn't so much a warning as it was a test. I was curious too to hear what you had to say. And this witness. Do you have any idea who it might be?"

"I've had to deal with people on the estate. Their livelihood depends on us, most of them live in cottages that belong to us, and there's nowhere else to go. A spot of revenge may be welcome in some quarters."

He was tiring. I could see it. I took the pitcher of water and poured him a glass, then gave him a little more aspirin.

"Shall I ask your mother to come back again?"

"No. She is worried. She thought she had us home safe, and now this." He paused. "How is Grace?" He hadn't asked about her recently. "I thought I heard screaming yesterday. I know it's been very difficult for her."

"She's managing," I replied diplomatically.

"I took Frederick from her. That's how she will always feel."

"You weren't thinking to step into his shoes?" I asked quickly.

"Certainly not," he said harshly. "She didn't deserve to be hurt so badly. And I'm sorry for it. It will always be at my door, that's all."

Lady Beatrice didn't arrive that day, although I shouldn't have been surprised to find her on the doorstep.

We were to have drinks at seven, and with two hours in hand before I should look in on Gordon again, I asked Lillian if she would care to walk into the village with me. But she demurred, saying that she had been asked to spend a little time with Grace.

"I find it hard to know what to say to her," I admitted. "She weeps so easily. I feel myself an intruder in a way. As if she would prefer to be alone with her grief."

Lillian, who had never been married, shrugged her shoulders slightly, and commented, "I don't know if that's wise, being alone, just now."

I left her to her duty and set out. As I opened the door onto the drive, something dark swung toward me, startling me. And then I saw that a large mourning bow had been placed over the knocker. The traditional way of announcing to the world that there had been a recent death in this house. I closed the door carefully after me and started down the drive toward the house gate and the lane beyond. I walked down that until it met the main road. The verges were rough, and so I kept to the road itself as I walked. I couldn't hear a vehicle or even a horse coming from either direction, and the quiet was absolute except for a crow or a rook calling from far away, the sound seeming to echo across the dale. Here the steep-sided Scarf followed the road, crowded a little by the trees that marched along on either side of it. I could hear it leap and dance among the stones in its bed. A restful sound. When I moved closer, to have a look, I could see the clarity of the water, right down to shadows moving in the eddies. Fish? Or simply the reflection of the leaves above?

Farther along I saw a kingfisher dart into the water and then fly up again, leaving a trail of sparkling droplets behind him.

I was beginning to think that the village was farther than a mile, when I saw the first cottage appear around a bend in the road that followed the bend in the stream. And then the road and the water ran among a string of houses. At a stone bridge, the road switched sides of the beck, leaving a short lane behind on the near side. It ended at a farmhouse gate. As I got closer, I saw there was a rectangular stone just short of the bridge, and I wondered if this had once been a stop on a coffin trail, where the fell residents rested a coffin they were carrying to the nearest churchyard, sometimes miles away. I didn't see a church ahead of me, no spire or tower rising above the cottages and shops, although there was a small chapel, Methodist by the look of it, right on the road.

Several people were standing in front of the General Store, talking, and just beyond was a pub called The Sheep Fold. The door to a lamp and candle shop stood open, and the warm smell of beeswax and oil wafted toward me. There was no electricity in the dales. A small boy was squatting by the beck, a stick in his hand, poking at something in the water.

The Neville house had been built of the lighter grist stone, while the village was the darker limestone, like Bald Willie and the outcropping.

People turned to stare at me as I passed, and I smiled, but got no smile in return, just that cold stare, both suspicious and unwelcoming.

Some cottages beyond the pub there was a slightly larger house with a brass plate by the door. Dr. Menzies's surgery. Why had he chosen to live and work here, in this tiny village? From what I'd seen, he was a good doctor. He could make a living anywhere. Perhaps he served several villages like this in the dale. But then I hadn't seen any but this one, not for miles, after we turned into Scarfdale.

On this side of the beck, there was a little square, where the lane leading to a few more cottages joined the street I was walking along. In the center of it, someone had put up a piece of wood shaped like a cross. And on it someone had burned names. It was a roughly done memorial. And someone had planted pansies around it in a circle. For remembrance. The wood had been smoothed but was still raw, and somehow that added to the sadness, an open wound, in wood.

I was looking at the names when I heard a door open behind me, and I turned. A young woman, perhaps in her late twenties, stood in the opening of the small cottage just behind me. She was looking directly at me, and I thought she might be coming out to speak to me. And so I smiled. Beside her the window on the street was open, and the lace curtains were stirring a little in the wind that seemed to follow the Scarf through the valley.

Or was someone twitching them for a better look?

Someone called, I could just hear a voice, I couldn't determine whether it was a low woman's or lighter man's. Whichever it was, she stopped, one foot poised to cross the threshold. And then she mouthed something, and I realized that she was saying *Mr. Neville?*

She was asking if he was all right. I was sure of it. Before the door could close completely, I nodded briefly, once. And then she was gone.

I walked on, coming to the end of the cottages, although the road traveled on, past a farrier's shop. I could see the flame he was working with the bellows. He glanced up, then returned to whatever it was he was tempering in the water bath, and I turned to retrace my steps. From the start I could feel eyes on me watching, as the villagers examined this visitor from the Neville house. But now I felt it so strongly that I turned to see who it was. Not on this side of the beck, surely. Across the beck there was a tall house, last one before the farm gates and the stone dark as its neighbors, that had a large garden to one side. There was no one working in the garden, nor as far as I could judge, at the lace-curtained windows. No telltale twitch. The ground rose rather abruptly beyond the outbuildings, and I could see something in the shadows of the trees. They thinned quickly, and the fell beyond was bright with sunlight, effectively deepening the shadows under the trees. I could see among them. Milk cows rather than sheep grazed there. And in the open door of a shed I thought I glimpsed a cheese machine.

Reminding myself that the village was naturally curious about anyone who lived in the Hall, that it had nothing to do with *me,* I moved on. In another house, a child ran to open the door and stare up at me, her thumb in her mouth. She was perhaps three or four, with pretty brown curls. I smiled at the little girl, just as her mother came, caught her arm, and pulled her away. The door was smartly closed.

A small black dog got up from beside another house, following me until I crossed the bridge again and then lost interest.

Midway over the bridge, I looked back to the house with the garden by its side. Just then I noticed another man just stepping into the pub, his back to me as he disappeared inside and closed the door. He seemed familiar, somehow, but I didn't recognize him. He was wearing the usual farmer's flannel shirt and brown corduroy trousers, the bottoms of which were stuffed into Wellingtons. But somehow he didn't look like a farmer at all, in the way he carried himself. An ex-soldier?

I moved on, not wanting to stare, and was quickly out of the village again and on my way back to the Neville house. I didn't see the young woman again, as I passed the square and her cottage.

Walking along the road, empty now, just me and a squirrel scurrying up a tree, that feeling of being watched returned. This time I refused to turn and look. If someone *was* there, I refused to give him—or her—the satisfaction of appearing to feel anxious. Still, this was a very lonely place, just a handful of animals, some birds above me in the trees, and the sound of the beck tumbling over its stony bed to keep me company as I walked.

I was in sight of the lane that led to the house, when I heard a loud rustling in the undergrowth, somewhere behind me and, I thought, on the far side of the beck. I found myself picking up my pace a little.

The sound grew louder, it was coming closer, that rustling. And it wasn't a fox after a hare or a squirrel. It was moving steadily, and quickly. And then it was at the beck, a wild splashing as something or someone leaped into the water, coming directly at me, and a little behind me still.

I whirled to face whatever was coming, then stood there, bracing myself.

Even as I did, a rather ferocious-looking dog broke cover and charged straight for me, teeth bared, growling deep in his throat.

Chapter Ten

HE WAS THE size of a mastiff, I thought in that first startled moment, and I drew in my breath sharply, lowering my chin so that my throat wasn't as vulnerable. The urge to run was overwhelming, but there was nowhere to go, and running would only excite it more.

Its lip was curled back, showing long white teeth, its hackles raised. I cast a swift glance around, saw nothing that could be used as a weapon, and realized I was about to be hurt rather badly.

No one knew where to look for me—

All this was happening in a matter of seconds, although it seemed that time had slowed.

Just as he was about to leap at me, I threw up my arms to shield my face. And in the same instant I heard a low whistle. And the dog *stopped*. Still growling, still showing me its teeth, holding me at bay from only feet away from me.

It wasn't a mastiff after all, but my racing heart still hadn't realized that. I couldn't determine the breed, and I didn't care, as I faced it and shouted, "Call him off. *Now!*"

Another low whistle, different in pitch, and the dog gave me one last look before turning and disappearing along the beck toward someone I couldn't see.

It took me several minutes to slow my breathing. But I made myself turn away and appear to cross the road quite calmly—while the rest of me fought down the shock. That was swiftly followed by anger. I was furious with whoever it was. If he could whistle the dog away on the brink of attack, he could have stopped him from ever crossing that beck. And he knew he could have done that.

And another part of my brain was beginning to recognize that the signals were very much like those a shepherd used to control the dogs helping him herd the sheep. But the animal didn't look like the usual sheepdogs I'd seen in the dales and elsewhere—the black and white small collie breed. This one was brindled, with black, and a good bit taller.

I remembered then. A similar breed was used by our own Army as messenger dogs.

I had never seen one on the verge of an attack like this one. I was still shaking rather badly when I turned in through the gates.

When I got to the house, the door was firmly closed. I had to knock, and the butler, Davies, came to admit me.

His eyebrows went up. "Are you quite all right, Miss?"

"I'm so sorry! I forgot to tell anyone I'd gone out." Then I asked, "I saw a dog just now, larger than the sheepdogs here, brindled with a black face, and yet it responds to whistles. Do you know who the owner might be?"

"I expect, Miss, that it's the dog Joe Harding brought back from France with him. I've been told he found it as a puppy, and has even taught it to herd sheep. He brought it back for his sister, who lives at his farm adjacent to the Neville land, but it's more his dog. Well, not too astonishing, after a war together."

I'd seen the farm, from the end of the street that crossed the beck and ran to the footbridge.

Men in the trenches adopted cats and dogs and even birds and rats, something to love and protect at the end of the day. I'd been told that an artillery company kept a deaf white cat, who never minded the sound of the guns, lying there while they worked. Some men took in French or Belgian dogs found wandering on the battlefield and trained them to listen for attacks at night, when their keener hearing gave more warning. It wouldn't be too surprising that these dogs were trained to whistles, where voice command could give away positions.

The question was, who was out with it today?

"Do you know what the dog is called?"

There was the hint of a smile. "Yes, Miss, I'm told it's called Cooper. It was called Gladys for a time, until it was determined that the dog was not a Gladys."

Gladys Cooper was the quite beautiful actress whose photo was popular with the men fighting in France. I'd seen dozens of them while preparing the belongings of the dead to return to the Army.

"Thank you, Davies. Has anyone looked in on Mr. Gordon?"

"I believe Mrs. Neville sat with him for a time."

"I'll go up, then."

The fever was worse, I thought, laying my palm on Gordon Neville's forehead, and he was restless. When I examined and then cleaned the wound, I could see from the bandages I'd removed that it had been draining. That could mean a variety of things, but in general a wound that was draining infection was a good sign. I would keep it under observation for signs of blood in the drainage.

He lay there silently, watching my movements. Then he said as I was gathering the used bandages, "Mark Caldwell came to see for himself that I was not malingering."

"And was he convinced?"

"He told me the room smelled of rot. Of gangrene."

"It doesn't," I told him. "And I should think I'm a far better judge."

Gordon smiled wryly. "Quite." Then he added, "I'm dry as a bone."

I found the pitcher of water, poured him a cup, and carefully raised him so that he could drink it.

"Where did you see most of the fighting?" he asked as I settled him again.

I told him, and he whistled. "That's impressive."

"I was a surgical nurse," I explained. "I worked with some very fine doctors. Together we saved a good many men from dying. Is there anything else you need?"

"The wound and the bone are aching. Shoulder is healing. More aspirin would help."

I was not as liberal with it as some doctors had been during the war. It helped with inflammation and with fever, but many were more careful about doses. After he'd taken it, I said, "Would it help, if you had more pillows? Now that your shoulder isn't hurting as much?"

"God, yes!"

We had put four or five more pillows in a chair, in case of need, and I brought those over to the bed and arranged them so that he was no longer lying flat on his back.

The shoulder was still sensitive—but it was still firmly back in its socket.

"That's much better. I should be able to get out of bed by tomorrow."

"Dr. Menzies tells me you are better off in bed. The minute you walk out that door, Inspector Wade will be here to arrest you. Besides, that arm still doesn't look good. The infection is still there. You are my patient and I can't risk you being moved too soon."

"At this point I'd much rather face a cell than another day shut up in this room."

There was a tap at the door, and both of us looked toward it, tensing.

I went to open it. Margaret was standing there. "I've come to amuse the patient. Mrs. Neville tells me he's restless and will be running down the stairs and out the door as soon as our backs are turned."

I smiled. "So he is." I turned back into the room. "You have a visitor. I'll leave you to it."

She touched my arm lightly as I left. I was walking down the passage when Grace Caldwell stepped out of her room. I greeted her, and she turned my way. I saw that she was dressed for riding.

"Hello," I said.

Grace Caldwell sounded very much like Gordon Neville when she said, "I've asked Arthur to have a horse brought around. I can't breathe in this house."

"I walked into the village earlier. It's nice weather for a ride."

She shook her head. "I wouldn't care if it were pouring rain. I see that room every time I come up the stairs, and it hurts so I feel light-headed. My parents are coming to take me to their house. I don't care what the Inspector says about leaving."

"I'm sure he'll have nothing to say about your going. You weren't even here—"

She was pulling her riding gloves as she walked toward me. "That's what haunts me most! We didn't need an outing. I could have been here, I could have talked to him, held his hand. Instead I was in some shop in Richmond looking at new china for Mrs. Neville's birthday dinner. We have perfectly good china right now, it was ridiculous, and the worst part of all is that I felt nothing. Absolutely nothing. Why didn't I know he'd been hurt? I'd have come home. I'd have been here." Her face flushed. "Why couldn't someone send a telegram to our hotel? Arthur knew which one it was. Why didn't he *send* someone? I'd have traveled all night—I'd have *walked* if I had to."

"From what the doctor told me, they hadn't expected your husband to die that night," I said gently to Mrs. Caldwell. "He couldn't judge the internal injuries—"

She turned on me. "I don't care if he'd only broken his thumb! I should have been here. I should have come back."

"I understand," I replied, trying to calm her.

"No, you don't. You aren't married, you can't possibly know what it is like to walk through the door and be told that the perfectly healthy husband you'd left only two days before has died. You have no idea what a shock that could be." A gloved finger, trembling with her anger, pointed beyond the stairs, down the passage when the family bedrooms were. "They were protecting *him*. Gordon. And I'll never forgive any of them. And neither will Mark."

Mrs. Caldwell walked on, down the stairs and out the door. I heard it slam.

I went to find Arthur Neville.

He was sitting in his study, and I tapped lightly on the door, not knowing if he was busy or simply trying to cope.

"Come."

As I came in to the room, he said, "Bess? Is Gordon all right?"

"The infection is still worrying. Dr. Menzies will come back tonight to have a look. No, what I've come to talk to you about is Mrs. Caldwell. She's terribly upset. We've all watched as she's tried to take in what happened. But she's turning bitter now. She tells me that her parents are arriving to take her to their house. It might be best if she leaves. I don't know what the funeral arrangements may be."

"He'll be taken to Maris Hall, his home, and be buried from there. But I understand from the undertaker that Inspector Wade hasn't released the body yet." He vigorously rubbed his face with his hands. "I expect he's still determined to press charges. The inquest will be Monday, in the village. None of us is to leave before that. Including Caldwell, who insists he wants to give evidence. God knows how that will be arranged—he wasn't even here."

"Have you heard anything more from Lady Beatrice?"

"I have. She'll be here tomorrow." Arthur grimaced. "Much as I look forward to seeing her, I don't know how much good it will do. Given the household at the moment."

"She's very persuasive," I said, speaking from experience.

"I don't think even my aunt can deter Mark or even Grace." He rose. "I'll have a word with Grace. I know how upset she is. This wasn't something any of us would have wanted to happen, not ever. I should have sent for her. But Menzies assured us that Frederick would live. At the time we did not want to worry Grace before she'd finished her journey. Then after nightfall, everything began to change. She couldn't have reached us in time if I'd sent a hundred telegrams." He stopped me at the door. "Sister—Bess. Do what you can to keep my brother out of the village gaol. If he comes from this house to the inquest, it might go a long way toward proving to a coroner's jury that he's innocent. If he's brought there from a cell—" He broke off. "Yorkshire men believe in the proof of their own eyes."

"Surely Gordon's well liked in the village?"

"When my brother enlisted, half the village went with him. Most of them didn't come home. There's some hard feeling about that. As if he should have kept them safe. I know he tried. My God, no one who wasn't there can even imagine what it was like."

He nodded politely and was gone.

I barely had time to bathe and dress for dinner. As I changed, I was grateful to Lady Beatrice's seamstress. I at least had a number of changes to make a good appearance at times like these. It would have been impossible to get suitable dresses here in time.

Unless of course the Colonel Sahib—or Simon—could be persuaded to bring them himself.

Dinner was quiet. Grace Caldwell stared at her plate most of the meal, tasting this or that but showing very little interest in the food.

And it was an excellent meal, given the ongoing problems of austerity. But there were gardens here in the dale, there were plenty of fresh fruits and vegetables. They provided lovely soup courses.

Still, it was difficult to carry on any conversation in the face of her grief. We made an attempt, then fell silent ourselves. The clink of silverware and fine china filled the handsome dining room, with its paintings of Neville ancestors and intricately carved wooden surround for the hearth. Where I was seated I found myself staring at it, and then realized suddenly that the subject of the carvings was an ark, and all the figures of animals moving two by two toward the ship were beautifully done.

Noticing my interest, Mrs. Neville said, "It's Italian. One of my husband's ancestors brought it home from a Grand Tour. The story is, he kept sending things from his various stops, and for months after he got back, they were still coming in on packhorses. The chandelier is Venetian, the mirror French, and there's a German painting in the library. The marble bust in the front hall was bought in Rome as well, although it is Greek."

I think we were all grateful when the meal was finished. We left the men to their brandy and retired to the small drawing room for our tea. I excused myself briefly to look in on Gordon Neville and be certain he'd had his own meal.

But when I got to his room, he wasn't there.

I stood there in the middle of the floor and stared at the empty bed.

Where was he? And how long had he been gone?

It was well after nine . . .

I'd last looked in on him at six thirty. Someone had brought his tray, and it was still there, on the table, covered with a linen napkin. The lamp had been turned down low, as it usually was when he was sleeping.

Oh, the silly man! I thought, exasperated and worried and knowing only that I dared not raise the alarm . . .

I sat down in one of the chairs by the hearth and waited.

It was a quarter to ten when the door began to open quietly. He slipped into the room, turned—and froze when he saw me sitting there.

He had a riding cloak thrown over his shoulders, and was wearing a shirt poorly stuffed into his trousers. His feet were clearly bare of stockings, thrust into boots.

In the staleness of the room, I could smell fresh air on his clothes.

"Where have you been?" I asked, not stirring from my chair.

"Bess—"

"You do realize, don't you, that if anyone had seen you, we would be hard-pressed to keep you out of gaol. As it is, we've stretched the truth thin to keep you here at all." I kept my voice level, neither angry nor condemning. Just pointing out the truth.

In reality, I'd have liked to subject him to one of Matron's scathing lectures when a recalcitrant patient kept the Sister wasting time that could have been better spent with others more in need of care.

It usually left the subject of her remarks reduced to better behavior.

I didn't think it would work here.

When I'd finished speaking, he moved into the room, and tried one-handed to return the cloak to the armoire. It fell twice before he managed to get it out of sight.

"Bess, I'm sorry. Everyone was at dinner—the staff busy in the kitchen, then having their own meal. I just wanted to breathe a little fresh air. My limbs still work, they aren't broken. I can walk."

When I said nothing, he added, "I live outside. I have an estate, tenants, even the sheep, to keep running smoothly. I'm simply not accustomed to lying in bed for days on end. Not since I had measles at ten."

He crossed to the lamp and turned it up.

"You haven't touched your food. Did it arrive before you left?"

"Yes. I told Ruth that I wasn't hungry, and I'd have you feed me later."

Ruth, apparently, was one of the maids.

As he crossed in front of me to sit gingerly in the other chair, I said, "Do you wish to eat now?"

He took a deep breath. "Yes, I expect I should. It's difficult to feel hungry when you've done nothing days on end."

I got up then and went to the tray. The baked chicken had been cut into small pieces, the vegetables and potatoes as well. The soup was cold, as was the tea.

I brought him the tray to balance on his knees. But he took the fork from me and with his left hand managed to feed himself, after a fashion.

That's when I noticed the long scratch on his left hand.

"How did that happen?"

He looked at it. "I expect I scraped it on one of the walls."

"How far did you wander?" I asked, appalled.

"All right, I went as far as the outcropping. I haven't been back—I wanted to see what I remembered, if anything helped me recall just what had happened there."

"And did it?"

"No. It's still a blank. I took the short way back, and had trouble getting over one of the walls."

"Anyone could have seen you! It's light until nearly ten!"

"They were busy in the kitchen—"

"Even kitchens have windows."

"No. It's below ground the land rises in the rear of the house. The kitchen has no windows on that side."

He finished the tray, and I set it back on the table. "All right. I'll stand at these windows while you get yourself back into bed. I dare not leave and let someone find you, still dressed."

I walked to the windows, standing there with my back to him. I heard him swear under his breath several times as he struggled to undress and get ready for bed. When I heard the springs creak under his weight, I turned and had just finished hanging his clothes in the armoire when there was a tap at the door, and Ruth was there to take the tray back downstairs.

I smiled at her, and thanked her, then closed the door after her.

"Thank you," he said from the bed. "Could I ask you to fix these infernal pillows? I can't make them comfortable again."

"And it serves you right," I said, but did as he asked.

Standing by the bed, I reminded him, "You took a terrible risk."

"I tell you, I need to remember how we came to fall," he said stubbornly.

"And what would I have told the Inspector, if he'd come?"

"I don't know."

I took his temperature. The exertion hadn't helped his fever. I thought it was rising too quickly now. And it was possibly the fever that had made him get out of bed and take such a silly chance.

I said, "How does the arm feel?"

"It's hurting."

"If the infection doesn't begin to heal, we'll have to transport you to hospital."

"No. I'll stay where I am."

"You may not have any choice in the matter."

I crossed the room to the lamp and turned it down again. "Try to sleep. It helps."

There was a silence from the bed. I went back.

"I keep dreaming about falling," he said. "I hear Frederick cry out. But we never hit the ground. We just—fall."

"It's part of the fever."

"I didn't think I was going to make it back here tonight," he admitted in a low voice.

"And then what? It would look like you aren't as ill as we've being telling Inspector Wade."

He didn't answer.

I left then.

He'd been terribly foolish. Criminally so, under the circumstances.

It was important that I make an appearance in the little drawing room. Taking a deep breath to relieve some of the tension I was feeling, I went down the stairs.

"There are times—" Margaret was saying when I walked into the sitting room where she and her mother-in-law, Mrs. Neville, and Lillian were gathered, going through a basket full of bed linens, choosing what to donate to a clinic near Richmond for the wounded who wouldn't return home for some months yet. I'd worked with many of such cases once the war was finished.

She broke off as Lillian said, "Hallo, Bess."

Mrs. Neville smiled at me. "Come join us. We've kept you busy, my dear. Hardly a way to treat a guest. How is my son's fever?"

"It hasn't got worse, for which I'm grateful. Still, I gave him more aspirin."

"And the shoulder?"

"I added to his pillows. He took that very well." That said everything— and nothing. If I had to lie again, I didn't want it to be known that I was doing so.

"Good news," she said nodding.

Margaret asked, "Have you seen Mark about the house?"

"I don't know where he is. I'm sorry. The last time I saw him, he was still in the dining room with Arthur."

She shared a glance with Mrs. Neville.

"I think they had words again. Arthur stepped in while you were upstairs. I could see that he was quite angry and trying not to show it. He said he was going up. I expect I should call it an evening as well."

I felt cold. Had Mark Caldwell seen Gordon coming back across the fell? Or even Arthur?

"Just leave the basket, my dear. There's tomorrow, we'll have it finished then."

Lillian said, "I think it's best that Grace should go with her parents. She'll be better away from all that's happened here."

"I hope that's true," Mrs. Neville said with a sigh. "I just wish she'd take Mark with her."

"I don't count on it," Margaret replied.

I said, "I can understand how upset he must be about his brother's death. And that he's grieving. But I don't understand why he's such an ill-tempered man."

Mrs. Neville hesitated. Then she said, "As a rule, I don't care to gossip, but you are the object of his temper at the moment. Lady Beatrice tells me he was unpleasant as a child. And he hasn't changed very much. His uncle was just the same, but he lost his wife at an early age, and it made him very bitter. I didn't meet Mark Caldwell until Grace was engaged to his brother Frederick, who I knew because he and Arthur and Gordon were friends. Mark is a very able man, by all accounts, but he tends to rub everyone the wrong way, which only makes matters worse."

Margaret said, "Mark Caldwell appears to get along better with horses. His stable at New Market is always winning."

"He isn't married? No children?"

"I'm told that in the spring before the war, he was engaged, but his family didn't approve of his choice, and during the war she married someone else. He's engaged again, and Arthur tells me the wedding will be sometime this summer." Margaret smiled wryly. "I expect none of us will be invited to attend."

Mrs. Neville had risen and was putting out the lamps as we started toward the door.

We said good night at the top of the stairs and went our separate ways.

Lillian said, as we closed the door to our room, "I think I shall have indigestion if we have another meal like the one tonight. My heart breaks for Grace Caldwell, but I wish she could make an effort. For her own sake as well as Mrs. Neville's."

"Mrs. Caldwell feels very alone here. But we don't know how to comfort her. And that just makes her isolation seem more real."

We got ourselves ready for bed, turned out the lights, and I heard Lillian breathing quietly while I was still awake, staring at the ceiling. I couldn't get out of my mind the image of Gordon Neville stepping quietly into the room, thinking that he was safe, that no one had seen him. But what if Mark Caldwell had?

We'd know in the morning when Inspector Wade arrived.

It was a little after one in the morning when I heard the distant sound.

I was still awake, but even so I couldn't quite identify what it was or where it was coming from.

And then I was rising from the bed, reaching for my robe and thrusting my feet into my slippers. There was no time to worry about my hair, falling over my shoulders and down my back.

I got to the door without waking Lillian and stepped into the hall.

There were voices now from below.

Someone had seen Gordon, and the police were here—

I hurried to the top of the stairs, prepared to speak to Inspector Wade if Arthur couldn't stop him from carrying out his intentions.

But when I got there, I stopped short and moved back into the shadows of the passage.

It wasn't the police at the door.

It was two or three men, speaking earnestly to Arthur.

I tried to follow the conversation, but they were speaking quietly now, as if he'd told them not to wake the household. And their local accent was nearly impenetrable because they were speaking fast and urgently.

Arthur, also in robe and slippers, was nodding.

I heard him say, "I'll have the fire bell rung. Let me get dressed, and I'll organize a party. But you've looked elsewhere?"

One of the men was explaining where the other parties had gone.

"Yes, yes," Arthur said, agreeing. "Yes, that's all to the good. Give me ten minutes."

There were nods of agreement, and the men had turned away before he could shut the door.

Then he was taking the stairs two at a time. I spoke so that he would know I was there.

"Is something wrong? You mentioned the fire bell."

"I'm so sorry their pounding woke you. No, there's someone missing from the village. The watch was roused, and we've been asked to join the search. The fire bell is just a way to reach the tenants in an emergency. I must go. You should return to bed, Bess. If there's any need for you, I'll come back at once."

"Yes, thank you." I let him go and went back to our room. Much as I wanted to help, I knew I'd be useless in such a search in the dark. I hardly knew the estate or the fell, could find my way in daylight to the outcropping, but that was it. In the dark, I would only be in the way, if I tried.

But I didn't go back to bed. I dressed in the dying light of the fire, and took out my coat, carrying it with me. For I had remembered that there was a garden room—Gordon had mentioned it—and I was sure a few of the windows there looked out on the fell rising behind the house.

But first I went into the room where Frederick Caldwell had been taken, and died. I had no fear of the dead, I'd worked too long and too closely with them. I knew that the windows in that room looked out on the front of the house, and I lifted an edge of the drapes to peer out.

I couldn't see the main road or the beck. But on the far side of the water the land rose through a narrow stand of trees that followed the Scarf. And I thought I could just see tiny pinpricks of moving light.

It was a search in earnest . . .

I got down the stairs without being seen. I wasn't even certain Mrs. Neville was awake, or that Margaret was still asleep.

The male staff had been routed out, and from the garden room I heard the bell as it stopped ringing. The room was dark, I hadn't lit a lamp, but I could hear the shouts as men came hurrying from the farms. Their torches wove and bobbed out there in the dark as they gathered, got their instructions, and spread out to search. I could see the lights moving among the sheep folds, rising steadily. A few latecomers, who had no torches, lit the flame version, and as the fire streamed high above their heads, they went not up the sloping darkness of Old Grumble, but straight. I thought perhaps they were intending to look where the land flattened.

I shivered in my clothes, and pulled on my coat against the night's chill. It was quite an unnerving spectacle. I couldn't shake the sense that they were hunting someone. This time for rescue, of course, but it had such a medieval air about it.

I heard a sound behind me, turned, and saw that Mrs. Neville had joined me. She too had taken the time to dress. She stayed there for quite a long time, without speaking.

Then she said decisively, "They'll want a hot soup, and tea. I must see to that." And she was gone.

It occurred to me that whoever had gone missing was thought to be in danger. There was an urgency about the movement of the lights on the fell-side, and Old Grumble seemed to blot out the stars. A high, uneven peak.

When I opened the terrace doors a little, I could hear that the men were communicating by the whistles they used for the sheep. Shrill and sharp, the sound carried. I shut the doors again.

I don't know how long I'd been standing there watching. Why such a determined search here, was there some reason why the grounds were being searched?

I'd opened the doors again, drawn by the sound. And I heard it change. A series of shouts, faint at first and then growing louder.

Whoever it was they'd hunted, they had found him . . .

The searchers began to turn back from the higher elevations, first one or two, then in greater numbers. I saw two men sit on Bald Willie, resting before starting the rest of the way down. Those closest to the house were moving toward the kitchen steps.

For their soup and their tea.

The sky was brightening a little, and the torches were being put out or turned off. Old Grumble blocked us from the better views of sunset, and the fell across the stream rose nearly as high, blocking sunrise. And so shadows were still deep in places.

I turned away, hoping to sleep a little before the house woke fully. On my way, I looked in on Gordon. He'd been restless in the night, the pillows were in disarray, the coverlet askew. He must have heard the summons and the fire bell. And no one had come to tell him what was going on. After all, it was his land, his responsibility . . .

Or his fault?

I stifled that little voice of doubt, and left quietly.

Walking down the passage, I heard footsteps on the stairs, surely taking them two at a time, because as I reached the top of the staircase, I nearly collided with Arthur.

"Oh—good. You're awake. Dr. Menzies has gone to one of the outlying farms. Can you come at once? Do you mind?"

"I'll just collect my kit—"

He looked away. "You won't require it."

Whoever they'd searched for was dead . . .

"Yes, of course."

We went back down the stairs but out the kitchen door, passing more of the searchers coming back.

They nodded to Arthur, glanced at me and away, then went down to the kitchens.

"Where will you put everyone?" I asked.

"There's a Servants Hall with a long trestle table. It's used for staff meetings, for the dinner we give to the tenant farmers and their families, that sort of thing." He'd replied almost absently, his attention on making his way toward the path across the fells.

The same one he'd taken with me and Inspector Wade—

As if he'd heard my thought, he said, "Inspector Wade is on his way. I want to get there first, if possible. He was out with a different party, thank God. That's why we have a little time in hand."

He was already setting a breakneck pace. I stumbled twice, and he cast an apologetic glance over his shoulder. But he didn't slow. I was glad I was a good walker, otherwise I'd have taken a nasty fall on the second misstep.

The outcrop was standing out against the brightening sky, a gray bulge that was ugly.

"Does—does it have—a name? That—place?" I found the wind to ask.

"That—? It's called Arnhead. The head of Arn. No one remembers who that was."

We could see the cluster of people already gathered above and below the outcrop. But I couldn't tell what they were looking at.

To my surprise, Arthur led me to the spot where the two men had fallen earlier.

The gathering parted as they saw us approach.

No one stood on the ledge. And I could see why.

A crumpled body lay there.

CHAPTER ELEVEN

I COULDN'T SEE who it was, but there was no doubt it was a woman, for a shawl covered her head and shoulders, and the tumbled skirts showed slim ankles and a woman's boots.

I'd thought it was a man they were looking for. Not that it would have made a difference, but I'd grown used to dealing with the broken bodies of men. Arthur stopped to allow me to go the rest of the way alone.

The black shawl was wet with blood. A slim arm lay to one side where someone had tried for any sign of life. I looked around the body, but in the dim light, nothing struck me as unusual or worth noting. Footprints would be impossible to see on the hard ground.

I went forward. She was lying on her side, head slightly fallen down, her hair and her shawl covering most of her face. When I moved the body very gently to put her back, I saw at once where all the blood had come from.

Someone had beaten her face with a stone or something as hard. The features, bloody and distorted and battered, were nearly unrecognizable. It was horrible, vicious damage. Done with the force of anger behind it. And she must have looked at her attacker as it was happening.

Had she fought? I lifted the hand I'd seen in the beginning. There were bloody, broken fingernails, and one had a bit of what appeared to be wool yarn heavy enough to have come from outer clothing. And the other hand was much the same, although it had been smashed with the same stone, possibly as she had tried to shield her face.

Knowing what to look for now, as I gently put the body back the way I'd found it, I scanned the space around her. And there, in the shadows of the side of the rock face, was an irregular bit of limestone.

I had been kneeling, so I now got up and walked over to it. Without touching it, I could see bits of hair clinging to it. And bloody bits of her face.

I pointed it out to Arthur, who had kept his distance, and saw the grimace of fury spread across his face.

Someone behind him spoke quietly, and Arthur said to me, "We must go. I don't think Wade should find us here."

"I can find my way back alone. You should stay. He'll expect to find you here."

He turned to one of the men. I remembered him, I'd spoken to him before, near the kitchen garden.

"Ed. Can you see her back safely?"

The farmer nodded, and we set off together. But not before I'd cast one last glance at the quiet, forlorn figure lying there as the first rays of sun broke over the eastern fell.

We said nothing for a time. It was easier going, downhill, but I had to watch my feet as we hurried. Until we reached Bald Willie, my back had felt stiff and vulnerable, waiting for a shout from the police telling me to come back at once.

But after the bench, the light was better. I said to my companion, "Does anyone know who she is?"

"Aye. Lettie Bowman's girl."

I had no idea who Lettie Bowman was.

He read that in my face. "Her was wet nurse to Mr. Gordon. Her had a stillborn babe, and plenty of milk. So Lettie was brought up to the House. But Judith is her name, her daughter. She lived with her mother in the village."

"If she lives in the village, what brought her to the outcropping in the middle of the night?"

"Mayhap she didn't start to go there."

He was right. She may have died there—but how she came to be there had died with her.

Men were leaving the house, on their way home to morning chores. No rest for them. But the soup and tea had done them good. They seemed less silent and more awake now. They looked at me as I came down with Ed, curious, but not asking what I'd seen. I was sure Ed would be asked those questions as soon as I was out of sight.

I thanked him for seeing me safely home, and he went down to the kitchens for his own soup and tea. I started down the passage on my way to the stairs. The sitting room door opened, and Mrs. Neville stepped out. Seeing me, she beckoned urgently, and I went to join her.

The room was empty. A fire was burning on the hearth, and I began to unbutton my coat as the heat hit me after the morning chill out on the fells.

"Tell me," Mrs. Neville said, leading me to the chair across from where she had been sitting.

I hesitated, ordering my thoughts, trying to keep my personal feelings out of what I could tell her.

"Don't hold anything back, Bess. Please. I need to know."

"It was a woman. She was lying on the ledge of the outcropping. And she was dead. Someone had battered her face with a lump of limestone. She fought back, while she could. There was no time to ask Arthur any questions—Inspector Wade was on his way. He'd been with another search party, and they'd had to send for him. But Ed—the tenant farmer—saw me safely back to the house. And he told me that he believed it was Judith, Lettie's daughter."

She had covered her mouth as the shock hit her. "Oh, dear God! Oh—*no!*"

Mrs. Neville sat there in shocked silence for all of a minute. I said nothing, letting her absorb the news.

She stood up. "I must go to Lettie. Losing her son in the war and now Judith—"

I had to stop her. "No, you mustn't. Not yet. Inspector Wade hasn't informed her. I don't know if anyone has told her yet."

"To the devil with Inspector Wade!" she said angrily. "At least he can't hold Gordon to account for *this* death!"

I bit my tongue. I was still the only one who knew that Gordon Neville hadn't been in his bed part of last evening. I still didn't know what to do or say about that. Duty said I must report what I'd observed. Not only as a nurse, but also as a person. If I spoke up now, it would be seen as Gordon's guilt. But was it? Inspector Wade was bent on charging him already, and this would seal Gordon Neville's fate. Did I have the right to withhold what I knew—because a man's life depended on it—until I could better judge that knowledge? Until I knew more?

There wasn't time to consider what my actions ought to be.

I still had to convince Mrs. Neville not to make a precipitous visit to the waiting mother in the village—the woman who had been wet nurse to her son.

And it occurred to me that Mrs. Neville mustn't go there with any suspicions about that son's guilt. Lettie Bowman would have enough time to hear what happened—what might have happened. She needed comfort now.

I said again, "It might not be wise to go before the Inspector has called—"

"Bess, I've known since one in the morning that Judith was missing. I had to see to the men doing the searching. Now I must be with her mother when the news is brought to her."

And that was a very different perspective. I'd been so worried I hadn't seen the visit in that light.

"Yes, of course. Even the Inspector can't fault that. I'll see to things here, if you aren't back by breakfast."

"Thank you, my dear. I'm so glad you're here. Now I must send word to the stables." She gave me an unhappy smile.

I stood there in the middle of the room, listening to her steps fading down the passage.

She was right, she'd seen the real need.

If I wasn't careful, I'd betray myself . . .

There was a tap at the door, and one of the maids came in with a tray. It held a small pot of tea, a single cup, and a dish of toast. "Oh," she said, looking around the room. "I was to bring her tea here."

"Ruth, isn't it?" She had taken trays up to Gordon.

"Yes, Miss."

"Mrs. Neville was called away. But I could use it myself."

"Are you sure, Miss? I can easily bring another pot."

"She had to go out. It will be all right."

Ruth nodded, satisfied. She crossed the room and set the tray on the small table by the arm of the chair where Mrs. Neville had been sitting.

As she was leaving, she said, "Is it true, Miss? What Ed was saying in the kitchen? That it was Judith?"

"I'm afraid so."

"How awful! He said her face—that he hardly knew her."

"I expect so," I said. Being circumspect.

"That's really terrible, Miss. She was nice. She lives—lived—some doors down from where my mum and dad live. We was of an age. I can't think why someone would want to do anything to Judith."

"Did she have any family?"

"There's her mum. She lost her brother in the war. Teddy, too. I always thought he'd marry her when he came back. But he never did. None of them did. They're all buried in France. They *say* they know where. I can't see how they do, with so many dead. I think they tell us that to make the families feel better."

"Who put up the cross in the village square?"

"That was Drake." She shook her head. "I never could think why his mother named him that."

Remembering her place, she bobbed a slight curtsey and was gone.

The tea was ready to pour. I was really grateful for it, and yet I wouldn't have the courage to ring and ask for any, given how busy the staff must be. I sat down in the chair and took a piece of toast.

The night and the morning washed over me. I found it hard to keep the image of Judith's face out of my thoughts.

Could Gordon have done such a thing, especially to the daughter of the woman who had nursed him?

But then who could? What had she done to deserve to die like that? And why, with the village and both sides of the dale, the woods along the stream—why with all those places available to the killer—had she died on the outcropping?

To put the blame on Gordon?

Or was that as far as he could reach, when he slipped out of the house?

But how did she know to come there, to meet him?

The questions circled in my head, in spite of the tea and the toast.

I finished more quickly than I'd have liked. I had to reach Gordon before the news broke. Asleep or not.

Draining my cup, I went up to his room.

He was still asleep.

I put a hand on his good shoulder and gently roused him.

He lashed out with his good arm, opening his eyes in alarm.

As he realized who was there, he frowned. "Bess? What time is it?"

"It's nearly seven. They'll be bringing you breakfast soon, I need to talk to you—"

He interrupted. "What was all the noise last night? I wanted to get up and find out, but I was afraid Wade had reappeared. But then he never came up to my room."

"It wasn't Wade. Someone from the village came to tell Arthur that there was a person missing, and it was necessary to broaden the search in this direction. Arthur rang the fire bell."

"Was he found? Who was it? I know most of the people in this dale."

"It was Judith Bowman."

He struggled to rise up in the bed. "*What?*" Wincing as he used both arms, he sat up. "Is she all right?"

"I oughtn't to be the one who brings you the news. But in light of last night, you need to know what's coming. I'm afraid she's dead."

"Dead? How? *Tell me.*"

"She was killed. Someone used a stone to batter her face. She fought as long as she could. But whoever it was, was stronger."

"Gentle God," he said softly. "Are you sure? Yes, of course you are, you're a nursing Sister! Did you see her? Did you look for any signs, anything that could tell you who might have been with her?"

"You went out last night. Perhaps you saw something," I countered.

I thought he was going to erupt from the bed. If he'd had use of both arms, he might have been successful.

"Are you suggesting that I killed her?"

"She was found on your estate. And you were out, while we were at dinner. It will look that way to many people."

He swore then, dropping back against his pillows as he added savagely, "Damn it, she was Lettie's *daughter*! I wouldn't have touched her.

I've known her all her life, I liked her. I always have. Why the bloody hell would I want to kill her?"

Calming a little when I didn't answer, he said, "How many people know I left my room?"

"I'm still the only one who knows. If Wade finds out, he will charge you with her death." As I said the words, I realized that if he had killed Judith Bowman, he would have to kill me now as well. I knew too much.

"I'll speak to Arthur."

"No! He's a solicitor. You'll put him in a terrible situation."

With his good hand he rubbed his eyes. "God, yes, I hadn't thought . . ."

"And don't put this on your mother's conscience. She doesn't deserve it."

"No." He closed his eyes. "I wouldn't hurt her, Bess. I didn't do it."

"You put all of us at risk because you wouldn't stay in your room. What possessed you? A breath of fresh air? I refuse to believe it."

Before he could answer there was a tap at the door.

"Just a moment." I quickly arranged the pillows, caught up the scissors that thankfully were to hand, and was cutting away the bandage on his right arm when I called, "Yes, all right. Come in."

The wound had opened. The bandage was soaked with bloody infection, where it had drained in the night. Or after heavy exertion?

Ruth came in. "Cook says, she's sorry about breakfast, sir, but she's had her hands full. If you mind having it this early, she'll send another tray later."

"No, that's fine. Tell Mrs. Jenkins I understand."

As she set the tray on the table by the bed, she saw the open arm. "Oh, my, sir, that's nasty."

"It won't heal," I told her. "And it's causing him to run a fever."

She looked away, as if it turned her stomach. "No wonder we cut up his food," she said to me. And with a nod she was gone.

"How bad is it?" he asked, lifting his head in an effort to see his arm.

"I think some of the infection is draining." I didn't tell him I'd sniffed the bandage to be sure it wasn't becoming septic. "Whether there is more to come, I don't know. I was hoping to see Dr. Menzies yesterday, but he was out at one of the farms, or so I'm told."

"There are any number of small holdings. Over the years we managed to buy out a number of them, but these are hardy people. They don't give up their land easily." He returned to the death of Judith Bowman. "Lettie Bowman's husband died in a mining accident soon after Jamie was born. He'd gone there for better wages than he could earn as a farm laborer. Mother kept an eye on the family. We wanted to send Judith away to school. She was bright, she could have been a schoolmistress. But she didn't want to leave her family." He shook his head. "She has no enemies. My God, how could she have?"

I had cleaned and wrapped the arm, washed my hands at the washstand, and said, "I can shave you. It might present a better appearance when Inspector Wade arrives."

I'd done just that often enough in the base hospital. Beards could spread infection. He wasn't quite to that point, but he badly needed a shave, the dark shadow of his beard giving him a sinister look. Inspector Wade's suspicions were already well established, he didn't need more to drive him to a decision.

Gordon had no wish to have me shave him. But I did feed him his breakfast. It was not an enjoyable task. Still, while I was working with him, I asked, "Where did you go last night?"

I hadn't told him where Judith Bowman was found.

And again, he wouldn't tell me.

I set the tray outside his door for collection, and went to my own room.

Lillian was just lacing up her shoes. "You're an early riser," she said smiling. "I don't know why I overslept."

I could tell her. She was worried and under stress. It took a toll when sleep eluded her, and she usually only shut her eyes in earnest in the wee hours. It was only a matter of luck that last night she had fallen asleep by midnight.

And so, because everyone else would know very soon, if they hadn't heard the news already, I said, "Before we go down, there's something you need to know."

"They haven't come for Gordon, have they? Lady Beatrice—"

"He's still safely shut up in his room." I wished for a key to lock that door. "No, there's been another incident. Let me tell you what happened."

Lillian listened as I went through the night's events. "I don't know the Bowmans. I'm so sorry, Bess, it must have been rather awful for you."

"I worry for the family. I'm sure they must be terribly distraught."

She looked across at me in the matching chair. "I seem to bring sorrow wherever I go. Death, unhappiness, painful memories I can't seem to forget."

"You couldn't have known this was to happen."

"I couldn't have foreseen tragedies," she said quietly. "That's true. It's just that no matter how hard I've tried, I haven't been able to make the aftermath any better. One of the reasons I'm so grateful to Mrs. Crawford for finding me a place with Lady Beatrice is that there were only the two of us. I could let down my guard."

I thought she must be talking about the children who had been in her care. And so I said only, "Yes, Melinda has such a way of finding solutions that work. I'm glad you have been so happy in Yorkshire."

She got to her feet. "We must go down. They'll be needing us."

When we reached the dining room, only Margaret was there. Mrs. Neville had left for the village, Grace was still in her room, and Arthur was still out on the fell.

"I was told about poor Judith," she said as we walked into the room. "It's horrid. Who could have done such a terrible thing? And Arthur isn't back. I don't know–"

"He'll be waiting for the Inspector," I replied. "In Gordon's place, he's the head of the family."

"Poor darling." She sighed. "He's been happy in Richmond. He loves his work. He's always said he wasn't cut out for farming. He's rather like his Uncle Harry. *He* was a solicitor in York. Harry wanted Arthur to come down and join his firm, but Arthur preferred to be his own man. And I don't think he really wanted to be that far from home."

We managed to finish our breakfast in peace. The toast was a little scorched, the rashers of bacon limp, and the eggs more than a bit cool. But considering what Cook had on her plate this morning, no one said a word. The marmalade, a good Spanish variety, covered the worst of the toast problems.

We were just rising when Arthur came in. He looked haggard, and a light rain had begun to fall, he said, creating more problems. "Wade came, ordered the body taken down to Dr. Menzies's surgery, then left."

I wanted to ask if the Inspector had found the stone that could have been the murder weapon, but I didn't want to bring it up in front of Margaret and Lillian.

"He's not a local man," Arthur was saying. "He doesn't seem to see things our way. At the moment, he appears to be trying to make a connection with my brother. He asked if Gordon and Judith were *lovers*. And if someone were jealous. She was a pretty girl. But she wasn't even out when we went down to university."

But she must have been by the time they'd come down. Until the war. Still, I said nothing.

Margaret went back into the dining room with him, while Lillian and I went to the sitting room that Mrs. Neville seemed to favor. It was more comfortable than the formal rooms.

Lillian was just starting to say something about Judith Bowman, when the anticipated thundering at the main door could be heard.

Inspector Wade had arrived.

Mrs. Neville hadn't returned from the village, Arthur had apparently gone directly from the dining room out to thank the tenant farmers for their work as search parties, and so Davies showed the Inspector into the sitting room.

They were continuing their conversation as Davies opened the door, and I caught snatches of it before Davies was free to announce the policeman, which is how I heard about Arthur.

"I don't need permission," the Inspector was saying sharply to the butler.

"Sir, I take my orders from the Family. I always have." And then, "Miss Crawford, Miss Taylor, Inspector Wade."

He withdrew abruptly, without asking if we'd care to take tea with the Inspector. Perhaps he already knew that we had no such intention.

Lillian was the friend of the family, I was the outsider. And so I looked to her as the Inspector came forcefully into the room. "I should like to have the staff ordered to the Servants Hall, and I will use the housekeeper's room to interview them individually."

She cast an urgent glance at me, and so I said, "Yes, I understand. May I ask why you wish to question them again?"

"There's no 'again,' Sister Crawford. There was a murder last night on the estate's land. This is a separate inquiry."

"I see. I don't know how they could help you, but I'll speak to the housekeeper. I have no authority in this house to order anyone."

Frustrated, he said, "I'll see about that." He stood aside, waiting for me to precede him to the door.

I hadn't a choice, and so I escorted him to downstairs. Mrs. Roper was in her room, according to the scullery maid, and I went across and down the passage to tap on her door.

She looked up as I came in, surprised to see me there, then a frown followed as she saw the Inspector behind me. "How can I help you, Miss Crawford?" she asked, ignoring him.

"Inspector Wade has come to speak to the staff. About last night. Could we ask them to wait in the Servants Hall, while he sees them in your room, one by one?"

She threw him a glance of irritation. "We're just starting to prepare lunch," Mrs. Roper said half to him and half to me.

"Nevertheless."

Mrs. Roper had no one to take her part, and so it was done. She closed the housekeeping book she had been working with and rose from her desk. She and I left the cozy little room smelling of spices from the cabinet behind her desk, and the Inspector stepped around to take her place in the chair. I heard it creak as he sat down, and saw her wince.

She collected the staff, telling them to remember their place and not to gossip, then returned to her room, to be interviewed first. Davies was already there.

Mrs. Roper indicated with a tilt of her head that she wished to speak to me, and we moved into the kitchen, where Cook was peeling potatoes for the pot.

"What is this about? Poor Judith Bowman?" I nodded, and she went on. "But we were all here at dinner. How could we know anything about that?"

"I have no idea when she died." Rigor hadn't set in, the body was still pliable when I'd had to move it. And cold, from lying out. Still, that was no help.

Mrs. Roper shook her head. "I don't like agreeing to this, with Mrs. Neville not here. Or Mr. Arthur. He went out to speak to someone right after wolfing down his breakfast, and that'll come to no good."

She had known the brothers since Gordon and Arthur were born, I thought, and still saw them as the boys they had been, grown men and ex-Army or not. I hadn't heard anyone give either Arthur or Gordon their courtesy military title. I didn't even know what rank they'd held. It was Mr. Arthur and Mr. Gordon, sons of the house.

"Mrs. Neville will understand," I assured Mrs. Roper. "There's nothing you could have done, once he'd made up his mind."

And then Davies was leaving her room, his face flushed. But before we could speak to him, one of the bells rang, and he turned toward the stairs.

The door was still open, and I heard Inspector Wade call Mrs. Roper's name. She cast me a look that could have been a martyr going to her fate, and walked away.

Remembering my promise to Lady Beatrice, I left the kitchen, intending to go and warn Gordon—as Mrs. Neville had asked—when I saw Ruth, the maid, by the stairs. Her face was pale, and she was wringing her hands.

I walked over to her, and she leaned forward to whisper, "Miss, I'm ever so frightened."

"What is it?" I countered swiftly, sure Ruth had seen Gordon leave the house last night.

"It's Judith. She came to the house around teatime, and waited for me to come out. She had a note for Mr. Gordon, and she asked me to give it to him."

My heart sank. Was that how Gordon Neville had known she would be somewhere, waiting for him?

"What was in the note?"

"I didn't look. She told me it was from her mum. And so I took it up to Mr. Gordon straightaway."

"Have you told anyone else this?"

"No, Miss! After I'd heard—I don't want to go to prison, Miss! I meant no harm!"

"Nor did you do any," I told her, touching Ruth's arm for comfort.

"I'm sure Mrs. Bowman was worried about Mr. Gordon. That's all. But if I were you, I'd say nothing about that to the Inspector unless he asks you directly. You haven't done anything wrong. After all, did you see Mr. Gordon go out last night?"

"No, Miss, of course not!"

"Then there you are. That's what he wants to know. And you can be perfectly truthful about that. Mrs. Roper is right, family affairs should remain family matters, unless you are asked a direct question. And then you must tell the truth."

"Even about that note?"

"Even about that," I said, taking a dreadful chance, but knowing it was the right thing to do. "I've been told that Mrs. Bowman was Mr. Gordon's wet nurse, before Judith was born. And she's kept an eye on both brothers. No one had thought to tell her that he was hurt, but not dreadfully so, and she must have been sick with worry, just hearing the bare details of what had happened when Mr. Frederick died."

Her face cleared a little. I was saying a silent prayer that I wasn't lying. But I wanted to know more about that note before I took any steps.

"She does care for him. And the family has been kind to them after Mr. Bowman was killed in that dreadful mining accident." Reassured, she gave me a wavering smile. "Thank you, Miss. I didn't know what to do."

"Best to keep it to yourself until someone asks. Until then, it's not to worry you."

"Thank you, Miss!" she said again, and as we heard the door to the housekeeper's room open, she sped away to the Servants Hall.

I quickly and quietly went up the back stairs myself, not wanting to rouse any suspicion by lingering to hear what Mrs. Roper was asked.

I reached the bedroom floor without being seen, and went directly to Gordon Neville's room.

He was lying awake, staring at the ceiling. When I came in, he said at once, "I think I heard a loud knock."

"You did. Inspector Wade is in the kitchens, speaking to the staff. I'm sure he's asking if you had gone out to meet Judith Bowman last night."

"But I didn't. I didn't see anyone. I took care not to. You don't know what I go through, here in this bed, my mind busy and not able to even care for myself. I had to get out of here if only for a bit."

"What did the note say, the one that Ruth brought up from Judith?"

He had the grace to flush.

"It wasn't from Judith. It was from Lettie. She was worried. She had heard that I'd been hurt in the fall that had killed Frederick. And no one had come to tell her I was all right."

I remembered the girl who had come to her door and seemed to want to speak to me. Was that Judith? I thought she'd mouthed the word *Gordon,* and I'd shaken my head. Indicating he was all right. But what if she'd taken that to mean he was badly hurt and might not live?

"Then let me see it."

He shook his head. "I threw it in the fire while you were hanging up my cloak. I didn't think it should be found if there was a search of my room."

Had he burned it?

If it was in any way incriminating, I was certain he would have done. "You've set a pretty trap for yourself," I told him. "Judith comes to the house with a message, you wait your chance to go outside the house, and hours later she's found murdered."

He was angry. "None of that is true! Why should I hurt someone I cared about? No, not in that way," he added. "I told you. But I'd visit Lettie sometimes to tell her about school and what I was doing. Judith was small, a baby, then a toddler. She'd come and cling to my knee and

I'd give her a sweet. God, she was Lettie's *daughter*! I'd hardly sow any wild oats in that direction."

He was brutally honest. But there might have been other reasons why he might kill the girl that had nothing to do with a lover's quarrel.

And that reminded me of something else.

"Does— Did she have a beau? Was she walking out with anyone while you were away, or as you came home?"

"I don't think so. Jamie's death hit both of them hard. I don't think Judith was prepared to leave her mother alone." His mouth twisted in a grimace. "God knows, most of the eligible young men in the village never came home. Who is there to walk out with? There's hardship because the men who supported all the families are dead. And a good many of the girls won't marry."

He felt responsible. He'd led those men off to war and hadn't been able to bring them back.

"Do they hold it against you, that you came back whole—and others didn't?"

He closed his eyes against the pain, and it wasn't physical. "I can't blame them. But the Yorkshire regiments took heavy casualties. Out of seven hundred men in one of our battalions at the Somme, only a bare two hundred lived to see the end of it. Wounded, dead, missing. I watched them fall. I carried them back through the wire when I could. I held them as they died. But I couldn't *save* them." The words were wrenched out of him, the guilt overwhelming.

How many officers had told me the same thing? They knew every face, they knew how every man died. God knows, they wrote the letters home that would follow the official notification that had arrived at a soldier's door. There was no forgetting . . .

But he had successfully led me off the subject of Judith and that note.

I said, "I had to tell Ruth that if she were asked a direct question about that note, she was to give Inspector Wade the truth. She's not a part of any of this. She doesn't deserve to be."

"No." A pause. "And what will you tell him?"

"I don't know," I said. "I still don't know what the truth is." And I left the room.

Chapter Twelve

I HAD LIED for someone in my care before. In Ireland. I had done it purposely, to keep him out of prison as well. But I'd known why. Because in prison he wouldn't have survived. For several reasons. And he was innocent.

Why was I lying for Gordon Neville? I wasn't sure about anything. My promise to Lady Beatrice? Of course. But I also believed that one was innocent until proven guilty, and I also didn't trust Inspector Wade not to bully my patient. And until I was sure about Gordon, I didn't want to do something I might regret, including handing him over without any evidence. I was fairly certain Arthur Neville would stand behind me, if I was in any trouble over it.

As well I could be. This made me an accessory to any crime Gordon Neville had committed. And that might well be two murders . . .

Unhappy about the whole affair, I went down the stairs.

I knew how Gordon had felt, if he was telling the truth about last night. I wanted to escape the house myself. But after my experience with that dog and his master, I didn't feel safe going off the grounds. And I wasn't comfortable on the fells, either. They had seen two deaths already.

And so I took refuge again in the library, a handsome room with a lovely ceiling, bookshelves, map tables, and comfortable chairs. A desk stood at the window end, with a view of a terrace and borders. I sat down in the first chair I came to, sinking into well-worn leather as smooth as the years could make it.

Remembering that I'd first seen Mark Caldwell here, I wondered where he'd disappeared to. He'd given every impression of staying at the Hall until the funeral.

About to make trouble, most certainly. And I wasn't sure he would care either way about Judith Bowman's death, unless it could somehow be tied to Gordon Neville along with Frederick's death.

Putting him out of my mind, I tried to think instead about what I should do, before I found myself in serious trouble.

The simplest answer was to tell the truth. But truth could have unforeseen consequences. That was my dilemma.

I tried to tell myself that I should never have come to Yorkshire—should never have stayed after I got there—and should have refused to come to Scarfdale at Lady Beatrice's request.

That didn't fly either. I was *here*. Wishful thinking would get me nowhere.

Either Gordon Neville was a consummate liar—and some murderers were just that. Or he was innocent. It was a toss of the dice at the moment.

I'd been lied to in hospital by men who wanted to return to the trenches before they were fully healed refusing to accept the need to stay another handful of days until they had got their strength back to the point where they could keep up racing across No Man's Land in the next attack.

It was a lie practiced by men in the ranks afraid to leave their comrades to fight and die without them. And by officers, who had come to believe that their men needed them to survive. I'd often had the task of telling a doctor what I believed to be true. Not what I felt was wrong. And yet I'd managed to hold back some of the men who were actually still too weak to fight. In spite of their vociferous protests and the doctor's skepticism.

This wasn't the same. There I only needed to draw on my best medical judgment to defend my position.

I was still quarreling with myself over that problem when there were sounds in the distance that told of arrivals. A motorcar that was not Lady Beatrice's was passing beyond the tall hedge at the end of the library's little garden. I had noticed the small turning off the main drive when I walked to the village, and from Bald Willie I'd seen how that led to the carriage house, where now the motorcar must be garaged.

Then I remembered the car that had just passed. Mark Caldwell was back.

I got up, walked out of the library, and went up a separate flight of stairs, to avoid him. But as I was walking down the passage toward our room, I heard a distinctive voice welling up from the front hall.

Lady Beatrice's fine motorcar was pulled up to the front door and she had made her entrance.

"Davies," she was saying, "you must tell me what is going on here. And Wilson is with me, is there room above the coach house for him, or must you send him down to that wretched pub?"

"There's room, my lady. Of course there is. As to what's happening, it's best that you speak to Mrs. Neville."

"There's a black bow on the door's knocker. Who's dead? Is it Gordon? You must tell me, I can't wait any longer."

"He's very much alive, my lady–"

"Then the rest can wait." She sailed into the hall, walked down the passage, and said over her shoulder, "Where's Anne? Mrs. Neville? Is she in the sitting room?"

He hastily closed the door and trotted after her.

"I'm afraid she's in the village with Mrs. Bowman—"

"Well, then, Lillian? Sister Crawford? Where are Arthur and Gordon?"

"If you care to wait in the small sitting room, my lady, I'd find them and ask Mrs. Roper to bring you tea." He sounded slightly harassed.

"Do that, please, Davies. And then I should like to go up to my room. We left in the dark. I'm not as young as I once was."

"Yes, my lady."

I didn't wait to hear any more. I dashed down the passage to our room. The door stood open, and Lillian was already carrying the last of our things to the smaller room next to ours.

"You should have let me help you," I told her, feeling a pang of guilt.

"I know, but I had such a strong feeling that she would come today, and the more I thought about that, the more I felt the need to make the change. She'll want to rest."

I helped her settle the last armload. "She's here. She just arrived."

"Oh, good heavens!" Lillian went to the mirror, smoothed her hair and her dress, and turned to me. "I must go down. Where is she, do you know?"

"The sitting room. Davies has sent for tea and is looking for us, I expect. There's no one else here."

She started briskly for the stairs. I went back into our former room, made a swift search to make sure that all was well. The bedclothes had been changed, there were fresh towels at the washstand, and the coverlet was as smooth as a calm sea. There was a fire on the hearth, and I'd send someone up with hot water as soon as I could.

Satisfied, I went after Lillian, following her down the stairs. I could hear her greeting Lady Beatrice and asking about her journey, and I slowed my pace a little.

Lady Beatrice was gracious, but by the time I'd reached the door, she was already asking, "Could someone please tell me what is happening? Just that cryptic message from Arthur, no news, only *I think you'd better come as soon as you can.* I had to ask Davies whether that black bow signified that Gordon was dead."

"I'm so sorry—" Lillian began.

I stepped into the room, and Lady Beatrice said, "Bess. That dress is very becoming. I promised you you'd like Mrs. Foster's skill."

"Yes, as it turned out, I am grateful indeed," I said, realizing she was intentionally shifting her attention toward me. Perhaps she'd rather not hear any distressing news from Lillian. "But perhaps you'd rather hear what we found when we arrived ourselves."

She pointed to a chair. "Please. I've been worried enough that I brought Dr. Halliday with me. That's what took an extra day."

"You did?" I asked blankly, unable to think of anything cleverer than that.

"Yes, we dropped him in the village. He wanted to speak to Dr. Menzies. Wilson will collect him as soon as the luggage is in."

"They know each other?" Lillian asked.

"I don't believe they do. Courtesy, you know, to let the local man see that there won't be any toe-trampling."

Or to learn the facts before ever setting foot in the house.

And so I told her, in the words I might have used for Matron, what had transpired. Leaving out only what ought to be left out, and not making any personal comments.

Except for her changing expressions, she didn't interrupt me. I was just finishing when Mrs. Roper came in with tea. She greeted Lady Beatrice warmly, and told her she had sent one of the maids up with hot water and some of Lady Beatrice's favorite bath salts, to make all ready for her.

Lady Beatrice thanked her, and when the door had closed behind the housekeeper, she said to us, "Well, I shall soon set this Inspector Wade to rights, and as for Mark Caldwell, he's no gentleman and never has been. I know his family, and I despise all of them." She moved to the tea table with accustomed ease and began to pour, firing questions at me.

"How serious is this arm wound?" I explained to her that deep infection needing surgery was the greatest fear.

"And what precisely killed poor Frederick?" Spinal and neck injuries from the fall, as far as I could see, and Dr. Menzies seemed to agree.

"But there must be something else behind this absurd notion that Gordon took him to that outcropping with the intent to kill him for taking Grace away all those years ago."

"I don't think he likes the people in this house—or in any house this size." God alone knew what he'd make of a Dowager Countess with the force of Lady Beatrice.

"Oh yes, I've met his sort. They come out of the collieries, acquire a little education, and begin to believe they know what is best for the rest of us. It's exactly what got the Czar and all those children killed."

I blinked. I hadn't quite thought of it in that way. But the Czar, Czarina, and the Romanov children had been reported shot in the basement of the house where they'd been taken, far from the palaces of St. Petersburg, because there was a new order sweeping through Russia. Another outcome of the war, because the Kaiser reportedly had sent the exiled Vladimir Lenin back to Russia from Switzerland, to foment Revolution and take the Russian Army out of the war. Which he had most certainly done well.

I said diplomatically, "I think you should speak to Mrs. Neville or Mr. Arthur before deciding on a course of action."

"Well, I intend to see Gordon straightaway." She finished her cup and put it down. "Since no one else seems to be here, perhaps you would take me up to his room."

We rose and walked with her. Lillian looked apprehensive. I knew how much she disliked confrontations of any kind.

I tapped lightly on Gordon's door, opened it, and said, "Your godmother is here, Gordon. Do you feel up to a visit?"

Lady Beatrice stepped around me. "Good day, my boy. What's this about you breaking an arm, and poor Frederick dying of his wounds?"

I don't think he was prepared for her. I saw him try to rally his forces as she crossed the room with brisk steps and came around to kiss him lightly on the forehead. "There," she said, straightening up to smile at him. "That will have to do by now. As for the police, I'll soon have them out."

"Aunt Bea, you can't—you'll only make matters worse," he said straightaway, for she left him no opening to greet her, taking charge as I'd seen her do so often before.

"And I shall be the judge of that." She turned, smiling, to us. "If you will give us a few minutes? I'd like to hear Gordon's version of events."

We left them together.

Mrs. Neville was just returning.

"I saw the motorcar outside Dr. Menzies's surgery, and Wilson brought me back to the house," she said, walking into the sitting room. Looking around her at the comfortable chairs and the peace there, she sighed. "I must ask Mrs. Roper to light the fire in the small drawing room."

"I'll speak to her, shall I?" Lillian volunteered.

"Thank you, Lillian. I see she's had her tea. Where is she now?"

"With Gordon." With a smile, Lillian left. Always looking to be useful, never easy in the company of the family.

"Yes, of course." Mrs. Neville took off her hat and set in on the sideboard. "Well, Bess," she said and gave me a wry look.

"How is Mrs. Bowman?"

"As you'd expect. She's lost both her children now. And she was terribly worried for my son." Sitting down in one of the chairs, she leaned her head back for a moment. "The village didn't take much note of Frederick's death. I doubt most of the people hardly knew him. They would see him on the fells, but there's no church in Scarfdale. And so we either held worship services here or traveled to the next village, which has a small chapel built in gratitude by some distant Neville who survived God knows what. Crusades?" She shook her head. "At any rate,

Frederick was a source of curiosity, of gossip even. But he didn't touch their lives. Judith did. Everyone had known her since the day she was born. And there are whispers now."

"Oh, dear." I hadn't realized I'd spoken aloud.

She lifted a deprecating hand. "Exactly. She died on our land. Gordon is already under suspicion for one death in that same place, and now there's another. Ergo, he must have committed both."

"But surely they know him? They know better?"

"Before the war, yes, very likely. But most of the village men went to enlist when Gordon and Arthur did, and too many of them didn't come back. Both my sons did, with scars on their bodies, probably in their minds as well—I've seen the signs—but they are *whole*. One man nearly lost his sight, two others have lost limbs, another had half his jaw shot away. The list is long. And there is—resentment. Why didn't Gordon protect them?"

"Why does he bear the whole blame?"

"He was their officer on the Somme. Arthur wasn't. And Yorkshire was hit hard."

The Somme was such a bloody battle that over twenty thousand men died or were severely wounded the *first* day. Over the long months of fighting that followed, no less devastating, the toll had climbed without pity. I remembered a letter from my father telling me that Ian was there, that he'd been wounded but was patched up and sent back. There was no time for healing, the Army needed any man who could fire a rifle. I remembered too a distraught doctor telling me later that there had been no time to save everyone, that he had to take only those with the best chance to live. And watch the others die. He shot himself when he came back to England. He'd managed to cope somehow as the war went on and he could serve. But the ghosts followed him home, and there were no wounded to keep him from seeing the dead.

"It would have passed in time," she said, referring to the resentment.

"The village depends on the house, and after a while, we might have returned to the old ways. This tipped the balance in the wrong direction."

"How does Mrs. Bowman feel?"

"She knows Gordon couldn't have killed Judith. I mean to say, *why?* There's no possible reason."

And then without knowing it, she blew away my peace.

"There's even a whisper going around in the village that someone in dark clothes was seen lurking near the old laithes barn late that night."

There was a possible witness.

I'd seen this same laithe from the outcropping, and Lillian had told me later that they were scattered all over the dales, these old barns. In the past, building a few secondary ones at a distance from the main barn made sense in the harsh winters, for man and beast and feed alike. All that was needed in place, to keep everyone alive.

Gordon hadn't told me he'd gone as far as that. Not as far as the outcropping, and that was nearer than the barn.

Yet behind the rumor had to be some truth.

Mrs. Neville was picking at the seam in her pretty blue skirt. "I was glad I could say with absolute certainty that Gordon was lying in his bed, in pain, and unable even to leave the room."

I looked away, fearing what she might read in my eyes. Doubt, not absolute certainty.

"And you might as well know the worst of it. Lettie had sent Judith out with a note to give to Gordon, asking to know if he was all right. She never came home. And now Lettie is blaming herself for letting her worry over Gordon send poor Judith to her death."

Shocked, I said, "You're saying that she believes if Judith had not gone out on such an errand, she'd be alive now?"

"Yes, sadly." She sighed. "That's why I was there for so long, comforting her. And there was no comfort I could give. Not when she was blaming herself . . ."

Mrs. Neville rose and walked to the door. As she reached for the knob, she turned and gave me a rueful look. "I didn't mean—I can count on your discretion, Bess?"

"Yes—you know you can," I replied at once.

And she was gone. Already regretting confiding in a relative stranger. But she had needed to tell *someone* before she had to face Lady Beatrice with this trouble so fresh in her mind. She had wisely sent Lillian away, not wanting to burden her with such knowledge.

She had no idea the burden she had given me to carry.

It didn't occur to me until I had wandered about the house on my own, unable to settle, that I had been too caught up in the knowledge I had carried to ask her who was spreading the whispers about seeing someone out in the night, close by where Judith had been killed.

Was it just a whisper, spread maliciously? Or was it true that someone had seen Judith leave as well, and in following her, had somehow caught sight of Gordon as well?

Mrs. Neville was already regretting her confidences. It was too late to go to her now and ask questions about them. Even for Lettie Bowman's peace of mind.

I opened a door into the large, formal dining room. I'd seen it before but had never had a reason to step in. It was quiet in there, the draperies drawn. A beautiful room with an elegant plaster ceiling, a blue-silver paper on the walls that reminded me of waterfalls in the snow, and the long table covered with a white gleaming cloth.

The first thing that caught my eye was the centerpiece of the table. It was an ornate porcelain masterpiece, a large blue bowl fluted in white and filled with a bouquet of exquisite flowers in colors so vibrant they looked as if they were real. At either side was a tall candlestick holder, with vines and tiny flowers and butterflies entwining the white porcelain to a fluted base for the dark blue candles.

I had seen Meissen pieces in some of my travels, and I wondered if this was another.

It was so entrancing that I moved closer, just as the door at the far end of the room opened, and Mark Caldwell stepped inside, book in hand, his attention on quietly closing the door behind him.

I stopped—and he did as well, as soon as he saw me standing by the table.

I said the first thing that came into my head.

"Oh. I'm sorry, I thought you were away."

"I was," he answered in the same way, as if he too were caught off guard. "I know I'm not wanted here. I've even taken my meals in my room." The ill-temper was back now in full force. "Still, I have no intention of going away until I know what happened to Frederick." His voice was cold, a cold anger that could be dangerous. I'd seen it before in some people.

"I'm sorry," I said again. "It's a grave loss for you."

I'd thought he'd gone to bring back Grace's parents. But he said now, "I sent the necessary telegrams. My responsibility, or I'd never have left."

Had he been here—in his room—when Gordon Neville so foolishly dressed and went out?

Before I could respond to that, he'd turned on his heel and left.

I had the room to myself again, but the tranquility had left with him.

I went away myself, to the only place I could be sure he couldn't follow.

Dinner was late—after two—and Cook must have been tearing her hair. The chicken was dry, the potatoes stiff, and the glaze on the carrots was beginning to seep into a sauce. And this only served to put supper off for another hour. It was after eight when we came through. No one seemed in the mood to linger over their drinks.

Dr. Halliday had arrived in time to dine with us, then gone up to have a look at Gordon's arm. Conferring with me afterward, he approved the treatment that Dr. Menzies had instituted, added one more ointment that he told me was showing some promise in treating wounds in a York hospital, then went up to his room.

"I shan't have supper with the family," he told me as he was leaving the sickroom. "At best I had two hours of sleep last night, coming up from York late, and then leaving at an hour that God never meant man to rise. I'm leaving tomorrow morning, if I can. I have patients in York who need me more than Mr. Neville. But you must be wary. A wound like that can indeed turn septic. A pity to lose his arm after he came marching home from war."

I went down to the kitchen and asked Mrs. Roper to send up hot water and to take up a second tray when the time came.

"May I ask what Dr. Halliday had to say about Mr. Gordon's arm? Ruth tells me she saw it and it was nasty."

"We're doing all we can. It wasn't kept clean after the break occurred. Sheep droppings and dirty bits of wool can cause all manner of problems."

"I just wish," she said pensively, "that we could go back the way we were. Before the party was planned."

"Oh—" I said, remembering. "Tonight is Mrs. Neville's birthday party."

"She's asked that we don't make a fuss after all. She told me this morning that Mrs. Caldwell is in deepest mourning, and it wouldn't be fitting to have even a small celebration."

Which, I thought, was typical of Mrs. Neville.

I didn't see Ruth while I was down in the kitchen. I wondered if she was avoiding me.

We were all there for supper, only Dr. Halliday missing. I wasn't sure there was room for him, anyway, as we were already eight in the small dining room, and without the friendly atmosphere of a dinner party, with the servants moving about, the candle stirring, the small dining room felt oddly crowded. Neither Gordon nor Frederick were here, of course, and yet they were much on our minds. Their empty seats were like ghosts in the room no one wanted to address. And no one suggested opening a window to let in the evening air.

It was about as pleasant as having a meal in a pit of vipers. Mark Caldwell was glowering, Grace, beside him, was staring at her plate, with nothing to say to anyone. Arthur's mouth was tight, Margaret seemed nervous, and so did Lillian. Mrs. Neville, doing her best to play the kind hostess, was finding it hard going. Lady Beatrice, on the other hand, said to the table generally, "I am sorry we find ourselves here in these extraordinary circumstances, it cannot be easy for any of us. But out of courtesy to the house, we must behave with decorum. Is it understood?"

I saw her glance sweep the faces across the table, resting for seconds longer on Mark Caldwell's.

That said, she opened the next conversational topic with a reference to seeing so many ex-soldiers begging on the road, and asking Arthur if many came to the house.

"We've seen a few. And done what we could. We're rather out of the way for anyone looking for work."

"Sad, isn't it? They fight for King and Country, then are abandoned when they are no longer needed. I've seen more than my share, unfortunately. There is little work to offer them."

When no one took the topic further, she turned to me. "I believe you worked with the wounded throughout the war. Is that not true?"

"Yes, I did."

"How absolutely fine of you to serve your country that way. I take it your parents agreed to let you train?" She already knew most of this about me, but she was making certain that the table stayed on safe subjects.

"They worried, of course, but as they knew I wanted to serve rather badly, they allowed me to sign the papers." I didn't add that we had had long discussions of the wisdom of volunteering, and I'd been amazingly persuasive in my arguments. I'd wanted that badly to train.

She said now to Margaret, "You did wonders, raising money for the care of widows and orphans. I've heard from friends just how marvelously you managed. It's a credit to you, my dear."

That topic failing quickly to interest anyone else, she turned to Grace. "And you, my dear. Shall we be seeing your parents soon? I remember your mother from your wedding. A lovely woman. I'm sorry to meet her again in these circumstances."

Grace didn't look up from her plate. "They are seeing to matters at home, Lady Beatrice. The church, the Vicar . . ." Her voice trailed off.

It was Lillian's turn to speak, but she was spared the experience by Davies conferring with someone at the door of the room, speaking softly to him.

Davies turned back to the diners, and said, "Beg pardon, my lady. But the Inspector is at the door. He wishes to come in and interview the family."

"Tell him we are at our meal, and we will speak to him when it is finished."

Lady Beatrice had taken it upon herself to respond.

Davies tried not to look at Mrs. Neville, his face rigid.

"Is that wise? To provoke him?" Mrs. Neville asked Lady Beatrice in a quiet, neutral voice. "The repercussions . . ."

"My dear, he's a policeman. He can wait." She looked around the table. "Hugh went foxhunting with Danny. Lord Broadhurst. He's the Chief Constable now." She spoke of this man in an ordinary tone of voice, stating mere facts. Not trying to impress anyone.

Mrs. Neville gave a barely imperceptible nod to Davies.

He said, "Yes, my lady," turned and walked out of the room.

But Mark Caldwell held a very different view of the matter. He began to rise. "I for one wish to speak to *him*." Referring to Inspector Wade.

Lady Beatrice, without raising her voice, said simply, "Sit down, young man. This is not your dinner table." As if he were an unruly child allowed to be among adults for the first time. That done, she turned to Arthur and began another one of her conversational ploys.

It was a long meal. I don't believe any of us enjoyed it.

And afterward, when we went into the salon where he was waiting, I could see that Inspector Wade was fuming.

As we took various seats, Lady Beatrice nodded to him, said with some authority, "Now then, young man, tell us what you need." As if he were a tradesman who had come to the house.

If he'd held strong opinions about wealth and aristocracy before, I thought to myself, they will have been heavily reinforced before this interview was over.

Gathering himself with an effort, he faced her squarely.

"And you are?"

"The Dowager Countess de vere Linton."

"And how are you connected with this family?"

"I am a family friend of long standing, and godmother to Gordon Neville."

He appeared to have come to the end of questions he could put to her. After a moment, he turned back to Arthur and said, "I have spoken to Mrs. Bowman."

I thought, *Here it comes* . . .

And fought to keep from glancing toward Mrs. Neville.

Walking to the hearth, where he would have a better view of our faces, he said, "She sent a message to this house by her daughter Judith just at sunset, Friday night. She *claims* she wished to ask after Mr. Neville's health, as she hadn't heard any recent news."

Inspector Wade left it there. Waiting for several seconds, to let that sink into our minds, he added, "Judith Bowman was at this house on Friday evening. And she never returned to her mother's home. Instead she was waylaid and brutally killed. On the land belonging to this estate."

I could see most of the faces myself. Arthur and Margaret appeared to be thoroughly shocked. Mrs. Neville had turned a little pale. Grace was paying very little attention, her mind somewhere else. Or so it seemed. Lady Beatrice was frowning. Mark Caldwell was flushing with anger.

He said, before anyone else could speak, "I've told you from the minute I arrived that there was a murderer in this house. Now perhaps you'll stop 'interviewing' us and make the necessary arrest."

I was thinking of Ruth, the maid, and how she would cope with this revelation. Because the Inspector would press the servants until he got his answer: who saw Judith and collected the message . . .

A sudden thought popped into my head, and before I could review it and be certain that it was wise, I spoke.

"Does Mrs. Bowman know that the message was delivered? If her daughter actually reached this house before she was stopped and killed?"

The Inspector glared at me.

"There was no message found on the daughter's person."

"Could the killer have taken it? To let it appear that the message had been delivered?" I'd kept my expression merely curious—or at least I hoped I had.

The others were looking at me now, including Grace.

"I don't know much about police matters, but I should think that it might serve the killer better, and cover up the time of death, if we thought she had reached the Hall and was turning back."

I could almost read his expression. Frustration. Anger. Even uncertainty. I expect he would have liked me to disappear from mind and memory, in a puff of smoke.

That was the trouble with truth, I thought in a corner of my mind. Once the genie was out of the bottle, it was difficult to stuff it back inside.

Only, this wasn't really the truth. It was just misdirection. But a necessary one, I believed.

I *knew* the truth. And I didn't want to see it become a weapon. Too many innocent people were going to be hurt before this was over. Some, like Lettie Bowman, already were. Still, I hoped that I was doing the right thing.

Chapter Thirteen

Lady Beatrice was regarding me with some surprise in her gaze. As if she hadn't expected me to take any part in the proceedings, and was not only caught off guard by my sudden interference but also rapidly reassessing me.

Mrs. Neville had quickly looked away, but not before I saw the flash of gratitude in her face.

Arthur, the solicitor, was quick to step in.

"I must say, Miss Crawford has asked a pertinent question. I'd like to hear your opinion of it, Inspector. How *do* we know if that message was actually delivered?"

It was like a game of chess, this whole inquiry, I thought. Move and countermove.

Traps and escapes.

Mark Caldwell cut in before Inspector Wade could find an answer.

"It doesn't actually matter, does it? She *had* come to the estate. She *was* killed on estate property. Before or after the message was passed is immaterial. The opportunity was here and was taken by someone. The only question I can see is, who did such a thing?"

"And why," Arthur put in. "There's generally a motive for murder, even among the mad. Why would someone wish to kill Frederick? Or

Miss Bowman, for that matter? Where is the connection between these two people that led to their murders within a week of each other?"

"Opportunity," the Inspector snapped, finally regaining his equilibrium after these attacks. "For the first time since the war began, these people"—his finger drew us together in a circle of guilt—"these people have come together. That's your motive and your opportunity."

"We should call in Scotland Yard," Lady Beatrice said firmly. "This is too difficult a matter to resolve without the assistance of the Yard. I'll ask Jonathan to speak to the Chief Superintendent." She turned to the Inspector. "His name. Do you know it?"

Inspector Wade said, "I am not ready to summon the Yard to Yorkshire, Lady Beatrice. I know this dale, and I am far better suited to look into these murders than a Londoner with no experience of them."

I thought he was surely fighting a rearguard action, and was about to go down to ignominious defeat before Lady Beatrice's passion for interfering.

But she said, "Yes, there is some truth to that. But you do understand. If we don't have a murderer in custody by Tuesday next, I shall ask the Chief Constable to call in the Yard. And as he knows me personally, you can be assured that he will listen."

This was Saturday. Only a handful of days . . .

"Thank you, Lady Beatrice," the Inspector said grudgingly. He wanted no support from her hands. Or anyone else's for that matter. He turned to Arthur. "I will bid you good night."

Without another word he walked out of the room, and just after, we could all hear the main door slam shut. With some force.

"Well I'll be damned," I heard Arthur say under his breath.

Lady Beatrice was already questioning Mrs. Neville. "Is any of this business about a note true?"

"I visited Lettie—Mrs. Bowman—today, and she was in an agony of fear that sending Judith out at such an hour, alone, made her some-how responsible for her daughter's death."

Margaret spoke for the first time. "I've walked down to the village and back, many times. And often alone. I never felt afraid. And she's lived here all her life. Very likely she never thought she would be un-safe."

"Yes, that's true," Mrs. Neville replied. "I mean, it isn't as if we have wild beasts lurking in the shadows of those sheep folds, or wild men either."

"What about these poor homeless beggars?" Lady Beatrice asked. "Are they desperate enough to commit murder?"

Margaret added, "She was alone, yes, but what use would it be to kill her—she wouldn't be carrying more than a few coins with her, if that. Hardly enough to keep a man alive for a day."

"I still think we need a more experienced man," Lady Beatrice said. Turning to the two men in the room, she added, "I have had a long and tiring day. Are the gentlemen returning to their port and cigars?"

Without glancing at Mark Caldwell, Arthur said, "I think not."

"Then shall we have our tea and then go up to our beds? I don't believe any of us are eager to continue this conversation tonight." And then, remembering that this wasn't her house to order about, she smiled at Mrs. Neville. "Don't you agree, Anne?"

"Yes, most certainly," she replied, and rang for tea. No one asked for a second cup. I excused myself to look in on Gordon Neville. I thought perhaps they might wish to discuss matters without me there.

He was restless, the arm draining, refusing to stop. His fever had not risen beyond what it had been last night, which gave me a little hope. But it was still too high for my liking.

While I worked, I said, "I expect your mother told you about what happened in the village?"

He said, more subdued than usual, "Yes. She did. Could you write a note for me tomorrow? I'll have someone take it down to the village."

"Inspector Wade knows about the note. I think we managed to distract him from pursuing that here at the house. Poor Ruth, she's caught in the middle, loyal to the family and endangering her own safety by keeping to herself what she knows did happen. If only you hadn't gone out that night—that puts you at risk, it drags the whole family into that poor woman's death, and people are having to lie on your behalf."

"I do realize that now. Too late to cry *Sorry* and expect anyone to believe me," he said soberly.

He was right, it was too late.

I didn't stay long. As soon as the arm was clean and dressed again, I left.

I was just passing the door to the room we'd vacated for Lady Beatrice when it opened, and she stood there in the doorway, a finger to her lips.

I stepped inside, and she closed the door afterward.

"How is Gordon's arm? Dr. Halliday is cautiously optimistic. But he has given Arthur a note for the police, in case that awful man tries to drag him off to a cell."

"I know how happy the Nevilles are to have that assurance." Although privately I wondered if Inspector Wade would honor it, even from a doctor with Dr. Halliday's credentials and training.

"Indeed." She led me over to the chairs by the fire. "Thank you as well, Bess, dear, for speaking up tonight. It was immensely clever—and quite true—what you told that man."

"I didn't intend to interfere," I said honestly. "I found myself speaking before I'd even thought through what I was trying to say."

"You are truly your father's daughter," she told me, leaning back in her chair, studying me.

"You know the Colonel?"

"No, I'm sorry to say. But Melinda is terribly fond of him and of your mother. I expect you know how highly she thinks of you. And as I think highly of Melinda and am fond of her as well, I had the good sense to listen to her when she wished to send you to Yorkshire."

It was high praise, but she had also got her way about things and could afford to be generous in her gratitude. The gown I was wearing this evening was further proof of that.

She was saying, "What are we to do about Gordon?"

"In what way?"

"I've known him since he was born, Bess. I find it extraordinarily difficult to imagine him killing anyone. Yes, I know, he was quite efficient at killing in France. He has the medals to prove it. But it is very different, I should think, shooting a Hun who has taken an oath to kill for his country and has you in his sights. And killing a man he's known since university."

It was true, most men came home from war and never harmed anyone again. The few who went on killing were either too damaged by what had been done to them in France to know how to live with peace—or able to kill long before they put on a uniform.

But as I had learned, people could see things quite differently. A man might convince himself that all the trouble or grief or hardship in his life could be removed by one simple act of murder. And want that badly enough to carry it out.

She looked terribly tired, and to change the subject I asked if there had been any problems with her surgery after I'd left to come here.

"Thanks to your excellent care—no, it was Dr. Halliday himself who said that, Bess, not I—although I completely agree—I am no longer on the mend. I am now fully recovered. Although Dr. Halliday has restricted my diet again. It appears that certain things don't agree with you after you've lost your gallbladder."

I smiled with her. And stood up.

"You must get your rest. I expect Lillian is asleep, but I can help, if you like."

She laughed. "My dear, I'm perfectly capable of putting myself into bed. Lillian loves to fuss over me, and I'll admit it's pleasant at my age to have someone who cares enough to want to make me comfortable. And so we manage quite well together."

Lillian was indeed asleep when I came into our room. Nights of sleepless worry had vanished with the arrival of Lady Beatrice.

As I turned down the coverlet to crawl into my side of the bed, I hoped I'd be as lucky.

The weather had changed by morning. The cool, pleasant days had given way to hot and humid air that seemed to hang above Scarfdale with no interest at all in shifting. By ten in the morning, the sun was hot on my face when I stepped into the gardens after breakfast. On the fells the sheep, all of them shorn by now, were sheltering in what shade they could find in the lea of the dry rock walls.

One of the maids said to me as I walked back inside, "It'ul storm now."

I smiled and agreed.

No one had lingered over breakfast, no one seemed to be inclined to talk about last night or the deaths or even how Gordon was fairing.

Dr. Halliday left for York just after breakfast. Wilson was to drive him to Richmond where he could take the train directly. Grace asked if she might go into Richmond with him, to order suitable clothing for her mourning. Both Margaret and Mrs. Neville volunteered to go with her on such an errand, but she told them firmly that she would rather do these things alone. At the last minute, Mark Caldwell insisted just as firmly that he would accompany her, as he wished to send another telegram. It was Sunday, but Arthur had reluctantly given Grace permission to stay in his house so that she could rest from her journey, buy what she needed on Monday, and return that evening.

He suggested hotels for Mark Caldwell.

In an odd way, her departure seemed to lighten the bleakness in the house, for her presence and her understandable grief were a burden we all carried for her. It was impossible to forget even for an instant how Frederick had died. Not that any of us wished to forget! But the respite allowed Mrs. Neville to see to household matters, while Margaret and Lillian entertained Lady Beatrice.

No one mentioned Mr. Caldwell's absence, but I for one breathed easier. It troubled me that he could remind me of Simon, even so very slightly, and be everything that Simon was not. I would have trusted Simon with my life, with the lives of my parents—I wouldn't have trusted Mark Caldwell not to stab me in the back as I left the room. Whatever anger and resentment he carried, whatever was on his soul, I was wary of him.

I saw the dog again later in the day.

I had walked to the gates of the drive for the exercise, accustomed as I was to being busy most of my day. From there I could almost see where the lane ended in the road that followed the Scarf into the village. And as I stepped through the gates without thinking, I glanced that way.

He was sitting upright on the lane some distance from me. As if on guard. Watchful. There was no one with him. No one to whistle him away. It was unsettling.

I turned back through the gates and went up the drive back to the safety of the house.

Mrs. Neville went again to visit Mrs. Bowman, taking another basket of food. I hadn't known she had carried one before, but as I took this one out to the motorcar, she said, "I know how much one loses one's appetite in times like this. I can't think she will even think of cooking."

I wondered if her neighbors wouldn't bring her dishes—it was common enough when people had lost a family member, but I thought Mrs. Neville's own sense of responsibility was adding to her concern for the family's wet nurse.

Did she wonder about Gordon's place in all that had happened? Or was she, his mother, sure that he had had nothing to do with either death? The upper classes had a way of hiding their feelings, of carrying on, making it impossible to be sure of what they believed or felt or thought.

Lady Beatrice was a master at that as well.

When I came into the sitting room after my walk, I saw that she had found a large table, an old family jigsaw puzzle, and was enthusiastically encouraging Margaret and Lillian to help her assemble it. It was an acceptable Sunday occupation. Even though we'd had no morning service, with the imminent departures, the pace of the house had slowed upstairs, but I could imagine that below stairs, work had lightened very little. I had glimpsed Ruth with an armload of sheets from Grace's room, hurrying toward the back stairs, before I'd gone for my walk.

I saw that the puzzle Lady Beatrice had chosen was a pretty scene in the heart of Paris, full of flowers and chestnut trees, mansard roofs and wet umbrellas as people did their marketing.

Margaret was doing her best to take on the role of entertaining her, but I saw her look up hopefully when I stepped through the door, as if I might have need of her elsewhere. Lillian, accustomed to working with her employer, was doing *her* best to please.

Lady Beatrice greeted me and said, "Ah, Bess. Can you tell us anything about these flowers in the stall outside that shop? Are these intended to be gladiolas? Irises? Roses?"

I had to come and look. To me the picture of painted flowers was indistinct enough to make it more difficult to assemble the puzzle, but I said, "Perhaps forsythia in that pail? It's tall and yellow. And yes, that could be gladiolas. I don't think *those* are roses. Something smaller?"

"Pull up a chair, my dear, and let's see what can be done here."

"I must change bandages again, I'm afraid. Dr. Halliday left strict instructions."

"Yes, of course."

And I escaped.

Dr. Halliday had awakened Gordon before going down to breakfast, so that he could leave directly afterward. He had reported to me that the arm looked less inflamed, and I was to watch it carefully for the next four and twenty hours.

I found the patient drowsing, the breakfast tray only partly touched. When I said his name, he opened his eyes and stared at me without some of the glitter of fever. A good sign!

"No peace, is there? In hospital, Sister would wake me to know how I slept."

I smiled. It was a common complaint among the patients. But we had so many in every ward, long rows of beds against either wall. And in the larger wards, sometimes we'd had to put beds down the middle, if there was a push on and the wounded were arriving in steady streams of ambulances. To attend them all, we worked early until late, and still had more to do for the very ill ones, those who couldn't feed themselves, or those too close to dying to be left alone.

I knew he was trying to ease the strain of our last conversation, and so I said, "Army rules."

He smiled. "Mother told me that Grace and Mark had gone into Richmond. Could I sit for a time? I shan't be able to walk."

I debated, then decided it might indeed be best if he sat up. At least while I was working.

His sheets needed to be changed as well, and I thought I could manage that, once I found the linen cupboard. It would be a reasonable excuse for allowing him to sit in a chair.

And so I helped him out of bed. He was weak at first, but quickly got his legs under him, making me wonder if in the still of the night he was walking about his room. There would be no one in the passage or in the room below to hear.

I dressed the wound, saw little or no change since early morning, and left it to air while I went to the bed.

Pulling first the coverlet and blankets away, I drew off the first sheet. Gordon said, "Here! What are you doing? It's the maids' work."

"And if someone comes in while you are sitting there as calmly as a well man, what are they to think?"

And then I saw it.

The crumpled bit of paper that was very likely the note from Mrs. Bowman, brought by her daughter.

For some reason I'd thought he'd had it with him when he came in from the fells, for he said he'd burned it in the fire on the hearth. Nor had I found it in the cloak's pockets, when I returned it to the armoire.

I reached for it.

He was out of the chair in an instant, and our fingers curled over the bit of paper at the same time. He towered over me as I leaned across the bedclothes.

I looked up at him, our faces barely a few feet apart. He didn't look away. Nor did he release his grip on the little knot of paper. It was hurting my fingers.

"Let it go," he said sternly. I could see the landowner and the officer in his eyes then. Certain of his right, unlikely to back away.

I challenged him anyway. "What's in it that you don't want anyone to see?"

"It was a personal message to me. It has nothing to do with you."

"Then let me summon your mother. Let her read it. Listen to me. She knows about this note. If it is brought up in the inquest, it would be far less damaging if she could say under oath what it contains."

"No."

What was in it?

I could believe it was from Lettie Bowman. She had said as much, and it made sense that in her worry and concern, she would write. But what else might it contain? A postscript from Judith that the police shouldn't see?

Can you meet me . . .

I'll be waiting at the usual place . . .

What was it I mustn't see?

It was an impasse. We stood there nearly face-to-face, leaning across the bed, our hands locked together. I could feel his breath on my face, he was so intense.

And then with a sudden, forceful movement, he managed to twist my fingers. And it hurt. In spite of my hold, in a reflex response, my fingers opened and he had the bit of paper, crumpling it even smaller in his left fist.

He straightened and started for the hearth. A fire hadn't been lit this morning, not with the weather changing so quickly, and while the house was still cool, it would be stuffy before very long.

Swearing under his breath, he tried to fumble one-handed for the matches in their pretty jar on the mantelpiece.

I got there in time to stop him, reaching for his arm. As he tried to shake me off, I said, "No. Listen to me. If you burn that now, and the inquest binds you over for trial, it could save your life to be able to show what is in it."

He hesitated.

But he didn't relinquish the message. Instead he turned, crossed the room to his desk, and opened a drawer. Shoving the bit in there, he half turned and said, "My keys. There on the tall chest."

I brought him his heavy ring of house and estate keys. Finding the one he wanted, he inserted it in the lock and twisted it. A tiny brass *click* followed.

There was no assurance that the message would rest for very long in that drawer. He was strong enough to rise as soon as I was out of the room, and put a match to it.

I'd done all I could.

It was on his own head if he refused to listen.

He walked back to the chair and sat down. I went on removing the remaining bedclothes. I'd just got it stripped when one of the other maids knocked.

She had come to take away the breakfast tray and was aghast to see me putting the pillow slips into the pile of linens.

"Oh, Miss, you shouldn't 'av. Let me fetch clean sheets, and I'll have it made up in a trice."

I smiled and thanked her, returning to rebandage his arm while she worked.

I asked him as she took the soiled linen away, "Is there any pain in that shoulder?"

"Twinges. When I forget. Otherwise, it's well enough."

He got into bed again on his own power, although it was left to me to arrange the pillows under his right arm.

"Sister. Bess," he said, once I was finished. "I know you have our best interests at heart. God knows why, we're strangers to you. But there are matters here that you aren't aware of. Be careful. Don't get caught up in something where you are vulnerable as a result."

"What matters?"

"Just let it go. I'll deal with it as soon as I can get out of this wretched room."

"That," I told him, "is going to depend on Inspector Wade. Not on me. If your arm begins to heal before he's got his answers, you may have to go to Richmond gaol until he does. I don't think he knows whether you are guilty or not. But you are the only logical suspect in these deaths.

If you aren't absolutely watchful, he will find a way to charge you and try you."

"How do you know so much about murder?" he asked, considering me thoughtfully.

"I don't. It's rather like nursing in a way. One is trained to think logically. To evaluate the patients individually, to consider all the possibilities from the symptoms that can be seen or must be searched for. To be objective. To collect information and put it to the right use. And do no harm." I smiled, remembering. "It has served me well, my training." I'd have to ask Ian sometime if this was how the police went about their inquiries.

I don't think he believed me, even though I was telling him the truth.

There was a skeptical expression in his gaze as I walked to the door.

The thought of that message, between my fingers, almost in my grip, so close and yet so easily taken from me, followed me down the passage as I left the room.

The thought occurred to me that I could enter the room when he was sleeping, find those keys, and unlock the desk. But I knew I wouldn't do that sort of thing. It was one thing to ask questions, another to cross the line into something I had no right to do.

Margaret met me in the passage. She had somehow escaped the great puzzle assembly.

Giving me a cheeky grin, she said lightly, "Mrs. Neville needs something from her room. It was as good an excuse as any I'd been able to think up."

"Lady Beatrice is trying to keep us distracted, she doesn't want us to worry. But I can't seem to stop worrying."

She put a hand to her face. "Nor I. I liked Frederick in many ways.

His death was a shock—doubly so because of the way it had happened, out there on the fell." She bit her lip for a few seconds, then added, "He and Arthur and Gordon came home safe from the trenches. I mean, the Germans failed to kill them. And then he is severely hurt all but on our doorstep—and then dies in his bedroom. In such a macabre, unforeseeable *fall*."

"Accidents do happen," I reminded her.

"Then why doesn't this feel like an accident? A terrible, wretched, senseless accident?"

"I expect it's the Inspector who makes everyone uncomfortable."

She smiled wryly. "I must tell you—I admired the way you stood up to him. It took more courage than I could muster—even Arthur was impressed. My only dealings with the police have been polite ones. The Constable on our street is a lovely man. Here—" She shook her head. "It's shockingly different. I find myself feeling guilty when he gives me that basilisk stare of his, as if *I've* done something wrong and he's aware of it."

"It's part of his police training," I suggested, trying to find a way to make it less frightening to deal with him. "Practicing that look in front of the mirror three times a day and four times on Sundays." Still, I'd never seen Ian with that look. Or some of the other policemen I'd dealt with. Inspector Wade was anything but objective . . .

The smile was real now. "I never thought—I shall tell myself that, the next time he stares at me."

I said, "Is it true that Frederick never was conscious, that he could leave no message for his wife?"

"Arthur said he would mumble things from time to time, but apart from saying he could not feel his arms and legs, no one could understand anything. Arthur was afraid it meant he was in great pain, but Dr. Menzies felt it was more his wounded mind still trying to function, unaware of the damage."

I'd seen it in the war, far too many times. A man barely alive, not yet fully unconscious, trying to speak. And what we could hear over the roar of the guns beyond us made no sense at all. I'd put my ear to their lips, and only once or twice caught a name.

"Thank you for telling me. I didn't want to ask Arthur."

"No. I don't know how he's managing to go on. He never wanted to be a barrister, he wanted to use his knowledge and experience helping solve legal issues for families who didn't know how the law could serve them. Not dealing with horrific crimes. It's one of the reasons I fell in love with him."

She walked on, and I turned into my own room.

I had it to myself for a change—unlucky Lillian was probably still trying to decide whether those were roses in the pail. But she and Lady Beatrice dealt comfortably with each other, and I didn't feel it necessary to rush down and rescue her.

I was glad that Gordon Neville hadn't burned that note, that he'd lied to me about that earlier. But why lie? And more importantly, would it ever see the light of day? That was the worry. I would have liked to tell Mrs. Neville that he'd kept it, but that would put her in a wretched position, if she asked to see it and he refused.

Well, there was nothing much I could do.

There was a tap at the door, and Mrs. Neville stepped in. I could feel myself looking like the cat with the mouse in his mouth—I'd just been thinking about her.

She said, "Bess, Lady Beatrice has taken it in her head to speak to Lettie Bowman. I can't possibly go with her, and Margaret is not particularly happy to accompany her. She doesn't know Lettie well. But a Dowager Countess showing up at her door is going to be a hardship for Lettie. She's not prepared to entertain, not in the midst of grieving. And Lady Beatrice can be, well, rather overwhelming."

"I wonder why she should wish to go there." Was she meddling?

Curious? Or trying to help without taking into account the fact that the woman was very likely still just coming to terms with her grief?

Mrs. Neville's eyes held a distinct twinkle suddenly. "You have spent a little time with her, I think. I don't believe the word *no* is in her vocabulary."

"Oh." I was caught off guard by her honesty. "I have to say you're right."

"Will you go with her? It's too much to ask, really, but it will be best for everyone."

"Of course. What about Lillian? Will she go with us?"

"I don't think so," she said, considering the question seriously. "You may even find it hard to insert yourself."

As I did.

CHAPTER FOURTEEN

I HAD TO explain to Lady Beatrice that my nursing instincts made me feel I should be sure Lettie was all right.

"She has Dr. Menzies just down the road," she reminded me.

I said, "He's a fine doctor, but I shouldn't think he was much of a comforter. And there's no Vicar in the village to offer consolation either. It must be terribly difficult for her." I meant every word, although it was also a useful ploy.

"Then come along, the motorcar is waiting. I'd like to have a rest before we dine."

Mrs. Neville had taken down a basket earlier, but she passed me a small bundle, warm in my hands as she stepped up into the motorcar. "It's a loaf, just out of the oven. I took some jam this morning, and a little butter."

And so I carried the warm loaf on my knees, while the open windows of the motorcar brought us heavy, warm air.

"A wretched day," Lady Beatrice commented. "I hope Grace is faring a little better in Richmond. She's an odd sort, you know. I never understood why Frederick and Gordon were so taken with her."

"I've only seen her as a widow."

"I expect it's something a man sees in her, that women can't."

This, coming from Lady Beatrice, was rather unexpected. I was glad that the Neville driver, in the front of the long Rolls, wasn't able to hear us.

And I remembered Diana, my wartime flatmate at Mrs. Hennessey's. She had a devastating smile, a way about her that drew people to her, men and women. She could flirt outrageously, and it was never taken as seriously meant. It was exciting to be in her circle, and the light could appear to go out of the room when she left it.

But Grace had something else. I couldn't quite put my finger on it. A way of separating what she was from what she wanted? Why had she chosen Frederick instead of Gordon, who stood to inherit the Hall? While Frederick was a younger brother.

The answer came into my head almost at the same instant. Frederick lived in a place that was just the opposite of quiet, bucolic Scarfdale. A place where she could shine as hostess, move in social circles, travel to Richmond and York and even London. Where she was admired and respected. Head of her own house, not under the thumb of another woman who had lived there longer and knew it more intimately.

Lady Beatrice was saying as we turned from the road into the lane, "I want to see this woman Lettie for myself. That note is disturbing. I'd like to know what was in it. A loving message—a need to hear Gordon was all right—or something that was too urgent to wait and worth the risk of sending her daughter out at sunset."

I nearly dropped the loaf of bread on my knees.

She turned her head and smiled at me. "It was you who questioned that message last evening. I've had all night and all day to think about it."

"I didn't mean—"

"I know you didn't, my dear. But the thought went into my head and stayed there. I found I couldn't get rid of it. You do remember that Lettie Bowman and I have something in common. I am Gordon's godmother, while she's his wet nurse. We have a bond with him that is hard to overlook in a time like this."

It was true. Godparents took their duties seriously, and I'd been told once by a wet nurse that holding a baby and caring for him and nursing him in those first weeks of life, keeping him safe and watching him grow, made him one of your own forever. Whether it was ever spoken aloud or not.

Feeling a little less awkward about putting myself forward to accompany Lady Beatrice, I also appreciated why she would have preferred to go on her own. I was young and had no experience of babies. They did.

"I'm glad you told me. Shall I find an excuse to leave you alone for a moment?"

"That would be so kind, my dear."

Lettie Bowman must have seen the motorcar drive up to her door. She came to greet Mrs. Neville, a little surprised to see her again, but nevertheless rather pleased. Her expression froze when our driver—Matthews was his name—helped Lady Beatrice to step down and then turned to me.

"I'm Gordon's godmother," she said at once. "My name is Beatrice Linton. I felt I wanted to meet you. We are both worried about him, even though he's fully grown."

It broke through the social ice quite nicely. As Lady Beatrice turned to me, she said, "And this is Sister Crawford. She came to Yorkshire to see me through a difficult surgery, and of all the unexpected things, I sent her down to care for Gordon while I finished my healing. Dr. Menzies has been so pleased with her care."

I stepped down, and handing the bread to Matthews, I took the hand that Mrs. Bowman offered me next.

"Do come in," she said.

I was sorry that we had troubled her. I hadn't seen her before, but her face now was drawn, pale, the eyes heavy-lidded from crying, and I wondered privately just how much of the food Mrs. Neville had sent she had felt she could swallow.

I took back the bread, and we went inside.

The front room was rather pretty, with a small dark blue horse-hair couch and two matching chairs, a thin carpet on the floor, tables against the far wall, and an old and tarnished silver candlestick in place of honor on the mantelpiece. It appeared to have come from a religious house, taken as a souvenir in some dim dark past.

We sat down, and Lettie offered us tea, although I didn't think she had the energy to prepare it. I said, "If you'd like, I could prepare it?"

"Oh, would you mind terribly? I don't seem to be getting to any-thing. I just sit and stare and listen for Judith coming through the door."

I found my way back to the tidy kitchen, and set to work. I could just hear the conversation in the front room even as I sliced the still-warm bread, buttered it, and found the pot of jam while the kettle boiled. How many times had I made tea in hospital, only vats of it then, and some-times too weak because the leaves were scarce? But no one had com-plained.

Lady Beatrice was asking about Gordon's first weeks. "I saw him at his christening, of course. All swaddled in a long white gown, lace ev-erywhere, and bright eyes that missed nothing. I held him, a warm little bundle, and he was as good as gold. You did a wonderful thing, taking him on."

"I'd just lost one of my own. I didn't think I could accept another baby. Not so soon. But I had the milk, and Mrs. Neville didn't. Mr. Nev-ille came himself and asked, and how could I refuse him? He was such a good man, and this was his first child. He was frantic with worry and trying not to worry me as well."

They talked on about that baby they had both shared, and as I was ready to bring in the painted wooden tray of tea things, I heard Lady Beatrice add, "And now this. After they came home safely from the war.

Scarred, yes, but alive. I had to come here and see for myself that Gordon would be all right."

"She says his arm was broke bad, and is infected."

"Yes. Bess works with it several times a day. Is that what you asked about in your message? How he was getting on? No one had come to say anything to you?"

"Oh, no, nobody came. I heard about Mr. Caldwell being so terribly hurt, and then dying. I heard Dr. Menzies's horse coming and going at all hours. I knew it was a good sign, that there weren't two dying in the House. But signs aren't always right, are they?"

"It was a nasty break, I can't lie to you there. Still, he'll be fine when it is stable enough for him not to do more damage than is already there. Anne says you may come and see him, if you like."

Lettie must have shaken her head. For she said, "No, I'm poor company now. I can't wrap my head around Judith not coming home. All her things everywhere, the neighbors coming in to cry with me. It seems she ought to be here by now, ought to come through that door saying, *Mum, I'm so sorry to be late, but I lost sight of the time.* And she'd give me a hug—" Her voice broke, and I could hear quiet sobbing.

It was time for the tea. I came down the short passage by the stairs and set the tray on a table. Lady Beatrice had just handed Lettie one of her lace-trimmed handkerchiefs. Lettie was staring at it as if she wasn't sure what to do with it.

The tea helped. It usually does.

We talked about Judith then, her childhood and her future. Lost now, but still mattering.

"She wanted to be a teacher. Mrs. Neville told me the family would send her to Richmond, for training. They believed she would be a fine schoolmistress, she said. But Judith didn't wish to leave me, not after my son Jamie died, and I was selfish, I kept her with me instead of encouraging her." A fresh bout of tears.

After a time a neighbor, her curiosity getting the better of her, came to the door with a covered dish of soup, and the last chance to ask about the message was gone. I did my best, took the neighbor, her cheeks a bright pink with embarrassment now, to the kitchen to put it in the cupboard.

We said our goodbyes. I think Lettie was ready for us to leave by then. She thanked us profusely, sent messages to Mrs. Neville about the bread, and we stepped out the door.

The tiny square was not that far away from where I was waiting to follow Lady Beatrice into the motorcar.

Something drew my attention there—I thought afterward that it was the dog dancing around a man's feet. I recognized that dog at once. My gaze moved up to the man beside him. The same person who had stared at me before across the Scarf running through the village. Too far then to be clear about him but feeling something familiar there . . .

And in a flash of memory I knew where I'd seen him before. The man with bandaged eyes, who had shared my compartment as far as York. Who had been met by a nurse who took him away.

The bandage was gone. I could see that clearly, I was too experienced to miss it.

The upper part of his face was pale, almost like the underbelly of a dead fish, as one of my patients had called it. A grayish white, but from lack of sunlight through the bandages, not from any feelings he might be having now.

We stared directly at each other. And then he called the dog, gave me a last malevolent glance, and turned away.

He remembered me as well. And I realized that he wasn't at all pleased that I remembered *him*. I was certain Joe Harding had recognized my voice when I shouted to call the dog off on my walk back from town. He was definitely the man on the train, I was sure of it. He couldn't see me then but he knew my voice, and had recognized my accent as I called off his dog.

When I had settled myself in the motorcar, I was about to open the little window to speak to Matthews, then thought better of it.

Lady Beatrice was saying, "It wasn't a very successful visit after all. Although I'm sure it offered that poor woman a little comfort to know how the family cared." The disappointment in her voice was heavy. She had intended to come home with the knowledge she had gone to find.

And Lettie had been her match.

"You'd think," Lady Beatrice went on, "that she might have told us how worried she was about Gordon Neville. That she had heard the news about Frederick Caldwell's and Gordon's injuries. Lettie was sick with concern. Anything. But she said nothing about it."

"She appears to be a private person. I expect that's why the Nevilles were ready to ask her to wet nurse the baby. She could be trusted with the heir."

"Yes, yes, that's true. One doesn't want to use a trollop for such work."

When we came to the house, Lady Beatrice thanked Matthews, thanked me as well, and walked on inside. Her back was straight and stiff, and I could see how her failure rankled.

I took my time getting down, so that she would be inside when I spoke to Matthews.

He was waiting patiently with the door wide for me, and I stepped out, then said, "Matthews. That man in the square with the dog. Do you by any chance know what his name is?"

He gave me an odd glance.

"That's Joe Harding, Miss. He's just come back from the war, after months in a clinic. Nearly lost his eyes, I've heard."

I suddenly felt the need to explain my interest. "I think he nearly set the dog on me when I walked into the village a few days ago."

"I shouldn't at all be surprised, Miss. He's a nasty piece of work, if you'll forgive me for being blunt. He was after Miss Bowman before the war." He moved his head slightly, looking up at the room where Gordon Neville lay. "I wonder if Mr. Gordon knows Harding's come home."

It was said in a way that got my attention.

"Should he be told?"

"Warned is more like it." He touched his cap, and closed the motor-car's door behind me.

The subject was closed.

The door to the house was still ajar, and I went up the steps and walked inside as Matthews got in behind the wheel of the motorcar and drove away.

I took off my hat and gloves, dropped them in our bedroom, and went straight to Gordon Neville's bedroom.

He was awake, staring at the ceiling with a frown on his face. He looked toward the door, saw that it was not someone else, and said, "I'm not in the mood for a browbeating."

I smiled. "Have I browbeaten you, Mr. Neville? I expect it's because I'm so used to unruly patients who refuse to listen to instructions and cause an inordinate amount of trouble for everyone else."

He tried not to smile, but it quirked around his lips anyway. "To what do we owe this bright mood? And can you open a window? It feels like the bottom deck of a troop transport in here."

"I'm afraid it won't do much good. It's very hot outside. With no breeze."

"We have such days this time of year."

I was straightening the bedclothes, in some disarray from his rest-less movements.

"Could I sit in a chair for a few minutes? These bedclothes are smoth-ering me."

"Yes, all right. I need to look at that arm."

We got him up between us, and he crossed to the chair without my help. I'd thought earlier that he must have been practicing late at night, and now I was certain of it. Except for his arm, still a serious break, he was nearly fit again.

I waited until I'd opened the bandages and was beginning to clean the arm before telling him what I thought I knew now.

"That message from Lettie Bowman. I believe I know now what was in it."

He stared balefully at me. "Did you come in while I was asleep and open that damned drawer?"

"That, Mr. Neville, would be underhanded."

He looked at me blankly. "Did or didn't you?"

I stopped what I was doing and said frankly, "No. I did not and would not."

"Then how have you come by this knowledge you are so certain of?"

There was less drainage this afternoon. The red lips of the torn skin where the broken tip of the bone had forced its way out were still red, but I tried to think a little less so. The new ointment that Dr. Halliday had left appeared to be working. But I didn't tell the patient that. He was intransigent enough as it was.

Cleaning the wound, I said, "I was in the village today. Lady Beatrice wished to offer her condolences to Mrs. Bowman, and I was asked to accompany her."

Gordon Neville was suddenly wary. "And what did she tell you?"

"Nothing more than that she had sent a message to you at the house, by way of Judith."

I could see him calculating. *Nothing new in that.*

"I've been in the village before, I walked there one day when I couldn't bear to be shut up in this house for another hour."

"Then you must know how I've felt."

CHARLES TODD

"Yes, but I was free to do that. You weren't. At any rate, someone set a dog on me. Then called it off at the last minute."

Something changed in him. The patient had vanished.

"Go on." His voice was harsh, his face hard.

"I believe it was Joe Harding. At least Matthews today told me it was. He wondered if you knew the man was back."

There was silence.

I took it to mean that the note had warned him.

"He's been in a clinic somewhere. Shrapnel in the eyes, I think. For he was on the train to York with me, for part of the journey. And he was met by a nursing Sister in York. How and when he came back to Scarfdale, I can't say. But he must have come back quietly."

"You said he had shrapnel in his eyes. How could he come back quietly?"

"The bandages are off for good. It happens sometimes. The bit of metal migrates and vision is restored. How perfect that vision is, varies of course. But some patients do return to sight. Others aren't so fortunate. The eye itself is too badly scarred."

He had listened carefully, although I was fairly certain he knew most of it. After all, he'd been an officer, he'd seen men blinded by shrapnel, he must have known why they hadn't returned to the line.

But his interest here was different.

"How long has he been back in Scarfdale?"

"I don't know. He'd got down at York. He'd have been taken to a clinic, a final evaluation, and then the matter of his official release from the Army. Then he would have to make his way back here, from York."

We weren't pretending that Joe Harding didn't exist. For some reason this was far too important to Gordon Neville than any pretense that he didn't know or care about this man.

He was doing rough calculations in his head. "The occasional small lorry comes through. The pub needs beer, the store all manner of merchandise. Other shops as well. It's unlikely that he could find a lift straightaway. He would know where to ask, all the same. And very likely someone would bring him through."

I continued to work, finally tying off the bandage to keep it in place.

"Why does he matter?" I asked then.

Gordon Neville came out of his thoughts with a slight movement of his head.

"That's not important."

"Then why should Lettie have to send you a message as soon as she herself was certain? Why send Judith out in the waning evening, if it could wait until the next morning?"

He took a deep breath. "There was trouble just before the war. I had to sort it out. He was convinced that Judith must care for him, and she didn't. He started to harass her, turning up when she went to market or went to visit a friend. Out for a stroll. With Lettie, finally, and *she* asked me to do something."

Why did I feel that this wasn't all the story? That he'd told me what he thought would satisfy me? Of course he'd think of Judith if Joe Harding had come back. It was natural. But there was something more recent. It was there in the room, in his tension, his suppressed anger.

"What rank did he have in the war?" I asked, curious. I'd been told the Yorkshire men had served together on the Somme . . .

"He'd risen to Sergeant. He received a battlefield commission in late July of '16, when we were losing officers and Sergeants at a pace we couldn't afford. I don't know if they stripped him of that later or not."

Sometimes such a promotion was temporary. In other cases the Army made it permanent.

I said, "Then he was in your battalion?"

"Yes." It was curt, inviting no more questions.

If I'd had a telephone and could call the Colonel Sahib, I thought in one part of my mind, he could find out what had gone on, during the fighting.

I was turning away to make my usual little packet of bandages and the like, to be taken out by one of the maids, and he caught my arm to stop me.

"Who else knows?"

"Davies. Matthews. I'm sure Lady Beatrice never glanced his way. And I said nothing to her on the way home." I was still stinging from the humiliation of being held at bay by the dog. I wouldn't have called her attention to a man in the square. But I didn't say that.

"Good. Keep it that way. I'll deal with this when I've got Wade off my back. For now there's nothing I can do. And I don't want Arthur to know. Especially Arthur. Do you hear me? Or my mother."

"Yes, I do."

"Do you think Ruth might have read that message, before bringing it up to me?"

I considered that. "I don't think she would. She might be curious. But if Judith simply told her that Mrs. Bowman was worried and wanted to let you know she was concerned for you, I have to think Ruth would have believed that."

"Yes. She wasn't in service here before the war. She came to care for her aunt in late '14, and when the aunt died, Mother took her in."

He rose, finding it hard not to use that right arm. "All right. Back to the torment of the bed."

And he got in, settling himself with weary resignation.

Sunday night, I dreamed about Somerset and home. We were in the garden, Mother and I, admiring a rose that we'd watched for days. And finally it had opened in the early morning, a drop of dew still fresh on a silky petal. Mother had called the Colonel Sahib to come and look, because it was as beautiful as the original in Melinda's garden, from which we'd taken a cutting to root. It had bloomed true. I called to Simon as well, but he didn't answer. He never came to see it. Mother said, "He must be at the cottage, darling. He will see it later." But I had a feeling he wouldn't, and I felt tears close behind my eyes.

A whimpering sound started in the dream. Making me turn away for fear my parents would see me crying, and want to know why. Embarrassed, I dropped to my knees, looking for a problem with a leaf, one that didn't exist, and I knew it didn't exist, but the whimpering was louder, and I didn't know what else to do.

A cry brought me out of the dream. I was still caught by it, I wasn't yet aware that the whimpering had come from beside me. But the cry had, and I turned quickly to see if Lillian was all right.

The room was dark, there was no firelight dwindling to a small glow in the heart of the coal, it had been too hot. And dawn hadn't broken, for the drapes were still black stretches against the wall.

A low moan followed as Lillian began to twitch, as if to fight off something.

I got up, and barefoot, I went to light the lamp and bring it closer to the bed. All the while, my mind was running through possible medical reasons for what was happening to Lillian

Yet when I carefully held the lamp high enough to see her clearly, I was surprised to find her asleep. And dreaming too.

Except that this wasn't a dream about roses blooming in a Somerset garden.

Her hands were knotted, her fingers digging into the sheet covering her, as if clinging for dear life, and her face was contorted in a grimace of pain.

I was reaching for her when the house seemed to shake under my feet, and there was a clap of thunder that seemed to roll on forever.

It brought Lillian out of her deep sleep with a start, her eyes wide as she looked up to see my face and the lamp looming right over her.

"What—" She cleared her throat. "What is it, Bess?"

I was about to say, *You were dreaming—and it was more of a nightmare.*

But the room was filled with a bright flash of light, and the next clap of thunder seemed to come right down the chimney.

The lightning hadn't struck the house. But on the fells, a storm was breaking the heat we'd felt building all day. And here in this narrow dale with its high sides, the storm was far worse than on most treeless mountainsides.

I quickly moved the lamp away, setting it beside the bed.

I'd jumped a little with each clap, and I was saying as I did, "It's a storm out on the fells. I thought I ought to wake you. I'm afraid it might be rather bad before it ends."

"Oh—thank you, Bess. I didn't hear anything, I was so deeply asleep."

I believed her. She had not slept very much at all, since our arrival. And she took no naps during today, to make up for it. Or take away the strain in her face. I had put it down to having to leave Lady Beatrice so soon after her surgery, even as she had arrived here to a tragedy that was unfolding.

I'd noticed too that she found it difficult to face confrontation and disruption. There had been enough of that here. She was a peaceful, honest woman who had given her life to the service of others.

Another clap of thunder shook the windows and made both of us jump.

I said, smiling, "Well, now we know why that fell is called Old Grumble."

She looked around the room, and I thought she might still be in the grip of whatever it was in the dream that had made her cry out. I'd had nightmares from the war. I knew too well how real they could seem.

I'd fought against tears in my own dream.

The room was hot, stuffy, but we could now feel the rain and wind lashing at the stone.

"I wish we could open a window," she said, throwing off the sheet and getting out of bed. Her hair was in damp tendrils around her face.

We walked barefoot across the carpet to the window and pushed back the drapes. But another brilliant flash of lightning made us drop the edges back in place and hurry away from the glass.

Retreating to the cold hearth, she said, "It would be lovely to have a cool lemonade. I haven't had one in ages."

I remembered them too. I couldn't recall when I had last seen a lemon.

"You were dreaming just before the storm came—" I began.

"Oh—I didn't kick you?" She was all apology, afraid she had somehow been unkind. "It was so hot in the room, I know it was difficult even to think about sleep, and I'm surprised I even drifted off."

"Not at all. I was just going to ask if you recalled it. I was dreaming as well, about Somerset and roses blooming."

"How nice! You must miss your family, Bess. You've been such a trouper about all this. I know Mrs. Neville is so glad you came. And of course Lady Beatrice, for all you've done as she recuperated. And look at all you do for dear Gordon."

She had neatly turned the subject.

The storm stayed overhead for another twenty minutes, and then we could hear it move down the dale, perhaps following the Scarf through to the next valley.

The rain lingered, and the wind, but that too began to dissipate as the room lightened a little with the summer dawn.

"I love the summers," she said thoughtfully. "I always have. There is something so bleak about winter, not only the weather but also the sense of being shut in for months."

"I remember India. There's a cold season, of course, but not anything like what Yorkshire must offer. Or Canada."

"I saw snow in Canada so deep one couldn't see over it. And it seemed so reluctant to melt. At the end of the winter, these dirty bits of hard snow were everywhere, unless someone removed them, a reminder wherever you looked."

"You were in South Africa as well, I think?"

"Not for very long, no. My family hardly had time to settle."

"What happened?"

Color drained from her face. "What—what do you mean?"

"You said you'd hardly had time to settle."

"Ah. Oh, I meant that the—the time had gone so quickly. It's hard to get used to foreign places, dealing with the people who often don't speak much of one's language, who lived differently, saw life differently. The poverty struck me. Yes, there was want in England as well, but in the places where I worked, you didn't see it every day. Devon. Essex. Kent. Worcestershire. You probably know what I mean, growing up in Somerset."

She had changed the subject again.

"I saw it in India," I answered. "It was sometimes heartbreaking to be told that neither you nor anyone else could change it. A part of life there."

She stretched and yawned. "Does it seem a bit cooler? I think I might try again to sleep."

And so we went back to bed, and let the quiet of the house drift around us again.

I fell asleep.

I don't think she did.

CHAPTER FIFTEEN

I WENT DOWN early, before breakfast, to step out on one of the broad terraces, to breathe in the cool, fresh air.

This was the one outside the library, where I knew I wasn't likely to disturb anyone else enjoying the morning.

But it wasn't. The air was still humid, heavy, as if the rain had only made it more sultry. Disappointed, I was about to step inside again, when my eye was caught by something on the broad step that led from the terrace down to the lawns.

I wasn't certain—I walked across the terrace to the step and looked down.

There were tracks here. Still wet from where someone had moved from the lawns to the step, then stopped and moved away.

I didn't need to know much about such matters to see what was there.

Three or four perfectly formed paw prints from a large dog.

And a partial print of a man's boot.

The sheepdogs didn't come into the house. They were quartered with the shepherds and men who worked the sheep.

I'd seen them at a distance, never close.

But they were surely smaller in frame, faster, and more active. This was a large print. That of a large dog.

With a half print of a boot, it was impossible to tell anything about the man, except that he wore workmen's heavy boots. Not a gentleman's shoe.

Had Joe Harding come to the house after the storm had passed? Before it was truly light?

Why would he do such a thing?

A taunt? Curiosity? Or was he looking for Gordon? Or was he looking for me?

Our dinner was quiet, desultory conversation—Mrs. Neville asked how the lambs had fared in the storm. Margaret asked her mother-in-law about something more appropriate to mourning to trim her black hat, in place of the emerald pin and feathers there now. I'd seen it, it was a handsome, frivolous thing that she wore with style.

As they were talking, Lillian joining in, Lady Beatrice quietly asked Arthur if he knew how Frederick Caldwell's affairs stood.

I went on with my soup, but I couldn't help but hear most of the short conversation.

"Well enough, as far as I know. He was asking my opinion of a few investments that had come to his attention, whether I thought it was too soon to leap into something. The war is barely over, we're still retooling in the factories, food shortages—I advised him to wait."

"Good advice, my own man of business has said much the same thing." She took a sip of wine, then said, "I expect Grace inherits?"

"I should think so. With the usual obligatory bequests to staff and the church fund, and so on. He drew up a will before marching off to war, as all the rest of us were ordered to do. I doubt there has been either time or reason to make alterations."

"Do you think Mark expects to receive a bequest?"

I could hear the surprise in Arthur's voice as he replied, "He has his own money. Although I have no idea how that stands now, of course. But I can't think why he should wish to deny Grace."

"He could marry her, and secure the family money that way."

I couldn't stop myself from looking up.

Arthur was staring at Lady Beatrice with some consternation. "Are you saying—do you have reason to believe that's the way the wind blows?"

I quickly dropped my eyes to my plate.

"He's never married. Gordon and Frederick were drawn to Grace. Who's to say that Frederick's brother wasn't as well. And just kept it to himself."

Arthur dropped his voice, but I could still hear it, for he was close enough to me.

"What are you suggesting, Aunt Bea?"

"I don't know that I'm suggesting anything. But both you and your mother have told me that Mark spent hours sitting by his dead brother's side. Sometimes with Grace, more often on his own, when you were conferring with Menzies and were distracted by the state that Gordon was in."

"My God." His voice dropped even lower. "Are you suggesting that Mark killed his own *brother*?"

"Why not? Cain killed Abel."

Just then Mrs. Neville said, "Do you know where it is, Arthur?"

He looked up, without the barest idea of what she was asking. Still trying to deal with the shock of Lady Beatrice's questions.

"Ah—um—I'm sorry, Mother, we were off into politics. I didn't hear your question."

She smiled. "I'm not surprised. You had that grim expression, a certain sign. No, no, I was asking about that portrait of Grandfather with your uncle Alex. Is it in the gallery still, or have we moved it? I wanted to show it to Margaret and Lillian."

He was still recovering. "Er—I think it's still in the gallery. We talked about putting it back on the south staircase. But that would mean moving the Turner. Gordon felt it fit the space better where it is."

I caught a glimpse of Lady Beatrice's face. She was cutting her meat with care, as if her mind were elsewhere. But when she looked down the table toward Mrs. Neville, her gaze was troubled.

After the meal I went up to dress Gordon's arm again. We were short of bandages, and I had to unpack a new box. When that was done, and he'd had his brief respite from the bed, I finished my work and gathered up the soiled bits.

"How hot is it outside? I'd hoped the storm had moved the heat along."

"Davies told me at breakfast that you could see a string of such days this time of year, and then the dales would go back to their usual pattern."

"He should know. He's always keen on weather. He has a barometer in the butler's office." He changed the subject then. "We haven't seen much of Inspector Wade."

"Don't think he will simply go away. I almost prefer him underfoot than skulking about where we can't keep an eye on him."

"Probably looking into Frederick's affairs. If there's murder done, there has to be a reason somewhere. Even if it doesn't appear straightaway."

It was too close to what I'd overheard at dinner. "I expect he will need to see a copy of the will, that sort of thing."

"It will be simple. Everything to Grace, after the usual bequests to staff."

"He really loved her, it seems."

"Besotted, is more to the point. Well, I was as bad as he was, before the war. I had never met anyone like her. The trenches have a way of stripping your mind of anything but survival. I got over her in the stalemate early in '15."

Surprised, I said, "The general impression that Inspector Wade was bandying about suggested that you'd killed Frederick to make her a widow."

He smiled grimly. "Even if I still felt the same as I did back then, she isn't going to choose Scarfdale as her new home. Peterborough suited her. But Frederick mentioned that he was considering opening the house in London now. At least for the Season."

"Would Mrs. Caldwell wish to move to London?"

"She said something about wanting to be there for the signing of the peace treaty. The King would be coming, with other royals. Parades. Parties."

But that was just coming up—and she was a widow now, in mourning.

Gordon echoed my thought. "Nothing will come of it now, of course. The day is almost on us."

I was just coming down the stairs after dressing the wound when I heard a motorcar pull into the circle by the door.

Someone must have alerted Davies, because he came quickly out of the door to the kitchens, and was there on the step in time to greet the occupants.

Mark Caldwell got out first, and I was reminded of Lady Beatrice's question, whether he had been or was still in love with the woman I could just see in the shadows of the interior.

He didn't look like a man who was desperately in love, but then he wasn't someone who wore his feelings on his sleeve—except for anger.

That he felt free to show in abundance. I could never tell what he was thinking when he was sitting passively. His face was closed. Almost secretive.

He was helping Grace out now.

And I stared at the woman who descended from the motorcar.

She had had her hair fashionably cut, for Mrs. Neville's birthday celebration. Now it was drawn smoothly back, leaving her face without any softness.

And she was wearing a beautifully cut traveling dress in deepest black. There was no doubt she was in mourning. But the whole picture was one of severe beauty.

I wouldn't have called her beautiful before, as grief had overwhelmed her features. But there was a coldness about her perfectly chiseled features now, more on display than they had been before she left.

It was as if she were throwing into our faces the fact that Wade had ordered her to stay—had ordered all of us to stay for that matter—stay in the same house with her husband's killer.

She brushed by Davies with a nod, stepped into the dimness of the hall blinking after the sun's brightness outside and didn't see me at first.

"It's as hot and breathless in here as it was in the motorcar." Her voice was querulous. "I can't lie down in this heat." She turned back to the door, starting to say, "Davies, will you ask one of the maids to draw my bath—"

It was then her eyes grew accustomed to the dimness and she saw me by the door to the main drawing room.

"What is it?" she all but snapped.

"I'm so sorry, Mrs. Caldwell—I was just coming down the stairs as you arrived."

"I shan't keep you."

I took that as a dismissal, and with a smile, I passed her to go down the other passage in the direction of the sitting room, just as Grace started up the stairs.

Mrs. Neville looked up as I came in. "I thought I heard a motorcar, but there was no knock at the door—"

"It was Mrs. Caldwell and her brother-in-law returning from Richmond. Davies was at the door to greet them before they could knock."

Lillian rose and excused herself. "I need to run upstairs for a few minutes, if you'll forgive me, Lady Beatrice?"

"Of course. I'll have a lie-down as well, I think. This heat is giving me a dreadful headache." She said to me, "Out in India, you had men who sat on the porch of the house and pulled the ropes of the great fans in the various rooms. Is that true?"

"Indeed it was. The fan wallah. The ceilings were high, and we didn't always get the best of the cooling even then. But it was better than nothing when the heat was at its worst."

"We shall have to find our own fan wallahs," she told me with a smile, and went up with Lillian. I wasn't completely convinced that Lillian had wanted to sit with Lady Beatrice. But she made the best of it.

I don't think anyone else could do much more.

I was going out for a breath of fresh air—not that I expected to find any.

Grace Caldwell had taken over the small sitting room to write notes on black-bordered cards, to inform anyone beyond the immediate family who knew Frederick and would wish to attend the funeral.

Lillian was reading to Lady Beatrice, who was lying down, feeling the heat—so she told us—and had taken up a corner in the library.

Margaret had gone down to one of the tenant farms to take a basket of food to a family whose mother had taken ill with a fever.

Mark Caldwell lurked in various rooms, avoiding or ignoring the rest of us, I wasn't certain which.

Arthur was in the estate office with the man who ran the Home Farm.

Mrs. Neville, beginning to look just the tiniest bit harried, met me at the top of the stairs.

"Grace has asked if we could bring forward supper tonight, as she's tired from her journey. Could you let Lady Beatrice and Lillian know of it?"

"I'll be happy to," I said, smiling.

She hesitated, as if about to say more, then shook her head slightly.

I said, "Mrs. Neville, may I ask you a question?"

"Yes, of course you may, Bess. Is it about Gordon's arm?"

"It's about Mr. Caldwell. I can't help, seeing how wretched he is here, wonder why he accepted the family's invitation to the birthday celebration."

I thought she was going to roll her eyes in a sudden flash of irritation, but she quelled it.

Hadn't she invited him?

"He was in Peterborough staying with Frederick and Grace. He had some business in the town, as I understood it, and there was to be a delay in getting the proper papers signed. Frederick was reluctant to leave him to himself while they were away, and so he asked Arthur if he could bring Mark as well." This time she did shake her head firmly. "I was against it. It was my party, after all. But what could I possibly say that wouldn't be absolutely rude?" Then as if regretting being quite so truthful about someone under her roof, she added, "Arthur told me Mark would rather stay in Peterborough, that he would politely decline. He wound up staying here instead. Not without objection of course."

"Oh, dear."

She took a deep breath. "Yes, exactly what I said when I saw him step out of the motorcar that evening. I must go and make peace with Cook. She's not taking this well."

I watched her walk away, and then tapped lightly on Lady Beatrice's door. There was no answer, no sound of voices. I opened it a little, expecting to see both of them nodding in their chairs.

Only Lady Beatrice was in the room, and she was asleep on the bed, a cool cloth over her eyes.

I shut the door as quietly as I had opened it and tiptoed away.

When I reached our door, I could hear voices, and I thought perhaps Margaret had come up to speak to Lillian. My hand was on the knob before I realized that it wasn't Margaret's voice, it was a man's, speaking to her.

I stopped, wondering if Arthur had come up to see her, when through the door I heard him say harshly, shouting, "Take those meddling women and go back to the Hall, or you'll regret it. Tell them what you like, but get them into that damned motorcar and leave."

Arthur?

I couldn't believe my ears. But Lillian was in that room, and host or no host, he had no right to speak to her that way. Anger rose in defense of her, and I was about to open the door and walk in, as if I hadn't heard anything, forcing him to stop berating her. Surely he wouldn't say the same to *my* face?

If he did, I was capable of protecting myself.

But the knob was jerked from my hand, the door was swung open, and the man in the room sent me reeling back against the passage wall behind me as he walked into me full tilt, his head turned for one last glance at Lillian.

"Get out of my way!" he said, one arm coming out to sweep me aside. I didn't know whether he mistook me for one of the maids or if he'd actually recognized me. Caldwell.

And then he was gone, striding angrily down the passage. I heard the door to his room slam with enough force to bring the paintings off the wall. And then the passage was empty and silent.

I gathered myself and walked into our room. Lillian was in the middle of it, shoulders slumped, hands over her eyes, weeping inconsolably.

When I gently closed the door behind me, she flinched, as if she expected another attack. Physical or verbal, I couldn't be sure.

I went to her, put my arms around her, and led her to the nearest chair. I got her seated, knelt on the floor beside her, and said, "Are you all right?"

Which of course she wasn't, I could see that clearly, but it was the first thing I could think of that didn't have to do with my anger at that vicious man.

"Oh, Bess," she said, her hands clinging to me as the tears rolled down her cheeks, "what am I to do?"

"Tell me what's wrong, and we'll find a way," I said, keeping my tone soothing and quiet, as if I were dealing with one of the frightened wounded. And all the while I could feel my own anger building inside me.

Lillian shook her head frantically. "Oh, no, please, it will be all right, I'm just terribly upset. It's nothing, Bess, truly. I don't know why I cry so easily. So silly of me."

But the tears were still coming, despite her protests.

I could feel her trembling as I held her hands. It wasn't just worry—the shouting—the orders to leave. Lillian Taylor was deeply frightened.

I asked as gently as I could, "Why did Mark Caldwell come up to our room?

Her face went even paler. "Oh—did—did you see him?"

"I literally ran into him. Or, no, *he* ran into me as he was leaving the room, and I was about to open the door."

That frightened her more. "He—he was looking for Lady Beatrice." It was a lie, and a very bad one. She was asleep next door. And I didn't think even Mark Caldwell would dare face down the Dowager Countess, whose son sat in Parliament. He wasn't a fool, and he didn't strike me as the sort of man willing to risk his own standing in society by attacking a family with political and social connections far above his own.

Lillian was a companion, by nature accustomed to do the bidding of others, with no resources and no power and no authority. And so Mark Caldwell had tried to use her to make the three of us leave.

If that was the case, he had reckoned without Lady Beatrice.

I said gently, "She's asleep next door, my dear, in her own room. He could have knocked if he wished to speak to her."

Her fingers gripped mine painfully. But the tears had slowed, and there was something in her face now that I couldn't read. A determination, a need. That same deep-set fear? "Please, Bess. Let it go. There's nothing wrong, truly. He wants us to leave, he wants a better room, he's tired of being here. It was just the heat and his frustration and whatever is going on with Inspector Wade. All of us are on edge, we're struggling to understand what's happening, and the waiting is keeping us awake at night."

Was it?

I was about to speak again when she shook her head. "I'm all right. When people shout at me, I just lose my wits, and dissolve into tears. It looks much worse than it was. Truly. I was that way as a child, I think." Then she added hastily, "It wasn't my parents, I didn't mean them. It was the children in my school, and the mistresses. I was so terribly *shy*. A *boo!* could set me off."

I found I didn't believe her. She was pressing too hard to beg me to let whatever it was alone. It was as if she would do or say anything to have the disturbance to her peace forgot.

I rose and went to the washstand to wring out a cloth in the pitcher of tepid water, then bring it back to let her bathe her face and cool her eyes. After a bit she rose, went to the glass to smooth her hair, and find a smile.

"I'm so sorry," she said again. "It's a wonder Lady Beatrice puts up with me."

I let it go. She didn't mean it, and I would give it too much importance if I told her it was nonsense to say such a thing.

"The reason I came in," I said, "was a word with Mrs. Neville in the passage. She tells me Grace would like to have supper put forward an hour. She's tired from traveling in the heat and would like an early night."

"I'm sure she would," she agreed.

But to me it seemed an imposition. She had only to retire early and have her meal brought up on a tray. For some reason, her new coldness or her feelings about the family and her husband's death made me wonder if she wanted to sit there at the table and make us see her bald grief.

I could see that Lillian was still badly unsettled, even as she was trying her best to persuade me all was well. And so I left her the room, to whatever peace and tranquility she needed before the evening meal.

What I wanted badly to do was have a word with Mark Caldwell. But I was also a guest here, I couldn't very well burst into his room and tell him what I thought of his behavior. Nor was I a talebearer. Even so, the question had to be, Should I speak to Arthur? Or to Mrs. Neville?

And the answer to that was clear. It would only make it more difficult for them to deal with him during our enforced stay, and add to the tension and worry for the Nevilles.

But the next question was there, waiting for its own solution.

If I said and did nothing, if it appeared that Mark Caldwell suffered no unpleasant consequences for his behavior, would he attack Lillian again? He already knew he could bully her.

If it were the heat and frustration and the waiting, he just might. Who else could he vent his anger on?

I found a quiet corner in one of the formal drawing rooms and tried to think about what to say to Lady Beatrice concerning what had happened. She could protect Lillian, she had no love for Mark Caldwell either. A put-down from her might well be the answer.

But she hadn't been a witness. I was, at least at the end of the confrontation.

After nearly three quarters of an hour, I still didn't know what to say to her.

Or even if I should say anything at all . . .

Perhaps that was exactly what Mark Caldwell was counting on.

Supper was exactly the sort of penance we were all expecting.

Grace took her accustomed place at the table, looking very much as she had on her arrival, although the traveling dress had given way to a more suitable evening gown. Lace at the throat and wrists, in spite of the heat, no jewelry—except her bridal rings—and no touch of color at all, a pale powder dusting her face.

I watched Arthur avoid looking her way. Even Mark seemed to be very annoyed with her.

Lady Beatrice and Margaret and I tried to help Mrs. Neville keep a light conversation moving about the table, but it was a struggle. Grace answered questions put to her   how was it in Richmond, just as hot?— did you find what you needed, my dear?—were you able to speak to your parents or your Vicar?

The answers were brief. "Wretched hot."

"Most of it, yes."

"They would have arrived by now, but my grandmother is unwell, and her doctor is in London. He has been conferring with my father. Frederick's death shocked her terribly. My mother is afraid we might lose her to her grief."

Oh, dear.

"I'm so sorry to hear that," Lady Beatrice put in, before Mrs. Neville could express her concern to the murmurs around the table as the words sank into the silence. "Would you like for me to call on the Chief Constable? I'm sure I could persuade him that there is absolutely no need for you to be kept here in constant reminder of your loss. And you could give your poor grandmother a little hope."

It was like move-countermove in a chess game that had no figures, only words.

Grace smiled then, the tragic heroine. "That would be very kind, Lady Beatrice. But I want to be here when my husband's death is fully explained. I owe him that."

Conversation lagged after that.

Grace went up to her room as soon as the ladies rose, but Arthur said to Mark Caldwell, "It's too hot for port and cigars tonight. Care for a turn on the terrace instead?"

He agreed, and while Arthur held the door for us, Davies scooped up the port and box of cigars and set them on the sideboard for the evening.

As soon as it was polite to do so, I excused myself and went up for a last look at Gordon's arm.

Mrs. Neville said, "Tell him I'll come to say good night."

I had the impression that the four women were glad to see me go. Not in any way that was rude or representing a dislike of me, but more the feeling that they wished to talk about matters that were too private to bring up before a relative stranger.

As I started up down the passage, I heard someone else going up before me, and slowed my pace a little. I was at the foot of the stairs when I was fairly sure that I heard Mark Caldwell's door open and close.

In that wing, the larger rooms looked out on the drive, and down the sweep of Scarfdale, the trees along the beck, the slopes of the dales on either side. The finest views from the house.

When I had finished with the dressings and salves, Gordon was sitting in the chair, staring rather morosely toward the cold hearth.

I went to the windows, but didn't open the drapes, stepping between them instead. I only intended to open one of the windows to see if there was any relief to be had before going to any more trouble.

The light was already going as clouds moved in from the west, enveloping what was left of it. In the distance I could see the desultory flicker of lightning, flashes that weren't storms so much as the disturbed atmosphere.

The window slid silently upward on well-waxed ropes, and I looked down.

The gates appeared to be closed—it was quite dusk now, colors already faded to that silvery gray that made it hard to distinguish real features, but one could still see a little. The shadowy presence of planting here and there, the paler line of the drive.

The air outside seemed to be as heavy with heat as the rooms inside.

Sighing, I reached up to close the window and then stopped short.

Movement caught my eye.

I had purposely left the light low when I'd finished Gordon's arm, the room seemed cooler somehow. And so there was no reason why anyone should look up toward the open window.

But I could look down.

The movement I had seen had too many moving parts.

And then I realized that it was a man with longer legs, and a dog with shorter ones.

Pacing—or keeping guard?

Had Gordon himself put a watcher on the grounds, knowing that Joe Harding had come back?

Impossible to tell.

"What is it?" Gordon asked from his chair.

"I was looking out, hoping for a little breeze. Did you set a guard tonight?"

"What?"

He was out of the chair, grunting as he put too much pressure against the broken edges of bone.

Beside me now at the window, he said, "The lamp."

I turned and put it out, then found my way back to the window.

"What did you see? Where?" His voice was low, harsh.

"I think—down the drive, just before the turning for the yard."

He studied the night.

"Your imagination," he said finally and was about to turn away. But as he did, I saw it again, and touched his good arm.

Following my pointing finger, he said, "Yes. All right."

And I knew he was seeing what I had seen earlier.

He swore, a helpless, furious sound beside me. I couldn't hear it, but I heard the tone of voice.

"Your man?"

"No. What the devil does he—"

He broke off.

There was movement nearer the house.

Gordon saw it as well.

Someone was moving quickly down the drive toward the man and the dog.

Impossible to tell, we were high, looking down—almost impossible to see shape or judge height or age. Just a dark, flitting figure.

It caught up with the man, and they moved away.

"Who was it?" he asked, low.

I shook my head. "I couldn't tell."

"One of the maids? I'd have sworn—but of course they grew up in the village—it can't be helped."

We waited. Five minutes? It seemed longer there in the darkness by the window.

There was a tap at the door of the room.

Ruth? Gordon's dinner tray was still there on the table . . .

"Just a moment," I called.

While I fumbled to light the lamp, Gordon was rustling the bed-clothes, getting between them as best he could.

As the light came up, I cast a quick glance at him. He would do.

I went to the door and opened it. "I was trying to bring a little air into the room," I said ruefully. "It doesn't appear to help."

"Still as a church mouse," Ruth agreed. "I stepped out just now but there's not a leaf moving."

"Where were you?" Gordon asked from the bed.

"The kitchen garden, sir. Cook wanted to know if there were any radishes for dinner tomorrow. I was glad to tell her no. I never did like them."

She picked up the tray and the bandages, wished us a good night, and was gone.

"Not her, then," he said quietly.

"No. She seemed to be telling the truth."

I went back to the window, intending to close it against any storm in the night, and looked down.

No movement at all.

It was as if we'd imagined that anyone was out there.

I reached up to pull down the window—and as my fingers were about to bring pressure to bear, someone came hurrying up the drive, veering toward the library terrace rather than the main door.

A long way from the kitchens, in this wing of the house.

I couldn't judge anything now but the motion, and I was about to summon Gordon, hoping he might recognize who it was.

The figure looked toward the west, where I'd seen the lightning. And in that same instance a brighter flash lit up the drive.

I drew in a breath.

Gordon said, "What is it?"

Before I could think about what to reply, the surprise sent the words tumbling out.

"It's Mrs. Caldwell—"

By the time he reached the window, the figure had reached the shadows of the house and vanished among them.

"You must be wrong."

But I wasn't. I was as certain of that as I was of the man standing next to me among the window drapes.

Again we waited. But there was nothing more to be seen.

Gordon turned and walked back to his bed.

"She doesn't know anyone in Scarfdale village," he said as he settled himself.

"No, I'm sure that's true."

"Turn down the lamp as you go, please. It's cooler in the dark."

I shut the window, rearranged the drapes so that early morning light wouldn't wake him, trimmed the lamp, and started for the door.

"Good night," I said as I went out.

He didn't reply.

I walked down the passage toward the stairs, my thoughts jumbled and trying to sort themselves out. Before I reached the top step, I paused, standing there by the corner of the passage wall, in the shadows, where I wouldn't be visible if someone came into the entrance hall below. Trying hard to recapture the image I'd seen so fleetingly.

What was I really sure of?

If I was right, and it seemed mad even to me, I told myself I'd just seen Grace Caldwell walk down the drive to meet Joe Harding and his dog.

And the dog never barked . . .

Or even growled.

The night was so still, I was sure I wouldn't have missed a sound that I'd heard only days before, along the beck, as that dog had held me at bay. I could bring it straight up out of my memory even standing here in the safety of the house, shivering a little at the vividness of it.

Gordon hadn't believed me. Who else would?

Even if I *was* right—what ought I to do about it?

It was the same quandary I'd felt earlier, as I'd comforted Lillian. Do I tell someone?

I was too deep in thought. I hadn't heard the soft footfalls behind me, I hadn't known anyone was there.

Until I felt the hands flat against my back, between my shoulder blades, giving me an almighty shove toward the stairs just beyond the toes of my shoes.

Chapter Sixteen

I HAD WALKED in the slick, heavy black mud of war-torn France. Slipping and sliding, in danger of losing my balance if I didn't mind where I was stepping next.

Something of that world must have come back to me. My right foot went out to counterbalance the shove—and met nothing but air. Even as it did, the buckle of my other evening shoe caught against something for the briefest of seconds. And I was sent pitching headlong. Not straight down the steps, but toward the elegant walnut banister.

There was no rope to reach for, as there sometimes was on the boards that led to the Sisters' quarters, for they were uneven and sometimes even worse underfoot.

But here there were the balusters. Heavy wooden hourglass-shaped decorative balusters that guarded the outer edge of stairs beneath that polished handrail.

And I was going to crash straight into them, because I'd been standing near the wall. They seemed twice as large as they really were, and I knew somewhere in the muddle that was my mind that I was going to be badly hurt. My flailing hands went up in front of my head, reaching out toward them, in a desperate effort to shield my face—and the jolt through my right arm and shoulder as they took the full force of my momentum made me cry out. My left hand scrabbled to catch a lower one, to swing me around, just as my head struck a rounded side.

My chest and right hip came down across the hard edge of a tread, knocking the breath out of me. Senses reeling, I came to a stop, and just lay there, pain everywhere as the shock descended.

It must have been a loud and fearful sound.

I could hear feet running from a distance, cries. They seemed to be miles away.

I lay there four or five steps from the top, closing my eyes against sweeping pain.

I heard someone shout to Davies, "Get Menzies, man!"

And then Arthur was taking the stairs two at a time, racing toward me, stopping to kneel or sit on the step just below me. I could hear his heart pounding, then feel his warmth beside me

"Bess," he said, trying to control his breathing and his own shock. "Can you hear me?"

His voice was gentle. I wondered much later if he thought I was dead.

Trying to find my way up through a dark cloud of pain and disbelief, I made an effort.

"Um."

"Help is coming. Tell me what to do before it arrives."

And then that moment of clarity when you realize fully what has happened, when you seem to see yourself in place, and know you are hurt.

I said, "Don't move me. Best."

"No—no." He must have been examining me visually, for he added, "There's blood on your forehead, where you struck the balustrade. Your left hand is bleeding, too. Your limbs don't seem to be hurt, but that right hand is twisted against the other balustrade."

The war, I thought. He's used to gauging what the wounded need, where to send them. He was doing it for me.

I just wanted to lie there in blackness.

More movement on the staircase, and Mrs. Neville's voice.

"My dear. I'm here. Help is coming."

It was what her son had said to me. It was comforting to hear again.

"Would you like a blanket?" Arthur asked.

"No."

I felt cold, could feel my body starting to shake a little with the reaction. That must be why he'd asked.

"Yes," I said now, and someone must have passed him a blanket, for very soon afterward it settled softly over me, warming me.

I was beginning to take note. "My hip hurts. Could you move my right limb a little?"

"Are you sure?" Mrs. Neville asked.

"Please."

They shifted my leg a bit, and the pain in my hip flared, then wasn't as harsh.

I tried to lift my left arm, crooking it a little. No breaks there. But my fingertips felt raw. Hadn't he said they were bleeding?

My neck felt as if it were jammed hard against my right arm, but my hairline on the left was trickling blood. I could feel it spreading down toward my eyebrow, warm and wet. Yes, he said—a cut.

I was afraid my right arm might be broken. It was aching so badly I felt sick. It was the same arm I'd broken as *Britannic* sank in the fall of 1916.

There was movement around me, and Mrs. Neville said, "Bess, Lady Beatrice has got her smelling salts. Would they help?"

"Yes. Just a little."

A hand under my nose. And a whiff of the salts.

They steadied my thinking.

The stairs were uncomfortable, the treads hitting my body in all the wrong angles, and yet I was afraid to try to move any farther. At the same time, it was getting harder to lie here in little short of agony.

Pain, I understood. I'd given so many wounded what relief I could. And so many times, far from enough. And they had endured, bringing tears to my eyes sometimes as I walked back to my quarters in the dark or the early dawn.

I tried to move my right fingers.

They were stiff, and my first efforts sent wired pain through my arm and shoulder. But I hadn't screamed. I tried the elbow. I didn't think I'd dislocated anything.

"Can you help me sit up?" I asked Arthur.

"Bess—are you sure it's wise?"

"Please. Carefully."

He was strong, but he was afraid he'd do more damage, and so it wasn't as smooth as I'd hoped. With one hand cushioning my head and neck as a lover might, he put his other arm around my body and slowly lifted.

I cried out as I changed position, and he stopped.

"More."

This time he managed to set me on a stair tread as Mrs. Neville, working behind him, brought my legs and feet around in the same movement, so that I was now upright. He was still cushioning my head and neck. As he slowly let them take their own weight, I saw the smear of blood on his white shirt cuff.

I could see down the long fourteen or fifteen stairs to the hall below. Strained white faces stared back up at me.

Margaret, her mouth open in shock, Lady Beatrice, pale but resolute. Lillian, her face streaked with silent tears.

And the staff, drawn from the kitchen by the turmoil, just at the edge of my vision directly below me. Looking up in horror.

Sounds from outside moved Lady Beatrice to turn and open the door before Davies could reach it, and a swirl of hot air came in with Dr. Menzies, his face grim as he looked at the crowded entrance hall. Then his gaze swept on to the stairs and he started up them.

Arthur and Mrs. Neville rose and moved to the top of the flight. I saw Arthur reach out and steady his mother as they did.

Below, Davies was heading the staff away to the kitchens, and Lady Beatrice was taking Margaret and Lillian back in the direction of the sitting room. Behind me I heard Arthur move away, giving me privacy for the examination to come.

Mrs. Neville said quietly, "I'm here, Bess."

And now Dr. Menzies was there beside me.

"A fall," he said. Stating a fact, then he was asking me questions, touching me, ascertaining what was wrong—and what was not. His hands were sure, gentle, and I tried not to wince or cry out.

Finally, he sat down just one step below me. His expression was grave.

"I don't know," he said thoughtfully, "why you didn't break your neck."

I attempted a smile. I didn't feel like talking. My jaw ached, I realized. From where I'd jammed my head?

He had brought his case up with him, and he opened it now, attending to the cut on my head, another on my arm, and two torn fingernails. "The rest can't be mended as easily. You will be very stiff tomorrow, and movement will be painful. I want you to stay in bed and rest. I will see to Gordon's arm."

"Nothing is broken?" I was fairly certain. But I wanted his assurance.

"There is a great amount of deep bruising into the tissue around your hip and where you injured your arm. But the bones appear to have no damage. I can't feel an edge or lump that indicates a crack or break."

That was good news. But I knew too that sometimes the damage wasn't apparent straightaway because of the initial trauma and swelling.

"We will take you upstairs and put you to bed. I will order a cup of tea for the shock, and then a drop or two of laudanum to allow you to sleep. I don't need to tell you that sleep is a healer, and you are not to refuse the drops. You can have more tomorrow morning, if needed, and again tomorrow night. But then we should rethink."

And finally, he asked the question no one else had had a chance to speak of.

"How did you happen to fall?"

Oh, dear.

Of course he had to ask—medically, he had to know what had precipitated such a thing.

His eyes were on my face.

"Did you trip on the hem of your gown?"

"No."

"Feel dizzy as you started down?"

"No.

"What then?"

I hesitated a second too long in my answer.

"I have a responsibility to you and a duty to the law, Sister Crawford."

I could hear Mrs. Neville's skirts rustle behind me.

His gaze was sharp now. "Were you pushed?" It was what the police would ask at some point.

"I don't know. I didn't see anyone. More to the point I didn't hear anyone coming up behind me. I was standing to one side of the staircase, thinking about a problem, and hands struck my back in a shove."

Mrs. Neville drew in a breath. I could hear it clearly.

There. It had been said.

"I will ask Inspector Wade to call on you tomorrow. In the meantime, Mrs. Neville, will you see that someone sits with her all the time? No exceptions? She will be vulnerable when she has taken her drops."

"Yes—yes, of course—" She cleared her throat. "I take full responsibility for keeping her safe."

"Will you ask your son and Davies to help me move her to her room?" he asked then.

"I'll turn down her bed as soon as I have rung for them."

And she was gone.

Dr. Menzies said nothing until she was out of earshot. Then he asked, "And why would you be pushed down a long flight of stairs?"

"How did you know?" I parried.

"You landed oddly. Jammed against the railing and balustrades. It isn't easy to fall in that fashion, if you trip or feel dizzy. Again. Why?"

But this wasn't something I could tell him, could I? I had to be truthful medically. The rest wasn't information he should be told. Not before the Nevilles and Lady Beatrice had learned of it. If at all.

"Who was downstairs when you came to your senses?"

"Most of the staff. The Nevilles. Lady Beatrice. Lillian was there."

"Who was not?"

"Someone on the staff? Mrs. Caldwell. Mr. Caldwell." I drew in a breath. "Gordon Neville."

He patted my hand. "Tell Inspector Wade. For your own safety."

Davies was coming from the kitchens, and behind me I heard Mrs. Neville speaking to her son as they came to the top of the stairs.

It was an ordeal, getting me to my feet, then half carrying me to my room. It was the half of me that hurt as well.

But we managed, and as the men withdrew, Lady Beatrice and Lillian came in. Lillian was carrying a small silver tray with teapot and cup, which she set on a table. With Mrs. Neville's help and a minimum of fuss, they got me undressed and tucked into bed.

It was when Lillian began to take off my evening shoes and stockings that another memory came back to me. The left shoe buckle catching . . .

But it hadn't. Someone had put a foot out and tripped me, to be sure the shove had done its work. A quick, unplanned move that had kept my feet from saving me.

I didn't tell anyone. I couldn't then.

I was brought my cup of tea, and then three pairs of eyes watched me dutifully swallow my laudanum. I had no idea what time it was—I was beginning not to care as I let myself drift into painless comfort.

I could hear them by the cold hearth. Mrs. Neville was drawing up a list of who would sit when.

"And Lillian won't be sharing her bed," Lady Beatrice told them briskly. "She will share mine when she isn't on duty."

No one argued.

And then Lady Beatrice came across to the bed. "Are you still awake, my dear?"

I let my eyes stay closed, and after a moment she moved away.

"Are you sure," I heard her ask Mrs. Neville, "that even Dr. Menzies believes she was shoved?"

"He brought it up himself."

"Very well, then. I think it's time we brought in Scotland Yard. This has gone on long enough, Anne, and we must face the truth. I'll send a telegram to the Chief Constable in the morning."

"I don't understand any of this," Mrs. Neville said despairingly. "What is happening, Bea? What is going on in this house?"

"It isn't our work to stop this. It's why we have the police." And then she must have turned to Lillian. "See if you can persuade her to talk to you. It would be best for all of us if we knew a little more information before that wretched man sets his foot back inside this house."

And the room was silent. I was too drowsy to open my eyes, but I thought I had heard the door quietly being opened and closed.

Then I heard a soft sigh as someone tried to make themselves more comfortable in one of the large chairs by the fire.

Lillian was to be the first to sit with me.

My last thought as the darkness took over was that she was the last person capable of keeping me safe.

———

I slept without dreams of falling again. Or if I had dreamed, they had slipped away with the dawn, leaving no memory of them behind.

But the moment I opened my eyes and tried to turn my head, it was all there again. The fall, the pain, the stiffness.

I must have groaned, for a shadowy figure rose from a chair and moved toward the bed.

It was Lady Beatrice. She looked tired, but she was dressed as elegantly as always, her hair in perfect order.

"How are you, this morning?" she asked quietly.

"I'm afraid to find out," I said truthfully.

"It's early. There's no rush to rise."

"How long have you been here?"

"We've all taken our turns." She went away and brought back the straight-backed chair where Lillian and I sat to put on our shoes. Drawing it close to the bed, she sat down.

"As a matter of fact, I chose the last duty of the night on purpose."

Ah. I knew what was coming.

"Who pushed you down the main staircase?" she asked without fanfare or warning.

"I truly don't know."

"I have accounted for everyone when those alarming sounds shocked us into rushing out to the hall."

"Have you?"

"Everyone except Grace, who went up early, Mark Caldwell, who did the same. And Gordon, lying in his bed."

"He couldn't have pushed me, surely."

"My dear, I have noticed the soles of his feet. He sits in his chair in the middle of the night. When you bring him water to bathe, he doesn't wash his feet. Or if he does, he is on them again later."

She was very observant!

"You said nothing about that?"

"No, why should I? He's an active busy man. Did you expect him to lie quietly and behave himself as the doctor ordered him to do?"

I smiled ruefully. "I've been guilty of letting him sit up while I finish cleaning his arm. It's been terribly hot, after all."

"Don't distract me, Bess. Three people. How have you crossed them?"

But I was thinking about feet. I hadn't heard anyone coming down the passage. Had the person who shoved me been barefoot? Who put out a foot to make certain the fall injured me? That would point heavily to Gordon. The only problem was, I didn't know any reason why he might want to kill me, given that I'd tried to treat him fairly. Except that I knew he had been out in the dark the night that Judith was murdered.

I'd been a witness to the quarrel between Mark Caldwell and Lillian. Was that a strong enough motive for murder?

I had no idea whether it would matter to Grace if she had seen me watching her walk down the drive to meet Joe Harding.

"Bess."

I brought my attention back to her.

"Tell me. I have come to know you. And care for you. If there is something wrong, you can trust me to see to it discreetly and directly."

I was beginning to think she believed I'd had a clash with Mark Caldwell. That perhaps he had upset me in some fashion. And that he'd retaliated.

For she said now, "Did you fall down the stairs in your haste to get away from him?"

I'd been right . . .

"No."

"Truthfully?"

"He was not chasing me down the passage."

She sat back, nodding. As if I'd confirmed something. I'd thought she was testing me to see if it *was* Mark Caldwell. Instead she was eliminating the possibility.

"Then we are back to why, aren't we?"

What to do?

Dr. Menzies expected me to tell Inspector Wade the truth. But what would he do with it?

I said carefully, "I'm a guest here."

"As am I as well. But you must think that there are two deaths to account for here, and now a third attack has been made. We are none of us safe, if you know something and fail to warn us."

Could I trust her?

I drew a long breath. "I know three secrets. And I'm not certain which of them sent me headlong down the stairs."

"Tell me the first one."

This was Gordon Neville's godmother. If I did, I'd betray him to her. But she was right. A third attempt changed things.

And so, quietly, keeping my voice level and unemotional, as if I were giving my end-of-day report to Matron, I began to talk to her.

I could see her eyes as I told her what I knew, and watch the changing expression in them.

She was annoyed with Gordon—as I myself had been—for taking such a foolish risk. She seemed to be telling herself that he couldn't possibly have known that Judith would die that night, but it didn't change the fact that he shouldn't have done what he did.

But even in the face of the chance he'd taken, she didn't suspect him of killing Judith Bowman.

When I gave her an account of the confrontation between Mark Caldwell and Lillian, there was a very different expression there. Anger—knowledge that I didn't have—I couldn't read it well enough to be sure. But I did learn that this was not about a better room. This went far deeper. And it explained Lillian's gallant effort to make me believe it was not important. It *was*. On a level I couldn't begin to comprehend?

I went on with my account, telling her about seeing Grace outside last night.

And like Gordon, she found that hard to believe.

"I've known her longer than you have, of course. And I can't see her in this light."

"I didn't mean to suggest an—an affair—"

"No, of course you didn't. But how does she know him? Why would she know him? How did he know she was here? It was very likely one of the maids who saw her at dinner, and decided to impress this Mr. Harding by trying to copy Grace's unfortunate appearance last night."

I closed my eyes for several minutes.

I'd done my best.

Opening them again, I found her gaze on me.

"Do you wish to go back to Somerset, Bess? We can fill the motorcar with pillows, as you did for me in York, and Lillian will accompany you on the train all the way home, to make the journey as comfortable as possible. She's good at that. She will take excellent care of you."

As if she wished me out of the way.

I was about to shake my head, and quickly thought better of it.

"Thank you for offering me the opportunity. But I would like to stay here and see this through."

It wasn't the answer she was after. Still, she didn't press me.

Not then.

Later in the morning I was feeling very much as Gordon Neville had done. I was heartily sick of my bed.

And so when Lillian came again to sit with me, I persuaded her to let me sit up, and then swing my feet over the side of the bed, preparing to stand.

She gave me a horrified look.

"Bess—look at yourself!"

I did. Where there was visible skin, it was darkly bruised, great patches of blue and purple and almost black. I knew there was more beneath my nightdress.

I was stiff in every muscle and joint, parts of me ached and parts of me hurt in a different way. But I needed to be on my feet and walk.

Lillian knelt by the bed and put on my stockings and shoes, so that I could stand.

It was painful, and I took in a deep breath to help me cope with it.

I managed to creep as far as the windows. Lillian rushed behind me with the chair that Lady Beatrice had sat in, and made me stop.

"Dr. Menzies ordered you to stay in bed," she reminded me, clearly worried.

"I know. But if I move a little—the stiffness will go away."

Outside it was sunny and there was a haze toward the east. Richmond lay that way.

"Is it hot again today?"

"I haven't been outside. But Cook told Davies she could boil a lobster on the back step."

I smiled.

She said, "I wish I knew what happened to you. I'm so afraid it has to do with my quarrel with Mr. Caldwell."

Without turning from the window, careful not to look at her, I said, "Do you think he would push me down the stairs for eavesdropping?"

She was pensive, considering the question. "His father might have—" she began and then turned white. "Why on earth did I say such a thing as that? We're all so unsettled, we can't think clearly."

"What do you know about the Caldwells, Lillian? If it could prevent another crime, you must tell me."

"They—they have a reputation. That's to say, they did. Frederick took after his mother, he was a much nicer man. But even he could be unpredictable at times. He wanted to marry Grace, I've told you that, and he set out to take her away from Gordon. Lady Beatrice knew them then. She said he was quite ruthless about it."

"So why on earth was he invited to Mrs. Neville's birthday celebration then?"

"The three of them—Arthur and Gordon and Frederick—survived the war, and they—I don't know. I think Arthur must have told his mother, let's include Frederick, as a mark of our return, and then we don't have to include them after that."

"It didn't disturb Arthur that Frederick had been so set on marrying Grace?"

"I expect he felt what Mrs. Neville felt—that it was just as well Gordon didn't win her. She would have made his life wretched and driven poor Anne out of her mind. Hugh knew her as a child, as I recall. The family is high church too." As if that was the final impression to leave behind. "An uncle is an archbishop."

I'd been led away from the main subject very cleverly. Again.

"It still seems odd—the first real family gathering in four years? And people included who weren't particularly close to the family."

Lillian sighed. "Yes, I know." She rubbed her hands together nervously. "I heard Inspector Wade ask Mrs. Neville if Gordon had invited Frederick Caldwell here purposely to kill him. Since the war hadn't got around to it. His words, not mine."

I was stiffening as I sat in the chair. Rising, I walked back across the room to the door, then turned and started back. It was painful. Everything was battered and bruised. That's how it felt.

Lillian said, "Bess. This isn't wise—Dr. Menzies—"

"It's all right, Lillian, I just need to loosen these tight muscles." I walked across the room again, paused, then walked back.

My brain was still a little foggy from the drug-induced sleep. And I was trying to walk and think clearly, and find a way to persuade Lillian to trust me.

And then I remembered something she had said at the beginning.

"You mentioned Mark and Frederick Caldwell's father—"

She put out a hand, as if to stop me before I could say any more. "No, I don't know anything about him! It was *hearsay*!"

"I don't think it was. You were about to say that *he* might push me down the stairs in a fit of anger."

"Please, Bess, don't ask any more questions, I beg you," she pleaded with me.

"Lillian. Were you governess to Frederick and Mark?"

This time I could see how taken aback she was. "When they were—no, Bess, no! I've never worked for the Caldwells."

I believed her.

"Then how did you know their father? It wasn't Lady Beatrice—she met the family through the Nevilles when the sons were in school and university together."

Lillian's eyes closed for a moment, then opened again bright with tears. "If I tell you, will you let it go? Nothing good will come of it, if you keep pressing for the truth. Just—let it be, let's go back to where we were in York, and forget that family again."

I waited.

She swallowed hard at a lump in her throat from the tears she was holding in with all the strength she possessed.

"I happened to know. Don't ask me how, I'll never tell you that, it would break a confidence that I have sworn to keep. The person who asked me to swear is dead, but I revere that promise and I will keep it. But I will surely lose my place."

Once more I waited.

She didn't turn away. She just simply stood there, a forlorn figure with nowhere to go and no one to turn to. Clinging to worn-out dignity.

"Their father is a murderer. Was. And no one knows what he did but me, now. I am so afraid that someone will remember me, that I was there, and do their best to see that I never tell."

"Lillian! Does Lady Beatrice know?"

"No."

Remembering something else, I asked, "Melinda. Mrs. Crawford. Does she know about this?"

"No. I have told you. I swore to tell no one. And I haven't."

I wanted to press Lillian to explain more, but I could see her curling in on herself, already ashamed to have said this much. I walked back to the bed and sat down on the edge. My hip had been hurting, but now my head and neck had begun to let me know they were there with a vengeance.

"I'm so sorry, Lillian." It was inadequate, that apology. But how to make up for what I'd just done to a woman I considered a friend?

Chapter Seventeen

Even though I'd learned more about what was disturbing Lillian's peace of mind, why the Caldwell family distressed her so, it had no bearing on what was happening here in the Neville household.

Mark Caldwell's father was dead. He couldn't touch Lillian, nor could he be in any way responsible for the deaths of his son or Judith Bowman.

What's more, his past couldn't be seen as marking his remaining son as a killer.

And so I tried to put all that aside, and look at what I did know.

It wasn't that easy.

Tiring quickly, I relented and let Lillian lead me back to the bed and tuck me under the sheet.

That seemed to help her pretend that nothing had been said that I felt I had to pursue.

I looked at her returning to sit in her chair, giving me a little space to drop into a light sleep.

She had carried a heavy burden most of her life, for some reason I didn't understand. Probably would never understand. It was somehow buried in a past she had worked hard to hide.

I fleetingly wondered if she had known Mark Caldwell's father when she was young, and perhaps had a brief affair with him. I could see how good her bones were in her face, how pretty her hair might have been, and how a vivacious, natural spirit might have made her vulnerable. It would explain why she had done nothing with the knowledge she possessed.

Yet, somehow I couldn't quite picture that image of her youth.

She had such a strong sense of responsibility and a strict moral view of life.

Housemaids and governesses, milliners and actresses—women struggling to make their way in a world where they had to earn their own keep were often seduced and betrayed, not just in books—*Jane Eyre* came to mind—but in real life. I had worked during my training in a women's ward where I had interviewed and treated women who had been terribly abused. I had watched them die of illegal abortions and mistreatment, one in particular who had been knifed viciously and wanted to die when she looked in the mirror after her bandages came off. I didn't see Lillian among them.

Sighing, I let it go. She didn't want my help, and I had to respect that.

Hearing the sigh, she looked my way and smiled a little. Thinking I was in more pain after my exertions, she asked, "Shall I mix another drop into some water, Bess? Would that help?"

"It's best to keep a clear head. I fear Inspector Wade might descend with breakfast."

"Will he come, do you think?" she asked, suddenly anxious again.

"I expect he must."

It was her turn to sigh. "What are you going to tell him?"

"The truth. I promised Lady Beatrice."

She made a little face. "Then, of course you must." After a moment she added, "And she is so often right, you know. I often ask her advice."

My breakfast came, as nicely cut into fork-size bits as the trays brought up to the master of the house. I smiled wryly at the thought—having watched him insist on feeding himself with his left hand as soon as he could manage it, I was about to embark on the same attempt. There was no hope of using my own right arm this morning.

I did find my mouth most of the time, while Lillian hovered between wanting to take my fork from me and help, and suppressed laughter at my mistakes.

It was good to see her in happier spirits.

The tray had hardly been removed, my hands and face washed to remove the remnants of the meal, and the napkin emptied of crumbs, when there was a tap at the door. Lillian was just helping me with my hair, pulling it back and knotting it behind my head. Stepping back, she gave me an encouraging look, and went to answer the summons.

It was an entourage.

Mrs. Neville came in, to be sure I was prepared for visitors, giving a final twitch to the bedclothes and settling my dressing gown collar more evenly. Then she turned to the door, nodded to someone outside, and Lady Beatrice sailed in. There was no other word to describe it—she was making certain that no one dared to try and keep her out.

Behind her was Inspector Wade, and behind him, Arthur Neville.

He gave me a half smile, and said, "Forgive me. I'm offering my service as your legal representative, and I hope you can accept me as such."

"Thank you," I replied. I was somewhat relieved not to have to face Inspector Wade's questions without a witness.

They arranged themselves around the room. Lillian moved back to the windows and Mrs. Neville joined her there. Arthur pulled up the straight chair that we'd used earlier, and offered it to Inspector Wade.

He took it as his due and sat down, notebook in hand. It was the first time I'd seen him use one, and it brought home to me just how serious this conversation was going to be.

Arthur stood a few steps behind him. Where the Inspector couldn't see his face, but I could, quite clearly.

We went through the formalities, identifying who I was, and why he was there to interview me, with the purpose of taking down my statement and having me sign it.

He asked if I had any reservations about allowing him to take it down, but that was purely a factor of my right hand still being bandaged and my right arm useless at the moment.

I quietly listened and agreed to each of his explanations.

Above his head, Arthur gave me a slight smile.

Inspector Wade prompted me. "Last evening, on the date shown at the top of this statement, I was . . ."

I repeated the words, then moved on. "I had just finished dressing Mr. Gordon Neville's arm, and had settled him for the night. I turned down the lamp at his request and left the room. Walking down the passage, intending to go down to the sitting room where I had left the family earlier, I paused at the top of the step. I had several matters on my mind, and before descending, I wanted to put them into some order before I forgot details."

Inspector Wade interrupted me. "We will come back to these matters in due course. Continue with events of the moment."

I nodded.

"As far as I could tell, I was alone in the passage, alone at the head of the stairs. I'd seen no one else in the passage nor did I hear anyone. It was quiet as well on the floor below, for the sitting room door must have been shut. Still, I had no idea anyone was behind me. The first inkling was a hand placed flat against my back, between my shoulder blades, and I was given a heavy shove."

"Describe the hand."

I frowned. "It may even have been two hands. I can't tell you if it was a woman's hand or a man's. It was there and gone so quickly, I was only aware of the pressure and the force." I tried to think. "Whoever it was, I was not expecting it, and I started headfirst down the steps. Because I wasn't standing directly facing the stairs—more likely at an angle there at the corner of the wall at the top of the stairs, not having taken the first step to descend, I was—" I looked for the right word. "Slightly at a slant." I could feel my muscles tense painfully as I looked back at what had happened next.

"Because of that, rather than a straight fall to the floor below, I collided with the balustrades five or six steps—I'm not precisely sure of the number—flat on my face, my feet behind me."

There. It was said.

"I don't know if I cried out. I was trying to protect my head, reaching out to stop before I struck the solid balustrade. Trying not to lose my senses and roll the rest of the way. Not coherent thoughts, just to keep from being too badly hurt."

"Was anyone behind you at the head of the stairs, when you could look back?"

"The way my head and arm were wedged, I couldn't look there at all. Someone could have walked back the way he or she had come—could have stood at the top of the steps to see the results of the push—or crossed the landing to go to a room on the far side of the steps."

We moved on to what I heard and saw next. Who came running, where they were standing, the position of the staff, who summoned a doctor. I was hazy on some of the details, however sharp they had seemed at the time. It was as if I had been in two places at once, seeing myself fall and come to a stop, and going through it physically and emotionally at the time it was happening.

I told him everything until I was put to bed and given my drops of laudanum.

He wrote busily but carefully. I couldn't help but notice that his script was large and not well formed. As if he had learned to write in a grammar school in his village.

It wasn't important. It was just that I could look down and watch the black ink scrawl across the page as I spoke. Stark and black and ugly.

Inspector Wade had caught up with me.

"I shall have to ask the others present in the lower hall at the time of your fall to give their own accounts. I have already done that with the witnesses present in this room."

I said, "I understand." Their memories had to be collected before they heard what I recalled, so that I didn't change theirs with mine.

Inspector Wade was regarding me with a curious frown. "Have you ever given the police a statement before?" he asked. Thinking perhaps that I'd been too calm and straightforward for one my age or with my background.

Hedging around the question, I said, "I have just finished the war years making regular reports to Matron about our patients, their responses to treatment, and any problems with it. I sometimes think she could have taught Scotland Yard a thing or two about observation and detection. But then men's lives depended on her skill."

"Don't be pert," he told me, giving me his basilisk stare.

"I'm not. I'm trying to explain my statement."

He said, "Is that all you wish to write here?"

"I think so. I tried to remember everything."

And then he read my words back to me. In a slow, careful, emotionless voice that did more for the grammar than the content.

"You have stated here that you heard no one in the passage approaching you. Was there someone there?"

"There must have been. It's the only explanation for the hand in my back."

"Could that person have been barefoot? In stocking feet?"

I wanted to glance toward Mrs. Neville, but I forced my eyes to stay on his. "It is certainly possible."

We signed the document then. I was first, then Arthur as my solicitor, and Lady Beatrice as witness, since she wasn't directly related to anyone under suspicion.

That done, he folded the statement, put it carefully in the breast pocket of his coat, capped his pen, and then folded his arms.

I braced myself for what was to come now.

CHAPTER EIGHTEEN

BEFORE INSPECTOR WADE could speak, there was a harsh rap at the door.

Arthur went at once to answer it, almost as if he thought it might be estate business that would take him away. I glimpsed his expression as he reached for the knob. He was not pleased by the interruption.

As the door swung open, I could see Mark Caldwell standing there.

"Mrs. Neville told me you were taking a statement. If that is the case, I should be here, as my brother—"

Arthur said, "It isn't about your brother's death. Or Mrs. Bowman's daughter. Miss Crawford was attacked and injured last evening. She has been ordered to stay in bed. That's the only reason we are in her bedroom."

Mark Caldwell's gaze moved from Arthur's face to mine, there among the bedclothes.

"Is that true?"

"Yes." I held up the bandaged hand and raised my other arm. As the sleeve of my dressing gown fell back to the elbow, he could see the bruising. Everyone could.

I thought he would have the good sense if not the good manners to leave, then, but he didn't.

"Who is responsible for this?" He moved into the room, staring from me to Inspector Wade. "And what does this have to do with my brother?"

"We have no idea, Mr. Caldwell. That's not what we are trying to discover at the moment. In good time, we will draw our conclusions. After the facts of *this* incident have been examined."

It took more than sternness to dislodge the man by the door.

In the end, mostly because Inspector Wade had not interviewed him yet about where he was and at what time, he was able to send Mark Caldwell—fuming at being thwarted—away.

It hadn't been much of a respite.

And I dreaded telling Inspector Wade about Gordon.

But to my surprise, he said, "I understand you saw someone walking in the drive last evening. Just before you were—attacked."

"That's true."

"Tell me what you saw."

And to the best of my ability, I did. Even seeing Grace Caldwell. Holding nothing back except the fact that Gordon Neville stood at the window with me.

When I had finished with my description, he asked what Gordon hadn't.

"Are you certain enough of what you saw that you would be willing to make a statement to that effect?"

Did I?

The room behind Inspector Wade was quiet. A different sort of quiet, when the witnesses were simply listening to question and answer. This, I thought in a corner of my mind, was more apprehensive.

Was I sure enough to damage Grace Caldwell's reputation?

I took a deep breath. "Someone came from the house. She walked down to where the dog and the man waited, and I never saw her clearly. In that one flash of lightning, I was surprised. The last person I'd have expected to be in the drive."

Inspector Wade turned to Arthur, then to Mrs. Neville.

"How would Mrs. Caldwell have known Lieutenant Harding?"

Mrs. Neville said, "I couldn't tell you, Inspector. I wasn't aware of any connection between them."

"Mr. Neville?"

I saw Lady Beatrice move slightly as the Inspector's gaze swept past her.

"Nor I." He frowned. "Lieutenant Harding served with us for a time. With Mrs. Caldwell's late husband. If he wished to offer condolences, why didn't he come to the door? And how did she know he was in the drive in the first place?"

"I'll be asking the staff if a message was passed." Turning back to me, he added, "Have you seen any indication of another contact between these two people?"

He had a rather rude way of insinuating that someone was withholding information. Well, hadn't I?

"No." I remembered. "I went out the library door to the terrace the morning after the storm, for a little fresh air. On the step, as I walked to the terrace's edge, I saw the wet imprint of half a man's boot, as if he'd rested a foot on there as the dog walked up and sniffed the air. I'd had a fright recently with a dog. Otherwise I wouldn't have thought twice about it."

There. No mention of Gordon and his feelings about Mr. Harding.

"Were the terrace doors locked when you went out?"

"Yes, I found them locked, opened them, and then closed them again afterward."

"And so you would have no way of knowing if someone had stepped out there before you. Perhaps when the man was there."

"Yes, that's true."

"And you have met the housemaids. You believe you would recognize them on sight?"

I didn't know them as I did Ruth, who had been so helpful.

"I believe so."

Wade nodded.

"Mrs. Neville. Would you please ask Mrs. Caldwell to step in this room for a moment, please?"

I thought Mrs. Neville would refuse. And then with resignation, she said, "Certainly." And was gone.

There was an awkward silence while we waited. No one wanted to break it, and yet as it wore on, it was more and more difficult to know just where to look. I kept my gaze on my hands. Arthur had gone to look out the window, where his mother had been standing, and Lady Beatrice was almost unnaturally quiet in her chair by the hearth. I was afraid she was wishing she hadn't come in here after all.

The minutes dragged by. Twice I looked at my little watch on the table by the bed, but I was beginning to wonder if it had stopped altogether. If in my daze last night, I'd forgot to wind it.

Surely I had done?

The door opened finally and Mrs. Neville came in. Her face was flushed.

"I'm so sorry, Inspector. Mrs. Caldwell is resting and doesn't care to speak to you or anyone else at the moment. She will give you time after dinner. Perhaps two thirty?"

"We shall see about that," he said grimly, and went out of the room.

Inspector Wade was away no more than five minutes.

When he returned, Wade said only, "I believe there is another point we have not discussed." But his eyes were hard and very cold.

I saw Lillian move deeper into the corner, her back against long drapes that had been pulled back to each corner, to let in light.

The room was stifling. Too many people as well. I felt an instant's light-headedness, and told myself it wasn't a concussion, it was just the stale air that was to blame.

Settled in his chair again, he said, "In the matter of Frederick Caldwell's death. I am given to understand that he was not left alone, for fear he might require urgent care at any moment."

"I wasn't here. It is what I have been told."

"Did Gordon Neville visit him?"

Arthur, once more behind Inspector Wade answered, "He was in the room when we carried Frederick to his bed. I told him in no uncertain terms that I wasn't having him black out with pain or be sick all over the floor. He looked ill and he was unnaturally pale. He went down to the study then, he said he needed a stiff whiskey. Later in the evening, as I was speaking to Dr. Menzies, I found Gordon in the room with the patient. I thought they were speaking, but when I came closer, I heard my brother call Frederick's name again and ask him if he could see or hear him."

It was coming, I could tell . . .

"And so he was with the dying man on the fells, and he was with the dying man in his room." He turned back to me. "I also have it on good authority that you are aware that Gordon Neville may have left this house on the night of the murder of Judith Bowman. That he received a missive from Mrs. Bowman and then went out to meet her daughter."

"I didn't know of a message until much later. I found him in his room, just returning from a breath of fresh air, as he put it. It was my view that he couldn't have got far in his condition. That it was possible he'd done what he confessed to doing. Stepping out for several minutes. I told him this was not to happen again."

"But he left his bed again, Miss Crawford. On the night you fell. In his bare feet, knowing that you believed Gordon Neville was settled, and he followed you to the top of the stairs, intending you serious bodily injury."

There it was.

"I can think of no reason why Mr. Neville would wish to harm me."

"On the contrary, you knew he had left the house, and you could place him on the fells the night murder was done."

"Here—!" Arthur said sharply. "Miss Crawford has told you that Mr. Neville had not had the ability to go far. It's a medical opinion, not a guess."

Inspector Wade rose. To the room at large, he said, "I am taking Gordon Neville into police custody as a suspect in two murders and an attempted murder. I will not be put off, and come here again for another fall. This will be ended now."

He walked toward the door. Mrs. Neville called out to Arthur to stop him, to Lady Beatrice to do something.

They followed him. I managed to untangle my sheets, find my slippers, and stand up. The room tilted a little, but I ignored it. Impossible to dress—there was no time. I went as I was. I'd forgot Lillian. She was in the middle of the room now, telling me that I wasn't dressed, I couldn't go with them. But stiff hip or not, my neck hurting with every step, I walked on.

I was nearly there when they opened Gordon Neville's door.

The Inspector was inside the room when I reached the door, speaking his name.

But when I could look between the shoulders of the two women blocking the doorway, I realized, just as Inspector Wade was discovering, that Gordon Neville was not in his bed or in any other part of that room.

Inspector Wade turned on Arthur, accusing him of warning his brother what might happen, and helping him to dress and leave. But I had seen the surprise on Arthur's face. It wasn't he who had warned Gordon.

Turning to me, he said, "And so much for your medical views of the threat to Mr. Neville's arm if he is taken into a cell. I've half a mind to charge you as well."

With that he turned and walked out of the room. We quickly moved out of his way.

Arthur said to his mother, "Was this your doing?"

"I wanted to. But I was afraid it will make him appear to be even more guilty."

I said, from where I was standing, my good hand holding onto the doorframe, "He knows that Mr. Harding—Lieutenant Harding—is back in the village."

They stared at me, now.

"Did you tell him?" Arthur asked coldly. Then, "No, of course not. You couldn't have known."

"Lettie Bowman warned him in the note she sent to the house by her daughter," Lady Beatrice spoke in my defense.

"That makes sense."

"What is between Gordon and this Lieutenant Harding?" Lady Beatrice asked.

"I think we ought to know," Lady Beatrice added.

"There's no time," Arthur began, coming out of that sudden and unexpected discovery that Gordon was gone. "I've got to find my brother before Wade does."

But Inspector Wade had found Davies and was organizing a search of the house. I could hear him barking orders there in the front hall, frightening the maids, one of whom was crying, with certain imprisonment if they let the master of the house escape.

I went past the head of the stairs, staying far away from the steps themselves, and hurried back to my room as quickly as possible, hurting though I was.

Opening the door, I said to Lillian, "Quickly, you must help me dress."

"Bess—"

"No, Gordon had left the house on his own. There's going to be trouble and possibly even another murder. It won't hurt me—"

But it did, changing from my nightdress and gown to undergarments and clothing. I bit my lip, clenched my teeth and my good fist, but it was finished, Lillian helping me with my stockings and my shoes.

She was talking rapidly, and at first I ignored Lillian, too occupied with what I had to do to make myself presentable.

And then I realized what she was saying.

"This Lieutenant Harding tried to have Gordon court-martialed during the war. As soon as he was an officer, he went after Gordon for slights, as he believed he'd suffered as he rose from the ranks. It's true, Bess, I've heard them discussing it."

She was a listener, a quiet ear a little away from the family she served, there ready to be of assistance, never putting herself forward, always keeping whatever she learned strictly to herself. Never using that information or even letting the family know that she possessed it.

"He's vindictive?"

"I don't know that I've ever seen him, truthfully. And so I can't speak to that. But he hates Gordon Neville. He would relish seeing him hunted down and taken away by the police."

"I don't think he's in the house—" I continued, "Go down the stairs and out to where Wilson is keeping the motorcar. I'll be down by the time you find him. You stay in the house in case Gordon comes here."

"I have no right to tell Wilson—" Lillian began.

I caught her hand in my good one. "There will be far more suffering in this house if those two men meet and fight. Taking a motorcar and driver without leave will pale by comparison."

Worried, clearly reluctant, all but wringing her hands anxiously, Lillian tried to convince me to wait. I had to lead her to the door, then shut it behind her.

There was a walking stick in a tall Chinese vase by the main door.

Along with an umbrella. I took the stick, and quickly went out to the steps, where Inspector Wade wouldn't see me. Then I closed the main door and waited.

It opened again just as Wilson brought the motorcar up the drive. And Lady Beatrice stepped out the front door. "That man can't order me about like the scullery maid. Where are you going with my motorcar?"

"I'm looking for Gordon. Lady Beatrice, Gordon's stood his ground, I think, in the face of the Inspector. He wouldn't hide somewhere in the house to be hunted down. He thinks he has only a short window of opportunity, and he's decided to take it," I replied.

"Foolish man. He can't fight this man Harding. He's not fit. Hallo, Wilson, help Miss Crawford into the motorcar. She's not fit to be driving either."

When we were in and Wilson had returned to the wheel, Lady Beatrice said, "Where are you expecting to look?"

"The village."

"My dear, he won't scandalize the village by challenging this Harding fellow in front of them. He's the lord and master here. And the day of horsewhipping is past."

Where then?

I couldn't walk as far as the outcropping. Even with every bit of my strength, if I tried, I'd have to stop long before I got there. And this motorcar couldn't make the journey any more than I could.

Where?

Where would they find the privacy to meet?

And I recalled the laithe barn I'd seen from the outcropping. It was some distance from there, but it was closer to the farm where I thought I'd first seen Mr. Harding.

Would Gordon and Joe Harding meet there?

I gave Wilson his instructions and leaned back against the seat. Every bone in my body seemed to throb. I closed my eyes, but the movement of the motorcar down the twisting drive to the gates made me dizzy. I had to open them.

Lady Beatrice was looking down at me. "This is foolishness, Bess."

Taking a deep breath, I said, "I don't know what else to do."

She nodded. "Nor do I." And then, under her breath, "Reckless, reckless man."

We had reached the main road, the large vehicle making short work of the distance I'd walked.

Remembering, I leaned forward. "Wilson. This man Harding. He has a vicious dog."

"Thank you, Miss."

We came into the village, took the left fork of the road, staying on the fell side of the river. And there, almost where the two roads came together over a footbridge for the right branch, we came to the muddy lane down which the Harding house was set.

It was a little larger than some in the village, a prosperous farm in fact. It might be Harding's sister's farm. Davies spoke to me about it when I'd asked about the dog. It appeared to be an independent holding, nothing to do, as far as I could see, with the Nevilles. Still, the lane that went to the farm and then continued past it, narrower and muddier, led to the old fell barn, where men could feed and keep stock alive in the worst weather winter could send to these isolated valleys.

Wilson hesitated at the gate that led to the secondary lane. It stood open—indeed, looking down the bonnet of the motorcar, I didn't think it had ever been closed. Saplings and briars and other wild-grown plants kept the arm that usually swung forward to shut it now locked the gate fast to the far side.

Here the Neville property must begin, for the barn was theirs. Had the Hardings kept this gate open for years, a bit of defiance toward the larger estate? Or was it something that one man had decided to do?

You can't shut me out . . . I'm here, like it or not.

I could see the barn ahead. Hopelessly ahead.

But at a word from Lady Beatrice, Wilson edged the motorcar forward. We barely scraped through the open gate without touching the paint, but limbs and leaves brushed the sides until we were through.

Rocking and bouncing over deep ruts and runoff, we plunged forward.

But some twenty feet from the barn we came to a large stone half buried in the lane, and one tire refused to mount it.

"As far as I can go, my lady."

"Well done. We'll walk."

I was grateful for my walking stick—the way was so rough Wilson had to offer Lady Beatrice his arm—and my hip felt as if it were on fire.

The barn seemed top-heavy, tall, rectangular, with straight sides and windows only where they were needed to pull up hay or feed to what must at one time have been a loft. We had a large barn on our property in Somerset, a different stone and in some way a pretty building compared to the stark, utilitarian shape of this one.

The large double doors, which would allow a wagon to pass easily through, were shut and slightly askew from what must be centuries of storms. But a side door was standing wide open, nothing in front of it to keep the snows out now.

A fleeting thought passed through my mind—the effort it must have taken to build these barns . . . and the need.

We hesitated some ten feet from the doorway, and then I moved forward. As I reached the threshold, I could hear voices inside, but it was dimly lit, dark in places, and impossible to know where these were coming from.

As my eyes adjusted, I finally saw them. Dwarfed by the high roof and missing loft flooring in many places, two men stood facing each other.

And the dog stood by one man's side, and I could hear that deep-throated growl.

"Call him off," Gordon was saying.

"Why should I?"

"This is between you and me, not the—"

At that point, something shifted, the heat, a tiny breeze—and the dog caught our scent.

He came at us with unbelievable speed, crossing the littered floor of the barn in great strides, his teeth already bared.

"Take her away," I shouted to Wilson, and braced myself, using the stick as a weapon straight in front of me.

Gordon was turning, shouting over his shoulder at Harding, starting this way.

But the dog must have had police training. Or family training, to keep the German soldiers away. For the dog stopped just as he had before, and stood there in front of me, holding me at bay.

As he'd done once before.

Realizing I'd stopped breathing, I took in a frightened gulp of air, and said in the tone of voice Matron employed when she was seriously displeased, "Call off that dog. We're armed, we'll shoot him if you don't."

We had only a stick, but Joe Harding wasn't to know that.

He must have believed me. After several seconds, he chose the dog's safety. And whistled him back. After a last long look at me, the dog obeyed.

I was unbelievably relieved. Stepping over the threshold, I limped into the barn. The dog made no other move toward me. But he watched me with intent.

"The police are on their way. Mr. Neville, you have left the house without permission. They will arrest you on sight. Mr. Harding, they have questions for you as well. Inspector Wade has already spoken to Mrs. Caldwell—"

I hadn't expected either one of them to heed me, much less believe me.

Gordon Neville said, "You have no business here, Miss Crawford. Go back to the house."

Lady Beatrice must have appeared in the doorway behind me. She said, walking forward, "You have witnesses. Like it or not, gentlemen. Finish what you have to say to each other. And we will leave."

The odd thing was, Joe Harding was no longer looking at Gordon Neville. He was staring at me.

Not because I had shared a compartment with him on the York train after he'd been put aboard by a nursing Sister.

"What do you mean?" Joe Harding asked. "Spoken to Mrs. Caldwell?"

Thinking quickly, I said, "I believe it was about the fact that she was seen in the drive with you last evening. Inspector Wade wished to know why a recently widowed woman would be having an assignation with a villager."

He stood there, eyes on my face still, as if he could look beneath the flesh and bone, and read my mind.

I added for good measure, "A woman, in fact, whose husband was recently murdered."

He moved then. A whistle at the dog, and he was marching straight toward the door we'd just come through. I stepped to one side to get out of his way, but Lady Beatrice stood her ground. He had to walk around her.

And then he was gone, through the door, his feet crunching in the thick grass and rubble as he strode purposefully and quickly away.

Gordon Neville was understandably furious. He was already lashing out at me as he crossed the littered barn floor, his voice harsh and grim.

"What the he—" He remembered his godmother. "What the devil did you think you were doing, interfering?"

I said, holding my ground, "Did you think you could possibly have fought with that man? With that arm already badly damaged? And because you aren't in your room where Inspector Wade can arrest you, Wade had every right to declare you a dangerous fugitive."

But he wasn't listening. "You don't know what is at stake here. You know nothing about this business."

So tell me then, I wanted to say. But I knew that would make no difference. Frustrated, I turned on my heel and walked off.

Past Lady Beatrice, whose expression was such a mixture of emotions that all I saw was the surprise and rampant speculation. Wilson had somehow managed to turn the motorcar while we were in the barn, and as he got out, festoons of broken grasses fell out of the doorframe, the windscreen was covered in dust and seeds and grit. The heat overhead was heavy, the sky an odd haze.

Wilson walked past me to Lady Beatrice, eager to get her away. But she was trying to reason with Gordon.

They came out, still talking across each other. He was too angry to listen, and she was earnestly trying to calm him down.

He looked awful. The effort he'd made after all that had happened, as well as his enforced idleness, had taken a toll he hadn't expected when his mind had urged him to act.

Standing by the motorcar, I called to them, "He has a head start. Does that matter?"

Lady Beatrice turned, uncertain what I was asking. But Gordon heard me, and he swore feelingly under his breath.

"My lady—" Wilson was urging her.

Lady Beatrice made a decision. Turning, she walked directly to the motorcar and got in. Over her shoulder she said, to him, "You can walk home or you can ride."

I followed her inside.

After a stubborn moment of pride and hesitation, Gordon beat his way through the tall grass that blocked the far side of the motorcar, and was able to open the chauffeur's other door, getting in beside him instead of joining us. He was holding his right arm awkwardly, and had to reach across with his left to bring the door fully closed.

Wilson began to drive, leaning forward, watching his wings and bonnet carefully as the heavy vehicle rocked and swayed like something alive. And then we were at the gate, squeaking through once again. I heard Lady Beatrice, who had been watching almost as cautiously, sigh with relief and lean back in her own seat.

By the time we'd reached the village, little knots of people were gathered here and there, trying to discover what was going on. They could see as far as the laithe barn gate, they even could tell we had gone beyond it. Two women and a driver. They must have seen Joe Harding walking away. It was not what they were used to, and their faces were worried. Or they knew more about the relationship between these two men than some of us did.

As we passed the little square and the candle shop, Mrs. Bowman was just by her door, her arms clasped tightly across her chest, her face drawn and worried.

And then the motorcar was beginning to move faster, and we were out of the village and on the road to the house.

"Gordon. Will you surrender to Inspector Wade? Before this completely destroys your public credibility? You know Arthur will have you out of there at once—I will speak to the Chief Constable myself. Jonathan will do what he can—the best barrister in London. Whatever is required."

"No."

It was curt.

The motorcar's purring motor was the only sound we heard the rest of the way.

And we didn't see Joe Harding. Not that we would have, if he didn't wish us to. I'd had a little experience of that earlier.

The gates of the drive were ahead before Gordon said, "If you will find me a whiskey, I'll deal with Wade."

CHAPTER NINETEEN

IGNORING THE CRY from my hip, I was out of the motorcar almost before it had fully stopped by the house door.

Leaving Lady Beatrice to Wilson and her godson, I went inside.

It was far too quiet as I stepped into the dimness of the front hall, stuffy and airless and somehow—I couldn't quite put a name to the sense of *waiting*.

Almost like hearing the first ranging artillery shell being fired, and not knowing yet where it would land . . . watching for it, needing to know where it was heading.

Ignoring that too, I went directly into the first room where I knew there was a drinks cabinet—the small drawing room—and took the first whiskey decanter I could see. I put an average amount in a glass for him, put everything away as tidily as possible for the moment, and was at the door when he and Lady Beatrice stepped over the threshold.

I saw that she was leaning heavily on Gordon's arm, as if events had been too much for her. But I glimpsed her eyes as I turned to him, and there was no hint of weakness or distress there.

She was intentionally slowing him down, and he dared not ignore her and walk away.

She straightened so that he could take the whiskey with his left hand. He drained it and handed me the glass.

Then he said, "They'll have searched the house, as Wade told them to. Aunt Bea, may I use your bedroom?"

Without a word she led the way up the stairs to her room. I followed them.

It was empty when we got there. But there was evidence too of a hasty search, the armoire door slightly ajar and the windows' drapes askew where someone had looked behind them. The bed was turned down, and I wouldn't have been surprised to see that someone had looked under it as well.

Turning to me, Gordon said, "You needn't stay. It's not your quarrel."

"It's rather late to suppose that," I said ruefully. "The Inspector is angry enough to bring charges against me." And what would my mother and the Colonel Sahib have to say about that? Or Cousin Melinda, who had sent me north. I put it out of my thoughts.

Gordon regarded me for a moment. "Just who are you? Really?"

"What's wrong, Gordon?" Lady Beatrice said, then.

"I'm not sure. Why did someone try to kill *Bess*, if she came only as your nurse for a surgical procedure?"

"Who told you I was attacked?" I asked quickly.

"Mother. Arthur. Lady Beatrice."

"I have kept secrets," I said. "Yours, for one. I saw someone on the drive, and no one believed me. Or rather, no one appeared to. I believe Joe Harding is somehow a part of what is happening. He also tried to frighten me away."

"His part in this has to do with old history, and the war. With me."

"What if that isn't all of it? What if there is something else he wants?"

He shook his head. "Then you don't know the man very well."

"Or perhaps you still see him as an old rival, and a thorn in your side in France. Not as the man he became in the trenches."

Something in his gaze changed slightly. Some memory, something. I had no idea what it might be.

"I think," Lady Beatrice said, "we might eliminate one of the discrepancies here. They are still searching somewhere in the house. It will be finished very soon. Grace is in her room."

I was just going to say something to Gordon when we heard someone say angrily, "No. That's finished. Over."

It sounded like Grace's voice.

Someone else answered.

"The front hall—" Gordon said and started that way.

Lady Beatrice caught his good arm. "Stop. Let's have a look before you fly down those stairs."

We moved quietly toward the landing on this floor. I wasn't tall enough to look down into the entrance hall, but I could see that the door was standing wide, and the voices were coming from there.

Grace was saying, "You don't seem to understand. There's a murder inquiry going on. Inspector Wade has come to arrest Gordon for my husband's death. Let him do his work—I can't be seen—"

"I live here."

"It doesn't matter. Go away for a month. Two. Until the trial."

"I've just got my sight back. My sister needs me to bring the farm up to what it was before the war. I'm needed here."

"Then stay here! Stay away from me, from the house—stay away and let the police deal with Gordon Neville." She was helplessly furious with him. "Why is it you want to hurt him so badly? So—so *personally*? Isn't it enough he'll hang?"

"And I'll be there in the room when it's done."

"You can't—that's not how—"

"So you may say. I'll be there. Wait and see."

"Oh, for God's sake, what has happened to you since you came back here? It's as if you changed overnight—I hardly recognize you."

"I saw the farm. There weren't enough people to keep it running, to keep the sheep, the dairy. My sister couldn't do it alone, there was only my pay to help her, and the Nevilles never lifted a hand for her. Four years. Four almighty years of neglect. And she never told me—she always said she was *managing*. That she was all right. But she wasn't. She was barely able to *survive*." The pain in his voice was heavy and very real.

"I don't have Frederick's money yet. Not until the will is probated. I only have my allowance and the legacy from my parents. Frederick controlled all that." She was pleading. "Try to be understand—"

"No, it's summer now. I need the money now. By winter we'll be in trouble, and no way to save anything that's left."

We could hear voices coming down the stairs now from the attics. The two people below heard them too.

Lady Beatrice said, "In my room, Gordon. Now."

Joe Harding was saying, "Don't play with me, Grace. I'm warning you."

And I heard the door slam shut behind him.

Grace Caldwell cried out in absolute, chilling frustration. And then we could hear her heels on the lovely patterned floor of the hall, and start up the stairs.

"Go," Lady Beatrice said. And we hurried, to be out of sight before she reached a point in the stairs where she could see us standing there, eavesdropping.

Her door slammed, ours was closed, and the parade of staff and Inspector Wade came spilling through the servants' staircase at the far end of the passage where the family rooms were situated. We could hear loud arguments, Inspector Wade's voice rising above the tumult, Davies interjecting reproof for the way he was addressing someone—Mrs. Neville, very likely. Gordon started for the door, then stopped. As the flow of feet and voices headed for the main staircase, Arthur was saying,

"That's enough. You've searched the house. Now search the village. He is not *here!*"

We lost the thread as they went down the stairs. And then the door slammed for a second time.

The hall fell silent at last.

"Well," Lady Beatrice said, moving toward a chair at the hearth, "I wonder if it's too soon to ring for tea." She turned to Gordon. "And how does Grace Caldwell know this Harding fellow?"

"I've no idea." Gordon glanced at me, and I shook my head. He took the other chair across from Lady Beatrice, favoring his right arm, rubbing it in a futile effort to ease the pain. It needed to be cleaned, dressed. I took the other chair at Lady Beatrice's dressing table.

"It makes no sense," he went on.

I said, "Did the Caldwells open their house as a clinic?"

"As I remember, it wasn't large enough to serve as one."

"Did Mrs. Caldwell do good work among the wounded?" Women of her position often visited clinics, brought small presents of tobacco or chocolates or even toothbrushes and shaving razors to the wounded men. It cheered them, of course, reminded them that they hadn't been forgot, but in a way these women also represented the England men were fighting for.

I had been in English clinics when the visitors had come through. I'd seen spirits rise among men who were in pain and facing more surgeries.

I said, "He was in a clinic for shrapnel wounds to the eyes. He was on the train to York with me, where he was met there by another nurse. No doubt to have his vision looked at before his final demobbing."

"Are you sure?"

"Yes. And the timing is right, isn't it? He was here ahead of me, but you didn't know at first that he had come back. That's why Lettie tried to warn you. If he came home and found his sister with the farm in desperate straits, he would have been very angry."

"I didn't know—I'd only just got home myself."

Lady Beatrice said, "That's why Lettie was trying to warn you. He wasn't simply home, he'd discovered the truth, and blamed the Nevilles for not doing anything to help."

I'd seen the farm, from the end of the street that crossed the beck and ran to the footbridge.

It had looked prosperous. Overgrown in places, perhaps, the drying of all the spring grasses that no one had had time to clear away. But the front door wasn't the measure of a farm. It was the outbuildings and the stock, and the people to keep both thriving. Joe Harding wouldn't have guessed, from a few brambles in the lane and front gardens, what he was about to see. He would have walked into his house, greeted his sister—and half an hour later, walked down to the barn—or out to his fields—or where his cattle and sheep were grazing.

And he wanted revenge for what he'd seen.

"Dear God," Lady Beatrice said, seeing the same images I must have been bringing up. It didn't take a prodigious imagination to follow a man's progress home. It must have happened in hundreds of farms and holdings and shops and places of business. There hadn't been enough men—or women—to keep Britain running perfectly in the face of the Great War.

Gordon said again, "I didn't know. I don't know what I could have done if I had. We barely survived. Feeding the Army helped, wool for blankets helped. I don't know what Mother did to keep us alive. She won't talk about it."

I'd been thinking about something else. "Going back to the birthday celebration. Why did Frederick and Grace come to share it?"

Gordon answered me. "Frederick and Arthur and I arrived home within a matter of weeks of each other. Two—three weeks? Arthur had written to Frederick, welcoming him home, and he said something about the fact that I was back as well, and we were in time to celebrate

Mother's birthday for the first time since 1914. He replied that he and Grace would like to come, just to welcome everyone home, before we scattered for our own lives. Something to that effect."

"Was it Grace's idea, I wonder?" I asked. "To meet Joe Harding again?"

"Who knows?" Gordon said wearily. "She won't tell us. Frederick is dead. I never thought—it never occurred to me that she might have found someone else. But of all possibilities? *Joe Harding?*" There was revulsion in his voice. And then he added, "I hope Frederick never found out. It would have killed him."

But hadn't someone told me that Grace Caldwell had looked at her choices between Frederick and Gordon, and decided that she preferred to live in Peterborough and changed her mind about marrying Gordon after all.

If that were true, I found myself realizing in alarm, she wouldn't leave Frederick for someone whose farm had nearly been ruined by the war, certainly not one standing at the edge of a village as tiny as Scarfdale.

"She's not in love with him," I said aloud. "I think she used him for her own ends. Lieutenant Harding. She could promise him money, respectability, a life very much like the one he envied here, at the Hall. Officer and gentleman."

"For what?"

"Helping her kill Frederick Caldwell."

They stared at me.

"And you, Gordon, quite by chance, gave him the opening."

Lady Beatrice said, "Bess. Do you realize what you are saying?"

"It fits!" I insisted. "What if Joe Harding got to the scene of the accident first. He might even have seen it happen. And he did something to Frederick, then left you alive to take the blame. We couldn't be sure whether there was a blow to the neck that damaged the spinal cord there. What if there was?"

"Why Judith?" Gordon insisted.

"She caught him coming to the house that night to speak to Grace after she returned from Richmond with your family."

"All well and good," he said, "as a piece of imaginary police work. Much as I despise the man, I don't see him killing a helpless man lying on the ground in the north of England."

"What did he accuse you of, when he tried to report you?" Lady Beatrice asked.

"That was different," he said shortly.

"Was it?"

He said accusingly, "You've talked to Arthur."

"Yes, well, I am guilty of that," said Lady Beatrice.

"What happened?" I asked her.

"Gordon had to kill a German machine gunner with his bare hands. His revolver had jammed, there was nothing he could do. The German had to be stopped, he'd already killed or wounded a dozen men. And so he did what had to be done. Later, it was reported that he had killed an unarmed German prisoner in anger because of the number of wounded and dead."

It had happened in the war. Machine gunners were hated, and there were whispers about what had become of some of them. Especially on the German retreat, when their well-placed and hidden nests could stop an entire advance.

If Gordon expected me to be shocked, he didn't know my long familiarity with the Army. Not even my father and Simon realized how many brutal and bloody events I'd witnessed or been told about in deathbed confessions among the wounded . . . The men didn't speak of it to anyone—and neither did the nursing Sisters.

"It's right now that matters," I said. "We don't have much time. You will have to decide about Grace, Gordon."

He'd loved her once. He didn't want to believe me. He wanted to think of her as having chosen Frederick in her heart and of being steadfast to her choice. He may have believed he was over his infatuation. But the feelings were still there deep inside.

Lady Beatrice said thoughtfully, "If any of this preposterous idea is true, then you owe it to Frederick to expose it."

Her godson abruptly got up—with some difficulty still—and walked to the window.

Lady Beatrice waited for a few seconds. "Gordon."

"Why should I? *He* didn't play fair, you know that. I've had to face it."

"She loved him best. You didn't stand in their way."

But it had hurt all the same. Both of us could see that, however he tried to hide it from us.

Lady Beatrice rose then. A tall, slim woman in a moss-green summer gown, her face set now. "Then I shall speak to the Inspector for you."

Chapter Twenty

GORDON, APPARENTLY, WAS all too willing to inform Inspector Wade that he, the man Wade was hunting, had just returned to the Hall in the Dowager's motorcar.

I heard the Inspector's horse come up the drive as I went down to the kitchens to see if there was any tea to be had. Both Mrs. Neville and Lady Beatrice had tried to ring when Mrs. Neville came directly to Lady Beatrice's bedroom, where we were debating what to do next.

Turning about, I went up the stairs as fast as I could hobble, and warned the gathering there.

I had just finished when Arthur came in behind me. His gaze went directly to his brother. "You shouldn't have come back."

"He won't make a fugitive of me."

"What am I to say to him?"

Lady Beatrice spoke before Mrs. Neville. "Put him in the sitting room. And have tea brought at once. Gordon will come down last. There won't be violence with the Spode service between us. Collect Margaret, and ask her to find an excuse to speak to Grace—above all, keep Grace in her room. Where is Lillian?"

"I sent her to wait in Gordon's room," said Mrs. Neville.

"Leave her there. And Mark Caldwell?"

"He stayed with the search. Every step of the way. I left him in my study with the whiskey decanter."

Lady Beatrice changed her mind with the swiftness of thought. "Bess and I would like to have a word with him. While we're waiting for that tea."

Like a general—reminding me strongly of Cousin Melinda—she made quick work of disposing of her forces. We were already going down the back stairs toward Gordon's study before a groom had taken Inspector Wade's horse and Davies had let him in the door.

Mark Caldwell was standing by the window, decanter in one hand and a glass half full in the other. He said, "Go away!" when he heard the door open, and when it didn't close because Lady Beatrice and I were coming in, he turned, his expression moody and angry, a volatile mix.

"What do you want? To gloat that the son of the house got away?"

Lady Beatrice went forward, took a chair, pointed to the other, and said, "Sit down, young man. I want to talk to you about your brother's widow. I'm worried, and since Frederick can't help me, I hope you will."

"She isn't my responsibility. Speak to her."

"But she is. Give me five minutes, and I'll tell you why."

He wanted to argue, to be rid of us, to drink in peace. He had Lady Beatrice to contend with instead. Finally, grudgingly, he sat down in the chair, without relinquishing either the glass or the decanter.

"I have seen great grief before. I have felt it personally. Tell me about Grace Caldwell's war."

"What?" He was completely lost.

"She lost her husband for four years. Knowing he could be killed or be listed as missing at any moment. How did she fill her time?"

"How do I know? I was in the trenches myself."

"Surely Frederick talked to you about his concerns for her."

He took a deep breath. "I don't—he tried to keep her busy. No children, she wasn't a pious person, to take comfort in the church. She had a horror of working with the wounded. But he convinced her to gather a group of her friends and take treats to the clinics. God knows there must have been enough of them already, and after the Somme, they were filled with wounded and dying."

"And did she?"

Something changed in his face. "Yes. There was a doctor—he had a title. Sir Robert something or other. Frederick worried about them."

"What do you mean, worried?"

"Her letters were full of him. He was in demand for surgery on the back, or some such. He moved constantly, and when he came back to Harrogate, she wrote of nothing else."

"But nothing came of it?"

"How do I know? If there was more to it than there ought to be, Frederick kept it to himself."

"Was it Sir Robert Pearson?" I asked.

"Possibly. Probably."

I'd met him. Handsome, tall, and broad-shouldered with a full head of lovely fair hair and large blue eyes, he had set the nurses atwitter when he stepped into the surgical ward. His skills won him an almost godlike reverence from the men he kept alive, but it was the blue eyes that made women want to speak to him.

And he had lost his wife in another outbreak of the influenza epidemic late last autumn.

"He's a very fine surgeon," I said, to keep Mark Caldwell from knowing what was in my thoughts just now. "There was some talk of a baronetcy as a reward for his war service."

"How does Grace know one of Gordon's neighbors?" asked Lady Beatrice.

"She doesn't know anyone in the dale except the family."

But she did.

He'd had enough questions. "I don't know what this is all about," he said, rising without spilling a drop. "Grace's family will be here tomorrow. I'll see her at the funeral and the reading of the will, and then my duty is finished. Speak to the Fairchilds, not to me."

He was about to walk out of the room when Lady Beatrice rose. "No, we've disturbed you long enough! Stay and drink your brandy in peace. I am so sorry there is nothing we can do about Grace."

Not *for* Grace—*about* her.

He caught the significance of that as we were leaving the room.

"What are you telling me?"

She smiled a little. "She really isn't the Nevilles' responsibility either."

Ushering me out the door, she closed it quietly behind her.

"Is this surgeon, Sir Robert, an attractive man?" she demanded quietly as we left.

"Very. He turns heads wherever he goes."

Lady Beatrice said, "I fear he may have turned one too many. And not even know that he has."

Inspector Wade was fuming. The tea had been poured, the little cakes someone had added to the tray were untouched, like the cups.

Margaret wasn't there, she had agreed to keep Grace occupied. Mrs. Neville was there, with Arthur, and the two of us walked in together. Lillian, as far as I knew, was still in Gordon's room, waiting for him.

And he needed that arm tended. In this heat, the infection could take a far better grip on the wound. It would have to wait.

Inspector Wade glared at us as Lady Beatrice and I came through. "I was told that Gordon Neville would be here to surrender himself to me."

Lady Beatrice took her usual place—no one ever wittingly sat in a chair she was known to favor—and regarded him.

"I am not a policeman," she began quietly. "But I can think for myself. I cannot see that your evidence is sufficient to take my godson to Richmond. Arthur, please help Inspector Wade explain his reasoning to me."

Arthur cleared his throat. "I expect the first question would be, why do you think my brother intended to kill Frederick Caldwell?"

She was merely trying to fill time before Gordon kept his word and appeared at the door. He should have been coming to the door *now*, by my sense of the time that had passed.

Inspector Wade was having none of it. I wasn't really listening to his tirade.

For some reason, my level of anxiety was rising. I glanced at Mrs. Neville. There was anxiety in her face as well. Her son had given his word. What was keeping him?

I couldn't wait any longer. "Let me see what is keeping him—"

Without waiting for permission or support, I walked as quickly as I could out of the sitting room and started down the passage toward the stairs.

I had the strongest feeling that Gordon Neville had decided to visit Grace Caldwell before keeping his word.

I had just reached the foot of the steps when a shot rang out, followed by another, and a woman's scream.

I thought I recognized Margaret's voice as the scream became a wail.

I reached the top of the stairs as Lillian was coming down the passage, and we both turned toward the chilling sound.

I had only just reached the door to Grace Caldwell's room, when it opened and Joe Harding cannoned into me with such force I was thrown back against the wall. Lillian was behind me, hitting the wall even harder, crying out.

There was a commotion downstairs, as people came running. I didn't wait, I plunged into Grace Caldwell's room.

There seemed to be blood everywhere.

In an instant I was thrown back to the war—to the forward aid stations where stretchers filled every space and we had to work by shielded lantern light to save as many as we could.

Margaret Neville, white and about to faint, had damage to her upper arm, where an artery had been sliced. I tore at her dress, ripping enough lace to tie off the wound as firmly as I could. She sank onto a small chest by the foot of the bed and started to cry.

I looked for Grace Caldwell. She was cowering by the armoire. There was blood all over her face, running bright down into her black gown and nearly vanishing from sight. I thought she was moaning, but she wasn't in danger.

Gordon lay on the floor. There was blood on his throat, and it was running fast.

I caught up a pillow, pressed it hard into the wound, and held it there. But blood was soaking the feathers, and I pulled something from the bed and changed my grip long enough to switch from pillow to what was once a cream-and-rose coverlet.

Someone was beside me. It was Arthur, used to battle, knowing enough about wounds to see what I was about. Only then did I see that the wound in Gordon's arm was bleeding too.

Mrs. Neville was working with Grace, who was struggling to stay in the protection of the armoire.

Lady Beatrice demanded, "I heard gunfire. Who was shooting?"

"Joe Harding," I said over my shoulder.

Inspector Wade seemed to hesitate—his prisoner Gordon Neville was on the floor, bleeding heavily, and Joe Harding, who had put him there, was in the wind. He couldn't seem to make up his mind.

Mark Caldwell, smelling of whiskey, was in the doorway now, shouting something.

Inspector Wade seemed to come to a decision. "Guard him," he shouted, pointing to Mark Caldwell, and then was off at a run.

The staff had come running. Davies or Mrs. Roper had had the presence of mind to catch up clean kitchen linens, and these were shoved into my hands.

"I've sent for the doctor," Davies said to me, and went to help Margaret.

Grace, hysterical, heedless of the tragedy at her feet, was fighting any aid or assistance. Lady Beatrice, stepping over Gordon's sprawling legs, walked straight to her and slapped Grace hard across the face.

Mrs. Roper began to comfort Margaret, an arm around her, trying to ease the shock of being shot.

Mark Caldwell seemed to be in everyone's way, as if he expected Gordon to get up off the floor and run.

I was already back beside the wounded man, working to stop the bleeding before it had gone too far.

Faces kept appearing in the doorway. One maid fainted. The heat in the room was choking, and I said to anyone who would listen, "Get everyone out. Now."

Davies turned to that task, sending the maids for hot water, more towels, and the aid box of the household, kept in the kitchens.

Arthur had gone to see to his wife's arm, making sure it was no longer bleeding as heavily, and then seeing how she was swaying, he lifted her bodily and set her in the ruins of the bedclothes. Mrs. Roper went with him to see to Grace Caldwell.

Someone had bathed Grace's face. There was a long red line through her pale hair, welling with blood every time the towel tried to press it away. But such wounds did bleed copiously I stayed with Gordon.

Margaret would have an ugly scar. It would depend on how well the wound could be sewn. The thought passed through my mind as I worked.

Gordon was still unconscious, and when I lifted his head to ease his neck, I could feel blood in his hair. Where he had hit his head going down.

Mark Caldwell was trying to ask Arthur what had happened, but Arthur ignored him, finally snapping, "Shut up and do as you were told."

Lillian came into the room. "I think I hear the doctor turning into the gates."

"Thank you."

She knelt by me. "Could I wrap a towel around that arm?"

"Yes, please. Thank you."

Gordon was beginning to stir. I said, "Don't. It's best if you don't."

I never heard the door knocker.

Davies must have been on watch. Dr. Menzies was suddenly there, pushing me aside and examining the neck wound. "Not the main vessel," he said. "Thank God."

Another scar, I thought in a corner of my mind.

Slowly but surely the chaos was becoming order. I got to my feet and surveyed the room. Margaret in the bed, eyes closed, wound seeping into the sheet beneath her, spread around her arm like an ugly flower. But safe for the moment.

Grace now sitting in the chair for the dressing table along the far wall, guarded by Mrs. Neville, whose eyes kept flitting to her son.

Lady Beatrice was by the window, on the other side of Grace Caldwell. Mark Caldwell, ever the angry brother-in-law, was leaning against the antique highboy. And then I saw him look at Lillian, and I was suddenly alert.

There was something in his expression that almost seemed to say, *Why wasn't she one of them?*

Speculative. And with something volatile there as well. An old and still very active anger. Or hatred.

I said to Lillian, still beside Gordon, "Go to your room and lock the door."

She gave me a frightened glance.

"Just do as I say. It will be best, with so many people milling around."

She rose, took a last look at Gordon, then her gaze found Lady Beatrice. Lillian gave her a wavering smile. And then she was gone.

I saw the movement, stopped almost at once, as Mark Caldwell nearly went after her.

The room was suddenly quiet.

After the urgency and the haste and the feet moving about Gordon's head, no one was crying or speaking or changing position.

My hip was on fire, my neck and right arm were aching. But we hadn't lost anyone. We could so easily have done.

Dr. Menzies moved to the bed to dress Margaret's arm as Arthur called her his brave girl, to endure so much pain so well. She was clinging to him with her other hand, as if afraid to let go.

Mrs. Roper went to the washstand and poured half a glass of water from the pitcher, bringing it to the bed. I watched Dr. Menzies put a drop or two into the water, swirl it several times to mix it well, and then hand it to Arthur, who helped his wife drink it down.

A sedative.

He asked for another glass, repeated what he'd just done, and handed it back to Mrs. Roper. But it required all three women to coax Grace Caldwell to drink it.

I realized that Gordon was staring up at me.

"What is it?" I asked. I couldn't quite read his expression. "Would you like a little water?"

"No." His lips barely moved.

"Should have told—someone—" he began in a low voice only I could hear. "Before the fall. He'd gone out with me. To talk privately, he said."

He was talking about Frederick Caldwell.

"It was Grace. He was afraid she'd had an affair during the war. He was afraid he'd lost her. I told him—I told him it served him right for taking her away from me. And then my footing went. He tried to stop me. From falling."

"But you didn't believe him?"

"Didn't want to. Being happy—being happy together always rubbed salt into an old—old wound. But I could at least believe she might have loved me with the same strength of feeling."

"What are you talking about?" Mark Caldwell demanded.

"About his wound," I said, not bothering to look up at him. "We can't move him yet."

But Arthur was now picking up his drowsy wife and starting toward the door and their own room. She lay against his chest, whimpering a little as the movements jarred her arm.

Lady Beatrice saw what Arthur was about, and moved to go ahead of him and help. They left.

There were no stalwart footmen to lift Gordon Neville and ease him into his own bed. The only one, just learning his trade, had run for the doctor and was now, according to Dr. Menzies, limping home.

I found bedding in the passage cupboard to make a pallet until we could do more. Mrs. Neville helped me arrange it.

There was a loud knock at the front door.

Mrs. Neville was the only family member here, and Davies was not around so she started for the stairs to answer the summons. Then thought better of who might be standing there, and from the doorway beckoned to me to accompany her.

We went down together. Inspector Wade, flushed from the heat, was standing there wiping his forehead and face with a wrinkled handkerchief.

Stepping in out of the sun, he said directly, "Have Davies ring the fire bell, if you please. Harding is bolted behind the farmhouse doors, and I understand he has a shotgun as well as his service revolver. I need as many tenants as we can muster, to help me bring him out."

Mrs. Neville protested, "The tenants aren't policemen."

"Some were in the war, they'll know what they're about—"

"But—"

"Madame. I can't trust the villagers. They know this man. Is that clear enough? I need men I can count on behind me. There is no time to send to Richmond for reinforcements."

Behind us, Arthur was coming briskly down the stairs. "Leave it to me, Mother."

Inspector Wade was looking up toward the landing. "Here, who is guarding the wounded?"

"Dr. Menzies is still with them," Arthur snapped in a cold voice.

Outside, a groom was just taking Inspector Wade's horse. Arthur called to him, ordered him to ring the fire bell, adding, "I'll be there directly."

The groom was gone, and Arthur said to Inspector Wade, as if he didn't know the house nearly as well as its occupants by this time, "This way, if you please."

Mrs. Neville watched them go. "I wonder if we might have a witch come and cleanse this house after that man has finally gone."

I smiled, thinking this sudden spurt of humor was good for her. But when I glanced her way, I could see she was quite serious.

Torn for a moment about where her duty lay, she chose the wounded. But she put a hand on my arm. "Bess, keep an eye on those men. If there's bloodshed, they will need you. Dr. Menzies is staying here until I am sure Gordon is safe."

And so I went after Arthur and the Inspector. I could hear the fire bell clanging as I came through the kitchen passage to the kitchen doorway.

The bell stood on a tall post in the yard, where it could be heard. And where it echoed across the fells, reaching those who were working the sheep.

Loud near too, as well. I stood to one side, fearful that Arthur would notice me and send me back inside. This wasn't woman's work. And Sister or not, I was a woman.

In some twenty minutes he'd collected a dozen men, and he was beginning to tell them what was needed—and why—when Mark Caldwell came out to join the group.

As they set off across the fells, the fastest way to their destination, I saw that there were pitchforks and shovels in some hands, and one broad-shouldered man of about fifty had an axe. I waited, and then trailed behind.

These were men used to walking the uneven ground in any direction, their long, almost loping strides carrying them quickly and surely. I was hard-pressed to keep up, and my hip burned with the effort. The heat was overwhelming, we were a sweaty and dusty lot when we reached the gate by the laithe barn. Spring grass seeds clung to my skirts, and briars had scratched my hands here and there where the haying hadn't been done in the barn's perimeter.

We could see the house now.

"Are you sure he's still there?" one of the men asked Inspector Wade.

He was craning his neck, looking for someone. A woman waved, and he turned back to the men. "Appears that nothing has changed. Separate, if you please, and circle that house. Doors. Windows a desperate man might leap from. I want him contained. But not at the price of bloodshed. He's Army, and he knows how to use his weapons."

He sent them off. Straggling into place, one or two talking together until they parted.

Once more I followed Arthur and Inspector Wade, this time to the front of the house. The woman who had waved was now walking away, head down. Something about her was familiar, and I tried to place her. And realized all at once that it must be Mrs. Bowman. She had kept watch while the Inspector gathered his men, making certain that Joe Harding didn't elude the police. That he was still in that house.

In position finally, Inspector Wade called to Mr. Harding to give himself up.

"Nobody died," he said loudly enough to be heard inside. "It isn't a hanging matter. Come out and tell us what happened in that woman's room."

Silence within. I stayed in what little shade a tree provided, and waited. For whatever was going to happen.

The heat of the afternoon was suffocating. But we stayed where we were. Someone from the village brought a pail of water and a long-handled cup, and passed it around.

Another hour dragged by. Another pail of water was passed around. My hair felt wet with perspiration, clinging to my face and throat.

Our prisoner, if you could call him that, was inside a thick-walled farmhouse, and it must surely be just a little cooler there. And so he could afford to let us swelter in this weather, then when it was dark, slip the guard of the tired, heat-worn men outside, and go. He'd have had time to decide what to do, whether to cut his losses and disappear, or stay and fight.

What was going through his mind? What had driven him to come back to the Neville house with his revolver?

Promises made—and not kept? The realization that he had somehow been used? The tumbling down of a dream he'd fabricated from lies told? I couldn't imagine, even though I tried to put myself into his shoes.

He was a hungry man, that much was clear. In the sense it was likely that war and France had changed his own view of himself. I'd seen it happen. Men who had lived in a world where life was narrow and opportunities were few arrived in Paris on medical leave, and suddenly wanted to be painters or writers, anything but walk behind a plow or spend their daylight hours in a factory or mine. They came back to the line talking of nothing else.

We waited another hour.

All this time, Inspector Wade had tried to speak to Joe Harding, to persuade him that there was no real ending to this standoff. His voice was rough with the effort now.

We could hear distant thunder now. A rolling through the dales, coming from Swaledale, perhaps, I couldn't be sure. The sun overhead was still brassy.

The water pail appeared again.

I couldn't see any of the men guarding the sides and rear of the house. They had found what shade they could, keeping watch from a distance. No one wanted to face a shotgun. Or be picked off by a single revolver shot.

As time crept by, Arthur came over to where I was sitting in shade that had moved with the sun.

"Go home, Bess. I don't think we'll need you here. Earlier—yes, I thought he would make a break. But he's waiting until nightfall. There's nothing for you to do, and it's wretched out here."

Dr. Menzies would be looking to the wounds in the house. And Mrs. Neville had asked me to go. To keep an eye on her other son as much as to be here if someone was hurt.

"How do the sheep survive this?"

"There are rills, tiny springs. They find water. The lee of a wall provides shade," Arthur replied blandly.

We both looked back toward the farmhouse. "I haven't even found out what happened in that room," Arthur said. "Margaret told me that when Harding lifted his revolver and was about to shoot Gordon, she threw up her arm in some mad notion of stopping the shot. Instead, the bullet tore through her arm on its way to Gordon's throat. It could well have saved his life."

"That was a very brave thing to do," I said, meaning every word.

"Yes," he said wryly. "And as foolish as it was brave."

"How did Grace come to be shot?" I asked.

"Margaret told me he was shouting at her, asking why the family never helped his sister; why she wasn't helping his sister now, and she finally gave it to him. He meant to kill her. Either she moved or he couldn't actually put a shot in her face. I don't suppose we'll ever know."

He wiped his forehead with a damp handkerchief. "We killed a lot of men in the war. I remember the faces of the ones I watched die in front of me. Too many of them, sadly. But a woman, that might have given him pause."

After a bit he went back to Inspector Wade and was earnestly trying to persuade him to do or try something. But he met with heavy resistance. I found myself wondering what the Colonel Sahib would do in such a situation.

The thunder had shifted, and the setting sun was banked in heavy clouds now. I thought once or twice that I saw lightning as well, but couldn't be sure.

And then an almighty clap of thunder came rolling down the stone wall–embroidered flank of Old Grumble, and the storm came pouring after it. The wind picked up, tossing and swirling anything that was free to move, and I had to hold my skirts as it ripped at them.

The rain came in buckets. We were wet through. Arthur pulled off his coat, trying to offer me a little shelter, but it was soaked almost at once. I left it over my head, protecting it as best it could.

The sky was black now, no lights showing in the house, nothing to give definition to the night except for thrashing leaves and branches.

We simply had to endure. There was nowhere to go, the village was now engulfed, and too far to seek shelter. The house in front of us was closed to us.

And then a rectangle of light appeared, seemingly in the middle of nowhere, evolving into the shape of an open doorway.

Someone was standing there—a woman, I realized. Joe Harding's sister. She was shouting to the Inspector, and he warily moved closer, expecting a trap.

I heard Arthur shout something over the noise of the storm, and watched his white shirtsleeves move rapidly toward the rear of the house. It was all I could do to follow. Tripping, sliding, somehow I kept him in sight. As soon as he reached the first man, he shouted encouragement, while reminding them to expect trouble.

Chaos followed.

Someone had brought a torch, and it was slashing through the rain, sweeping the back walls of the house. Lightning, close by, washed out the torch light, laying everything bare, and then dropping it back into inky darkness.

I heard a shotgun fire, somewhere in the rear of the house, but I couldn't see anything or anyone.

Shouting, then, someone screaming words I couldn't make out.

And then more chaos.

Men came charging toward me, and I moved out of their way as they raced at the heels of someone. Heading for the village? Looking for the next sanctuary?

Suddenly the sweeping crowd of men stopped, and it was over.

Joe Harding was down.

When they had subdued him, they dragged him to Inspector Wade, who had taken his time coming up, leaving it to the tenants to handle the situation.

I was there as someone flashed the torch into the grimacing face. There was a cut over his eye, and his nose was bleeding into his mouth. His eyes, wild and staring, swept the crowd, found me, and then passed on.

I moved forward, saying to Inspector Wade, "He's been hurt. He's entitled to medical care."

But no one was listening. "Take him to the Hall," he said, and I saw Constable Woods appear, his handcuffs already clicking around the wrists of the still-struggling man.

Where had he been in recent days? Constable Woods?

Chapter Twenty-One

It was a sorry crowd of people who converged on the kitchen doorway of the Hall.

Hearing the commotion swelling toward the house, the anxious maid who went to the door slammed it shut and went to find Davies or Mrs. Roper.

It was Davies who came back with her.

Dripping wet, muddy feet tracking the scrubbed floors of the Servants Hall, the butler guided the crowd of men who had been at the farmhouse toward the large room used for servant and tenant affairs.

Something was said about tea. It seemed to bring some order. Their prisoner, now guarded by Constable Woods, was seated roughly into a chair. I went to him, but he turned his head and refused to be helped

Ruth touched my arm.

"Sister? You're to go up to Lady Beatrice."

I looked around the room. There seemed to be no need for me, although I could see signs of the struggle to capture Harding. The tenants, scuffed up at the farmhouse, seemed to wear their wounds proudly.

I was still very wet, feeling the weight of my clothing and the hair clinging to my shoulders. It was cooler in the house too, as the wind rose with the peak of the storm.

Ruth came running after me with towels, handing them to me before racing back to the kitchens.

I climbed the stairs wearily, my hip no longer on fire, aching now instead, and my neck and right shoulder throbbed.

Lady Beatrice got up quickly from her chair as I opened her door.

"Dear God, Bess?"

"He's in handcuffs. The tenants are downstairs celebrating. No one got badly hurt, although Dr. Menzies ought to have a look."

"I've been frantic—all these hours of waiting—" She pulled me to a chair, and went to a small decanter on her dressing table. "You need this. No argument."

And I was handed a small glass of sherry. While I was sipping it, she went to my room, found my dressing gown and some clothes, brought them back, and helped me strip out of my wet things.

A towel around my hair, I sat down again and tried to tell her an abbreviated version of events. She listened attentively, asking questions and making comments.

When she was satisfied, I could ask the question uppermost in my own mind.

"Grace Caldwell—Gordon, Margaret—are they all right?"

"Margaret and Grace are sleeping. Margaret was worried about Arthur, and we decided to give her something more to help her rest. Grace, on the other hand, was alternately crying over her wound and seeing herself as the victim here. Dr. Menzies persuaded her to rest. That left Gordon to be dealt with. We finally got him to his own bed, when the doctor was certain there would be no risk of his wound opening again." She smiled. "Davies, the gem that he is, remembered an invalid chair that had belonged to an aunt who lived here toward the end of her life. Of course it was still in the attics, he'd seen it there during the search. Brought it down, cleared away the cobwebs, and he simply wheeled Gordon to his bed."

I smiled. "That's such good news."

"Dr. Menzies is staying the night. No emergencies or other demands on his time, thank heavens." She considered me. "I'll order a hot bath, and you can go directly to bed. Dinner will come up in good time. I imagine the staff will have its hands full for a bit."

The bath sounded heavenly. But the last thing I wished to do was go to bed.

"I must dress and go back down to see what is happening about their prisoner."

She tried to persuade me, but this time I stood my ground.

I arrived in the Servants Hall to find that the tenants had been sent home to dry themselves, and only a handful of people were still there.

The prisoner was seated in the chair. Someone had dealt with his face, but the bruises were beginning to show up. His hair was still wet, and his clothes, but there was a blanket over his shoulders.

Constable Woods stood to one side, while Arthur was standing behind Inspector Wade, his arms across his chest, and his expression quite stern.

The Inspector had just begun his questions. I was used to his pedantic preparation for them, and knew I'd come just in time if I wanted to know anything. I did stay close to the door, where I wouldn't be in the way—or noticed.

"—and so Constable Woods has been in Richmond making substantial inquiries about each of those involved in events here. Telegrams to Harrogate, to various clinics, to York and Somerset and London, as well as the War Office."

He hadn't mentioned Scotland Yard. The logical place for any county policeman to turn if he required assistance in an inquiry.

I remembered suddenly that Lady Beatrice had all but told him he was incompetent, insisting that the Yard be called in.

That had stung this man. And he had tried to find answers we couldn't—or wouldn't give him.

I wished for a chair. But I didn't move.

Inspector Wade was saying, "Sister Crawford, for instance, is the daughter of a high-ranking military officer, and her service with the Queen Alexandra's is above reproach."

I could see the prisoner staring at me out of the eye that hadn't begun to swell and blacken.

"Margaret Neville is the daughter of a bishop whose views are neither startling nor new. But his faith and his reputation are sterling, and his family goes back to the Plantagenets." That last word had a twist to it, as if he despised the Plantagenets.

No one said anything, not even Arthur.

"Which brings us next to Grace Caldwell."

I held my breath.

"She is the daughter of a minor county family, known as a beauty in her youth, and when she married Frederick Caldwell, it was considered a very fine match. Indeed, it was thought that Caldwell had been very fortunate to win her hand, as she could have had her choice of husbands." There was a pause, and then, "He was the wealthiest of her suitors."

Someone had come in behind me just in time to hear these comments. I smelled whiskey as he too exhaled in surprise. Mark Caldwell.

Still speaking to Mr. Harding, but for the benefit of the assembled group, Inspector Wade pointed out exactly when and where he had met Grace Caldwell.

I didn't need to hear the rest, but I listened. Grace had rallied her small group of married women who tried to do their bit by bringing a little brightness to men who were in hospital for long and painful surgeries. One was outside Harrogate, it was for those blinded by gas or shrapnel. Another was the surgical clinic where Sir Robert had worked.

The more he fascinated her, the more she found excuses to call at the clinic. And soon thereafter, she had befriended a man who claimed to have served with her husband in France. Lieutenant Harding. And she had spent time reading to him, talking to him, showing personal rather than a general interest in the man. It had been noted by the Sisters, and they had felt that it was inappropriate. This was the last year of the war. Though a good-looking man, it was very possible that the patient would be blind for life, and nothing was done.

But he recovered his sight and traveled back to Yorkshire and found his farm in ruins. The postmistress in Richmond remembered the letters that had come first from Harrogate, then York, and finally the bitter one from Scarfdale.

"I didn't kill him," Harding said, suddenly breaking his silence. "But I saw them fall, and I went to the bottom of the cliffs to see what was what." He cleared his throat. "I moved the bodies. Looking to see what could be done. I thought Caldwell was dead, until he groaned. Neville's arm looked like the very devil. I left them both."

There was something in his voice that made me think he was telling the truth.

"She told me after she arrived at the house that he'd never agree to a divorce. She wanted me to kill him so she'd be free. For me, I thought. But when I saw him there on the ground, I didn't feel it was right. He died anyway, and I wanted her to be grateful. And so I let her think I'd see to it he didn't make it."

"But you killed Judith Bowman."

He took a deep breath, looking down, his expression hidden. "She saw me moving the bodies. My sister told me that Judith was there, at the farm, that afternoon. She saw me move them and then walk away, leaving them to wake up on their own. I liked Judith. Before the war, I'm sure she could have been mine. But that was before. And I'd already told Grace that I had done as she asked and I couldn't risk Judith telling Grace otherwise. Or anyone else that I was there, for that matter. And then today—" His tone of voice changed for tired disinterest in anything but fact. "And then today, Grace told me that she didn't love me, she was going to wed Gordon as soon as her mourning was finished. It wasn't the truth, but she knew how I felt about him and she was goading me. Still, I saw red, and I shot her. Then I had to shoot the other two to get out of that room."

Behind me Mark Caldwell swore feelingly. I heard the door open and close, and he was gone.

There wasn't much more that anyone could do that night. Cook managed to feed the two policemen and their prisoner, and then the family and the invalids.

Wilson was asked to drive the three men to Richmond. Late as it was, no one asked them to stay. And Lady Beatrice agreed to the use of her motorcar.

The house settled into a quiet night.

But not before just after dinner, Mark Caldwell went to Grace's room, woke her up, and told her precisely what he thought of her. The shouting match could be heard because he hadn't bothered to close the door. Lillian, who had gone to look in on Margaret, also heard every word and was fearful for Grace, she told me afterward. And so she had lingered close by. Despite her own feelings about the man in that room.

She was still in the passage when he stormed out of the bedroom. He saw Lillian in the shadows, and in his anger and frustration, he put his hands around her throat and told her it should have been done long ago.

Her scream jolted me, and I got there first, for I had taken my meal in my room, too spent to find it easy to be a part in what was surely a difficult evening meal.

It took all my strength pulling a strong, angry man away from a woman twice his age and too frightened to fight back.

But as a nurse I also knew where the nerves would go numb, and Arthur was there just as Mark Caldwell let Lillian go and came after me. He was shouting something, I was trying to protect my aching arm, and the words were lost on me.

Arthur hit him, shocking him into stepping back. I realized all at once that this man could kill. And as if to corroborate that revelation, I heard the echo of what he'd barked at me in a voice twisted with frustration and anger. *I thought I'd rid myself of you on the stairs—I thought you'd take that stupid fool with you and go the hell back to York.*

Arthur must have heard him as well. A witness . . .

He said sharply, "Get control of yourself, man."

"She," he snarled, pointing at Lillian, "made my father's life a misery. He never found her. He never knew who she might have told. Frederick encountered her—and he did nothing. He was too besotted with winning Grace. Brother or not, he never had the stomach for it."

He wasn't talking about me now. He was still glaring at Lillian, still too wrought up to stop.

Davies came running, with Mrs. Roper. Lady Beatrice was just behind her, still clutching the table napkin in one hand. I heard others on the stairs.

Somehow they got Mark Caldwell into his room and locked the door. Lady Beatrice had taken Lillian away, and Mrs. Neville was trying to be sure I was all right. Grace, sitting in her bed, staring out her open door, said nothing. Indeed, seemed uninterested in the scene in the passage. I wondered if she had taken more of the drops than she should have done, to dull her own pain.

Mrs. Neville noticed, reached for the door, and swung it closed. She said, her face drawn, "How did this happen in my house? I just wanted my sons safely home, I wanted to celebrate a *happy* birthday after four years of dreading the knock on the door, the telegram with my name on it. I just wanted to be free of all that fear, and never have to look back at it."

I wanted to put an arm around her, to comfort her. But I didn't think it would help.

I said, "They are still here. Arthur and Gordon. And Margaret, too."

"But my peace is gone." Mrs. Neville gave me a crooked smile, and said, "Forgive me, I must speak to Gordon . . . He'll be worried."

And she was gone down the passage.

I watched her walk on. Then I turned and went back to my own room. Blessedly, it was empty.

And so there was another passenger in Wilson's motorcar. Bound tightly—it appeared that Constable Woods possessed only one set of handcuffs—Mark Caldwell was held over for disturbing the peace and attempted murder.

It was late when it was all finished. The rain had stopped, but the night was airless again, and we sat in the sitting room like mourners at a wake.

Mrs. Neville asked her son, "Will they charge Grace when she's fit to travel?"

He sighed. "I have no idea what Wade will decide. Harding didn't kill Frederick. Well, he didn't actively take the man's life. It will be argued that he moved the body, causing a fatal outcome as a result. Hard to prove."

I was still of two minds about that, having seen the body. But I let it go. There was already a charge of murder for Judith.

"What I don't understand," Arthur said then, "is why Mark attacked you, Lillian? I thought he hardly knew who you were."

She was stricken. Her face flushed and then went pale. Turning to Lady Beatrice, she silently begged for support.

But this time it wasn't forthcoming.

Lady Beatrice was uncharacteristically unhelpful.

"I think the time has come to do something about this, Lillian. The man is dead, he can't hurt you. Nor can his son. And Frederick is dead, what you have to say is not going to hurt *him*." She turned to Arthur.

"Will you find paper and pen, and take down what Lillian is about to tell you. I want it as legally binding as you are able to make it, and I want it witnessed by everyone here in this room. When that is done, I will see to it that it is put into the right hands."

Lillian protested vehemently, to the point of tears, but Lady Beatrice wouldn't listen.

"This has torn your life apart long enough. You have been forced to take work where you could safely find it, you have been accused of attempted kidnapping, you have been hunted and sought relentlessly. It will stop now." And then she ruined the whole effect by adding, "You'll thank me tomorrow. Wait and see."

I wanted to look in on Gordon and Margaret, even on Grace. But my curiosity or my fatigue was pinning me in my chair.

When the story began, I had no inkling what it would do to my life . . .

CHAPTER TWENTY-TWO

LILLIAN'S VOICE SHOOK as she began to speak, her eyes on her hands, twisting in her lap. If she had been wearing heavy rings, as Lady Beatrice often did, they would have cut into the flesh as her fingers writhed.

"My father owned a globe of the world, and he had stereopticon photographs of places he wanted to see. After tea, he would bring these out and tell me all kinds of stories. I don't know if half of them were true, but I was enthralled. When I'd finished my training as a governess at the Misses Quinn's School, I was employed by a young couple to care for their child on their journey to South Africa. It was the most exciting thing I could imagine, my father came to see me off, and I was a good sailor, I loved the steamer." She looked at Lady Beatrice. "I kept a journal, you know. About the ship and the ports. I was going to post it to my father as soon as we landed in Cape Town. But he died of a fever before I arrived. The news was waiting for me. My mother had died when I was ten, and so I was very much alone. Still, I had the family I was working for, the baby, and my new life. I kept writing in the journal."

Lady Beatrice was about to ask a question, changed her mind, and waited.

But Mrs. Neville asked, "How old was the baby?"

"Three years old. His Nanny hadn't wanted to leave England. And so I was more or less Nanny to him then, although I had begun to teach him things. He had a lively little mind, and we would explore the garden and collect things, then I'd tell him about them. A feather, an insect, whatever we found on our walks. Sometimes we would take something to tea with his parents, so that he could show them." She smiled, and her face changed. "It was the happiest time of my life. Except of course growing up with Papa. I thought it would go on forever, watching him grow, teaching him until he was given a tutor or sent away to school. I could count the years ahead, thinking what I would do and how I would teach him, and it filled me with a wonderful sense of responsibility. He wasn't my child, but I could give him knowledge and shape his life, and know that when he was a man, he'd be as fine as his father."

The joy faded. "It was rather silly and young and naïve of me even to think that. But I believed it, I truly believed it. This was my first posting, and I knew that I had done the right thing by choosing to become a governess. Later I wondered if his parents indulged me, knowing how much I cared for their son, letting me give him so much of myself."

She seemed to lose the thread of what she'd been trying to tell us, overwhelmed by these memories.

Lady Beatrice said, "What changed, Lillian? You came home with a different family, the Burtons, I recall, and left their employ shortly afterward. Why didn't you stay with the child in South Africa?"

Her hands were writhing again.

"I didn't mention that they were a military family, his parents? The father was an officer, this was his latest posting. I was told he was being watched by the Army, that if he went on as he'd begun, a career officer, he would do quite well. It isn't easy to earn a promotion in peacetime, you know. But he'd been given one before leaving England, and there would be another when the regiment left South Africa."

Having known some of the regiments that had served in South

Africa, I wanted to ask the father's name, but it was not my place to interrupt.

"One night, the father came home early, and he was quite upset. I was asked to take the child up to the nursery and stay there with him. Later on, I heard angry voices downstairs, and I thought someone had come to the house. Later still, I heard the mother crying, and her husband trying to comfort her. The next morning, a man came to the house, and I saw him. We were in the garden, the boy and I, and the man came over to where we were watching a butterfly. He frightened the child, he frightened me. I picked him up and ran inside just as the mother came running out, shouting at the man. It was terrifying, I didn't know who he was, why he was upsetting everyone, but two of the grooms came then and made him leave. Then the father was sent for, and he went away after talking to his wife, to speak to his commanding officer. I didn't see the man again. When I asked the mother who he was, and why he'd come, she said it had to do with her father in England. She said he was an evil man, she didn't want him to come near her boy, and that was why she had sailed with her husband, she had been too frightened to stay in England without him."

Mrs. Neville rose quietly and poured a little sherry in a glass, taking it to Lillian. She dutifully sipped it, but it didn't put any color in her face.

"A fortnight passed. Everything seemed to be all right again. But I could tell it wasn't. There was a closer guard on the house, and we were told not to go too far into the garden to explore. I began to find things in the house to talk about. A number of families must have lived there through the years, for I found dolls in the attic, and a little wooden train, and a toy sword. His father brought him a rocking horse, the cleverest thing imaginable. And it became his dearest possession, and it kept him from asking to go out into the garden."

Looking around at the expressions of Lillian's witnesses, I could see how they had become more than that, now able to picture the little boy and the garden, and the rising tensions in the family Lillian loved so much.

She took a deep breath. "It was the Queen's birthday, and there was to be a special celebration, parades and an Official Dinner and even fireworks later. I was told to keep the child inside, the doors locked, because his parents were invited to events. They had considered taking us with them, then changed their minds and went without us. I expect they thought it was safest to leave him behind." Tears filled her eyes. "I don't think I shall ever forget that night. We were to expect them by two in the morning. I had put the child to bed, but he was naughty, he missed tea with his parents, or some such, and I stayed with him for a while, reading to him. When I went to my room, I found myself pacing, I couldn't settle. Two o'clock came, and they hadn't come *home*."

The last word—*home*—was a cry of pain and grief.

She was weeping now. "They came to the house close to four in the morning. His commanding officer, the officer's wife, the chaplain—I didn't know who some of them were. And they told me there had been a terrible accident. That someone had shot at the carriage, but had hit the horse instead, and he bolted. The carriage overturned; they were killed. *Killed!* They wouldn't let me see the bodies. I was told it was too horrid, for me or the child. The caskets were sealed. I was all he had, then, I did everything I could when he cried for his parents, not understanding at all. The father's commanding officer saw to everything, he didn't tell me anything, of course, I was only the governess. I trusted him to see that everything was done properly, and some of the post wives came to sit with us and play with the child, but that only confused him. He would look for his mother, and cry when it wasn't she coming through the French doors. I tried to explain that he was best left to my care, but they wanted to help, and they thought they should help."

She buried her face in her handkerchief, weeping inconsolably. Lady

Beatrice and Mrs. Neville went to her, and after a bit, she was calm enough to go on.

"It was perhaps ten days after the funeral. Some men came to the door, I didn't know who they were. Lawyers, one of the women told me. They were the family's lawyers—or acting for them in South Africa, I expect. They talked to me. I didn't understand half of it. And then they were telling me that I was to be paid for my services to the family, and if I so chose, I would be offered transportation home, as well. But I told them I couldn't leave the child. He'd just had his fourth birthday, I was all he knew, and I'd expected to go on taking care of him. That's when they told me that his grandfather had sent someone to South Africa to bring him home, and my services were no longer required."

Holding out her hands, as if pleading with them still, she told the men what she had been told by the child's mother, that the grandfather was an evil man, and she herself had left England out of fear of him.

"But they refused to listen. I was told that I was lying, that I only wanted to keep the child from rejoining his family. I was told that I could face prosecution, that I was unfit to care for so young a child. And then they brought in the man who had come to fetch the child. But he hadn't just come. He'd been here *before*. He'd been the man in the garden. He asked if he could speak to me alone, that I was confused and uncertain with so many people trying to tell me what was right. I didn't want to talk to him, but I thought if I did, he would see that I was the right person to travel with him. But he already had a Nanny, an older woman with a sour mouth. And in that room where no one could hear him, he told me that if I stood in his way, I'd die too, and he would see to that, just as he'd seen that the boy was orphaned." She closed her eyes. "I didn't stop begging. I went to the Colonel, I went to anyone who would listen, but no one would. And in the end, I was told that if I made any more protest, I would be taken into custody and charged with trying to keep the child for my own. The house was closed, the child taken away screaming, I was given payment for my services, and told not to return to England for five years. That I would be arrested as soon as I stepped off the ship. I never saw the child after he was taken away, although I tried to find out when his ship was sailing, I wanted to go there and let him see I hadn't deserted him. But when I got there, policemen were waiting for me. And I was dragged away. When my money ran out, I discovered that no agency would take me on or find me employment, that the police had listed me as an unfit person. I finally found employment with the Burtons' friends, and then other families who wanted a governess but couldn't afford the agency fees to find a suitable one. I came home to England six years later, using my mother's maiden name. Taylor, no longer Winfield. I tried to find out what happened to the child, but I couldn't, and I was too afraid they would find me, if I pushed too hard. And so I went to Canada with another family. And eventually Mrs. Crawford came to me, asking if I would be interested in becoming Lady Beatrice's companion."

"And you never found out any more about the child?" It was Arthur who asked.

"He might as well have vanished. But I saw the man who had taken him away from me. And I found out who he was. Only, he saw me in the crowd of people watching the cricket match, and I knew he remembered me. I left the cricket match in some haste, telling my family that I'd got a touch of the sun. He found out where I was working, and in the park, he came up to me and told me that he would just as soon kill me then and there. But if I didn't keep my mouth shut about South Africa, I would have a rather nasty accident, and the child with me at the time would suffer as well."

I couldn't stop myself. "The name of the man who threatened you?"

She looked at me, and I wasn't sure she was going to answer. But she had got this far, and she had a reason now to tell us the truth.

"Mr. Caldwell's father. Mark Caldwell's father," she said a second time to be sure she was clear about his identity. "He's dead now, of course. The child's grandfather knew Caldwell and had him travel to South Africa in his place. For many years, I believed that Frederick Caldwell was the child they'd taken away. But he wasn't. He told me once when I met him in Harrogate, walking in the gardens of the Swan Hotel. He was at university, a young man. I didn't expect him to remember me, I just wanted to know, finally, that—that they had been good to him. In spite of what had been done. But he just stared at me, then he told me that the child had died on the ship back to England. Of a broken heart. And that if I ever mentioned the matter or his father to anyone again, he would see that I was taken up for a madwoman and put in an asylum."

There was a heavy silence in the room.

One didn't speak ill of the dead. At least that was what everyone tried to remember. And Frederick Caldwell had died in this house.

But I think her words changed forever how we would henceforth view that man.

Mrs. Neville had been right. This house needed a cleansing of spirit.

And then something I'd heard came back to me.

"Lillian," I said, breaking into everyone's thoughts. "Lillian, did you go on keeping a journal after the voyage to South Africa?"

"I'd got into the habit," she said, apology in her voice. "I'd meant that one for my father, to share the journey with me. And I just couldn't face the truth that he would never see it. I went on writing until I was with the Burtons and no longer had the heart to write about the life I was living then. Or pretending to live."

Arthur said quickly, "Do you have those journals? Still? Did you keep them?"

"They went through my things when I was leaving the house. To see that I hadn't stolen anything, that's what they said to me. But I think someone must have told them about the journal—I never made a secret of it, everyone knew it was for my father. There was the lady's maid to the child's mother. She wanted several pieces of the jewelry being sent back to England. To remember her by, she said. They let her have those. And they found the first journal, the one from the ship. It was in my baggage, and they took it. They didn't know that the one I'd been writing in since the voyage was in my handbag. I was sorry to lose the voyage. It had meant a lot to me. But I had the years with the child in the other one, and it was very precious."

"Where is that journal now?" he asked quietly.

"It's in my belongings back at the Hall. In the bookshelf in my room. I used to take it out and read it before I went to sleep. But after Harrogate, I couldn't bear to remember anything about that time in my life."

Lady Beatrice cast a stern glance Arthur's way. As if to say this wasn't the time or place. He wanted to pursue the matter, the trained lawyer in him already thinking ahead. But after a moment he subsided.

"I'm glad it's safe," he told her.

He had taken down her words, and now he read what he'd written. We watched. Lillian seemed calmer, as if sharing her burden had taken a little of the weight from her shoulders. As if she could finally grieve now, without fear. Her shoulders drooped with fatigue, and I could see her hands were trembling.

But she waited until he had finished his survey, and then she signed the statement. Each of us went to the table after that and wrote down our names as witnesses.

For the first time, Lillian seemed to realize what he held in his hand, waving it a little to dry Lady Beatrice's extravagant signature.

He smiled at her. "It's only to keep you safe," he told her. "It will be locked in my vault at the office. But a letter will go out to the Caldwell family—what's left of it. To the effect that criminal proceedings will be instituted if any of that family ever comes near you again."

She didn't return the smile, frowning instead. "But that man is dead.

The one who shot them and took the boy back to England. He can't be charged with anything. Ever."

"Nevertheless. It will keep you safe."

Thanking him, she said, "I'm so very tired. Would you mind if I went up?"

"Of course not," Lady Beatrice told her. "And I shall follow you in just a moment, I need to speak to Arthur about the inquest."

I said, "Let me see you up to your room. I need to speak to Gordon and look in on the others." I glanced at Mrs. Neville. It was still rather warm in the house, nothing like it had been earlier, but noticeably so. "And perhaps Mrs. Roper can make you a glass of warm milk?"

"Yes, I shall speak to her myself," Mrs. Neville said, moving to walk Lillian to the door. "That was very brave of you, my dear."

They were still talking as they moved away.

I said to Arthur and Lady Beatrice, "Will this really protect her?"

"It will. I'll see to it. I'll speak to Jonathan as well."

I thanked him and left him with Lady Beatrice. We got Lillian settled, and the warm milk made her drowsy. I went to look in on Grace. I didn't think she was asleep, but the pretense was enough. The cut from her forehead deep into her hairline was inflamed and open, with an ointment or salve the only covering.

Margaret was asleep, and what I could see of her arm assured me it was being well taken care of.

Gordon wasn't asleep. And Dr. Menzies was there, so we couldn't talk privately. He looked tired and tense, but his color was a little better than it had been earlier.

I went on to my own room. The motorcar would be here tomorrow. We could return to Lady Beatrice's house, and then to York. I could find my way home from there.

Lillian was asleep. I wrote a letter then. To Cousin Melinda, telling her a little about what had happened in Yorkshire. I wasn't sure what I ought to tell my parents. I couldn't sleep, and writing was cathartic. When I finally slipped into bed it was very late. Or very early. I could see the room brightening as I closed my eyes.

The inquests were held in the Servants Hall, the only room large enough in this part of Scarfdale. I knew what Mrs. Neville was feeling as people tramped in and out, gave evidence or heard it. We'd hardly vacate our rooms before the staff would be set to scrubbing away what had happened. But one can't remove what's in our memories.

In each case, the prisoner was bound over for trial. Joe Harding for murder and assault. Mark Caldwell for assault on the person of Lillian Taylor. Inspector Wade, vengeful to the end, seemed to relish charging Grace with her role in what Joe Harding had done. Arthur was of the opinion that this would not be tried in a courtroom.

"But her reputation is ruined. Her family will see to it she is sent off to Canada or America instead of put in prison. In the hope people will forget."

And so the day after the inquest, bag and baggage we left the Hall and Scarfdale. Amidst a flurry of embraces and promises to write, Wilson drove Lady Beatrice back to her home, the faithful Lillian at her side.

The Neville chauffeur drove Margaret, Arthur, and me to Richmond, where I spent the night and took the train south early the next morning.

I watched the landscape change as the train rolled south, county after county, until Bristol was ahead, and I was collecting my things to disembark.

And there were my parents, standing ready to help me off the train while the guard collected my luggage. Simon wasn't there. I'd hoped he would be, but I had told myself not to be disappointed if he wasn't. After all, he hadn't had to come to Yorkshire to keep me out of trouble.

I didn't ask where he was.

We talked about Yorkshire on the drive home, and when that subject palled, my parents told me all the little things that had happened at home in my absence.

They didn't mention Simon either. Not even a word in passing, as in *I told Simon*—or *Simon suggested*—or *Simon liked the new cat*—

It was as if he'd gone out of our lives. Moved out of the cottage while I was away.

I listened to their voices as they laughed and talked and made me feel I'd come home.

Was there an undercurrent?

Yes, there was. I'd missed it, trying to decide what to tell them about Yorkshire and Lady Beatrice. Trying not to think about Simon. Trying to be happy with a homecoming that was beginning to feel less and less like one.

We turned into the gates, the motorcar pulled quickly around the two bends, and there was the house, just as I'd left it, although one of the roses climbing the wall had finished blooming.

As we stopped by the door, my father said briskly, "I'll take in your cases. Iris will have the tea tray in the sitting room."

Mother waited for me to get down, and as we started toward the door my father had just passed through, she said, "Bess, dear—"

I put up my hand. I didn't want her to say any more. It was there in her voice, a tenseness, now that we were home and I wouldn't cry in the motorcar. I could hear it. I managed to break in. "It's all right, Mother. Truly."

Simon had left the cottage . . .

She looked at me sharply. "No, I was going to say—Melinda is here. She got your letter and set out at once. By train! She wants to talk to you—us—and your father sent Simon up to London on a pretext. Something— Bess, there's something in the letter you wrote to her from Scarfdale."

The anxiety she had been trying to keep bottled up inside was beginning to show in spite of her efforts not to frighten me.

"What is it? What's wrong? Mother?"

"I—it has to do with Simon, Bess. We'll have to decide what to tell him."

And then Melinda herself was coming through the doorway, her step firm and her face calm. "Clarice. Let the poor child come inside and drink her tea. Hallo, my dear. I must say, I'm delighted to see you safely out of Yorkshire. I had no idea a simple gallbladder could lead to murder. My apologies for that."

Bewildered, still in some pain, and tired from the journey, I tried to make sense of what was happening, and it must have shown on my face.

Melinda smiled. "Simon is safe, Bess. You may be sure of that. It's just that we have to find a way to tell him that he is, without stirring up an old and bitter anger in him. And that, my dear, is where you will be the most enormous help. He trusts you, he will listen to you."

But would he?

I'd lost his trust . . .

Somewhere in Ireland.

But they didn't know that.

I said, "I wish you would just tell me what you're talking about—"

It was Melinda who linked my arm with hers and led me into the house as my worried mother followed us. "You couldn't possibly know, of course. But it's the story Lillian Taylor told the Nevilles and you. *They* couldn't possibly know—I don't think Lillian herself knows—but it has to do with Simon Brandon. And we've protected him all these years, your parents and I, from that man who sent Mark Caldwell's father to South Africa to kill Simon's father and bring Simon home with his mother. Only it didn't happen quite that way. She was killed too. And he was brought home to live with the grandfather who made Simon's life so wretched he ran away from home when he was fourteen. And joined your father's regiment. That saved him, Bess. That made him the man you know."

We had stepped into the house, dim after the brightness of the sun. My head was whirling.

"Is—is that why you sent me to Yorkshire? Because *Lillian* was there?"

"No, of course not. I'd pieced together Lillian's story from other sources I'd managed to uncover. But she had never spoken. I thought it very unlikely that she would ever speak. You were only to be there a few days. Any risk that she might tell you what she knew was minimal."

Suddenly I saw where this was going. "Simon is a *Caldwell*?"

"No, thank God. His mother's aunt married into that family and her brother, the child's grandfather, knew Caldwell and his reputation. His father was Andrew Brandon. And a very fine man. And he married a woman who loved him and their child with every ounce of her being. The child didn't die, Bess, whatever they told Lillian to keep her quiet. And he's in London on an errand for your father, something to keep him there while we decide how and what to tell him. Now drink your tea, and we'll find a way to free Simon from his past."

As I took the cup that Mother held out to me, its warmth cradled in my hand, I had one clear thought. Whatever this was about, I'd do everything I could to help. For Simon's sake. Without reservation.

But down deep inside me there was a little voice saying over and over, *He'll be able to leave then, without hurting my parents—they'll understand—they'll feel it's for the best. And I will never know what I did wrong . . .*

ABOUT THE AUTHOR

Charles Todd is a mother-and-son writing team and the *New York Times* bestselling author of the Inspector Ian Rutledge mysteries, the Bess Crawford mysteries, and two stand-alone novels.